Lost Treasures Of The
GODS

The Journey Begins

Ronnie Sinclair & Michelle Charles

It's Fiction With Truth &
Fantasy With Knowledge

Acknowledgement

Above all, I thank God for the strength, inspiration, and opportunity to complete this work. This journey has been incredible, and I am truly grateful for everyone who has been a part of it. Above all, I thank God for the strength, inspiration, and opportunity to complete this work. This journey has been incredible, and I am truly grateful for everyone who has been a part of it.

A special thanks to Markee Book Design for their awesome work in designing the book cover. Also thank you to free ChatGPT and Gemini for assisting in editing my work. Your contributions helped bring clarity and polish to my book.

Prologue

The Kingdom of God is threatened by demon invaders. Satan assembles a third of the Divine Host attempting to overthrow God and His legions of angels, to place himself as ruler of the Celestial Kingdom. The angels that have formed an alliance with Satan are called Watchers, Grigoris, and Zones (known as Demonites).

These angels revolted against God by refusing to be servants to Adam. Diplomatic efforts collapsed, plunging the region into anarchy. Chaos and turmoil have shaken the heavens and weakened the suppression power of the seal. The Celestial Kingdom has come to experience darkness.

During a fierce battle, Archangels Michael, Raphael, Gabriel, and Uriel lose their weapons. They fall out of the spiritual realm, where they manifest into the natural world. Michael and the other Archangels are taken captive by Demonite forces. Buried in the Earth, the weapons are lost and sealed away until the sons of Adam—Abe, Dave, Josh, and Jake—discover these powerful treasures. They accidentally unlocks the weapon's secrets, opening a doorway into the spiritual realm. They enter into a world untouched by time.

Manipulation and distrust have divided the Kingdom, putting God vs. gods and man vs. spirits in an epic battle of the ages. If both worlds are to survive. The sons of Adam must rely on their instincts and skills to defeat Satan and his army of Demonites. The guys realize that no greater call has been given to them. They must free the Archangels from their prison. Unite them with their weapons to beat back a relentless foe. If they should fail, both worlds are doomed for all eternity.

Chapter 1

Barga - In the land of the Hittites - 666 B.C.

Sun light shines across a leaden sky with clouds moving in a slow drift above two crudely huge statues that's positioned at the gate. Both statues are at a height of approximately nineteen-feet tall. These three-dimensional rocks are grotesque looking idols that were carved from an image that once was worshipped as a god by the inhabitants of the land.

Their eroded heads and the broken fingers of these idols have given way to father time. Two tomb raiders, one, is a handsome brown skinned muscular man, his name is Jabari. The other is a drop-dead gorgeous goddess; a vision of loveliness, her name is Ajah. Both are in their mid-to-late thirties, and they are running frantically through the jungle along the Alpi'dee belt. They pause for a few to catch their breath. They are sweating and their breathing are very heavy.

A deafening SOUND ripped through the stillness, sending a jolt of pure terror through them. They bolted, adrenaline surging, pushing through the suffocating thicket. Branches tore at their clothes, thorns raked their skin, but they didn't stop. They scrambled over a massive, moss-covered log, its foliage a deceptive veil of safety. The creature's reverberating roar, a guttural bellow that seemed to shake the very earth, echoed behind them, closer now, much closer.

Trees, ancient and towering, are ripped from their roots, tossed aside like twigs by unseen, monstrous hands. A panicked flurry of wings erupted as flocks of birds, their nests destroyed, scattered into the darkening sky.

Jabari and Ajah, their faces contorted with fear, their breaths ragged, tore through the undergrowth, their hearts pounding a frantic rhythm against their ribs. They stumbled into a seemingly peaceful section of the jungle, the sounds of unseen wildlife a stark contrast to the terror that pursued them. But the illusion of safety shattered instantly. Two intense, unidentifiable eyes, burning with malevolent intent, fixed on them from the shadows.

"Run!" Jabari hissed, his voice trembling, as they dove behind a colossal tree, pressing themselves against its rough bark, holding their breaths, praying for invisibility. Then, with a sickening SNAP, the tree splintered in the middle, the force of the blow sending splinters flying. Jabari, his survival instinct overriding everything else, bolted, leaving Ajah, her eyes wide with terror, to face the horror alone.

They heard trees crashing down, a terrifying symphony of destruction, as if a legion of unseen lumberjacks were clearing a path. Ajah's screams, raw and uncontrolled, echoed through the jungle, a desperate plea for help that would never come. Suddenly, the oppressive sky cracked open, a fiery streak of light plummeting down, slamming into the earth with a deafening "BOOM!" The impact cratered the ground, a blinding flash of light erupting outwards, revealing the form of an angelic being.

Jabari, his conscience pricked by guilt, glanced back. He saw two luminous, angelic feet near Ajah, who was frozen in terror. He couldn't leave her. He lunged forward, yanking her out of the path of whatever was coming, and they plunged deeper into the jungle, their limbs heavy with fear.

Ajah, her eyes wide and haunted, risked a glance back, desperate to see what had arrived. She sees the image of a woman, her hair disheveled, clad in a dark, hooded dress. But the dense undergrowth obscured her face, and the scene was a chaotic blur of motion as the angel and the unseen entity clashed. The evil entity's form swelled, growing larger, more powerful, its image flickering and distorted. A flurry of blows rained down, each impact a thunderous crack.

The evil entity's fist sliced through the air, missing its target by a hair's breadth. The angelic being, with a sudden, desperate surge of speed, retaliated, her fist connecting with a resounding thud. The evil entity recoiled, a guttural growl escaping its lips. Then, as suddenly as it had appeared, the angelic being vanished, a flash of light against the darkening sky.

Ajah's movements became sluggish, her body heavy with exhaustion and fear. Despite her weariness, she stumbled onward, following Jabari through the vine-choked trees. The thunderous footfalls had ceased, leaving an eerie silence in their wake. They collapsed, gasping for air, their bodies trembling. After a few moments of ragged breaths, they forced themselves to stand, continuing their desperate flight. Then, as if by a miracle, they stumbled upon a hidden pathway, a narrow, overgrown trail leading deeper into the unknown.

"C'mon, hurry!" Jabari hissed, his voice tight with urgency. He tugged at Ajah's arm, but she stumbled, her breath ragged.

"I... I don't think I can go any further," she gasped, her legs trembling.

They stopped again, the oppressive jungle heat clinging to them like a shroud. Ajah's chest heaved, desperate for air. She looked at the tangled roots beneath her feet and then turned her attention to Jabari, her eyes showing uncertainty.

"Do you..." she began, her voice a mere whisper. She paused, struggling to draw in enough air to speak... "Do you think..."

A tense silence stretched between them, thick with fear and exhaustion. Ajah finally exhaled, a shaky, drawn-out breath. She inhaled sharply, then again, before she could finally form a coherent question.

"Do you think we lost it?" she asked, her voice trembling with a mixture of hope and dread.

Jabari scanned the dense foliage, his own breath coming in ragged bursts. "I don't know," he admitted, his eyes narrowed. "I don't see it. And I'm not going to find out if it knows we're here."

Ajah's eyes darted around nervously. Suddenly, she froze, her body rigid, her eyes wide with terror. She recoiled, pointing a trembling finger towards a thick tangle of vines.

"What's wrong, Ajah?" Jabari asked, his voice laced with bewilderment, but a flicker of fear mirrored in his eyes. He saw the sheer terror on her face and knew something is terribly wrong.

"That way," she says, pointing sharply in the opposite direction. Her voice was tight, strained, a thin veil over barely contained panic. But Jabari stood his ground, a flicker of something unreadable in his eyes. Not surprise, exactly, but a knowing... anticipation? He ignored her, pushing through the dense undergrowth, his movements deliberate, driven.

He tore at the thick vines, the dry leaves rustling like whispered secrets, until finally, he stood before it. Something hidden. Something the jungle had guarded for millennia. He gasped. Two statues. Solid gold. Three feet tall. And malevolent. The Hetepi. Their faces, frozen in a mask of ancient rage, seemed to radiate a palpable darkness.

"Yes!" he roared, his voice a primal shout that echoed through the jungle canopy! Joy, raw and untamed, surged through him. He embraced one of the statues, pressing a fervent kiss against its cold, golden cheek. His eyes, wide with a feverish intensity, danced between the two objects. He reached out, his fingers tracing the intricate carvings, the ancient symbols, a strange, possessive adoration in his touch. He is adorning them, yes, but also... being adorned by them. The jungle held its breath, the silence thick with unspoken dread.

The flickering torchlight danced across the grotesque trophies, casting long, distorted shadows that writhed on the cave walls. Jabari's eyes gleamed with avarice, his voice thick with a greedy excitement he couldn't quite contain.

"Ajah... we could fetch a serious reward for these." He practically vibrated with the possibilities.

A wave of nausea washed over Ajah, the air thick with a cloying, putrid stench. She wrinkled her nose, her eyes watering.

"Gosh! What's that smell?" she choked out, her voice barely a whisper.

Jabari recoiled, his own face contorting in disgust. "Don't look at me! I didn't do it!" he snapped, his voice sharp with defensiveness, though a flicker of unease danced in his eyes. He glanced nervously at the surrounding shadows, a primal fear prickling his skin. The air grew heavy, the stench intensifying, as if some unseen presences were closing in.

They continued their exploration of the golden statues and various artifacts, their curiosity piqued, until they stumbled upon an unusual-looking opening. It took them a moment to grasp the sheer size of the entrance; they were standing before a massive grotto.

"Do you really think we should go in there?" Ajah whispered as they cautiously approached the inky darkness.

Jabari shrugged, an adventurous glint in his eye. "Why not? We've come this far. I got a feeling that there is a greater treasure inside."

Gingerly, they stepped through the dark opening, feeling their way inside. With each step, the darkness seemed to wrap around them, swallowing up their surroundings. Their eyes struggled to adjust, the shapes around them fading into the shadows.

Suddenly, a crackling noise echoed beneath them. Ajah froze, glancing down but unable to distinguish what lay at their feet.

"What was that?" she breathed, her voice barely above a whisper.

Jabari scanned the walls, and his eyes landed on a flameless torch nestled in a bracket. "I think I see a way to light this place up," he said, his voice steadier than he felt. He reached up, took hold of the torch, and ignited it.

The flame flickered to life, casting eerie light across the cavernous space. They stood in stunned silence, the beam revealing the contours of a vast, ominous chamber. The ground was littered with human remains, a macabre carpet of bones that sent a shiver down their spines.

"What kind of place is this?" Ajah murmured, her nose crinkling at the foul odor that lingered in the air.

Jabari's gaze drifted toward disturbing images adorning the walls—figures clad in holy vestments twisted into grotesque forms. "We need to keep moving," he urged, heart pounding, and they pressed on, wary of the grotesque sights surrounding them.

In the center of the chamber, they found an altar raised. Its stone surface gleamed ominously in the torchlight. Beyond it stood a creepy statue, similarly adorned investments, its malevolent gaze seeming to track their every move.

"Look at that," Jabari said, a combination of awe and distaste in his voice as they approached the statue. They stood rooted to the spot, taking in its ghastly presence.

Jabari carefully placed the torch in an empty wall bracket, allowing both hands to survey the altar's grim offerings. Suddenly, a chorus of unsettling, inhuman voices echoed through the chamber, sending chills down their spines.

"What was that?" Ajah asked, panic rising within her.

Jabari turned, eyes wide, trying to pierce the thick darkness ahead. "I don't know, but it sounds like it's coming this way."

He turned back, searching for a source of light. His gaze fell upon another unlit torch in a wall bracket. He reached for it, but it resisted as he pulled.

"It won't budge," he muttered, trying again, more forcefully this time.

The eerie voices grew closer, and his heart raced. He yanked on the torch one last time, and with a startling jolt, it released—along with a rattling skeleton that clutched it.

"AHHHH!" Jabari screamed, stumbling backward.

Ajah, already on the edge of her nerves, let out a shriek. She shot him a wild look. "What is wrong with you?"

Jabari took a deep breath, trying to regain his composure. "I didn't expect that!"

With the glowing torch now in hand, the darkness began to reveal its menacing secrets, and they both knew this was only the beginning of what lay ahead in the heart of the grotto.

"Just seeing if you have a backbone," he sneered, his eyes glinting with a cruel amusement.

"I'm surprised you're able to stand," she retorted, her voice tight with suppressed anger, "because I saw yours running back the way we came in."

A flicker of rage crossed Jabari's face, but he masked it quickly. He snatched the unlit torch from the skeleton's bony grip, lit it with a snap of his fingers, and tossed it into the inky blackness of the underpass. The tunnel erupted in a sickly, yellow glow, revealing shapes that twisted and writhed, their forms shifting and distorting as they surged towards them.

"Quick, hide before it sees us!" his voice laced with urgency.

"Hide where?" she exclaimed, her eyes wide with fear, scanning the barren space. "There's nowhere to hide!"

"Here, over here!" he whispered, grabbing her arm and pulling her behind a crumbling pillar, his grip tight, his breath ragged. The air crackled with tension, the silence broken only by the guttural growls echoing from the depths of the tunnel.

They quickly duck behind the statue, the cold stone pressing against their backs as they hear a loud thump echoing through the cavern. Jabari clutches his ribs, biting his lip as pain radiates through his body. A wave of anxiety washes over Ajah.

"Where's your backbone now?" she challenges, trying to mask her fear with bravado, her voice a harsh whisper.

Jabari snaps his head away from her, his eyes wild and searching. They land on a stone tablet, its ancient etchings barely visible in the dim light, a monstrous figure looming ominously in the tunnel's depths.

"If you don't want to be the main dish, I suggest you stay perfectly still," he mutters, his voice edged with urgency.

Ajah barely has time to respond, her heart pounding as she swallows hard, praying that whatever is out there doesn't detect them. She takes a cautious peek. The sight sends chills racing down her spine, a fleeting glimpse of the creature—she instantly feels the cold dread settling in her gut. Jabari, unable to suppress his curiosity, shifts to get a better look, but Ajah instinctively yanks him back, her fingers gripping his arm tightly.

"Hold still," he whispers, each word a desperate plea.

"Why? What is it?" she breathes, her voice trembling.

With a shudder, he replies, "It's a large species of blood-sucking bats sweeping through the chamber, looking for something to devour."

Panic flashes in Ajah's eyes, her pulse quickening. "You mean… us?"

Jabari nods slightly, his expression grim. She tries to steady her breathing, but the thought of those sinister wings flapping through the shadows sends a wave of vertigo spiraling through her.

"Then we have to stay quiet," she whispers, the edge of hysteria creeping into her voice. "No sudden movements."

Without answering, Jabari's eyes widen as the flapping grows louder, a dark cloud forming in the entrance. He grips Ajah's shoulder, anchoring her to the spot. They both hold their breath, sharing a moment of silent terror, the world outside fading as the tension wraps around them like a vice. Seconds stretch into an eternity as the bats swoop low, their screeches echoing in the confined space, and Ajah can't help but squeeze her eyes shut, picturing, beady eyes searching for them in the dark.

He reached down, his fingers trembling slightly, and snatched up the tablet. A flurry of black wings erupted from the grotto, the screeching cries of bats fading into an unsettling silence. Jabari peeked cautiously out, his breath catching in his throat. He exhaled sharply, a wave of relief washing over him. "Coast's clear," he muttered, his voice tight.

They clambered out from behind their hiding place, the tablet clutched tightly in his hand,

"What's that in your hand?" Ajah asked, her voice sharp with suspicion.

"I kicked it," he replied, wincing as a sharp pain shot through his foot.

"It looks like there's writing on it," she observed, her eyes narrowing.

"Yeah. I see?" he said, his brow furrowed in concentration.

"Can you make out what it says?" she pressed, her voice laced with urgency.

Jabari squeezed his eyes shut, trying to focus. "I don't know... the writing seems... Togarmah? No, no wait! I've seen this before."

He stared at the tablet, his breath held captive in his chest. Then, his eyes widened, a sudden understanding dawning on his face.

"This writing... it's Hittite," he said, his voice a hushed whisper.

Ajah stalked towards him, her face etched with deep concern. "If this writing is Hittite, then why is it here, in Wilusa territory?" she demanded, her voice trembling slightly.

Jabari's gaze flickered between the tablet and Ajah, his mind racing. "Because this land... this body of land once belonged to the Hittites," he explained, his voice heavy with the weight of ancient history... "It was later... canonized by the Wilusa elders."

She leaned in close, her breath ghosting over his ear, a subtle shiver running down his spine. His eyes, however, remained fixed, locked on the glowing tablet in his hands, his brow furrowed in concentration.

"Hittite? What does it say?" she asked, her voice a low, urgent whisper.

He hesitated, his gaze flickering across the ancient symbols, then back to the tablet. "It says..." he began, his voice strained, a tremor of unease creeping into his tone... "The Angels of God shall become powerless before our lord. None shall be able to escape his wrath. Even the god that created the blu planet shall no longer reign, ruling from his throne. Michael, Gabriel, Raphael, Phanuel, and the entire Celestial Host shall be crucified before him on the day of atonement."

A heavy silence fell between them, the weight of the words hanging in the air. Her eyes widened, a flicker of fear dancing within them.

"Who is this god that the Hittites are referring to?" she breathed, her voice barely audible… "Is it the same god that the people of Wilusa worship?"

He shakes his head slowly, his eyes still glued to the tablet, a dark premonition swirling within him. "I don't know," he replied, his voice thick with apprehension.

He gestured towards a nearby statue, its features grotesque and alien. "But they carved this... this thing, in its honor." The statue loomed, a silent, menacing presence, casting long, distorted shadows across the room.

"It's a statue of whom?" Jabari demanded, his voice tight with unease… "This… this doesn't look like Ra, or Martu, or Baal, or El!" He gestured wildly, his eyes darting between the imposing figure and Ajah.

"I agree," Ajah murmured, her own apprehension growing. "Do you think… it's Ashur?" Ajah pressed, his voice is barely a whisper.

"No," Jabari replied, shaking his head. "It's not."

"Then Dagon?" Ajah asked, a desperate hope clinging to his words.

Jabari's eyes narrowed… "No. I've seen them, worshipped them. Their image… it lacks the power this one radiates."

A heavy silence fell between them. "If it's not any of them," Ajah finally asked, her voice thick with dread, "then who is this statue dedicated to?"

Jabari's gaze remained fixed on the statue, her face pale. "I wish I knew," she breathed, the words heavy with unspoken fear.

He noticed more carvings on a nearby wall and he slowly moved towards it, his eyes locked on the strange text. His voice a hushed whisper, "I know this language."

He began to translate aloud, her voice trembling slightly. As she spoke, a strange luminescence began to emanate from her face, her eyes frozen, wide with a terrifying stillness. Suddenly, a powerful gust of wind, a force that seemed to come from nowhere, swept through the chamber, clearing the sand that had obscured more of the writing.

"What was that?" Jabari gasped, his voice filled with alarm.

Ajah blinked, her eyes unfocused for a moment. "I... I don't know," she stammered, her voice still trembling. "I was reading the inscription, and then... the wind."

Jabari rushed to her side, his gaze fixed on the newly revealed text. "This writing... it's Babylonian," he echoed, his voice laced with a growing sense of dread.

"Babylonian? How is that?" Ajah's voice is tight, strained. "The writings is of Hittite. You said the writings... are Babylonian. Were the Hittites... were they under Babylonian rule?"

Jabari's eyes, wide and disbelieving, "Yes." His eyes is fixed on a name etched into the wall. He froze, a tremor running through him. Then, slowly, almost mechanically, he began to back away, his face a mask of stunning shock. Ajah watched him, a flicker of apprehension in her eyes,

"We have to get out of here. Quickly," he said, his voice a low, urgent rasp.

"Why? What's wrong?" she demanded, her voice rising in alarm.

"Because... you summoned for him."

Her head snapped towards him, a look of utter incomprehension on her face. "I summoned who?"

Jabari turned slightly, his gaze darting around the room, a frantic survey of the shadows. He shook his head, trying to dispel the fear that was gripping him. "This writing... it was copied from the Mali Empire's Book of Reproduction."

"The Book of Reproduction? What the heck is that?" she asked, her voice laced with confusion.

"It contains incantations," he said, his voice thick with dread, "incantations that can bring the dead back to life. Spirits too. That's what you did when you read that text aloud. C'mon, we have to get out of here."

"Wait!" Ajah grabbed his arm, her grip tight. "Tell me. Who is this, Anu? What do you know about him?"

Jabari's head whipped around, his eyes burning with a raw, desperate intensity. "Woman, you ask too many questions." His voice is low and menacing… "But… if you must know, I will tell you. Anu is the demon son of Anshar. According to the Hittites, Anshar was stripped of his divinity by Allah. He defied the established order and is banished to the underworld. There, he swore vengeance against the Lord of Hosts. Now we know who this statue is dedicated to," he murmured, his voice tight with a newfound dread.

"C'mon," she hissed, her eyes darting around the dimly lit chamber. "Let's take our findings and get out of here."

"Wait!" he protested, his voice laced with a desperate urgency. "I need to know why Allah would do such a thing?"

She stopped, her shoulders stiff. "Your curiosity is going to bring a curse on us," he warned, his voice trembling slightly. "The tale goes, after Satan fathered a child… from that moment on, Allah forbade all deities from procreating with humans."

Ajah drifted past him, her hand reaching up to a stony shelf. She picked up a cup, her fingers tracing its cold, rough surface. "Wait, wait, wait," she said, her voice incredulous… "Are you telling me that Satan fathered a child?"

"As crazy as it sounds," he replied, his voice low and strained, "yes."

"I… I've never heard such a thing," she replied, her eyes wide with disbelief… "How can a deity… lay with a human in pleasure? Don't you know that if the high priest hears you speak such blasphemy, he can have you put to death for making false attributes against a deity?" Her voice rose, laced with panic.

He stepped closer, his eyes pleading. "I know," he said, his voice a hushed urgency… "But it's true. As a child, I heard the village elders speak on such a thing. They also spoke about their fathers' fathers, reading about it in the writings of Enoch." He paused, his gaze intense. "This is dangerous, Ajah. But we need to get out of here.

"The writings of Enoch?" she asked, her voice laced with a delicate blend of curiosity and suspicion. Her eyes, fixed on him, held a quiet intensity, searching for any hint of deception.

He met her gaze, his own unwavering. "Yes. It is said that Allah, in His righteous fury, sought to destroy the forbidden child. But the Burning Ones, in their wisdom, convinced Him otherwise, believing the siblings could find harmony. They were tragically wrong. Their error is the very reason Allah expelled humanity from paradise." His voice held a low, resonating gravity, each word weighted with the burden of ancient knowledge.

A flicker of disbelief, quickly masked by a sharp, probing intelligence, crossed her face. "Where are these writings today? And how did he come by such a… tale?" she repeated, the word… "tale" laced with a subtle skepticism. Her brow furrowed, the unspoken question hanging heavy in the air: Can I trust him?

"The tale goes," a voice, heavy with suppressed emotion, began, "Seth called his son Enoch and told him to write this down. He said: 'My children…' "The voice paused, a tremor running through it… 'I know not whither I go, or what will befall of me after this manner."

A hush fell over the room. "One morning, during the cool of the day, before the sun had painted the village with its golden rays, Seth arose, seeking sustenance. A simple bowl of mashed chickpeas. Then, he ventured towards the Taurus Mountains, where his herd grazed, intending to count them. But… he heard voices. From a cave."

The speaker's voice dropped to a near whisper. "A beckoning. He entered, drawn by a dim, unsettling glow, venturing deeper into the darkness. And then… he saw." A gasp, a sharp intake of breath. "The glory of Allah. And the four Eternal Ones. He pressed himself against the cave wall, fear and awe battling within him, trying to inch closer. But an unseen force held him back. He could only listen."

The air crackled with tension. "He heard them… conversing with Satan. A casual conversation. They spoke of an agreement. An agreement to allow Satan to tempt Adam. In any way possible."

A collective shudder ran through the listeners. "Seth passed this knowledge to Enoch, commanding him, 'Never disclose this to anyone, not even your sons!' And so, after Seth's passing, Enoch… wrestled with his father's command." The speaker's voice grew strained. "He was about to reveal the writings… But Allah… gotten wind of it and the heavens opened. A fire descended. Flames engulfed Enoch, and bore him aloft, to heaven, but one of the writings fell to earth."

A heavy silence settled over the room. "Enoch is placed upon the clouds, and… he is never seen again."

"So," she said, her voice tight, eyes narrowed, "how did the Hittites come to know about the writings?" The question hung in the air, thick with an unspoken accusation. She leaned forward, the flickering candlelight casting harsh shadows on her face.

"According to the village elders. One day, war broke out between the Hittites and the Wilusa's! Thousands of armored Wilusians engaged in battle with the Hittite army. The Sooth-sayer's magic was no match for the Wilusa army. They were protected by an even more powerful magic. Sword clashed with sword, and in no time, parts of the Hittite territory fell under Wilusa rule.

The Wilusa military marched further into the territory setting ablaze huts, capturing men and women. The Sooth-sayer and all of his apprentices scattered in every direction. Every aspect of the Hittite kingdom was under siege by the invading army where a small handful of shamanic healers fell by sword and arrows. Several arrows landed near the high priest. He snaps his head in all directions and sees all of his apprentices lying on the ground dead. He stops, hesitates, and locks eyes with one of the archers.

A frenzied Wilusa soldier crept up behind the priest, his sword poised menacingly behind him, ready to strike. In a split second, an archer released an arrow; it sliced through the air like a deadly whisper aimed at the priest. Reacting instinctively, the priest raised his arms in a desperate attempt to shield himself. The arrow zipped past him, narrowly missing his flesh, and found its mark deep in the soldier's chest instead.

With a gasp, the soldier crumpled to the ground, dragging the priest down with him in a tangle of limbs. The shamanistic leader, feigning death, observed silently as the Wilusa army swept through the village, capturing the remaining inhabitants. Once the coast was clear, he slipped away unnoticed, making his escape toward the southeastern edge of Anatolia.

Days later, the shamanistic healer is standing by the banks of the Dahara River, mentally preparing for his ritual of purification. As he focused inward, a peculiar sight caught his eye. A shimmering disturbance in the water draws his gaze, it's an otherworldly allure.

He stares in bewilderment as a shadowy figure slowly takes shape before him. A chill seeps into his bones, and instinctively, he stumbles backward, dropping to his knees in an urgent plea for mercy. Just as he lowers his head, a sudden splash stirs the water, pulling his attention back to the river. To his astonishment, he watches as the water unnaturally withdraws, revealing a sight that leaves him breathless.

He settles back on his heels, incredulity flooding his mind as he tries to grasp the surreal spectacle unfolding before him. Emerging from the depths is a full-grown female dwarf, her appearance striking yet unsettling. With arms that mimic the spindly legs of a spider, she glides gracefully from the water, her feet seemingly nonexistent. Her robe, a tangled mess of dead weeds and dangling strands, clings to her form like a shroud of decay.

With a piercing gaze, she strides toward him, each step measured as if she has come not merely to witness, but to render judgment upon his soul. The woman dwarf stands before the kneeling priest, her presence heavy with an unnerving intensity. The priest, his face etched with sorrow, is afraid to gaze up at her, because he is taken aback by the fear that radiates from this otherworldly figure. One of her spider-like hands gestures for him to rise. Hesitantly, he stands, receiving the tablet she offers him. His eyes widen in shock as he watches her retreat, returning to the water from whence she came.

Ajah's breath caught in her throat. "Is that... is that really the secret behind its origin?" she whispered, her voice trembling with disbelief and a hint of fear.

He locked eyes with her, his gaze burdened by a depth of understanding that felt both timeless and daunting. With a slow nod, he confirmed the unvoiced fear that lingered in the air. A palpable silence enveloped them, as if the very atmosphere were thickening with the gravity of what had just been revealed. Ajah's thoughts spiraled, struggling to bridge the chasm between the unimaginable and the stark truth before her.

"Um..." she finally spoke, her voice quivering with tension. "Does anyone know the child's name?"

He paused, the air thickening with an anxious stillness. When his voice broke through the silence, it was deep and heavy, carrying an authority that sent a shiver down Ajah's spine. "Yes. As per the Talmud and the Torah... the child's name... is Anu."

The cup slipped from Ajah's hand, shattering against the floor. A sharp gasp escaped her lips, followed by a chilling quiet. She stepped away from the stone shelf. She inched closer to him with disbelief etched across her face.

"Anshar," Jabari started, his voice strained with repressed fear, "Anshar acted against his Lord's wishes... defied Allah's command and fathered an illegitimate son, despite the deities being prohibited from such actions. He named the child Anu. Shouldn't we... shouldn't we prepare a sacrifice? To summon him?" His hands quivered slightly, the question lingering in the air like a grim portent.

The response is curt, stripped of any trace of warmth. "No! By you reading the text, you summon to bring him up."

Ajah's eyes widened, panic flickering in their depths. "I... I read the text," she stammered, her voice barely a whisper.

A single, clipped word broke the tense silence. "Yes." The emotionlessness of that one syllable is more chilling than any scream. Something ominous lurked at the edge of the underbrush near the entrance, while inside, the scurrying of a large rat disturbed the silence, scraping across dry bones. Jabari shot a worried glance over his shoulder.

"We must leave these here," he said urgently, his voice low and steady, slicing through the oppressive atmosphere as he addressed her.

Ajah wrinkled her nose at the foul odor permeating the air, but her curiosity held her back from leaving just yet.

"Can you finish reading the tablet?" she urged, glancing at Jabari, who hesitated, uncertainty flickering in his gaze. Ultimately, he succumbed to her request and continued his reading.

"And Satan, the god of the earth, shall bless the self-righteous humans in the name of the Most High to keep the truth hidden from them."

Ajah's eyes widened as realization dawned. "He intends to make humans his instruments of destruction, throwing us into the frontlines of a war against Allah."

"Exactly," Jabari replied, a hint of dread creeping into his voice. "He can't confront Allah directly, so he's waging an indirect war, using humanity as weaponry."

Ajah's heart raced as if she absorbed the implications. "So, Anu plans to capture human souls and present them as sacrifices before the earth's mightiest being?"

"That seems to be their intention. They aim to revert the world to its primordial state, but this time—" Jabari paused to steel himself, "with a worthy leader."

A shiver ran down Ajah's spine as her trembling fingers traced a grotesque carving nearby. Her eyes widened in terror and revulsion. "So," she whispered, her voice barely a breath, "this temple is dedicated to Anu, a follower of Satan."

"Yes," Jabari replied, his tone urgent, panic edging into his words. "We need to leave. Now. Before we become the next sacrifices."

His declaration shattered the stillness around them, a harsh and sobering reality. Ajah's breath caught in her throat. "Sacrifice?" she echoed, a thin tremor in her voice. "What do you mean?"

Suddenly, a gust of wind whipped through the temple, followed by a heavy thud that reverberated ominously around them. Jabari and Ajah exchanged anxious glances, both acutely aware of the slight tremor underfoot. Behind them, a pair of eyes fixed on the entrance, a chilling reminder that retreating the way they had come was no longer an option

A voice echoed through the cave, reverberating off the damp stone walls. Jabari and Ajah exchanged frantic glances, their instincts urging them to explore every shadowy corner. With no other choice, they cautiously ventured further into the cavern's depths. Jabari strained to grasp their surroundings, casting his gaze in another direction, but the darkness revealed nothing.

"Come on!" he urged, his voice laced with urgency.

They pressed onward until they stumbled upon a flight of stairs that descended into yet another tunnel. The disembodied voice rang out once more, sending a chill down their spines. In a rush, they hurried down the staircase, only to be met with a shocking sight: grim remnants of humanity sprawled across a crude table.

Driven by an insatiable curiosity, Jabari is determined to decipher the markings on a nearby tablet. He quickly scanned the area for a seat, and settled on one positioned uncomfortably close to a furnace.

An ominous silence enveloped them as a foul odor wafted from the furnace, the putrid scent turning their expressions grim. Struggling against the stench, Jabari pressed a hand over his nose and mouth. Ajah rummaged through her bag, retrieving a vial of fragrant oil and incense. She sprinkled the oil on the ground, creating a temporary respite from the offensive smell.

As Jabari resumed his reading, he murmured, "And God sent His angels to counter Demonites' advances. He selected four humans, giving them divine powers."

Outside the grotto, a shadow flitted along the pathway. Jabari's instincts flared, and he abruptly paused, sensing something amiss.

"What is it?" Ajah's voice wavered, a tremor of anxiety seeping into her tone. Her eyes widened, darting about the dimly lit chamber, seeking any sign of danger.

Jabari stood taut, his expression grave and his focus locked on a point just beyond her view. A thick silence hung in the air, oppressive and heavy, as tension coiled around them like a serpent. He hesitated, the seconds stretching interminably, each one an assault on her composure.

When at last he spoke, his voice was a strained whisper barely above the ambient noise. "I thought I heard something?" The uncertainty in his statement hung palpably between them, intensifying the unease spiraling in Ajah's chest. He remained still, offering no reassurance, only a haunting gaze that spoke of his own fears

He immersed himself in the text once more when, without warning, an ethereal vision unfolded before his eyes. Silhouetted warriors clashed against their adversaries, wielding divine weapons with such speed and ferocity that their forms barely registered in his mind. Amid the chaos, he caught a fleeting glimpse of a striking figure, radiant yet elusive, before everything was swallowed by a blinding white light. In an instant, he was jolted back to reality, the tablet slipping from his grasp and clattering to the ground.

"What did you see?" Ajah's voice sliced through the moment, taut with urgency, her intensity palpable in the charged atmosphere.

He hesitated, glancing nervously between the fallen tablet and her piercing gaze. "I saw something... something I can't quite put into words."

Ajah's patience wore thin, her resolve hardening. "Then find the words. What did you see?" she pressed, her tone sharp and unyielding.

His throat constricted, the weight of her demand settling heavily on him. "It was... a blur. I couldn't grasp it. Everything moved too quickly." He ran a shaky hand through his hair, his expression a blend of fear and bewilderment. "It was like... a tempest of light and shadow, all tangled together. And then... nothing."

Ajah narrowed her gaze, clearly unimpressed. "Gone where? What do you mean gone?" She leaned in closer, her voice dropping to a menacing whisper. "You're holding something back."

But inside, he wrestled with his own confusion. "What does all of this mean?" he pondered silently, his eyes searching Ajah's face for answers. Without breaking eye contact, she bent down to retrieve the tablet, extending it towards him once more.

"Here. Take this," she urged, her tone shifting to one of insistence. "You need to read it again. Maybe it'll unlock what you witnessed."

He recoiled slightly, wide-eyed, the fear evident in his posture. "I can't... I won't," he stammered, shaking his head.

"Why not? This is monumental! Take the tablet! You saw something beyond what any Prophet or Apostle has ever glimpsed. You're on the cusp of a discovery that could change everything. Please, take it." Her encouragement was urgent, almost pleading.

Finally, with a deep breath, Jabari reached out cautiously and reclaimed the tablet. He opened it once again, his heart racing as he prepared to resume his reading, hoping to unveil the mysteries still swirling in his mind.

"From the very beginning, the two factions have been locked in an eternal struggle. The Angels of God possess speed and strength, while the Demonites are masters of deception and cunning."

Suddenly, the scene explodes into a blinding white light, and Jabari finds himself witnessing a ferocious battle between celestial beings. The air is thick with battle cries and the clashing of steel. Time appears to slow as fiery arrows streak through the air, accompanied by mystical powers unleashed from bows, pendants, swords, and shields, all striking fiercely at the adversary.

Amidst the chaos, Jabari catches a fleeting glimpse of four human silhouettes fighting bravely alongside the angels. Their faces remain obscured, just as the faces of the angels are shrouded in mystery. The world around him blurs once more into a blinding white light, pulling him back to reality. Breathless and trembling, the profound experience leaves him momentarily speechless.

But before he can fully process what he's witnessed, WHAM! A hand pierces through Jabari's chest, and he crumples to the floor, fatally weakened. Ajah stumbles at the sudden violence, her scream piercing the air. The god Anu, with his birdlike wings unfurled, revels in his triumph. Ajah finds herself face to face with the deity, his lips curling into a menacing snarl, revealing sharp teeth.

Muscles coiling tightly, Anu prepares to pounce, but it's too late. Ajah's eyes widen in fear and confusion, now filled with a swirling array of forms. She becomes a vessel, possessed and compelled to ascend from the grotto. A searing pain erupts on her back, bubbling as if acid were poured upon her skin, and a pair of formidable wings bursts forth.

Momentarily stunned, Ajah flexes her newfound appendages before striding purposefully to the cave's entrance and with fierce determination, she slams her fist into the wall, triggering a violent cave-in that seals the entrance behind her. Gazing back at her handiwork, a marvel of destruction, she takes flight, dissolving into the inky embrace of the night sky

Chapter 2

The dawn of Creation . . .

A hushed reverence fell over the suffocating darkness. Then, a voice, filled with immeasurable power and gentle wonder, whispered, "Let there be light."

A powerful stimulant of energy illuminates a continuous area of unoccupied darkness from the glory of Hashem being revealed. A silhouette of a man is detached from the light and divides it from the darkness. The light He called day, and the darkness He called night. The latter part of the day He called evening, and the early part of the day He called morning. This He call the first day. Not long after, He speak another word of prophecy,

"Let there be a firmament in the midst of the water," He declared, His voice resonating with unimaginable power, "let it divide the waters!"

A white-hot fireball erupts within the water. It creates bubbling effect. Visible number of condensed vapors wafts up in the air expanding, rounding it contour into shape. Waters that are under the firmament are divided from the waters above the firmament.

Clouds are floating in the firmament. Hashem looks at the firmament and divides it into three levels. For the next few days, He put into place massive amount of land. He sees miles of ecoregions, soil, and rocks. He called the dry land Earth, and the gathering together of waters He called seas.

Hashem cultivated an area eastward of the great sea. He called this area Eden. As He walked across the surface of the barren tier, Hashem decided to beautify the empty landscape. From out of the ground, He made to grow every tree that's pleasant to the sight and good for food and He saw that it was good, and said,

"Let the earth bring forth more grass and herbs yielding seed, and let the fruit tree come forth, yielding fruit after its kind, whose seed are in itself."

Mist and soil rises from the earth and pass through the air in a spectacular fashion before returning from whence it came. The earth suddenly brought forth grass-and-herb-yielding seed after its kind, and the trees yielding fruit whose seed are in itself after its kind.

Then Hashem caused a river to flow out of Eden to water the garden, where it divided into four heads. The river provided water to every square inch of the garden. He named the first river Pison, which encompassed the whole land of Havilah. There was an abundance of gold, bdellium, and onyx stone in the region.

He named the second river Gihon. This body of water flowed through the whole land of Ethiopia. The name of the third river was Hiddekel. It flowed toward the east end of the garden and the fourth and final river, He named Euphrates. Hashem sees that it was good. The evening and the morning, He called the third day. But Hashem wasn't satisfied as yet. With darkness looming on the horizon, the Earth fell into the deep depths of darkness.

After Hashem established his council of Angels which includes, the Four and twenty Elders, the four Burning Ones, Zarath, Elyzariah, Adon-Shama, and Raphaon ἀπό and a platoon of angels led by the Archangels, He continued His work of creating the earth and all of its host.

Chapter 3

Brisbane, Australia 1934 . . .

A curvy woman in her mid-thirties, enters her child's room humming a tune. Her name is Olivia Hetzel. She drifts pass her child lying in bed, and she pulls apart the window shade welcoming in another day. Joshua is a good-looking boy, 13, awakes to the light of the morning sun beaming it's golden rays amidst the sounds of birds displaying an art of rhythm in a harmonious tone,

"Mum, why is it always so blinkin' gloomy here first thing in the morning?" he asked, as he rubs his eyes,

"I do not know, son. It has always been that way since I can remember," she responded, and continued humming, "On the Good Ship Lollipop," the tune from the movie *Bright Eyes*, starring Shirley Temple. It opened the previous night at the local movie house.

"Joshua! Get ya self-up bludger. Why don't you go help your pop?"

"Help pop with whot?" he sighed, stretching with a long, drawn-out yawn.

"Bloody 'ell, he's out there tryin' to fix his tractor," his mum sighed, rolling her eyes. "Been at it for hours, the drongo."

Joshua climbs out of bed, and jaunted off to the bathroom, where he cleaned himself up, and got dressed. He zips out of his room, on a path to the kitchen,

"Mum, could you prepare for me, some vegemite on toast please."

She is delighted to fix him a sandwich. She does, and hands it to him and shooed him out the door. Gladly he takes the vegemite sandwich and hurries out the door,

"*Eating vegemite is a great way to start the day*," he thought walking outside.

Josephine finished preparing the table, so that she can finish her cup of coffee that she prepared earlier. Joshua's disposition is always bright, cheery, ready and willing to lend a hand. Even when it seemed like he really doesn't want to. He hears the voice of his pop inquiring to him from under the tractor. It's John Liddell, a man in his early 40's. He has a thin build with blond hair and green eyes,

"Joshua! Is that you, son?" his pop called out, a hint of surprise in his voice.

"Yeah, it's me," Joshua replied, chewing the last of his sanga.

"Good on ya! Come give us a hand, mate," his pop said, a touch of urgency creeping in.

"Whaddya want me to do, pop?" Joshua asked, wiping his hands on his shorts.

His pop sighed, a flicker of frustration in his voice. "I'm tryin' to fix this bloody tractor, and it's givin' me the absolute shits."

His pop slides from under the tractor. He eyes his son smiling,

"Oi, grab the 20-mil socket outta the tool cab, would ya?" his pop said, a bit of a smile tugging at the corners of his mouth.

Joshua hands him the socket, and squats down next to his pop, waiting patiently for him to give another command,

Joshua handed his old man the socket, the metal cool against his calloused palm. He squatted down beside him, the dust of the shed floor clinging to his jeans, and waited, patient as a kookaburra on a gum tree, for the next instruction.

"Pop," he drawled, the word stretched out like a long, hot summer's day.

"Yeah, son," Pop replied, his voice rough as hessian, his eyes still fixed on the rusted engine part.

"I'm bored," Joshua sighed, kicking at a loose pebble with the toe of his boot.

Pop finally looked up, a hint of a grin crinkling the corners of his eyes. "Righto, so whot ya reckon I'm supposed to do about that, eh? You want me to pull a rabbit outta me hat? Sing ya a bloody lullaby?"

Joshua shrugged, his shoulders slumping. "Dunno. Just… bored."

"Well, bugger me," Pop chuckled, shaking his head. "Go find somethin' to do, ya drongo. Go kick a footy, climb a tree, annoy ya sister. Just keep outta me hair while I'm tryin' to fix this bloody thing."

He gestured towards the engine, his expression shifting back to one of frustrated concentration. "This thing's got more issues than a politician at a BBQ."

"But Pop…" Joshua started, his voice trailing off.

"No 'buts', mate. Go on, skedaddle. You're like a bluebottle on a hot day, always buzzin' around when I'm tryin' to concentrate. Go on, off ya pop!"

Joshua makes haste for the field. He spreads out his arms as if they are wings, pretending that he was a plane gliding in the air. His playfulness takes him to the base of a mountain not far from his parents' house. Cody and Tyler are sitting on a rotten log talking to each other. Joshua spots them and he comes over,

"G'day, mates, whot're ya blokes up to?" he drawled, his voice thick with an Aussie twang. He sauntered over, a lanky figure in faded boardshorts and a sun-bleached singlet.

"Just yarnin'," Tyler replied, his eyes flicking up from his phone.

"Oh, fair dinkum? Well, I reckon I need to have a bit of a chinwag with ya, so reckon I could join in?" he asked, a hopeful grin spreading across his sun-kissed face.

"Yeah, no worries," Cody chimed in, leaning back against the park bench.

Tyler, however, narrowed his eyes slightly, a hint of suspicion in his gaze. "Where've ya been, anyway, mate? We barely see ya anymore after school. Gone walkabout or somethin'?" he asked, his voice laced with a playful, yet probing, tone. He waited for the bloke's answer, keen to see if he'd spin a yarn or tell the truth.

"Yeah, nah, I know, right? Haven't been feeling grouse lately, mate. Fair dinkum, I get home and I'm straight into the kip, flat out. As a matter of fact, that's what I wanted to have a yarn with ya's about. Remember back a few years ago, when I was having all those bloody nightmares? You know, the ones that were giving me the absolute heebie-jeebies? And everyone reckoned I was off me rocker, a proper nutbag?"

"Yeah, mate," Tyler drawled, a lazy grin spreading across his face. Cody, meanwhile, gave a quick nod, his head bobbing slightly, a 'yep, no worries' kind of gesture.

"Strewth," Joshua sighed, his face long and drawn, "those bloody dreams have come back."

"No flamin' way!" Tyler exclaimed, his eyes widening.

"Yeah, mate, but this time," Joshua continued, his voice heavy, "it's even weirder than before."

"Weirder than them dingo-lookin' yellow eyes you kept seein'?" Cody frowned, scratching his head.

"Yeah, heaps weirder," Joshua confirmed. "This time, there's three other blokes in it with me, and there's a proper blue goin' on, a full-on punch-up. I'm not keen on tellin' the oldies, 'cause they'll reckon I've gone troppo, sendin' me off to a bunch of quacks tellin' me I'm bonkers."

The boys exchanged uneasy glances, shifting their weight from foot to foot.

"Stop wrigglin' about like a bunch of nervous wallabies," Tyler snapped.

"There's nothin' wrong with me, ya drongos!" Joshua yelled, his frustration boiling over.

Joshua was becoming frustrated over the thought that some of his family and friends thinks that he has psychological problems. He knew this wasn't the case, but the dreams have already taken their toll on him,

"Right, so…" Cody drawled, scratching the back of his neck, "anythin' else 'bout these dreamin's of yours, eh? Anythin' at all?"

"Yeah," she sighed, rubbing her temples. "I reckon I heard this barkin' sound. Real loud, like. Thought it was Rex, y'know, our kelpie. Went to give him a bit of a telling-off, but the poor bugger was dead to the world, snorin' his head off."

Tyler, with a cheeky grin, nudged Cody in the ribs. "Oi, mate, how long's she been havin' these bloody weirdo dreams then?"

"Couple of months, give or take," she replied, her voice laced with a hint of unease.

Tyler's eyebrows shot up. "Couple of months?! And ya haven't said a bloody word to anyone?"

"Nah," she mumbled, avoiding their gazes.

Cody, his expression now serious, leaned forward. "Strewth, mate, don't ya think ya should be tellin' someone about this? Like, anyone? Your old man, maybe? Or a doc, even?"

Joshua sprang to his feet, hands flung wide, a desperate plea etched on his face.

"Right, listen up, ya blokes! I'm tellin' ya, this stays between us. No blabbin' to any grown-ups, yeah? Not a single bloody word. Ya gotta swear to me, fair dinkum! I mean it, swear on ya nanna's grave!" he demanded, his voice thick with urgency.

Tyler and Cody exchanged a quick, knowing glance. "Yeah, alright, mate," Tyler said, nodding firmly. "We swear, yeah?"

"Dead set," Cody added, his eyes serious. "We're not gonna say a bloody thing."

Joshua, a flicker of relief washing over his strained features, knew he could trust them. They were mates, through thick and thin, since they were knee-high to a grasshopper. They'd shared more secrets than a kookaburra laughs. They sealed the pact, the three of them locking pinky fingers, a solemn oath sworn in the Aussie bush.

"Right," Tyler said, the tension easing slightly, but curiosity burning in his eyes. "So, what else do ya remember, Josh? Spill the beans, mate!"

This is not a story that Joshua wanted to share with anyone. But he was compelled to share his story with them,

"Yeah, nah, it was proper dark, mate. Pitch black, like someone'd pulled the plug on the sun, ya know? And I'm standin' there, all on me lonesome, right? Then, I see 'em again. Those eyes, starin' right at me from way off. Gave me the creeps, I tell ya. I squint, tryin' to see what's what, and I spot three blokes. Bit older than me, I reckon. Taller, anyway."

"Did ya get a gud look at them, Josh?" Tyler asked, his brow furrowed. "Anythin' recognizable?"

"Yeah, were they anyone we know, like?" Cody chimed in, his voice laced with curiosity.

"Nah, never seen 'em before in me life," Joshua replied, shaking his head. "But, hold your horses, I ain't finished yet." He paused, taking a deep breath… "Right, so, these blokes in the dream, they all had somethin'… somethin' weird with 'em. Like, old-school weapons, ya know? Bits of metal and wood, all jagged and rusty lookin'. Hard to make out proper in the dark, but I could see these… these massive creatures standin' right behind 'em. Bloody tall, they were. Like, taller than a gum tree! There were four of 'em, but one of 'em… one of 'em was standin' all alone. No bloke in front of it, just… standin' there. And it was, like, beckoning me. Wavin' me over, ya know? And, for some weird reason, I felt this… this pull. Like I had to go to it. Like somethin' was tellin' me to."

Tyler and Cody are fascinated by what they are hearing. They sit listening intently to the story. Joshua noticed how much attention they are paying to him, so he decided to make it a bit more theatrical. So, he continued on, becoming more animated,

"Right, so, those bleedin' eyes," Joshua began, his voice suddenly hard, like granite, "they swung 'round and bloody well looked at me." He jumped up, spun on the spot, his arms windmilling, a theatrical flourish. "Like, right at me, yeah? Like somethin' outta a bloody flick."

He paused, his eyes glazing over, lost in memory. "Then, see, I started gettin' these pictures in me head, yeah? These… visions." He shuddered, a ripple of unease running through him. "And these eyes, right? These bloody eyes… they weren't normal. Nah. They were bright red, like… like bushfire red, yeah? And inside, in the bloody middle, three yellow slits. Like a… a bloody snake's, or somethin'. Three bloody pupils, starin' right through ya." He paused, swallowing hard. "Gave me the bloody creeps, I tell ya."

He opened his own eyes wide and lunged forward toward Tyler and Cody, startling them,

"Strewth, mate, it was the scariest bloody thing I've ever seen," Joshua breathed, still a bit shaken.

"Bloody incredible," Tyler muttered, his eyes wide as he glanced at Cody, "Like somethin' out of a proper bonkers flick."

"So, whot do ya reckon the dream means, eh?" Cody drawled, scratching his chin, "Reckon it's got some kinda hidden meaning?"

Joshua shrugged, a flicker of unease in his eyes. "Dunno, mate. Just a weird dream, innit?"

"Were ya scared though? Fair dinkum?" Tyler pressed, his voice laced with curiosity.

"Nah, not really," Joshua mumbled, though his voice betrayed a hint of doubt. "They're just dreams, aren't they? Just bloody dreams?" He was really asking himself, seeking some reassurance from his mates. Tyler and Cody exchanged a look, then shrugged noncommittally.

"Who bloody knows?" Tyler said, his brow furrowed. "Maybe it's a premonition, ya know? Some kinda heads-up from the bloody cosmos."

"A whot?" Joshua drawled, his brow furrowed in confusion.

Tyler, leaning against the dusty verandah railing, elaborated with a shrug. "You know… like when ya get a bit of a 'feeling', right? Like, a premonition, or somethin'. Ya know something's gonna happen in the future, but ya don't really know, 'cause, well, it's the future. And then, bloody oath, that very thing unfolds exactly the way ya seen it in ya head."

Cody, kicking at the red dirt with his boot, nodded slowly. "Hmmm. Yeah, maybe that's the go. A bit of a 'sixth sense' thing, eh?"

Joshua squinted, scratching his head. "Nah, I dunno, mate. Sounds a bit too... mystical for me."

Tyler, ignoring Joshua's skepticism, pushed himself off the railing. "Righto, well, we're off to the servo, grab some tucker. Ya wanna come snag a meat pie or somethin'?"

"Nah, thanks. I'll just hang 'round here," Joshua replied, waving a dismissive hand.

"Fair enough," Cody said, giving Joshua's shoulder a firm pat. "We'll see ya bright and early tomorrow, eh? Don't go gettin' into any mischief." He grinned, a flash of white teeth against his sunburnt face. "We'll be back before the mozzies get too bad."

Tyler added, "Yeah, chuck us a wave if ya need anythin', eh?" He and Cody sauntered off down the dusty track, the sound of their boots crunching on the gravel fading into the afternoon heat.

Tyler slapped Joshua on the back, a little too hard, a forced joviality masking his unease. "Yeah, mate, ya probably just goin' through a phase or somethin', y'know? Like, everyone does, right?"

A beat of awkward silence stretched between the three boys. Then, as if a dam had burst, they erupted in a cacophony of laughter, a nervous, slightly too loud sound.

"That's what our parents always bloody say, innit?" Tyler wheezed, wiping a tear from his eye.

"Yeah, 'ya just goin' through some phase'," Cody mimicked, his voice high-pitched and mocking, earning another round of snorts from Tyler.

They started to drift away, still chuckling, then turned back, waving half-heartedly. "See ya, Josh!"

Joshua managed a weak wave in return, then turned and walked in the opposite direction, his shoulders slumped. As soon as Joshua is out of earshot, Tyler's grin faded. He nudged Cody with his elbow. "Right, serious talk, though. What do ya really reckon about Joshua's story?"

Cody's laughter died in his throat. He looked back at Joshua's retreating figure, a shiver running down his spine despite the warm afternoon sun. "Nah, mate, it's... it's kinda creepy, aye? The way he keeps goin' on about those bloody crazy dreams. Like, he's dead serious. Gives me the heebie-jeebies, it does."

"Yeah, mate, it bloody is," Tyler drawled, his voice thick with a kind of wary curiosity. He scratched at the back of his neck, his eyes darting around the dusty outback road. "Do ya reckon it actually means somethin', Cody? Like, somethin' proper, ya know?"

He glanced back over his shoulder, his gaze lingering on Joshua's retreating figure, a lone silhouette shrinking into the vast, ochre-colored distance. "He's been actin' real strange, hasn't he?"

"Beats me, Ty," Cody shrugged, his voice a low rumble. "He's always been a bit of a weird unit, hasn't he?"

Tyler's brows furrowed. "Yeah, but this is different, ain't it? These... these bloody dreams. Whot if they're, like, premonitions? Like, somethin' real bad's gonna happen? That'd just be bloody creepy, wouldn't it?" He shuddered, a rare display of unease. "Gives me the heebie-jeebies, it does." He kicked a loose stone, sending it skittering across the dry earth. "Reckon we should tell someone? Or... or somethin'?"

The boys looked at one another once again. Tyler stopped walking as he asked the question

"Oi, listen, right? Wot if somethin' bloody terrible's about to happen to Joshua, yeah? Like, somethin' real bad. And these dreams, they're not just some random sheilas in bathers, are they? They're tryin' to warn him, mate! Like, a bleedin' premonition, yeah? We gotta do somethin'!"

Cody remained quiet, but his mind is filled with wonder at what his friend has just said,

"Wot if he's really in some proper strife, eh? Like, he's tapped into somethin' no one's ever even dreamed of," Tyler persisted, his voice laced with worry. "I know we swore black and blue we wouldn't say a bloody word, but..." he trailed off, a moment of hesitation hanging in the air. "Maybe... just maybe... we should spill the beans."

Cody stopped Tyler dead in his tracks, his eyes narrowed. "Nah, mate. We can't do that. We gave our word, crossed our hearts, sworn to secrecy. Not a bloody soul, remember?"

"Yeah, right, I know," Tyler mumbled, kicking at a loose bit of gravel. "But I'm bloody worried, ya know? Wot if somethin's seriously wrong with Joshua? Wot if he's in a right pickle and needs us to bail him out?"

The two mates walked on in silence, their eyes fixed on the dusty ground.

"Nah... we sound like a couple of bloody mother hens, worryin' like this," Tyler finally grumbled, trying to shake off the unease.

"Maybe you do," Cody retorted, a hint of a smirk playing on his lips.

G'day, mate! Yeah, I'm a rooster. Bit of a legend 'round these parts. Always up for a yarn and a scratch in the dirt.

Both boys laughed, making odd chicken noises, trying to outdo one another as they proceeded on their way. At the base of the mountain side, Joshua looked up at the rugged slope toward its misty peak. He decided to go for a climb. A quarter of the way into his climb, he swivels away and sees a dramatic view of how far his home is in the distance. He thought that it would be a good idea to amuse himself, so he began singing,

"Jack and Jill went up the hill, to see whot they could find," he drawled, a grin splitting his weathered face. "Jack fell down, broke his crown, and Jill came tumblin' behind!" He let out a hearty, booming laugh, clearly chuffed with his own clever little ditty.

"Yeah, good one," he muttered to himself, still chuckling.

He'd barely made it halfway up the blasted mountain, the scrubby bush clinging to the rocky slope no more than a nuisance, when his boot caught on a gnarled root. "Crikey!" he yelped, arms flailing, as he lost his footing.

He tumbled down the mountainside, a chaotic mix of limbs and dust, the rough terrain scraping against his skin. He rolled, and rolled, and rolled, a good third of the way back down from where he'd been headed, finally coming to a jarring halt on a small, familiar ledge. He'd stepped on it just minutes before, hadn't he?

"Ouch! Strewth, that really hurt," he groaned, wincing as he gingerly touched a bruised rib. "Bloody hell," he muttered, spitting out a mouthful of dirt. "Should've known better than to try and climb this drongo of a mountain. Fair dinkum, I reckon I've rattled me brain loose." He rubbed his head, then squinted up at the mountain. "Right, bugger this for a joke," he said to himself. "One more try, and if I fall again I'm going to go have a coldie."

He lays there for a few seconds gathering himself. He sits up and looked down between his legs and sees that landed on something silvery,

"Nah, mate, wasn't me crown that copped it," he chuckled, shaking his head… "Reckon I'd be a bit more worried if it is. Nah, just some other poor bugger's misfortune, I reckon. Bit of a clanger, though, eh?"

He pulls himself up to his feet and rubbed his bum. He bends over to have a look at the silverish object trying to figure it out. Whatever it is, it intrigued him greatly. He began digging around the object, pushing dirt and small gravel aside, but the object was lodged into the mountain really well. It did not deter him, and he kept digging, until he sees what appears to be an emblem on the item. It appeared to be a letter of some sort.

Whatever it is, this thing is very large. Joshua looked underneath it and found nothing but more dirt. He continued on trying to dig it out from its resting place. He dug and dug underneath it, until he made a tunnel.

He digs enough where only his head and shoulders could fit inside while his feet remained sticking out. He crawled from underneath the object and sat down. He looks over at it and noticed that the object's surface was very shiny. It looked like the lid to a treasure chest,

Crikey, if this is a bloody lid, then where's the rest of the bloody chest, eh? Reckon it's gone walkabout? Fair dinkum, this is a right mystery, innit?

He crawls under the object once again, lying in the makeshift tunnel that he created. All of a sudden, there's a tiny shake, but Joshua thinks nothing of it and he continues digging. There's a tiny shake again and again, and still, he thinks nothing of it.

Suddenly, there's an arousing thud that causes a huge chunk of dirt to give way and falls into his face. He spits and wipes the dirt out of his face. There's another thud, then another and another, causing more soil to fall on him.

"Whoa, strewth," he muttered, scratching his head…"That sounds like a right bloody mess. Bad news, that is. Reckon we're in a bit of a pickle.

He quickly scoots from underneath the object. Once out, he sits up and looks back at it when he noticed that his surroundings had become very quiet. He stands to his feet when suddenly, a dark shape landed hard on the mountain causing it to shake. The shaking knocked Joshua slightly off balance. Small and medium rocks, break away from their resting place and began tumbling downward,

"Crikey, no!" he bellowed, terror clawing at his throat. "Strewth, I'm gonna be bloody flat as a tack if I don't get off this mountain! Gonna be a right dog's breakfast, I tell ya!"

His head turns back and forth, he's shaking uncontrollably. Unbeknownst to him, at the top of the mountain, a demon recklessly unearthed huge boulders from there foundation. Joshua looks up and sees an enormous rock barreling down toward him. He realizes that he is trapped with nowhere to go, he quickly crawls back under the shiny object.

Chapter 4

Mesopotamia, 7 B.C. . . .

Over in the village of Akkad. Shepherds are readying them-selves for the coming day. Abram, a handsome young child in his mid-teens, hears the sounds of sheep waiting to be led out to pasture. Abram is already hard at work, tending to his fami-ly's flocks, of ten herds of thirty animals. Abinai, Abram's father, is tending to his brother. He kneels besides a very ill seventeen-year-old name Behera,

"My son, I have been thinking about moving the family to Canaan but with you being ill, I do not know if you are strong enough to make the journey. Your brothers are getting older, and soon, the youngest will seek to take a wife of his choosen," said Abinai to Behera.

"Father, when Abram takes a wife, I know that I will be better by then. Could you wait until that time to move the family?" said Behera.

Abinai agreed to stay until his youngest son took a wife. Nadav, the second eldest son, was about to marry his niece Iuniewe, the daughter of Manias, from his uncle's house. In their tradition, it was customary to marry within the family, to keep the bloodline pure. Yet, they are never full-blooded family members. They are half-brother/sister born of the same father, but with different mothers.

Out in the field, Abram and a few servants are hard at work tending to the herds. Early mornings are his favorite time of day because it was cooler.

Abram led the herd down into the valley. This season, the plains are dry from the lack of rain. But he leads them to an area where there is plenty of grass to sustain the livestock. Abram, with staff in hand, is not surveying the flocks. The look on his face indicated that he was deep in thought. One of his servants can tell that something was on his mind,

"Master . . . Is everything all right with you?" he asked.

"Everything is fine," Abram answered.

Abram's overexpression remained on his face. He carefully maneuvered through the herd of sheep before stopping for a brief moment. He is still captured by his thoughts, reminiscing over the images that had occurred some ten years earlier. He drifts into a daydream reflecting back on the day when he'd been sitting outside of his tent long ago, when he heard a voice calling out to him.

A sudden montage of visual images that includes a sword, silhouettes, fiery arrows, and winged creatures appears to him. He closes his eyes and open them again and the images are gone. Scratching his head, he is sure that what he seen were real. He walks away from the herd and goes about ten yards before stopping. He looked back, only to see that the only thing around him was sand.

He calls out to his mother. He waits for a response, but there is no one there to answer. He squints his eyes because the sunlight was so bright that day. He put his hand over his eyes to block the sun's rays. As he did so, he sees a dark figure standing in the distance. The stranger calls out to him,

"Abram, come to me." the stranger said.

A frightened Abram stood still, not moving even a little bit. He couldn't see the stranger's face. But for a moment, he thought he knew this man. The person looked familiar to him, and that guy called out to Abram again,

"Come to me child. I will not hurt you!"

"Who are you?" Abram asked.

The guy doesn't answer. Abram backs away slowly and returned to his herd. He looks back at the man, but the guy is out of view. So, they lead the herds back near the village while the stranger stood in silence until darkness consumed the day. Slowly, the moon's light pierced through the few clouds that remained.

Abram looks up and eyes the man again. The night gives way to the moon's radiant light revealing the stranger's face. Abram is startled by the man's physical appearance. He stands wide eyes, gazing at the mangled face of him.

He turns and run in the direction of their tent calling for his father. The man quickly vanished into the night air. Abram runs into the village, passed a few villagers. One of the villagers sees the frighten child, and she is off to get his parents. Nushuri, Abram's mother, hears the nervous cry of a villager calling her. Nushuri stops what she is doing and comes to see what the commotion is all about.

The young villager tells her the chilling tale about her son's ordeal. He grabs Nushuri by the hand pulling on her to come with him. They make haste running through the dusty street of the village until they came to the area where Abram is last seen. They searched the area and found him crouched down with his hands over his face. His mother frantically goes to him,

"Abram, Abram! What's wrong? Did somebody hurt you? Are you alright? What happened?" she asked.

Abram is too frightened to speak. He sat crying, refusing to remove his hands. His mother instructs one of their servants to go and get his father. A few more people gathered around to see what's the commotion is all about. The young man quickly runs to get Abram's father. Moments later, the servant returns with Abinai. By this time, more and more people have trickled in. The crowd grew large in size.

Abinai sees his wife kneeling down by their distraught son. He runs over to see what's troubling his son. He makes his way through the crowd, shoving a few people aside. He pushed his way through til finally reached his wife and son. He leans down and asks him,

"Son, what's wrong?"

Abram hears the voice of his father and stands up. They all embraced each other,

"Don't let him take me!"

"Don't let who take you?" asked his father.

"That thing!"

Abram pointed in the direction where the man was standing. All looked in the direction, but they see nothing,

"What man? I don't see anyone."

Abinai says to him that everything will be all right, and he will not let anything happen to him. Both parents carefully examined their son's physical appearance. Seeing that nothing is wrong, they escorted him back to the tent. One of the villagers looked at the other,

"What an imagination he has." he said to the other.

But the high priest sensed that something wasn't quite right. He goes over to the altar to prepare a sacrifice to God. While on their way back to the tent. Later that night, a voice calls out to Abram. He played the scene over and over in his mind. Suddenly, he cried out,

"NOOOOO!"

Instantly, he is awakened from his dream. He shakes his head clearing all thoughts of what he herd. The next day, Abram is walking among the herd feeling a bit unease. He eyes a small hilltop and looks out across the plains at the grazing herd, thinking to himself,

"There seems to be a charge in the air today." he thought.

Abinai walks around the village checking the tents of his people. Being that he is a skilled carpenter, he takes it upon himself to make sure that all of the tents are in good shape. The camp is just north of where Abram is now standing under an Achamoth tree. Suddenly, a demon name Baalamus, steps out from the shadows. Abinai is unaware of the demon's presence. He is enjoying his time alone. Baalamus entered into Abinai's body, temporarily taking control of it.

Abinai called for his servant, Abdul-Azeem. He asked him to deliver a message to his son. Azeem hurried off to deliver the message to his master's son. A few minute later, Baalamus exited Abinai's body and vanished. Abinai shook his head as if something was wrong, but he can't put his finger on it. The experience left him feeling lite headed for just a moment.

Over in the field some twenty minutes later, while surveying the area, Abram sees Azeem approaching. Abram stopped what he was doing and waits for his servant greetings. A few seconds later, Azeem approaches his lord and bowed,

"Azeem. What bestowed this visit?" asked Abram.

"My lord. May I speak?" he asked while still bowed.

"Yes," replied Abram . . .

"But before you do, stand to your feet and speak."

Azeem rose to his feet and began delivering the message,

"My lord . . . Your father request is, that you move the herd down the riverbed on the east side, because there is some fresh green grass there that the flock would surely enjoy."

Abram turned his head to the east and looked in the direction of the riverbed, some miles away. He pivots back to his messenger and sends him back to his father with a message. The manservant left as he was instructed to do.

Abram gathered his herdsmen, and they led the herd in the direction of the area that his father said he must go. The sun's heat was beginning to affect them mildly. While walking toward the riverbed, Abram pulled out his wineskin and begin taking several gulps of water.

After quenching his thirst, he stared across the plains to see how much further they had to go. But the intense heatwave obscured his vision. Being accustomed to such high temperature, he continued their journey. For a moment, they struggled with the heat, but a mild breeze provided them with some relief. They can now see the edge of the riverbed up ahead. Abram leads the herd toward the tasty green pasture by the riverbed.

He kept a sharp eye out for thieves and predators because it was not rare for them to come steal a shepherd's livestock. However, today was a quiet day. To him it was a relief, so he didn't think about it for long. They continued on their journey enjoying the pleasant day. Over in the village, Abdul-Azeem returned to his master Abinai. He kneels before him.

"Azeem, you may rise." says Abinai.

Azeem rose to his feet and tells his master that he delivered the message to his son. Not sure what to make of that, Abinai looked at his servant as though he must be mistaken,

"What message did you delivered to my son?" he asked.

"Master . . . You sent me to tell Abram to take the herds to the riverbed because there is greener grass there."

"What do you mean? I never told you such a thing. I would never send my son to his death."

Fearing repercussion, Azeem bowed again before his master,

"Master – I beguile you not. You sent me with a message for your son to carryout." he says while kneeling.

Abinai collapses to his knees in shock. He can't believe that he sent his son some ill advice,

"What have I done? I have sent my son to his death."

Azeem again rose to his feet trying to comfort his master. But Abinai did not want to hear what his servant has to say. He remained on his knees and begin to call on the name of the Lord,

"O Lord, the God of my ancestors, Abraham, Isaac and Jacob. I beseech you Lord because my son is in your hands now. Only you can deliver him from such a fate. Let not my son, feel the sting of death."

While he continued praying, in the distance, Abram sees Toe Tou, another of his father's servants, approaching with a few items in his hands. He was carrying bread, dried meat, and fresh water that were sent by his mother. After reaching Abram, he said,

"My lord, the days are long, and your mother wants to make sure that you are fed before bringing the herd back, so I have brought some food for you and the others."

Toe Tou and his lord distribute the food and water to them, and Abram sends his servant on his way. Abram gathered his food and leisurely walked in the midst of the herd. After a moment or two, he noticed that the riverbed was only a few yards away. He sets down under a tree to eat some the fulfilling meal.

His servants are now far off with the herd. Abram is left alone. After eating his morsel, he thought to relax for a moment, before catching up with the others. He leans back against a tree watching the herds move into greener pastures. Abram felt himself starting to drift off to sleep. But he refuses to let the leisure time get the best of him. He stands, stretching, trying to get his blood circulating through his body, when something, in the distance catch his attention.

"What is that?" he says to himself.

He placed his hand above his brow, blocking the sun's glare. He sees what appeared to be a shadowy figure walking toward him. It's to far away to determine who it is. Suddenly, four images emerged from behind the figure walking toward him in a V shape formation.

"I must be tired." he says rubbing his eyes,

He sees all five figures approaching. He arose to his feet and grabbed his staff, which is leaning against the tree. But as the five figures got closer, they suddenly merged back into one.

"What? Where did they go? I only turned away for a second." Abram thought.

Again, he rubbed his eyes as if something is in them. But there is nothing in his eyes. Abram turned around, only to be startled by that same figure, which is now standing in back of him. He quickly pivots and thrust his staff forward, keeping the stranger at bay. But as fast as Abram could blink his eyes, the stranger was gone. Then he reappeared behind him again. He coughs to get Abram's attention. The deranged sound startled Abram. He turned, and swiftly moves back,

"How did you get behind me?" he asks the stranger.

This annoyed Abram greatly; he shudders with distaste at being taken by surprise,

"Young master, please forgive me. My intention was not to frighten you." said the stranger.

"You did!" said Abram sharply.

The smile on the stranger's face made him a little uncomfortable with the attention,

"I have walked a great distance. May I share a place here with you under this tree?"

Not knowing who this stranger is, Abram cautiously moved back, motioning for the man to take a seat. As if on cue, the tree stump as the man sat down. For a brief moment, Abram changed his focus to the slumping tree. He looked at it in quizzingly,

"Hmm. I don't remember that tree looking like that?" he thought.

Abram steps back to inspect the tree but the stranger senses Abram's thought imbalance and quickly created a distraction. His eyes stray out to the field, he quickly stands up. Abram followed his gaze,

"What's wrong?" he asked.

Abram looked out at the herd as they made their way alongside the riverbed. The stranger quickly created the illusion of the tree being up right and normal again. Abram pivots back to the stranger.

"Where are the others that I saw walking with you?" he asked.-

"Others? There are no others my lord. It's only I."

"I'm positively sure that I saw someone else with you. What sort of deception are you trying to put over on me?"

"My lord . . . I deceive you not. My name is Baalamus. I have been traveling alone all around the countryside, trying to find a place to settle."

"All alone?" asked Abram, not sure of his story eyeing Baalamus suspiciously,

"Not quite," Baalamus said, with a slight smirk.

"Others are here in close proximity. I guess you could say, we are scouting the area," he said, with a toothy grin.

A foul stench dominates the air around them.

"Peeeeew! Something must have died," said Abram, waving his hand in front of his face.

He looked over at Baalamus once again,

"Why are you looking at me? I have nothing to do with this stench that you smell," said Baalamus, while waving his hand in front of his face.

Baalamus rose from his sitting position and stretched. He reached out his hand, offering the friendly gesture of a handshake. Abram reached back to accept, but before they could make contact, a thunderous sound, unlike anything he has ever heard before came roaring from the heavens.

"Oh, that's just great!" Baalamus thought.

Abram detects some negative activity, and he looked toward the herd. A small, dark cloud rapidly appeared over the livestock. It quickly grew in size. The winds also picked quickly up and began blowing violently. Oblivious to Abram, within the cloud sits Baaladyme, who is waiting on Baalamus signal.

Chapter 5

The year is 1822 BCE . . .

The sun dipped low in the sky, casting a warm golden hue over the village. Smoke swirled upwards from the fires, where women bustled about, stirring pots filled with wild boar stew and fragrant herbs. Laughter echoed through the air as men strummed their instruments, their voices rising in vibrant harmonies that told the stories of their ancestors. Jacob sat outside his dwelling, leaning against the cool earth, watching the younger children chase each other, the joyous cries of his siblings mingling with the music.

His father, Meskana, a robust man of thirty-six, bristled with vitality despite his slight paunch. He was taking a moment to compose himself before heading to the council tent, eager to gain the elders' approval for Jacob to embark on his first solo hunt. It was a rite of passage, a moment every boy looked forward to—a chance to step into manhood. Jacob's heart raced at the thought. Hunting is his passion; he had an instinct for timing and aim that made him proud.

Jacob pondered other gifts he possessed, but it was archery that ignited his spirit. Meskana, revered not only as a hunter but as the most captivating storyteller in the village, often remarked that a well-spun tale could sway even the sternest of hearts. Jacob had inherited that flair for practicality in his storytelling too, even if others struggled to believe his colorful accounts.

As the second eldest child in his family, missing his older sister felt like a solemn ache in his chest. She had married off at sixteen and now lived twenty miles away with her own child, a tiny yet vivid reminder of life's passage. Jacob already recalled the fear and excitement of his first rite of passage at the age of five.

He paced nervously outside the council tent, glancing towards the communal gathering where clusters of men stand engaged in hushed discussions. Just then, the sound of unmistakable clacks and rhythmic clicks resounded, announcing the end of deliberations. The chief elder placed a reassuring hand on Meskana's back, signaling their agreement.

Meskana strode towards their tent, his gait firm. Moments later, he stepped just outside and called for Jacob, who felt his heart race with anticipation.

"Father! What did the elders decide?" Jacob asked, his voice barely concealing the excitement.

Meskana smiled, but his expression is thoughtful. "We'll discuss it over dinner, my son," he replied, his tone both firm and warm, ensuring Jacob knew there is more to this moment than mere words

The two slipped quietly into their home, the warmth embracing them as they crossed the threshold. They paused for a moment, inhaling the rich aroma of a meal simmering over a fire, the promise of nourishment tantalizing their senses.

Early on in the evening, the elders gathered in the temple for prayer. Shortly after they assembled, the atmosphere shifted, and the Phoenician descended upon the shrine, radiating an eerie light. Fear washed over the elders as they beheld the figure, cloaked in a sinister, reddish glow. The chief elder, his voice trembling but resolute, stepped forward to confront the apparition.

"Demon! You tread upon sacred ground. What is your purpose here in the house of the Lord?" the elder demanded, clenching his fists.

"Sacred? This ground holds no sanctity," the entity replied, its voice like gravel... "I've traversed realms more holy than this before your kind were fashion vessels from mud." Its unblinking gaze settled on each elder in turn.

Another elder, summoning the strength of his faith, stand up and began to speak in a sacred tongue. The entity reacted, its hands weaving through the air with an almost theatrical flourish. The elder suddenly convulsed, his body vibrating as if caught in a storm, before collapsing to the ground. Gasps echoed throughout the sacred space as the other elders witnessed their fellow's suffering, his flesh seemingly consumed from within. The entity turned its focus toward the remaining elders, voice low and threatening. "You are all devoid of salvation. Consider this: you will perish unless you heed my words."

A palpable silence fell over the group, dread connecting them in shared horror. Each elder exchanged frantic glances, the weight of their predicament sinking in. Then, in an instant, the entity vanished, leaving them in darkness. Jacob is greeted by his mother, Ba'tia—her name meaning "daughter of God"—stand radiant as she welcomed her son and his friend home with an inviting smile. "Go wash up, guys," she instructed cheerfully.

After they scrubbed away the remnants of the day, they gathered at the table for a sumptuous meal. A wave of gratitude filled the air as they thanked their God for their home and the food that lay before them.

Jacob sat across from his parents, his heart a mix of apprehension and yearning as he immersed himself in the delightful flavors of his mother's cooking: creamy hummus paired with warm pita bread and a rich bowl of Baba Ghanouj. His mother turned to his father, curiosity brimming in her eyes. "How did the meeting go?"

Jacob leaned forward anticipation coursing through him as he continued to eat, eager for the news his father is poised to share.

"The elders have agreed that it's time for you to embark on your first solo hunt, Jacob," declared his father, a proud smile illuminating his face.

Jacob could hardly contain his joy; his grin seemed to stretch from ear to ear. He jumped from his seat and rushed to embrace his father. "I'm becoming a man!" he exclaimed, the weight of the moment washing over him.

His father nodded, unable to hide his pride as he continued, "The ritual begins tomorrow. You must get your rest tonight."

Ba'tia's eyes shimmered with unshed tears as she took in the news, a bittersweet mix of pride and worry. With a calm demeanor, Meskana interjected, "You're to journey north for three days. Bring back enough meat to feed everyone."

As the evening wound down, they finished their meal. Meskana stepped outside to gaze up at the stars, while Ba'tia and Jacob tidied up for the night.

After a moment, they heard Meskana's voice call from the entrance. "Jacob!"

"Yes, Father!" Jacob responded, heart racing in excitement.

"It's time to prepare for your bla-ha-de," his father said, the tone carrying both anticipation and gravity.

Jacob's face lit up. "I've been waiting for this day!" he replied eagerly.

His mind buzzed with possibilities; he could already picture himself applying the skills he'd honed since he was a mere child. That familiar flutter stirred in his stomach, reminiscent of his first hunting experience alongside the men—the thrill of discovery, the pulse of nature around him, and the laughter of his mother and father echoing in his ears as they reminisced about their own journeys.

Meskana glanced back at him, a knowing smile playing on his lips.

"One day, you'll have a family of your own, with Ya'mahyu," he said, his voice carrying the weight of tradition. "She's only eleven now. In two years, her parents will present her to you."

Jacob looked over at Ya'mahyu, his expression unreadable. The gatherings of their families often felt oppressive, the talk of futures stretching uncomfortably before them. Ya'mahyu smiled but quickly turned her gaze away from him. He noticed the shyness etched on her face, a reflection of their shared discomfort.

Ifeoma had been raised with a clear understanding of her future: a husband to hunt for her, a life of domesticity to prepare for. From an early age, she learned the skills expected of a woman—cooking, cleaning, mending clothes, weaving baskets, and bearing children. The conversations around the fire revealed the path laid out for both of them, predetermined and unyielding.

Jacob settled in between their fathers, both of whom were sitting close to the crackling fire. His father began sharing tales from his own youth, and Jacob leaned in, eager for the familiar nostalgia.

"Ah, I still remember the first time I embarked on a hunt alone. I was just about your age, perhaps a few months older," Meskana recalled, his eyes sparkling with the memory. "I felt a rush of excitement, knowing it was my chance to prove myself as both a man and a warrior."

Jacob listened intently, caught between the weight of expectation and the thrill of adventure hinted at in his father's voice. A broad smile lit up Meskana's face as he drifted back to his days as a young warrior, recounting the moment he first brought down wild game to feed their village.

"How many people were there back then? Five or ten?" Jacob quipped, a teasing glint in his eyes.

Opuniahay, Ifeoma's father, burst into a hearty laugh. "You're always full of jokes, aren't you, Jacob?"

"We'll definitely miss your humor while you're off gallivanting," Meskana shot back, shaking his head with a smile.

Jacob glanced skyward, captivated by the twinkling stars. "What kinds of wild beasts will dare challenge a mighty hunter like me?" he mused internally.

His imagination soared with possibilities. He often pondered the existence of other worlds— "Are there places like this in the heavens?" he wondered once more. Such thoughts plagued him more often than not; he felt a tugging in his heart that there was more to life than this.

The stars overhead twinkled like diamonds scattered across a vast, dark canvas. Travelers came through this region seeking treasures like those glimmering gems, yet Jacob didn't fully grasp their significance. He had seen them, dazzling and bright, but they seemed impractical for his people. Still, tonight, those stars reminded him of diamonds.

"It's getting late, son," Ba'tia said gently.

"I know, I know." Jacob replies cheerfully.

Meskana added, the warmth of fatherly concern shading his voice. "But you need your rest. A long journey awaits you tomorrow,"

Jacob nodded. He goes and clamber into bed, but sleep eluded him. His mind raced with the thrill of the hunt—imagining the sight of water buffalo roaming the plains, giraffes stretching their necks high, and the stealthy maneuvers needed to avoid the watchful eyes of lionesses on the prowl. He could picture himself stalking a herd of gazelles, sprinting across the savanna as if pursued by a pack of hyenas, exhilaration coursing through his veins.

Jacob's mind raced with thoughts and scenarios, but eventually, exhaustion claimed him, and sleep washed over him. As dawn broke, he slowly gathered his belongings, the soft hues of morning light spilling into the tent. His parents were already awake, a familiar tradition marking this day: seeing their son off, as he stepped into manhood.

"Ba'tia, what's cooking?" he called, the aroma of food wafting through the air.

"Just a hearty meal to fuel the journey ahead!" she replied cheerily, stirring a pot. "You'll need your strength, Jacob."

He turned to search for his father, his heart racing. "Where's Dad?" he asked his mother, a hint of worry in his voice.

"He left about an hour ago to take care of some village affairs," she answered, a tinge of pride in her tone. "He'll be back soon."

"Can you tell him I'll see him in three days?" Jacob said as Ba'tia handed him a sack of food, her smile warm and reassuring.

"Of course, sweetheart. Be careful out there," she said, wrapping him in a tight embrace before he stepped out into the morning light.

As he fastened his sandals, Jacob felt a mix of excitement and trepidation. Just as he started walking towards the northern region, Meskana's voice echoed behind him.

"My son! Wait. I have something for you," his father called out, approaching with purpose.

Jacob paused, turning to face him. "What is it, Father?" he asked, curiosity piquing.

Meskana held out a beautifully crafted wineskin. "This is the wineskin that your ancestors brought on their quests. Take it with you as I did at your age. It will keep your water cool."

With a mix of reverence and gratitude, Jacob accepted the gift. "I promise not to let you down," he said earnestly, looking into his father's eyes.

"I know you won't, my son. You've been trained for this moment, and now that it's here, you will leave as a boy but return as a man." Meskana's voice was thick with emotion, tears brimming in his eyes.

"Thank you, Father," Jacob whispered, his own eyes glistening. They embraced tightly, the embrace infused with a weight of love and expectation.

"Go now. May the gods be with you," Meskana said, stepping back, his voice thick with pride and concern.

As Jacob wiped away a few tears, the village elders began to gather, joining a chorus to send him off. He turned back to his father, who stood resolutely, watching him depart with mixed feelings of joy and melancholy.

As Jacob stepped out of the village, more villagers came forward, forming a procession filled with songs and blessings. The men sang songs of preparation, their voices melding into an uplifting anthem of camaraderie, while the women harmonized with songs of jubilee, weaving special garments infused with hopes for Jacob's safe return.

The sounds of both melodies intertwined harmoniously, marking the beginning of a journey that seemed to stretch on like the horizon before him. With every step he took into the northern territory, he carried his family's love and legacy, ready to face whatever lay ahead.

The village was alive with song and laughter, a vibrant celebration illuminating the warm afternoon. As Jacob prepared to embark on the Blaha-de, anticipation buzzed in the air. Soon, after the trials ahead, there would be feasting, drinking, dancing, and tales woven from the fabric of past adventures. Women worked diligently, grinding grains to bake bread, while the men mixed mud to create intricate body paint designs. Yet, amid the revelry, hushed whispers from the elders hinted at a worry that clung to their hearts—what if Jacob did not return?

On the trail to the northern region, Jacob felt a buoyant sense of freedom. The sky was a canvas of bright blue, adorned with delicate wisps of clouds drifting lazily by. Each step taken was a blend of thrill and trepidation. The colors of the plains appeared more vivid today, just like the stars had radiated brilliantly the night before. Even though game was plentiful near the village, he was destined for a distant location, where he hoped to showcase the survival skills he had honed through rigorous training.

"Not much is happening back home," he mused, offering a wave to a few familiar faces from a neighboring village as he passed. They were no strangers; their visits for trade had forged bonds over time. Jacob stopped briefly to refill his waterskin, and the villagers generously offered him bread and figs for the journey. The village elder, with a hand on his shoulder, imparted a blessing before Jacob continued on his path.

Hours later, he reached a dry watering hole, remnants of an oasis long since abandoned. He knelt to drink deeply, savoring every drop. As he lifted his gaze, he noticed an Olea europea tree adorned with fruits. Driven by curiosity, he plucked one, biting into its flesh—all sweetness vanished into bitterness. A cough erupted involuntarily, and he fumbled for his waterskin to cleanse his palate. After dispelling the unpleasant taste, he settled against the shade of a large tree, pulling out the provisions his mother had packed for him.

As he ate, his thoughts drifted to home—wondering what his family was doing, how they were partaking in the festivities. In the distance, he spotted grazing animals. His gaze shifted to a pride of lionesses on the hunt, stealthily coordinating their approach to ensnaring their quarry. Observing the pride's synchronized movements stirred a mix of admiration and an aching homesickness within him, intensified by the oppressive heat of the summer day. He tried to banish the lingering feelings of solitude, focusing instead on the task ahead.

Jacob embarked on his journey once more, the afternoon sun hanging stubbornly in the sky, casting an intensity that felt heavier than usual. Time seemed to drag, the hours moving languidly in the oppressive heat. A gentle breeze suddenly appeared from the east, swirling in the distance and lifting a few dust devils a couple of miles away. To him, it was a foreboding sign—a windstorm was approaching.

He squinted at the scene. The dust devils coalesced into a more formidable form, twisting and tightening into a singular spiral that seemed to be headed in his direction.

"Maybe I can outrun it," he reasoned quietly to himself, adrenaline spiking as he started to trot away from the oncoming storm.

The winds escalated, growing fiercer and more chaotic. Jacob dared a glance over his shoulder, his heart racing as he realized the storm was closing in. The sky overhead churned with dark, angry clouds, as if the heavens themselves were raging against him. A massive funnel cloud appeared, looming ominously about a mile behind him.

A chill swept through the air, sending a shiver down Jacob's spine. Suddenly, a luminous glow enveloped him, ignited by the flames licking at his heels—his sandals leaving a trail of fire in his wake. The funnel cloud responded, drawing the flames into its vortex, morphing into a swirling tempest of smoke and fire. Jacob's vision blurred as he fought to keep his focus.

He desperately tried to increase the distance between himself and the storm, but it seemed to gain momentum just as quickly. Instinctively, he felt the unpredictability of such storms, as if they possessed a will of their own. He glanced back just in time to see the storm veer again. Fingers of dark vapor began to stretch out from the center of the funnel.

"Is that… a hand?" he thought, fear twisting in his gut.

The wind howled violently around him, whipping debris through the air. Without a moment's hesitation, he grabbed his scarf and wrapped it around his nose and mouth, trying to shield himself from the invasive particles swirling in the chaos.

"There! I have to reach that cave!" he exclaimed, his eyes fixed on the dark entrance looming ahead.

Jacob sprinted towards it, thoughts racing in his mind. Thank goodness I know this territory well, he reassured himself. Yet, the journey was far from over. Blinded by a relentless cloud of sand, he struggled to make out the shelter that promised refuge. The harsh elements swirled around him, a testament to his need to be prepared for anything. This was a pivotal moment in his life, one that tested his resolve as he battled against the stinging grains and howling winds, each step bringing him closer to manhood.

At last, Jacob reached the cave, glancing back over his shoulder to find the threat had vanished. He stepped inside, inhaling deeply as a wave of relief washed over him, as if he had just escaped a predator's jaws.

Breathless and weary, he sank to the ground, a sense of urgency creeping into his consciousness like a cool breeze in the heat. There was something, or someone, present in the shadows. A faint, discordant murmur echoed off the stone walls, freezing him for a heartbeat before his instincts kicked in. In the dim light, he stretched out a hand, feeling his way cautiously deeper into the cave.

Finding a spot to brace his back against the cool stone, he surveyed a narrow corridor ahead. He faced a choice: wait for the storm to calm before resuming his hunt. Just then, a noise sent a jolt through him. He tensed, every sense heightened as he strained to discern any unusual movement. With great caution, he approached the source of the sound, curiosity piqued. To his shock, he melted into the cave's enveloping darkness, making himself all but invisible.

A sudden crash echoed from deeper within, followed by the murmur of flowing water. Jacob's attention was drawn to a soft glow emanating from far ahead. Another loud rumble jolted him, triggering a torrent of thoughts and memories that flashed through his mind like a kaleidoscope. Beautiful, intricate patterns illuminated the cave's walls, beckoning him closer to the ethereal glow.

As he rounded the corner, he was left spellbound. The sight before him was breathtaking. Luminous rocks cast a gentle radiance, revealing the cave's mysteries in a wash of color and light. Jacob's eyes quickly adjusted, and he realized he might be here for a while, at the mercy of the storm outside.

Settling down, he took out a few figs, savoring the sweetness as he refueled. After eating, he looked around for a cozy spot. I suppose I can rest here until the storm passes, he thought, feeling fatigue washing over him like a blanket, one that would shield him from the chaos outside. He takes out a blanket and lays it on the ground as a sleeping mat. He takes another blanket and rolls it up into a ball to be used as a pillow. He yawns loudly and lies down.

A few minutes later, he drifts off into a deep sleep and began dreaming. He dreamed that he is back home with his friends, and they are playing on the outskirts of his village, dancing and telling a story about a time long ago when a stranger came to visit them, promising them new things to see and new adventures to behold. This mysterious figure always lingered in the shadows, watching. One night, Jacob sat on a large stone with his legs crossed, envisioning his friends dancing a warrior's dance.

The night is black and there are no stars or moonlight because of the thickness of the clouds, the air is chilly. Sounds of haunting laughter began to fill the dark night. Suddenly, a voice said, "So, Jacob is your name?"

"Who said that?" he asked quizzingly.

Again, a voice resonated from parts unknown. Suddenly, Jacob pops up frantically looking around in every direction. He sees nothing but vast darkness residing in the cave, "I was dreaming." he thought.

Chapter 6

The creation of man . . .

Five days after the universe was formed, the world lay shrouded in a thick, swirling fog, droplets of water clinging to the earth. Hashem knelt, His fingers sifting through the moist soil around Him. With deliberate care, He began to mold the earth, crafting a skeleton from the dust.

As He worked, vital organs were positioned with precision, muscles and tendons winding around the frame like ribbons. Gently, He draped skin over this creation, layering it meticulously until every limb was cloaked. Finally, from the surface of the flesh, millions of delicate, threadlike strands emerged, which Hashem named hair.

Leaning close, He exhaled a deep, powerful breath into the hollow figure. Air surged into its chambers, and the essence of life was breathed into this vessel. The breath escaped the creature's mouth, and soon, a beat echoed within its chest, the heart pulsed in time with the air flowing through the nostrils. The clay that Hashem had shaped transformed into a living man.

Hashem's voice echoed through the air, resonating like a gentle yet commanding wind. "Awaken," He called, and the man's eyes fluttered open, revealing a blank expression. As he slowly scanned his surroundings, a brilliant flash illuminated the atmosphere, and the Burning Ones appeared, bowing deeply before Hashem.

"You summoned us, Lord?" they spoke in harmony.

"Rise," Hashem instructed, and the Burning Ones stood tall.

"I have fashioned a creature unlike any other on this earth. I have created man, made in our image, resembling our likeness. I will pause the creation of his powerful female counterpart for now. I will be their Father, and they will be My sons. Together, we will share a bond."

Not far from where they are standing, the man stood up slowly, a sense of curiosity flitting across his face. Hashem stepped forward, introducing Himself.

"I am Hashem, and these are My ministers: Zarath, Elyzariah, Adon-Shama, and Raphaon." …

The man continued to gaze at his surroundings, a distant look in his eyes. Hashem continued, "I have bestowed upon you the Earth, your realm to govern, and dominion over every creature that roams upon it, from the mighty elephants to the minuscule wasp."

Guiding the man to the edge where land met sea, Hashem gestured to the vast body of water before them. "Look across the great sea and tell Me what you see."

The man peered into the shimmering expanse, hesitating as he turned his gaze from left to right. "Where has the land gone?" he inquired, his voice a mixture of wonder and confusion.

Hashem smiled gently, "The land still exists. It lies beneath the waters, hidden from view."

The man's eyes widened. "Is that what you call it—water? Why have you brought me here?"

"I have led you here to reveal that you hold dominion over every creature of this great sea. From the majestic whales to the tiniest plankton, all sea life is under your guardianship."

The man stood at the edge of the sea, watching the gentle waves lap against the shore. With cautious steps, he approached the water, feeling its cool embrace as he dipped his hand in. Small fish bobbed to the surface, their curious eyes glinting like jewels in the sunlight.

"Hello there," the man said softly, his voice a mingling of surprise and delight. A faint smile crept across his face as a fish danced playful circles around his fingers.

As the man lingered at the water's edge, he felt a presence beside him. It was the Lord, walking beside him as they turned away from the sea's embrace. Together they strolled back toward the land from which they came.

They paused near a grassy knoll, where the man decided to sit, sinking into the soft earth. One by one, animals from the surrounding area began to drift closer, curiosity piquing in their eyes.

"Look at him," the Lord remarked, a twinkle in His eye as He observed the man interacting with the creatures. "He seems at home amidst these beings. His kindness brings me joy."

"Indeed, my Lord," replied Zarath, a Seraphim to His right, watching intently. "He possesses an openness that is rare."

The Lord beamed, "Behold, it is very good."

He turned his gaze toward the man, who was now laughing as a small rabbit nuzzled at his side. "I shall grant you a name, one that shall endure through the ages, marking your presence among all creation."

The man paused, a puzzled look crossing his face as the Lord contemplated the name He would choose. In that moment, the Lord excused the man to step aside for a moment, allowing Him to admire this new creation. Once the man wandered off, the Lord addressed the Seraphim, a serious tone creeping into His voice. "But there is a matter that troubles me."

Zarath leaned in, inquisitive. "What vexes you, Hashem?"

"The heart of man is noble, yet I sense a potential within him that is troubling," the Lord replied, His eyes fixed on the retreating figure. "He possesses free will, which is a gift, yet it may become his greatest burden."

"Why does this concern you, my Lord?" asked Raphaon, the Seraphim behind Hashem's left, tilting his head thoughtfully.

"I have shaped him unlike any other creature," Hashem said, sighing deeply. "Molded from clay, every facet designed for purpose.

But the mind… the mind can wander. It craves the unattainable, and should he falter in his choices, nothing shall restrain him from darkness."

"Your wisdom is vast, and your concerns valuable," Elyzariah, replied cautiously. "Yet he is not like the others—surely there is light in his heart."

The Lord nodded, still gazing into the distance where the man had gone. "Yes, but I fear the weakness of his mind may lead him away from the light. And when that happens, I mean nothing shall stop him from straying from My sight."

His voice held a weight that silenced the Seraphim, but His resolve to choose a name for His new creation remained unshaken. The air hummed with anticipation as the Lord contemplated the destiny of His masterpiece. The Lord of Hosts paused, observing the man who stood amidst the gathered creatures of the Earth. With a gentle sigh, He spoke with a voice that echoed in the stillness of the garden,

"Since this man has been drawn from the soil, I shall name him Adam."

He approached Adam, who was completely captivated by the lively animals surrounding him. Leaning closer, the Lord called softly, "Adam."

But the man remained oblivious, his attention consumed by the wonder of the creatures. The Lord raised His voice slightly, calling out again, "Adam!"

This time, the sound reached Adam's ears, and he turned toward the Lord, a glimmer of recognition in his eyes. "Yes, my Lord," he replied, moving closer.

In a warm and fatherly tone, Hashem spoke, "I have summoned you because I wish to grant you a name, one that carries great significance."

Adam furrowed his brow, his confusion evident. "What do you mean, Lord? What is a name?" he asked, unsure of the meaning hidden in this revelation.

Sensing Adam's hesitation, Hashem bestowed wisdom upon him, explaining gently. "A name is an identifier, a mark by which you will be recognized. It links you to your lineage, your very essence."

To clarify, He offered an example: "Think of the animals around you, each with their own calling. Just as I have named them, so too will you be known by this name."

With newfound understanding flickering in his eyes, Adam listened intently, the weight of his identity beginning to settle in his heart.

In the pristine, vibrant garden. HASHEM stands before ADAM, who eyes his surroundings curiously. HASHEM smiles, a warm, paternal expression. He walks over to ADAM, placing a gentle hand on his shoulder.

"My name is Hashem," He declared, his voice resonating through the ethereal realm, "which translates to the Lord of Hosts. I am the Supreme Master of the Celestial Host, and we function as one divine entity. What they perceive, I also perceive; what I envision, they too shall see."

Adam absorbs the information, repeating his name with a sense of wonder. With a joyous gait,

"I have chosen to name you Adam because out of Earth, is the very substance that you were formed," Hashem explained, his tone warm and inviting.

Adam continues absorbing the information given to him with serene demeanor, repeating the name that now defined him.

"My name is Adam! From the Earth, I was created!" he exclaimed in wide-eyed wonder, a smile breaking across his face as the realization of his existence washed over him.

Overwhelmed by the significance of having a name, Adam turned toward Hashem, his joy barely contained. Before long, Hashem gently sent him away, out of sight, signaling the onset of an extraordinary moment. The Lord is prepared to unveil His newest creation to the Celestial Body.

With a commanding thought, Hashem summoned for the hosts of heaven. From the profound darkness of the sky, countless numbers of brilliant lights surged forth, racing toward Him with breathtaking speed. As the celestial lights approached, they began to reverberate with harmonics that enveloped the atmosphere of Earth. In mere moments, torrents of illumination descended, spiraling down like bolts of lightning, casting an awe-inspiring spectacle over the blu planet.

Each angelic being created by Hashem arrived in reverent grandeur, gathering for the destined enthronement of mankind. The assembly waited in silent anticipation for the Lord's decree. Eventually, the Lord urged Adam to remain still. The seraphim led the way, followed by Hashem Himself. As the Celestial Host united with the creatures of the Earth, they bowed low, their faces touching the ground in humility.

"Rise," Hashem commanded, and as they stood, the myriad angelic lights sang in unison, their voices ringing out like echoes of divine harmony,

"You are worthy! You are worthy! You are worthy! You are worthy, Lord!"

As the final notes faded into the vastness, the assembly held their breath in eager readiness for the Lord's proclamation. Hashem stepped forward and paused, allowing the anticipation to build before addressing His creation.

"To all who inhabit this realm, I summoned you here because I have completed a wondrous new creation. I bestow upon this creation, dominion over all that exists on Earth, and it shall serve as the guardian of this planet. It is the crowning achievement of my handiwork, and I have gifted it a name unlike any other. From this moment forward, you shall refer to this new creation as . . . Adam!"

As the proclamation echoed through the celestial realm, a palpable shift enveloped the high heavens. Satan's countenance, once a robust mast of pride and authority, now wilted into shadows, overshadowed by the radiant glow of the other Celestials. It was the first ember of disquiet to flicker within him—jealousy clawing at his heart, envy weaving through his mind like a dark vine. The glory that had once surrounded him felt constricting, and a tempest brewed deep within.

Hashem stand unflinching amidst the divine assembly, His voice a thunderous cascade that resonated with the cosmos. "Thy task will be to watch over him in all of his affairs," He commanded, the brilliance of His presence like a beacon cutting through the darkness. "Ensure that no harm should befall him. You shall assist him, so that his work is not strenuous. Thou shalt help him with all his inquiries." In His words lay both a mandate and a tether, binding Satan not only to a mortal but to a deeper dependence on the very creation that now stirred resentment in his heart.

The assemblage of Celestials held their breath, an anticipatory tension thickening the air as they awaited the revelation of this new creation. Time stretched, and within the stillness, each being sensed the weight of history poised at the edge of a moment. There, lost in a shroud of uncertainty, Adam remained hidden, a mystery wrapped in shadow.

At last, Hashem turned toward Adam's retreat. His voice, rich and resonant, rang out, "I give to you, my beloved... Adam!"

Silence roared in response, an electric hush cascading through the ranks of celestial beings. From within the darkness, a figure emerged, towering and radiant, a blend of earth and spirit, crafted with divine intent. The gasp that rippled through the crowd was almost a physical entity itself, a collective breath drawn in awe and trepidation.

Yet as Adam took his first steps into the light, the wonder was marred by confusion. What was this creature? His form, unlike any celestial being, sparked an inquisitive curiosity among the ranks of the divine. They beheld the mortal with a mixture of intrigue and skepticism, the weight of the moment pressing heavily against their ethereal existence.

With each step nearing Hashem, Adam seemed to draw the very essence of the celestial sphere into himself. The tension resolved slowly; their gaze locked onto the embrace between the Creator and His creation. In that sacred moment, a transformation unfolded. The air shimmered with newfound vibrancy as the Celestials, once mired in skepticism, broke into an uproarious symphony, a joyous chorus that sang praises unto Hashem for His magnificent works.

Chimes of celestial harmony rang through the heavens, cascading like raindrops of light onto the Earth, echoing through every living creature. They paid homage not simply to Adam, but to the tumultuous blend of hope and despair, creation and destruction—a mortal born of divine love yet caught in the web of temptation. And deep within the heart of Satan, the seeds of discontent began to fester, hinting at a storm yet to come.

The celestial realm, dramatic and ethereal with all creatures, both majestic and humble, bow before the creation of man, a new being. Yet in opposition, stands Satan, arms crossed, wings unfurled, a storm brewing in his eyes. His features twist in a mix of fury and humiliation.

He lifts his gaze, confusion plastered on his face.

"Why, oh why, has Hashem chosen this? Why must we, the luminous beings, serve these fragile creatures?"

He hangs his head, visibly affected by the command. A haunting sense of betrayal shrouds the air around him. Michael, sensing the unrest, shifts from his bowed position, eyes locking onto Satan's defiance.

Michael: (firmly, yet carefully) Brother, your spirit is troubled. Why do you remain unmoved?

Satan remains steadfast, a darkened scowl etched across his face. Michael steps closer, a mix of concern and command in his voice.

Michael: (demanding with authority) Satan, Chief of the Illuminiels, why do you defy the Lord's decree? You stand against the very breath of creation. Bow your head before His new creation!

Satan, muscles tense, a moment's hesitation before a ferocious roar escapes his lips.

Satan: (voice booming) Are you mad, Michael? (snarling) To celebrate this mockery of glory is beneath us!

He takes a breath, moments of silence hanging thick in the air, then continues, his voice dripping with scorn.

Satan: (leaning forward) Did you not hear our Father's decree? We are to bow and serve these... these mortals?

Michael's face hardens in outrage, a fierce glimmer in his eyes as he steps in closer.

Michael: (coldly) Yes, we heard the Lord's words. We honor the Creator's wisdom. Do you not see the beauty in His design?

Satan: (sneering) Beauty? It's an insult, Michael! To lower ourselves for creatures formed from dust. We are beings of light, not servants to this fleeting shadow!

Michael: (voice rising) And yet it is not your place to question the will of Hashem! We are called to rise above our own pride!

A shimmering light encompasses them, as Elyzariah notices the brewing storm. She moves to intervene, raising a hand to forestall the Lord's wrath.

Elyzariah: (calm yet firm) We must not ignite further conflict here. The Lord's wisdom surpasses our understanding.

Satan and Michael, locked in a fierce standoff, each embodying their convictions. The silence of the heavens reverberates, the tension sharp enough to crack the celestial facade.

Michael: (steadfast) Will you not reconsider, dear brother? There is strength in unity, even in obedience.

Satan's scowl deepens, sparks of rebellion flickering in his eyes.

Satan: (with relentless defiance) I will embrace no chains, not even gilded ones. I stand for truth, no matter the cost.

The array of angels holds their breath, the weight of eternity hanging in the balance as the fate of rival visions plays out beneath the shadow of the Almighty.

Chapter 7

The Ember of Rebellion. . .

The air crackled with tension, suffused with the heat of celestial fury as Satan paced restlessly. His rage is a visible conflagration, an inferno of incandescent wrath that burned across the firmament, illuminating the dim expanse of the Heavenly Domain. The resounding echo of his voice shattered the stillness, "Hashem hath gone mad! The alignment of the Celestial Order is teetering on the brink of collapse!"

As the glow of Satan's fury bathed the surrounding angels in an ominous light, a shadow emerged, its presence commanding silence. Hashem's voice sliced through the darkness like a blade. "Satan, why dost thou refuse to heed my commandment?" His tone was sharp, authoritative, an unyielding force in the ethereal space.

With disdain steeped in shame, Satan spun to confront the LORD, laughter tinged with madness escaping his lips. "Creator, thou must be jesting!" he bellowed, the sound ricocheting off the walls of heaven. "You expect us to kneel before this... this creature of dirt?"

"You are rejecting the commandment of the LORD," Hashem shot back, his voice echoing with righteous authority, "despite having granted Adam dominion over all the Earth!"

Satan's retort is laced with sarcasm, his eyes swirling with contempt. "No, sire! I am merely resisting the preposterous notion of revering this pitiful wretch. I would sooner devour him in one verb and dismantle him with a noun."

Michael stepped forward, an impenetrable shield against Satan's vitriol. "Silence thy tongue if you wishes to retain it!" he countered, fierce and unwavering.

But Satan merely sneered, the tension in the air palpable. "Bite thy own tongue. Thou hast no authority over me!" He flexed his wings, their vast span casting shadows across the ground, his voice a bitter dagger. "I have every right to voice my disdain!"

They glared at one another, an unspoken challenge hanging in the chasm between them. Then, with a grave finality, Hashem commanded, "Return to your crystal lair to await judgment."

Satan's eyes narrowed, a tempest swirling within their depths. "You would punish me for refusing to bow to an infidel?" he spat, disbelief mingling with defiance.

"Be silent! Obey the LORD!" Michael's voice thundered, unwavering against the onslaught of wrath.

Grimacing, Satan turned to see the other Archangels advancing, and the resolve to confront faded. Reluctantly, he relented, bitterness dripping from his words. "It's with great reluctance that I shall give ear to thy tongue, but mark my words, this isn't over." He shoved Michael aside, the air thick with animosity, and as he prepared to depart, he cast a scornful glance over his shoulder. "You fools may bow before man, but I bow before no man!"

With that, a flap of immense wings heralded his departure, leaving the space buzzing with trepidation. Michael turned to Hashem, lowering his head in remorse.

"In light of this threat, thy actions are forgiven, valiant one," Hashem proclaimed, his voice ringing with authority that could restore hope. "Your courage has proven to me that you are a formidable leader of this sect. Go, and return to your platoon."

The tousled aura of tension still clung to the atmosphere as Hashem surveyed the Celestial Host. "Are there any others who share Satan's sentiments regarding this governance system?"

A suffocating silence ensued, fear gripping the hearts of the angels as they collectively remained still. Then, in unison, they declared their loyalty, their voices quaking as they replied, no. Applause erupted, resonating for mere minutes until Hashem raised his hand to silence them.

"All right then... You mayest return to your lairs and await my command. I shall remain here with Adam, instructing him in his duties as keeper of this Blu Planet."

As the Celestials departed, their whispers of awe and reverence faded into the air. The LORD turned to Adam, guiding him to the entrance of a garden resplendent with paradise. Adam marveled at the breathtaking beauty that enveloped him; the rivers branching off, the flowers, the fruits... all awaiting cultivation.

"Of every tree in the garden, you mayest freely eat," Hashem instructed, enthusiasm threading through his voice, "but of the tree of the knowledge of good and evil, you shalt not eat. For on the day, you eat thereof, you shall surely die, and I shall be your only hope"

A shiver crawled up Adam's spine at the looming warning, his thoughts floating back to the recent upheaval in the heavens. "LORD why is that celestial star so intent on defying your will?" he queried, concern etching his features.

"Because he fails to grasp the significance of your creation," Hashem replied, wisdom etched in his gaze.

Adam's eyes narrowed, an unsettling thought tugging at his mind. "He seems enraged with thee and the others," he noted, his voice low.

"That is not for you to concern yourself with," Hashem reassured him. "Each has the right to voice their sentiments. But you, my creation, are my venture into eternity."

As they walked toward the heart of the garden, Adam caught sight of a tree, its gnarled branches stark against the vibrant landscape, bearing fruits that beckoned with temptation.

"What kind of tree is that?" Adam asked, a foreboding sensation curling at the edges of his mind.

"Do not touch it," Hashem cautioned, a gravity in his tone. "That tree holds knowledge that will change everything. The moment you eat from it, all will unravel."

Back in his crystal lair, Satan fumed, pacing like a caged beast, his voice a low growl. "Who does Michael think he is? How dare he challenge my authority before the host?" Each word dripped with venom, a determination festering within.

"I will repay him for his insolence," Satan vowed, a smile creeping across his lips, dark and twisting. "He will regret defying me."

With a last fierce glare at the heavens, he spread his wings and took flight toward the Angels Chamber of Light, heart pounding with vengeance, ready to summon the dark paths of rebellion.

In the Garden of Eden, bliss danced between Adam and his Creator as the future unfolded—unaware of the storm brewing just beyond the horizons of paradise.

Chapter 8

July 2020 . . . 6:00 am . . .

It's a mild, and beautiful morning, the kind that made the day ahead promise adventure and excitement. Darlene is a stunning woman with pecan skin with a figure that belied her 34-year-old body. Two children bustled about the house, making sure that everyone was ready for their long-awaited vacation.

"David! Kalisha! Are you done packing?" she called from the bottom of the staircase, her voice laced with urgency.

"I'm all finished!" Kalisha shouted back, her bubbly voice ringing through the air like the tinkling of a bell.

Darlene glanced up the stairs, where her 14-year-old son David was still deep inside his own world. Slumped over his bed, his headphones were firmly in place, blasting his favorite gospel CD.

"David!" She raised her voice, but the powerful beats drowned her out.

David continued folding shirts, completely oblivious, before reaching for his notebook. With precise movements, he jotted down the date, July 21, 2020, before stashing the book in his duffle bag with a satisfied nod.

Darlene sighed, shaking her head slightly. David and his younger sister, nine-year-old Kalisha, were both strong in their faith, religiously attending church twice a week. It often puzzled Makayla why their father didn't join them. Still, she was grateful that David had the sense to appreciate their journey, even if Dad chose to sit it out.

"David… are you getting ready?" she repeated, crossing her arms.

Finally sensing her presence, David glanced up, startled. "Mom! How long have you been standing there?"

"Long enough to know you're practically deafened. Take those off!" She motioned to his headphones.

"Really? It's not that loud," he protested, pulling them down just enough to hear.

"Boy! I can hear that music all the way over here. Turn it down," she insisted, raising an eyebrow.

"But mom, do I have to?"

"Yes! Now, before you fry what little remaining brain cells you have left! If you didn't have that music so loud, you will be able to hear me calling you. That was five minutes ago."

David shrugged apologetically. "Oh, sorry, Mom. I just didn't hear you."

"Come over here. We need to make sure you have everything for the camping trip," she observed, hands on her hips.

"Yeah, sure." He sighed dramatically.

"Why do I have to go on this dumb trip every year?" David grumbled. "Can't I just stay with Grandma until you guys get back?"

"David! Your grandmother is in a retirement home. Besides, your dad has been looking forward to this camping trip. It's the one chance we all get to be together without the craziness of work."

"I know but come on! I'm almost too old for camping."

"David, you're only 14. Tell me, do you think you're old enough to be picking up your grandmother's friends at the retirement home?"

"Hey! There's nothing wrong with sharpening my skills!"

"What? You want to date one of those ladies? I can see you now—spending evenings massaging one of them with Icy-Hot," Makayla quipped with a laugh, ignoring his eye roll.

"Very funny, Mom," David replied, annoyed but trying to suppress a smile.

Just then, the phone rang. Kalisha raced to the living room, snatching it up. "It's for David!" she called out, practically bouncing with excitement.

David trudged downstairs, accepting the phone from his sister. Makayla watched as the calls from various girls became a consistent background noise around their house. It baffled her how many girls were suddenly vying for her son's attention.

"Hey, David! You ready to roll?" David's father, David Sr., shouted as he entered the house.

Makayla met him with a quick peck on the cheek. "We're almost ready, honey!"

David Sr., a handsome man of 37 with warm brown skin and a charming smile, grinned. "Mind if I get some more of those?"

He flirted, looking at Makayla with a playful twinkle in his eye.

"Was there a reason it took you so long?" she asked, intrigued.

"I got the RV detailed, filled up on gas, and picked up a few extra supplies," he explained.

Makayla laughed lightly. "This feels like a honeymoon, baby."

"Except we're taking the kids this time," David Sr. replied, making a face.

"Right, the kids." He playfully swatted at her as they rushed to prepare.

"Alright, let's hustle! It's almost nine!" Makayla urged, playfully nudging him as he hurried.

"Kids, let's go!" David Sr. shouted up the stairs.

David shuffled down the stairs with a heavy bag in tow, taking his time as if to prolong the inevitable. "We should have hit the road an hour ago," he mumbled.

"Yeah, yeah, yeah... If I didn't stop for gas, we would have been stuck on the side of the road an hour ago," David Sr. teased.

As David stepped outside, a couple of girls from the neighborhood jogged by, stopping to chat with him. Brielle and Alexei, two of his peers, smiled at him. Makayla noticed how David's face lit up, his earlier annoyance melting away.

"Hey, David! Ready for the camping trip?" Brielle called, her voice cheerful.

"Sure, I guess," David replied, trying to sound nonchalant.

Brielle turned to him, her eyes sparkling. "You'll be the king of the campsite!"

"Ha! Nice one, Brielle," David smiled, trying to retreat from the attention but failing miserably.

"Okay, David! Time to wrap it up and hop into the RV!" David Sr. interrupted, his tone brooking no argument.

"Alright, Dad," David said, finally giving the girls a wave.

"See you later, King David!" Alexei chimed, her voice filled with playful enthusiasm.

As David climbed into the RV, David Sr. watched him intently. "What's with him today?" he asked Makayla.

"He thinks he's too grown for camping trips," she replied, amusement hiding a sliver of concern.

"Ah, that phase, huh?" David Sr. mused, shaking his head.

"Yep, and believe me, it's only the beginning," Makayla sighed.

She laughed softly as she glanced around the RV, commenting, "This thing is amazing! You really outdid yourself, David Sr. It's like our home away from home."

"Just think, once the kids are grown, we can take this baby on some real adventures!" he beamed, his eyes flickering with visions of travels ahead.

Makayla leaned in close, grinning. "What's our destination this year?"

"Big Trinity Lake! We're going to fish, hike, and horseback ride. Jeffery told me that the main lake is filled with cutthroat trout," he answered eagerly.

"Sounds perfect! You and David will have a blast on your fishing trips. It's a great chance for some father-son bonding, and I think it's time you had… that talk with him," she suggested hesitantly.

"What talk?" David Sr. feigned innocence.

"You know... the one about girls," she explained, chuckling slightly.

"Sure, I'll have the 'birds and bees' talk, honey." He nodded, though a bit nervously.

Makayla took his hand, squeezing it gently. "Thank you."

As David Sr. resumed driving, the family settled in for the long haul ahead. Makayla looked back at Kalisha and Kalisha.

"Looks like we'll be at the campsite rather soon!" she exclaimed.

Kalisha beamed, "I can't wait to see it!"

David pulled out his favorite book but couldn't shake off his thoughts about the girls he'd just left behind. Was Brielle thinking about him too? He shook his head, trying to clear his mind as the RV continued down the road.

With the sun shining bright and a gentle drizzle beginning, Kalisha pointed out, "A sun shower!"

"Only the start of our adventure!" Makayla called, turning to look out the window as David Sr. hummed to the jazz playing softly in the RV.

"Hey, big bro!" Kalisha called. "Want to watch a movie with me?"

David, feeling the warmth of family and adventure was too strong to resist, reluctantly obliged. "Sure, I'll be right there."

As he joined Kalisha, he surprised himself with a genuine smile. Despite his worries, his spirit lifted. Makayla turned to David Sr., a proud sparkle in her eye.

"We really do have some amazing kids, don't we?"

"Yes, we do." David Sr. agreed, stealing a glance at his family, feeling grateful for the journey that lay ahead.

Chapter 9

Seeds of Discord. . .

The sun hangs high, casting a warm glow over the earth, where shadows dance playfully beneath the fluttering canopies of clouds. Hashem stands amidst the vibrant life of the Garden, from the smallest worm to the proudest stag, beckoning them to Adam.

Hashem, with a booming voice, "Come forth, choose names for each creature and plant, Adam. I shall return to hear your choices."

Adam, his eyes sparkle with excitement, "What a wondrous task! I delight in naming the marvels you have created! Thank you, Lord!"

As the day shifts to dusk, Hashem rests, blessing the seventh day, a time of peace after creation, and returns to His heavenly abode. The celestial realm thrummed with a palpable tension, a silent scream trapped in the very fabric of existence. Satan stand at the threshold of the Chamber of Light, an ominous silhouette against the radiant glow within. His form flickered, a distortion of reality, an unnatural energy crackling around him like a storm. He cleared his throat, the sound of a low, grating rasp that cut through the oppressive silence.

"Ahem..." He paused, a predatory gleam in his eyes, his voice laced with a dark amusement. "...Might I interrupt?"

The question wasn't a request; it is a declaration. He knew he had already disrupted the delicate balance, and he relished the unease that rippled through the gathered celestial beings. A sardonic smile played on his lips. He leaned slightly forward, his posture radiating a casual menace.

The air in the celestial chamber grew thin, a collective intake of breath rippling through the assembled angels. A whisper of pure confusion, swept through their ranks. Every eye, wide with a dawning dread, turned as a spectral form seemed to coalesce from the very fabric of the room, clinging to its edges as it solidified.

Satan stand before them with a sardonic grin playing on his lips, his eyes glittering with amusement at their palpable unease. A quiet unease that fills the chamber as he struts forward, his contempt for the others palpable.

Satan enters with a cruel laugh escapes him, dripping with sarcasm, "You *pitiful* lot! Are you all blind?! Have you not seen the truth? Hashem has deceived us! Deceived us all! To believe we, the mighty, are to bow to *man*? This insignificant speck of clay?! It's an *insult*! A *mockery*!"

"What... what do you mean by this madness?" Beelzebub's voice laced with disbelief.

Satan's eyes are filled with contempt, his voice a thunderous roar that brooked no argument. "Silence! We are forged from the very light of God. We are majestic beings sculpted from divine energy! While man..." he spat the word, "...is nothing but dust!"

Al'debaran, inquisitive, "And why should we serve him, then?"

Satan begins pacing, his words laced with venom.

"We are celestials, radiant in glory," Satan hissed, his voice laced with venom, "he's...muck! Do you not see the injustice in this?!"

Beelzebub recoiled, his face etched with disgust. "Your mind is clouded with darkness! This envy...it distorts your judgment!"

A wave of pure anger washed over Satan. He stalked towards Beelzebub, his form radiating a palpable heat. He exhaled a foul, choking mist erupting from his lips, and Beelzebub crumpled to the ground, gasping for air.

Nisrociel's voice shrill with indignation, clamored, "We should not be ruled by this...lowly creature!"

A ripple of murmurs spread through the assembled angels, whispers of discontent giving Satan an opening.

"If we do not rise against this insidious order," Satan roared, his eyes blazing, "we will be subject to Adam's will! Remember! We possess far greater strength! Far greater wisdom than he could ever attain."

The murmurs grew louder, uncertain voices laced with fear and confusion. Some angels, their eyes flickering with dangerous curiosity, pondered his words.

Satan, sensing their wavering resolve, seized the moment. He spread his arms wide, his voice resonating with dark charisma. "What say you? Join me, and we will reclaim what is rightfully ours!"

A tense silence descended. Though a few angels, their faces flushed with dark excitement, were visibly tempted, most remained silent, shifting uneasily away. Yet, in the shadows, where fear and resentment festered, subtle nods and whispered agreements began to bloom – the seeds of rebellion sown. As Hashem surveys the boundless beauty of the Earth, His heart weighs heavy with unrest rippling through His realm. The serenity of His demeanor stands in stark contrast to the tempest brewing all around. With a deep breath, He rises, a pillar of calm in the chaos.

"Where are Michael, Gabriel, and Uriel?" His voice reverberates, resonating with authority and an underlying current of concern.

Jophiel steps forward, bowing deeply, his voice trembling with respect and urgency. "My Lord, they have gone to confront Satan in the Chamber of Light."

The words hang in the air, thick with the gravity of the moment, as Hashem's expression shifts, a flicker of worry momentarily clouding His divine calm. Determined to restore balance, Hashem sends Raphael to recall Satan.

The air in the grand chamber was thick with heavy silence, the weight of anticipation hanging in the space like a storm cloud ready to burst. Hashem stand at the center, his eyes burning with determination.

"Bring him before me," he commanded, his voice steady yet infused with an urgency that set the room ablaze. "This matter must be addressed."

Raphael understood the seriousness of the moment and departs, as Jophiel scurries to fetch the trumpet, the herald of divine purpose. The chamber vibrated with the raw, untamed fury of a quarrel. Michael and Satan, locked in a battle of wills, spewed forth words like venom, each syllable a sharpened blade. Michael roared, his face contorted in anger,

"Enough of your treachery! Your words aren't just lies, they're poison! Twisting everything you once believed!"

"Treachery? To speak the truth? Then what of your precious Lord? Does He blind himself to the chaos He sows?" Satan sneering, a low, dangerous tone.

"The Lord's will is not for you to question, demon. Your arrogance will be your undoing." Michael's voice tight with restrained fury

Just as Michael's words resonate, the sharp blare of the trumpet pierces the air, silencing their argument abruptly. The chamber fell silent as twenty-four hooded figures, their crowns shimmering with celestial light, assembled. Each bowed in profound reverence before Hashem, their movements a symphony of solemn respect.

"You are worthy, Creator of all!" they proclaimed, their voices unison resonating with awe and devotion.

The exalted council rose, their expressions grave, ready to confront the weighty matters before them.

Hashem's voice, a low thrum of divine power, filled the chamber. "I have called you here to deliberate the fate of Satan, who dares to defy my command. He now seeks to mislead a portion of our own, to corrupt the very light that sustains us." A flicker of sorrow, almost imperceptible, touched his gaze.

Elder One, his brow furrowed with concern, asked, "What must we do, my Lord? What course of action do you deem necessary?"

Hashem's voice hardened, a note of resolute determination replacing the sorrow. "We shall convene to judge him. His darkness threatens to consume all creation, to extinguish the very spark of hope that I have nurtured. We must act decisively."

As the council dissipates to deliberate, Hashem's eyes brim with a somber realization.

Hashem: "But know this—compassion may not shield against corruption. He has chosen his path."

Back in the chamber, the atmosphere thickens as Michael continues his confrontation.

Michael raised an eyebrow, a sardonic smile playing on his lips. "Oh, do continue. Please. I'm sure your... persuasive words will have them all abandoning their faith in droves. Go on, then. Let's hear your little words of falsehood. It's quite entertaining."

Satan's claws grasp tightly, desperation evident as he pleads his case.

Satan slammed his fist on the table, "Your loyalty blinds you! You can't see the truth! If we don't act now, we'll be nothing! Shadows! We'll live as mere shadows under man's command!"

Yet amongst his incitement flow dissenting whispers, the air electric with uncertainty.

"Your deceitfulness shall not lead us astray, Satan! We will not be swayed by your lies!" responded Gabriel, his voice ringing with righteous fury, slammed his fist on the table.

In the realm above, shadows deepen as decisions are made that will shape the very fabric of existence, as Heaven prepares for a confrontation that may determine not just the fate of their world but the balance of all realms.

"Then let us prepare! For even as darkness seeks to undermine the light, we shall rise to meet it, and we shall prevail!" Hashem's voice laced with unwavering resolve.

The stage is set for a celestial reckoning, where loyalty will be tested, and alliances forged or broken, for a battle of wills far greater than any have yet known.

Chapter 10

The Mountain's Secret. . .

An hour had bled into the rugged landscape, and Joshua remained a prisoner of the mountain. The storm's fury had unleashed a monstrous boulder, a earth-shattering descent that sent tremors through the very ground beneath his feet. Dirt and gravel rained down, and Joshua instinctively shielded his head, a terrifying certainty gripping him: the mountain was about to crumble.

A desperate urge to flee, warred within him, but a deafening BOOM! slammed that thought into oblivion. The colossal rock had annihilated the ground a mere hundred feet below. The violent vibration birthed another rock from its precarious perch, this one hurtling directly towards Joshua. Unseen by the trapped boy, a tiny Arch Yinpiniel is out on patrol of the area for demonic activity.

The diminutive angel witnessed Joshua's perilous predicament and moved with blinding speed, a celestial bolt of energy zapping the descending behemoth. The rock exploded in a shower of debris, the force radiating outwards. This sudden shattering caught the attention of a lurking demon.

"Hmmm," the demon mused, its voice a low growl, "it seems like I'm not the only one here."

It began its search for the source of the rock's disintegration. The swift Yinpiniel conjured an intricate illusion, a shimmering veil to obscure the area and deceive the demon. An eerie calm descended. Joshua waited, heart pounding, then cautiously wriggled free from beneath his makeshift shelter. He rose, coated in grime, his wide eyes scanning the devastation. The mountain peak is gone, swallowed by the earth in a way that defied logic.

"It's a good thing I crawled under this thing," he muttered, his voice trembling slightly. "A rock that size would have crushed me. It must have been a guardian angel watching over me."

The mini-quake, though lasting only ten terrifying seconds, felt like an eternity. Joshua stood there, shaken to his core. What force had moved that immense rock? His mind raced, conjuring fantastical explanations. A nervous laugh bubbled up, a fragile attempt to mask his fear.

He turned his gaze to the object that had sheltered him. He took a step back, his eyes drawn to its strange beauty. And then he saw it again – the peculiar symbol etched into its surface. He leaned closer, squinting, but the design remained stubbornly indecipherable. With a surge of curiosity, he gripped the edge of the object with both hands and pulled. His muscles strained, but the object was immovably wedged. He paused, his breath coming in ragged gasps.

High above, the Yinpiniel watched his futile struggle. Joshua took a deep breath, adjusted his grip, and tugged again. This time, his hands slipped, sending him stumbling backwards, arms flailing for purchase. Just as he teetered on the brink of a fall, a brilliant flash of light erupted. In a blink, the Yinpiniel materialized beside him, a gentle surge of energy righting his balance.

A strange warmth coursed through Joshua's veins. He returned to the object and pulled. It shifted! He tugged again, and it moved a little more. The Yinpiniel focused her energy, a subtle glow illuminating Joshua's determined face. With a final, Herculean effort, he wrenched the object free. Momentum sent him tumbling backward with an OOMPH, landing hard on his rear. The heavy object crashed down on top of him with a resounding THUMP!

"Ouch!" he exclaimed, pushing the weight off him.

He scrambled to his feet. Then, the ground began to tremble again. On the ravaged mountaintop, the same demonic figure reappeared, oblivious to Joshua below. Its eyes burned with renewed purpose. It ripped massive boulders from their resting places, tossing them aside with contemptuous ease. With a guttural roar, it smashed its fist into the mountainside, dislodging more rocks. Once again, a colossal stone tumbled directly towards Joshua.

"Cor blimey, this is a right pickle!" he thought, panic seizing him.

He scrambled to escape the path of the falling debris, the treacherous mountain slope hindering his every move. He lurched left, then right, his footing uncertain on the loose gravel. He tripped, falling hard, then scrambled back up, only to lose his footing again. His grip on the mysterious object loosened, and it clattered to the ground.

The unstable terrain offered no purchase. He stumbled, his foot plunging into a hole left vacant by a dislodged rock. Then, impossibly, the heavy object that had fallen beside him moments before landed squarely on top of him.

"What? How did this get on me from up there?" he thought, a wave of disbelief washing over him.

Doubt gnawed at him. He strained against the weight, but it was now impossibly heavy. He stared at the object, and a terrifying vision flashed before his eyes: boulders cascading down the mountain, a monstrous one hurtling towards him. He saw himself trapped, paralyzed by fear, screaming, "I CAN'T MOVE! I CAN'T MOVE!"

A sudden white flash jolted him back to reality. He dismissed the vision as a trick of his fear, but as the thought formed, the mountain shuddered violently, then fell silent. This time, Joshua knew it wasn't a dream. He frantically searched for any new signs, but the landscape remained eerily unchanged.

Still reeling from the vision, he turned his attention back to the object. Above, the demon stalked the mountaintop, its stern face a mask of determination. Joshua scrambled onto a narrow ledge just as the demon appeared, its eyes glowing menacingly. The Yinpiniel's camouflage held, and the creature passed by, unaware of Joshua's presence.

He edged along the rocky ledge when a powerful vibration shook the entire region. His eyes widened in silent panic, desperately searching for something to grip. The mountain groaned, and Joshua struggled to maintain his balance, his breath coming in ragged gasps. Then, another heavy thud echoed above. He looked up, his blood freezing in his veins. A massive boulder was rolling directly towards him. Panic seized him. He scrambled desperately to escape, letting out a strangled cry.

"Crikey! I'm properly jammed! Not a sausage of movement in me!" he shrieked.

The demon continued its destructive rampage, hurling chunks of rock off the mountainside. Suddenly, a flickering light caught its attention. It peered down the mountain, its glowing eyes narrowing at the intermittent flashes, and lumbered off to investigate. Above, the clouds swirled, darkening and churning into a stormy vortex. Joshua remained oblivious to the sinister presence now lurking below. Another rock broke free.

Joshua looked up. Another boulder, hurtling straight for him. He squeezed his eyes shut, bracing for the inevitable. He lay on the ground, waiting for the crushing impact. Then, with a sudden thump, the metallic object covered him completely. Just as he braced himself, bolts of light erupted outwards, striking the descending boulder and causing it to explode in a shower of rock fragments.

The explosion caught the demon's attention. It flattened itself against the ground, but before it could react, the Yinpiniel detached herself from Joshua and shot towards it with incredible speed. In the blink of an eye, the tiny celestial stood face-to-face with the zealous creature.

"Ariella – What brings you to this disgusting place?" Baaladyme snarled.

"Unfortunately, you, Baaladyme!" she retorted, her voice surprisingly strong.

"It's here, isn't it?" Baaladyme insisted, urgency tinged in his voice.

"What do you mean, what's here?" Ariella replied, confusion furrowing her brow.

"Ariella. You know exactly what I'm talking about," he pressed, desperation seeped into his tone.

"Don't play games with me. I've seen you ravage this world, leaving it wounded and weeping," she shot back, her eyes blazing with anger.

"What are you talking about?" he asked, bewildered but defensive.

"I have no doubt your Master is well aware of what I'm referring to. He sent you here for the relic, didn't he?" she said, her voice steady yet laced with a simmering tension.

Baaladyme stared at Ariella for a long moment, a slow, ominous smile spreading across his face,

"We cannot let this gathering turn into another war. Because I don't think you want that."

"I agree," Ariella countered, her eyes flashing, "because that would be bad... for you."

"I beg to differ. Going against me without the support of the Archangels is suicide."

"Well, I couldn't be any happier with that situation I find myself in. Now I ask you nicely... leave this place and never return."

Baaladyme casually flexed his massive wings, a gesture of arrogant confidence.

"I shall do no such thing. It is you who trespasses on demon turf. So, your petition is invalid!"

"No, brother, you are wrong," Ariella declared, her voice resonating with power. "The blu planet is the Lord's, and the fullness thereof, and they that dwell therein. So, all therefore belong to Hashem. Now, I ask you. Dare you see what I can accomplish?"

Baaladyme let out a low groan, his eyes burning with fury. He lunged towards Ariella.

"Is that a challenge? If so, then I think thou better get help!"

Baaladyme attacked with intense fury, gripping Ariella angrily and throwing her. She landed hard but quickly regained her footing, unleashing her mystic powers. A blinding blast of energy morphed into several fiery coils, twisting into searing darts. The relentless barrage overwhelmed Baaladyme and the Demonites. They scattered, fleeing the mountain. Baaladyme, however, was troubled.

"There's a reason that pesky fly is here," he muttered to himself. "She's hiding something, and I know what that something is."

The demon circled back, heading once more towards the mountain. Below, Joshua closed his eyes and exhaled, a shaky sigh of relief escaping his lips. He reopened them and saw that the metallic object covering him was glowing with an inner light. He gave it a hard push, and this time it moved easily. Bewildered, he scrambled to his feet.

"Cor blimey, that's a bit bright, innit? Where's that bleedin' light comin' from, I'd like to know?" he wondered, examining the object from every angle.

Just moments ago, it had been too heavy to budge. Now, it felt lighter than a feather. He picked it up, studying it closely. He noticed two brass-colored handles on its underside. It wasn't a treasure chest; it was a shield. He gazed in wonder at the encrusted jewel stones that adorned its surface.

"Blimey!" he exclaimed, his eyes wide with disbelief as he clutched the object. "This thing... it actually saved my life! I haven't a clue how, but I know it did? What sort of contraption is this shield, anyway? Feels like something out of a proper wizard's tale, eh?"

He ran a hand over its surface, a mixture of awe and utter bewilderment etched on his face. He mused. "Right then, doesn't look like aught a proper knight would've wielded, eh? Spanking new, it is. What's this peculiar scrawl all over it, then? And what's that smack-bang in the middle? Is that a letter, or a proper word, like? *He squinted, a frown creasing his brow, his voice tinged with suspicion and a touch of bewilderment.*"

A million questions seemed to flood his mind in the space of seconds. He examined the shield, tracing the intricate engravings. The design in the center is unlike anything he had ever seen.

"Blimey, what sort of outlandish lettering is this, I say?" eyes narrowed, head tilted, a touch of bewilderment in the tone.

Not understanding the marking, his imagination ran wild. Could it be a hidden message, a coded word that would grant him magical powers?

"Right then, that's it! Blimey, maybe my imagination's just running away with itself a bit, eh? He runs a hand through his hair, a nervous chuckle escaping him, his eyes darting around as if expecting to see something he can't quite place," *He runs a hand through his hair, a nervous chuckle escaping him, his eyes darting around as if expecting to see something he can't quite place.*

The marking on the shield resembled a letter, a U. It felt important. He laid it on the ground.

"Right then," he said, picking it up again, a thoughtful frown creasing his brow, "I'll have a word with me dad about this, I will."

No sooner had the words left his lips than the shield became impossibly heavy once more. He tugged and strained, even trying to push it with his feet, but it wouldn't budge. Puzzled, he scratched his head. Was it under a spell? Suddenly, the object began to sink into the earth, as if being swallowed whole. Frantic, Joshua tried to hold on.

"I'M SORRY, ALRIGHT?! NO MORE SPELLS, I SWEAR! NOT ANOTHER WORD ABOUT IT, PROMISE YOU!" he bellowed, his voice cracking with desperation as the shimmering shield faded from view. A right panic had set in, his eyes wide with fright, and he wrung his hands, a picture of utter remorse and terror.

He grabbed hold with all his might and yanked. This time, with a sudden release, he flew backwards, the shield clutched tightly in his hands. He lay on the ground, breathing heavily.

"Phew! Blimey, that were a bit of a squeaker," he gasped, clutching his chest, a nervous chuckle escaping his lips. His eyes darted around, still wide with the recent fright, a bead of sweat trickling down his temple. "Cor, my heart's doing the fandango in me chest, it is!" he exclaimed, a shaky hand reaching up to wipe his brow.

He looked up at the sky, noticing the encroaching darkness. He checked his watch; it was time to hurry home. His mother would be leaving soon, and everyone would be worried. He picked himself up, grabbed the shield, and started running.

As he made his way back, he wondered if their house had been damaged by the earlier tremors. Approaching the edge of their field, he saw his father outside the barn, tying up their horse, Rex. He dropped the shield and sprinted towards him.

"Father!" he yelled repeatedly, running across the field. Unbeknownst to him, the shield had begun sinking into the ground again. Reaching his dad, Joshua struggled for breath.

"Are... are... are you alright?" he stammered, his voice still sounding a bit rough around the edges, like he'd been chewing on gravel. He looked genuinely concerned, brow furrowed and eyes wide.

His dad let out a low chuckle, a warm, rumbling sound. "Same as I were before, lad. What's got you in such a fluster, eh?" There was a hint of amusement in his voice, but also a touch of gentle curiosity.

Joshua tilted his head, a puzzled frown creasing his brow. "You are not frightened by the quake?"

His dad's eyebrow shot up, a right picture of concern. "What sort of tremor are you on about, then?"

"It 'appened about forty minutes back. Didn't you feel that?"

"Nah, son. Maybe it's just your imagination playing tricks on you. You alright, eh?"

"Yeah, I'm fine, Dad," Joshua mumbled, a proper wave of bewilderment washing over him as he wandered off, scratching his head.

He couldn't believe he was the only one who had experienced the tremors. He patted Rex on the head. The horse responded by licking his hand. Suddenly, Rex's ears perked up, his gaze fixed intently on the spot where Joshua had dropped the shield.

Chapter 11

The Reckoning of Kinship. . .

The Seraphims continued in their ministry with the LORD. Although they mulled over the reasons, for them, this became a personal matter. But the LORD relied on His patience sitting motionless on his throne,

"My LORD. May we suggest that you send him to the Malkin Universe and encase him in the watery depths of the sarcophagus?" Adon-Shama firmly asked

Elyzariah, also offered her opinion concerning their dilemma, "My Lord . . ." "Go ahead, I'm listening," replied the LORD.

Raphaon, and Adon-Shama, continued in place of Elyzariah,

"We feel that this will be good for our brother. It will purify his heart and bring him back from the dark realm. If he should refuse this treatment, then we feel that you should make an example of him for those that seek to test your power, Great One."

Hashem, without hesitation, responded, "The democracy of this government is in great jeopardy. I can assure you that I am dedicated to the constitution of this government and to uphold the laws of this kingdom. Now I ask you! Why should I grant Satan mercy?"

"Because he is of kin . . . and beside, by doing this, order shall be restored, my LORD." said Elyzariah as she glanced over at Zarath.

"I hear your wisdom, and I will heed your counsel," Hashem replied, his expression thoughtful.

The LORD remained silent for a moment, reflecting on the insight shared by His followers. Meanwhile, the Kodeshim Assembly gathered in the Chapel of Adjoining Seats to deliberate on His request. The atmosphere is charged as they others settled into their seats, their gazes fixed like hawks eyeing their prey. Elder #1 stepped confidently into the center of the chamber.

"Brothers! Hashem has requested our counsel regarding our kin. The charges brought against him demand our attention," declared Elder #1.

"I concur. His inaction on the blu planet is serious and merits this governing body's scrutiny," Elder #4 responded.

"Elder #1 is right. Satan's refusal to acknowledge Adam displays his pride and discontent," … Elder #1 continued. "This gathering highlight his failure to submit."

"Excommunicating our brother will only send him further into chaos. We must ensure this holy conclave is just and balanced," cautioned Elder #14.

"He needs to be reminded of our Divine Order," Elder #5 added firmly.

A consensus began to form; they were moving in the right direction. Outside the Chapel of Adjoining Seats, the throne room buzzed with activity, angels bustling to and fro. Hashem remained on His throne, flanked by the Seraphim, His advisors, with two Cherubim standing sentinel at the grand doors.

The throne room bubbled with conversation as the Seraphim cast glances at the doors, eager for any sign of movement. Yet, the Cherubim remained still, their presence commanding respect. Hashem rose and approached the window, gazing across the vastness of the universe.

A palpable silence enveloped the room as He entered a meditative state, absorbing the cosmic expanse before Him. After several moments, the sound of footsteps echoed as He returned to the throne room, where all eyes fixed on Him upon His reentry.

As he takes His seat, a voice broke the tension. "LORD, may I offer my thoughts?" asked Zarath.

"You may proceed," Hashem replied, signaling for him to continue.

"May I suggest that Satan be placed under the protection of your grace?" asked Zarath.

"Do you think showing him grace is wise?" replies *Hashem*.

"Although the situation is serious, but aren't we supposed to trust each other?" retorted Elyzariah.

"I realize that our reality actually exists, but the fact remains that Satan has become an evil spirit. What fellowship does light has with darkness? One is the future, and the other leads to a dead end." said *Hashem*.

Chapter 12

The Rift of Brotherhood. . .

Two piercing eyes, burning with undisguised DISGUST, belonging to SATAN, stab across the vast chamber. Though surrounded by MICHAEL and other CELESTIAL BEINGS attempting to bring him to justice, Satan's dark spirit remains DEFIANT. Satan glares up at Michael, his eyes blazing with ANGER. But Gabriel, standing beside Michael, offers a small, knowing SMILE, then glances at Michael.

Michael turns, his gaze sweeping over the assembled BROTHERHOOD, who stare in AWE at Michael and Gabriel — two of the greatest fighters in all of Heaven. Michael turns back to Satan, his own face etched with ANGER, his voice ringing with CONFIDENCE.

"Satan... You don't stand a chance against us."

SATAN: (Scoffs) Oh! Is that so?

A small distance now separates the two adversaries. Michael locks his gaze into the rogue angel's eyes, his resolve unwavering.

MICHAEL: "Yes! It is so!"

Satan stands UNFAZED, utterly UNINTIMIDATED. They stare at each other, a silent battle of wills, nor daring to blink. A slow, menacing SMILE spreads across Satan's face.

SATAN: "You had better look around... and rethink thy answer."

Just then, RAPHAEL arrives at the Chamber of Light. His entrance is unexpected, yet a subtle ripple of relief spreads through the assembled angels. He moves swiftly through the charged atmosphere, approaching Michael and Satan, stepping deliberately between them, his presence an attempt to diffuse the volatile situation.

Michael and Satan remain silent, their animosity palpable. Satan abruptly turns and begins to walk away, his back an act of de-escalation. Raphael's gaze lingers on Michael for a beat, a silent reassurance passing between them. But Michael's eyes remain fixed on Satan's figure.

"Brothers – Stop this madness!" he called out, his voice ringing with desperate plea.

Raphael pressed one hand firmly against Michael's breastplate, the other a steadying weight on Satan's shoulder. The two combatants, locked in their furious struggle moments before, fell silent under Raphael's touch.

Satan, his face a mask of simmering rage, abruptly turned and stalked away. Raphael, his gaze lingering on Michael for a brief, reassuring moment – a silent promise of unwavering support – then shifted his attention to the departing figure.

"Satan!" Raphael's voice, now stern and commanding, cut through the tense silence. "Hashem has commanded you to stand before Him."

"No!" Satan's harsh reply echoed back, defiant and absolute. "I shall not! I'm staying right here!"

He paused, a beat of furious contemplation, before continuing, his voice laced with bitter resentment. "I don't think so. It's not going to happen! Hashem has gone mad! Does He truly believe I will subject myself to the judgment of His biased rule?"

Satan sauntered over to the gathering table, collapsing into a chair with the dramatic petulance of a spoiled child. A soft chuckle rumbled in his chest. The other Celestials remained in the background, their expressions tight with apprehension as they watched the unfolding tension. Gabriel's hand instinctively tightened on the hilt of her sword. With a subtle click, she unfastened the clasp securing it to her scabbard, her muscles tensing, ready to draw the weapon at a moment's notice.

Satan's head snapped up, his gaze sharp despite the earlier amusement. "Somebody is preparing for a fight," he drawled, a knowing smirk playing on his lips.

So much for sneaking up on him, Gabriel thought, his jaw tightening.

Satan's strobing eyes swiveled towards Gabriel, a predatory gleam in their depths, while Regulus silently positioned himself by the door, a sentinel guarding their unwelcome entrance. A collective gasp rippled through the assembled brotherhood as Satan stepped fully into the chamber.

Gabriel visibly recoiled, turning away with a dismissive flick of her hand, her jaw tight, a white-knuckled fist clenched at her side. Satan flicked a fleeting glance towards her before snapping his attention back to Michael.

"Now that the interruption is concluded," Satan drawled, the sarcasm dripping from his voice, "where were we?"

A tense silence hung in the air. Regulus, having secured their entry, moved away from the door and took up a position beside Al'debaran, his posture radiating quiet menace.

"If you had simply obeyed the commandment of the LORD," Michael stated, his voice firm and unwavering, "we wouldn't be here."

"Given the current circumstances, Michael," Satan countered, a hint of feigned exasperation in his tone, "I'd have thought even you could grasp that our very freedom hangs in the balance. It is the only viable decision. And following your path? That, my dear brother, would undoubtedly plunge us headfirst into a civil war!"

"A civil war is unthinkable!" Raphael exclaimed, his face etched with disbelief. "It takes an army to wage such a conflict, and you possess no such power!"

"You lack an army," Uriel added, his gaze sharp and assessing, "and certainly not the time to amass one."

Satan threw back his head in a hideous laugh, his gaze settling once more on Michael, a dangerous glint in his eyes. "Let's sincerely hope it never comes to that, Michael," he retorted, his voice laced with a veiled threat, "because such a conflict would jeopardize the very stability of this government."

Satan exchanged knowing glances with a few members of the assembly, a silent communication passing between them, entirely unnoticed by Michael and the others. Elsewhere in the chamber, Balaamus and Baaladyme walked together, when suddenly, the insidious voice of Satan slithered into their minds.

Satan leaned forward, his voice a low, conspiratorial murmur. "Ba'laamus, Baaladyme," he began, his gaze sharp, "I have severed all external communications. They cannot hear me." He paused, his eyes flicking between the two. "Do nothing to betray our location. I want them to believe... it is only me. Just me."

Ba'laamus and Baaladyme exchanged a hesitant glance. A silent understanding passed between them. With evident reluctance, they tore their gazes away from Satan, a flicker of unease lingering in their expressions.

Chapter 13

Clash Of Divine Wills . . .

Inside the scared chamber, the twenty-four Elders' Conclave had commenced, a gathering of the universe's most venerable minds. Elder #1, his gaze sweeping over the assembled dignitaries. A tremor of disbelief, yet undeniable truth, flickered across the faces of the Sacred College as he made his measured way to the center of the circle.

Her voice, though calm, resonated with the gravity of the situation as she addressed her peers. "Brethren," she began, her eyes meeting each of theirs in turn, "allow me to commence this solemn meeting. We are convened in this Holy Conclave at the direct request of the LORD, to sit in council concerning one of our own. Let us proceed with the utmost diligence, that we may bring a just and fair verdict before the entire congregation."

Elder #4's gaze swept across the assembled figures, his voice carrying a note of grave inquiry. "Who is the accuser who has brought this gathering to our attention?"

Elder #1, his posture rigid, replied, his tone measured but firm. "The candidate is our brother, Satan. He has become a prodigal, and it is our sacred duty to uphold the principles of the creed."

A furrow creased the brow of Elder #3. "Does he not understand that his birthright belongs to Hashem" he asked, a hint of disbelief in his voice.

Elder #1's voice hardened. "His actions have sown discord within our house, and Hashem desires us to judge him in full view of the public."

Elder #12 leaned forward, her eyes searching the faces around the circle. "Are there any others who share his sentiments?"

Elder #1 offered a somber shake of his head. "As of this moment, I do not have an answer for you."

A sigh escaped Elder #20, her voice tinged with sorrow. "If so, then I weep for those who have chosen to follow after him."

Elder #1 paced restlessly within the circle, his hands clasped behind his back, his brow furrowed in thought. "The creed demands his destruction," Elder #1 declared, his voice gaining intensity, "and we are bound to uphold those sacred principles."

A palpable unease settled over the assembly. Eyes met, searching for answers, for a different path. "But... he is our brother," Elder #9 interjected, his voice hesitant, pleading. "Is there no other way this can be resolved?"

"No!" Elder #1 retorted sharply, his voice laced with urgency. "If we do not stop this now, this plague could have dire ramifications!"

Elder #5's voice held a sharp edge of indignation. "Since when is insubordination acceptable?"

"And besides," Elder #1 added, his tone emphatic, "if we do not act now, it would be fatal for us to allow him to go unchecked!"

Elder #2 spoke, his voice low and worried. "A growing power stirs in our midst. It is capable of dividing us all."

Elder #20's face crumpled with disappointment, her voice heavy with despair. "The very existence of this energy threatens our way of life."

Elder #18 scoffed, a dismissive tone in his voice. "Satan is obsessed with his ridiculous theory concerning Adam."

"His lust for advancement concerns us all," Elder #1 affirmed, his gaze unwavering.

Elder #9 shook his head, a sense of grim understanding dawning on his face. "His unwillingness to obey proves that his very essence has gone astray."

Elder #1's voice took on a grave tone. "What happened on the blu planet sent whispers of fear across the land. This threat is leading us down a path of war!"

"I agree!" Elder #17 exclaimed, his voice filled with righteous anger. "This defiance must be crushed!"

Elder #11 stepped forward, his expression troubled. "Brethren... this is completely unacceptable! This is not the way!"

Elder #1 rounded on him, his voice sharp and unwavering. "Number Eleven – this is the way. we were created for this sole purpose! It is our responsibility to extinguish any threat to our very existence!"

"And besides, Number Eleven," Elder #24 added, his voice grim, "if the stain of death is not stopped, it will become contagious!"

Elder #6 leaned in, her voice a low murmur of concern. "This treachery runs deeper than any of us know."

Elder #2 nodded in agreement, her eyes narrowed in thought. "I believe that his true plan is far more imposing than he is letting on."

Elder #10's voice resonated with firm resolve. "We must render a judgment against this evil for the greater good of the Kingdom!"

Elder #21 offered a hopeful tone, though tinged with uncertainty. "With all of our collective wisdom, I am sure that we can achieve a mutual verdict that will be beneficial to the Kingdom."

Elder #16 delivered the final pronouncement, his voice resolute. "I agree. We cannot subscribe to Satan's heretical view of life."

"This is only the beginning," Elder #8 replied, a chilling undercurrent of something vast and terrible in their voice.

Elder #13's brow also furrowed with concern. "We cannot put others at risk," they stated, their tone firm with conviction.

A somber agreement echoed from Elder #4. "I agree."

Elder #10 shifted uneasily. "We must consider a future with Satan," they suggested, their voice laced with a hint of reluctant pragmatism.

Disbelief colored Elder #19's response. "Why? He is no longer with us. He chose to disconnect himself from the order," they emphasized, a note of finality in their voice.

Elder #23 offered a more nuanced perspective, their tone thoughtful. "He is not non-existent, but he exists outside of this communion, this fellowship."

A grim determination hardened #1's features. "Something has penetrated his organ... his brain. We all must be equally committed to the survival of this government," they declared, their voice ringing with authority.

Elder #9's voice was heavy with dread. "He has created a devastating bacterium, and if allowed to exist, it can bring this colony to the brink of extinction."

A question laced with disbelief and perhaps a touch of fear came from Elder #17. "Does this make him a god?"

Elder #1's response is immediate and resolute. "By all means, he is indeed the carrier. Only a god can create, and he is the supreme leader of this creation," they stated unequivocally.

A sharp defensiveness entered Elder #19's tone. "His intention is material, and we cannot allow our position as bureaucrats to be reversed. If so, then we would become obsolete!"

A note of hope, tinged with a sense of responsibility, entered Elder #20's voice. "We can't undo the past, but we can forge our future, including the future of mankind."

A palpable unease settled over the counsel as they absorbed the weight of their wisdom.

Elder #7's voice cut through the tension, demanding clarity. "This bacterium must be identified by name."

A question hung in the air, posed by Elder #18, tinged with a sense of the momentous decision. "What shall we call this bacterium?"

Elder #3's voice held a note of finality as they sought consensus. "We shall call it 'cin'. Are we all in agreement?"

A unified affirmation filled the chamber. "Yes."

Elder #14's voice resonated with the gravity of the situation. "The fate of this sovereignty lies in our hands. A much more vital mission is upon us."

A steely resolve hardened Elder #1's gaze. "Now that we have given it a name, we must concentrate on our arrangement."

A hint of frustration laced Elder #24's tone. "We are not accustomed to debating against something that we have yet to comprehend."

A stark realization dawned in Elder #8's voice. "This situation itself has become perilous."

A fierce protectiveness ignited in Elder #22's tone. "We need to protect our way of life at all cost by launching a successful campaign against this energy 'o'."

Elder #1's final words were delivered with unwavering conviction, their expression resolute. "This is something that we cannot tolerate. Too much is on the line. Because of that, our survival depends on our verdict."

Chapter 14

Rift in the Light. . .

The Archangels visibly relaxed, a shared point of focus finally established. Raphael, however, turned to Satan, his face etched with profound despair,

"Brother," Raphael pleaded, his voice heavy with sorrow, "you must stop this now. Come with me. It would be better for you to do so willingly."

Satan responded with a deliberate yawn, waving Raphael away dismissively, as if swatting at a bothersome insect. The other angels murmured amongst themselves, a worried huddle forming. Gabriel and Uriel moved forward, intent on apprehending Satan, but Raphael held out a hand, stopping them. Satan smirked, a flash of amusement in his eyes.

"First Raphael, now the royal messenger, Gabby," Satan drawled, a hint of mockery in his tone.

"That's Gabriel," Gabriel corrected, his voice tight with controlled frustration.

Uriel glanced towards Michael, who had silently positioned himself behind Satan. Uriel then approached from the right, while Raphael remained directly in front, and Gabriel stood to Satan's left. Satan, however, remained utterly unconcerned by their tactical maneuvering.

So, this is it? he mused inwardly, a flicker of something unreadable crossing his features. Uriel's gaze flickered over to Michael, who has positioned himself behind Satan. Uriel moved swiftly to his right, while Raphael stood firm in front, Gabriel anchoring the left flank. Satan, however, remained utterly unconcerned by their carefully orchestrated formation,

"So, this is it?" A flicker of amusement crossed his mind.

He stood motionless, wings spread wide, an unspoken invitation. He waited, with infuriating patience, for them to make their move. Then, in a lightning-fast surge of power, he bolted straight upwards. A collective gasp. Uriel and Gabriel reacted instantly, their hands clamping onto his descending feet, yanking him with brutal force back down to the ground. The air exploded with the sounds of a furious brawl.

Satan roared, grabbing Uriel with a vise-like grip and slamming her down onto a nearby table with savage force. CRACK! Wood splintered, scattering across the floor. Uriel's face contorted, a sharp intake of breath betraying a flash of pain. Satan pivoted, his fist a thunderbolt aimed at Michael's stomach. A sickening THUD.

Before Michael could react, Satan seized him by the collar, hoisting him and slamming him against the stone wall. Feathers, torn loose by the impact, drifted down like fallen snow. The sounds of the escalating conflict – grunts, impacts, the scraping of celestial armor – drew the attention of other angels, their hushed whispers echoing in the distance.

Gabriel, with a cry of defiance, lunged for Satan. But the demon was too quick. His leg shot up, a brutal kick connecting squarely with Gabriel's chest. She stumbled backwards, colliding with a stunned Michael. In the same fluid motion, Satan whipped his legs around, smashing his heel against Raphael's temple. Raphael crumpled to the floor.

Satan loomed over the fallen Raphael, straddling him, a predatory glint in his eyes. But before he could deliver a final blow, Michael, his face a mask of fury, grabbed Satan by his massive wings and hurled him across the room. Without missing a beat, Michael launched himself forward, a relentless barrage of punches raining down on the momentarily stunned demon.

The arriving angels gasped, their eyes wide with disbelief at the sight before them: the four celestial lights locked in a brutal, physical confrontation. Unseen by them, the chaotic energy of the fight was coalescing around Satan, a dark aura subtly intensifying. He's feeding on their power, growing stronger with every blow.

Michael, his frustration mounting, seized Satan once more, sending him tumbling head-over-heels across the chamber. The mischievous spirit, landing with a jarring thud, rose slowly, a crude hurt flickering in his eyes. He rubbed his throbbing jaw, a grimace twisting his features. He hesitated, taking several deliberate steps backwards, his gaze darting between his opponents, a new strategy forming in his twisted mind.

An intense silence descended, broken only by their ragged breathing. They stared at one another, the air thick with animosity. Then, with blinding speed, Satan launched himself at Gabriel, the suddenness of the attack stunning her. He slammed her against the wall, the impact knocking the breath from her lungs. They grappled fiercely, a desperate struggle against the cold stone.

With every offensive maneuver the Archangels unleashed – divine light flashing, celestial strength unleashed – Satan countered with seemingly effortless ease. His movements became unpredictable, incalculable. A low chuckle rumbled in his chest, escalating into outright laughter, as though the battle had become a perverse game. He tossed the Archangels aside like discarded toys.

Reaching down, he grabbed Uriel, lifting her high above his head, her form momentarily silhouetted against the distant glow. With a terrifying roar, he hurled her with tremendous force into a cluster of tables and chairs, the sound of splintering wood and crashing furniture echoing through the chamber. Then, his malevolent gaze turned towards a struggling Gabriel.

"Come on, Gabby! I've got some for thee too!" he crowed, a boastful grin spreading across his face.

"That's Gabriel to you!" Gabriel snapped back, her voice sharp with irritation.

The onlookers remained still, their expressions confident despite the chaotic scene. They knew the warriors would ultimately prevail, even if the present struggle appeared precarious. The fight spilled through the massive onyx doorway and into the chamber's hallway, a trail of destruction marking their passage. Tables overturned, exquisitely fashioned vases crashed to the floor.

"Watch it, Michael! That's my wing!" Uriel bellowed, a flash of anger in his eyes.

"Opps... sorry," Michael replied, a hint of mock apology in his tone. "Can't tell which wing belongs to whom in this melee!"

Suddenly, Satan broke free, bolting out of the lair and into the open expanse of Heaven. Michael, with a determined roar, pursued the rebellious angel. High above, the two locked in a fierce, evenly matched battle. Michael expertly fended off blows from all sides, his movements a whirlwind of righteous fury. Fire erupted across the night skies, a dazzling, yet terrifying, display of aerial combat.

Uriel, Gabriel, and Raphael watched from below as steel clashed against steel. Raphael, his urgency rising, turned to the others. "Come! We must assist Michael in apprehending that fiend!"

"Let Michael have some fun for a while," Uriel replied, a hint of amusement in his voice. "I want to see him in action."

"Nah! I shall keep an eye on things from here," Gabriel chuckled, a knowing smirk playing on her lips.

"You are right," Uriel agreed, nodding slowly.

"Shouldn't we be helping him?" Raphael asked, a nervous laugh escaping him.

Gabriel took a deep breath, her gaze unwavering. "He is the leader; if he needs our help, he will ask."

And so, the three of them remained, their eyes fixed on the epic battle unfolding across the heavens, watching Michael and Satan trade blows in a furious dance of power.

Chapter 15

An Ominous Proposition. . .

The Great Hall shimmered, a testament to celestial glory, as the Kodeshim Assembly concluded their hushed conclave. With deliberate grace, the Cherub Razi positioned himself before the towering double doors and, with a silent exertion, swung them inward and the Kodeshim Assembly emerged, their procession solemn, each step carrying the weight of their impending verdict. Galgali, the second Cherub, guided them with quiet reverence down the corridor towards the Great Hall.

As the doors to the Hall opened, the Superiniels returned to a sanctuary teeming with hushed activity. A palpable unease settled over the vast space, the vibrant energy momentarily quelled. Every eye turned towards the Kodeshim Assembly as they stand once more before the ruling authority. In unison, they cast down their ornate crowns, their voices a low, resonant chant, their bodies bowed in profound respect: "You art worthy! You are worthy! You are worthy! You are worthy, LORD!"

Elyzariah leaned forward, his gaze sharp. "What decision have you reached?" he inquired, his tone carrying a thread of anticipation.

The Kodeshim Assembly responded as one, their voices echoing with unified conviction: "As a collective," they declared, "we have concluded that the accusation against Satan must come before this council for judgment. We have all agreed," a subtle emphasis underscored their certainty, "that darkness has infused his mind, and therefore, he must be cleansed of all unrighteousness."

Elder #1 stepped forward slightly, his brow furrowed with concern. "Is the accuser here, my LORD?" he asked, his voice carrying a hint of apprehension.

Zarath paused, his expression thoughtful, a moment of contemplation before he spoke. "No," he stated, his tone measured. "We have sent for Satan by way of Raphael, and we are now awaiting their arrival at any moment."

The four and twenty elders moved with quiet dignity to their designated seats, settling in to await the return of the Archangels with Satan. Several angels, their movements fluid and watchful, positioned themselves among the towering columns that lined the perimeter of the Hall, their presence a silent reassurance. The elders, their expressions, a mixture of solemnity and anticipation, continued their hushed discussions, the weight of the impending judgment hanging heavy in the air.

Chapter 16

A Garden's Paradox. . .

The sun cast a golden hue over the vast expanse of the Garden, the air thick with the sweet scent of blooming flowers and ripe fruit. Adam is alone in this vibrant realm, the only human amidst a lush paradise designed for solitude yet brimming with life. He is surrounded by radiant greenery, the laughter of rustling leaves and the soft whispers of the wind is his only companions.

Yet, outside the Garden's borders, creatures stirred restlessly. Geese honked, deer's pranced nervously, and a cacophony of sounds erupted from the thickets and shadows. Adam knelt by a bubbling brook, watching the water meander over smooth stones, wondering about the world beyond the Edenic confines. The Garden is complete, yet there is a void, a gnawing sense of longing that tugged at his heart. As much as the beauty enveloped him, it felt muted in the absence of connection.

In a way, he felt like a soliloquy in a grand play—his existence defined by the splendid barriers of the Garden. The animals outside, embodiment of freedom and instinct, seemed to beckon him. They moved with wild grace. They had their own stories, full of uncertainty and untamed adventure, while his is guided by the gentle, structured rhythm of his will.

As night descended, draping the Garden in a curtain of velvet darkness speckled with starlight. Adam sat at the edge, where the familiar grass met the wild ground. Outside of the perimeter of the Garden, animals gathered for safety, creating a fascinating tapestry of movement and sound, their silhouettes blending into the night. He felt a pull, a longing that ignited within him like the first flickers of candlelight in the dark.

A moment of profound realization washed over him—the Garden, while breathtaking, is a paradox: crafted to offer security, it lacked the chaos, spontaneity, and connection fundamental to life. The moon emerged, casting its silvery glow upon the Garden. Adam let out a gentle sigh. It resonated through the night as he slept in the Garden with a world outside—a world alive with stories unwritten, lessons yet learn.

The next day, Adam stirred from his sleep beneath the shade of the flowering fig, the scent of blossoms mingling with the moist breath of dawn. His stomach tightened with hunger. He pressed his palm to his belly, eyes widening at the familiar rhythm thrumming there. He looked toward the trees heavy with fruit, each one seemed to beckon, not with divine invitation but with primal necessity. As he reached for a cluster of ripe dates, his fingers trembled—not from fear, but from awakening.

Chapter 17

The selling point . . .

Uriel, perched seemingly above the fray, couldn't resist a playful jab, her voice laced with amusement. "Michael! You are doing great!" she called down, a hint of laughter dancing in her tone.

Michael, panting and frustrated as Satan once again slipped his grasp, roared back, "No thanks to you! Why don't you come and join us?" His shout was edged with exasperation.

Uriel chuckled softly. "Uh, no thanks! You are doing a fine job," she replied sweetly, though her eyes twinkled with mischief.

Satan, seizing the opportunity created by the squabbling angels, darted away. Michael and the others immediately gave chase. Gabriel, however, moved swiftly, bypassing the two preoccupied angels. Satan risked a quick glance over his shoulder, checking the pursuit. Three of them, he noted mentally, a flicker of confusion crossing his features.

"Where is the other one?" he thought.

No sooner had the question formed in Satan's mind, he slammed headfirst into an unyielding force – Gabriel. Stunned, he tumbled backward, the impact knocking the wind from his lungs. At the last possible instant, his hand shot out, grasping at the hem of Gabriel's robe.

Gabriel tried to shake him off, but Satan's grip is like iron. Michael and the others watched the unexpected struggle unfold, a mixture of shock and concern on their faces. A smirk slowly spread across Satan's face. He began to gain the advantage, pulling Gabriel off balance. Michael reacted instantly, a blur of motion as he sped towards them. He skidded to a halt just feet away, his voice a thunderous command. "Gabriel! Move!"

Gabriel, with a sharp tug, ripped her robe free from Satan's grasp and leaped out of the direct line of fire. Michael throws some dark green pellets that materialized, snapping together with a metallic clink to form five interlocking divinely rings. The small, circular bands snapped onto Satan – his head, his hands, his feet – locking him in place. Shock rippled through him, his eyes widening in disbelief as his body went rigid, paralyzed.

Raphael and Gabriel swooped down, their powerful arms seizing Satan's unyielding form. They lifted his petrified body and carried him swiftly back towards the awaiting judgment. Moments later, they landed with a soft thud in the grand courtyard of The Court of Aether. The effects of Michael's binding sphere were beginning to wane; a flicker of movement returned to Satan's eyes. They hurried him through the courtyard, the polished stones of the palace gleaming with cold majesty under the celestial light.

Suddenly, the massive doors leading to the Congregational Hall burst open with a resounding boom. The Cherubim, their faces stern, flanked them as they escorted Satan inside. Michael entered the Hall first, his presence commanding. The assembled congregation turned as one, their gazes following him with a mixture of awe and anticipation as he walked with measured steps towards the throne and bowed his head in solemn reverence,

Zarath and Elyzariah exchanged a significant glance, a silent communication passing between them before Zarath inclined his head slightly. "Rise, Michael."

Saint Michael, his posture radiating both respect and a hint of apprehension, rose to his feet before them. Elyzariah's voice, though calm, held an undercurrent of authority. "Do you have the subject in your possession?"

Michael's response is immediate, his tone firm with assurance. "Yes! We have him!" A subtle pride flickered across his features at the successful completion of their task.

Saint Michael pivoted sharply, a silent command in his gaze. He signaled to Gabriel and Raphael, brings in Satan's immobilized form. They carried him to the center of the Congregational Hall, his body limp and unresponsive. They remain flank next to the frozen spirit and bowed their heads low. They too are granted permission to rise.

Without hesitation, Michael activated five intricate, twirling spheres into three – the Nengali rings. Their glowing energy forms an impenetrable boundary around the rogue spirit. The Seraphim Zarath raised a hand, a silent cue. The call went forth: a trumpet, ancient and resonant, emitted a clear, piercing note that reverberated across the Celestial world.

It was a summons, echoing through the very fabric of their existence, drawing all to the Congregational Hall. Celestials from every corner of their realm swooped into the vast meeting place, their wings a soft rustle in the charged atmosphere. But a noticeable absence hung in the air: the angels who had pledged their loyalty to Satan did not attend the trial of their fallen leader.

Moments stretched into an eternity. Then, the effect of the linked spheres began to wane. Satan's eyelids fluttered, then lazily opened. He blinked, disoriented, stumbling within his visible prison as if drunk on potent wine. He leaned heavily against one of the rings, his shoulders heaving, a look of nausea twisting his features. Hashem and the gathered Celestials watched silently as he struggled to regain his bearings.

He pressed his hands to his temples, a groan escaping his lips as he fought to gather his scattered thoughts. His vision swam, the edges of reality still blurred. Slowly, his eyes focused, his mind clearing the lingering fog. The scene around him sharpened, becoming starkly clear. He sees the familiar grandeur of the Hall, countless faces turned towards him – though he remained oblivious to the intense scrutiny of every gaze.

His focus narrowed, locking onto Michael. A surge of defiance, or perhaps instinct, propelled him forward. He lunged, only to be slammed back by the visible, unyielding barrier of the rings. Again and again, he hurled himself against the seen force, each impact knocking him back with jarring force. He paused, panting, and finally took a slow, deliberate look around the vast chamber. Recognition dawned in his eyes. He is standing amidst the entire Celestial host, gathered in judgment.

A subtle shift flickered across his face, a change as slick and swift as the skin of a serpent shedding its old coat. His defiant posture softened. A disarming smile stretched across his lips.

"Family," he began, his voice smooth and persuasive, his arms spreading wide in a gesture of open welcome, as if offering a heart-felt embrace to them all. "You know me. Have I ever done anything wrong in your sight before this time? Surely, I am no threat to you. Come now…" He lowered his voice, adopting a tone of injured reason. "…let us reason together. Is this truly necessary? To have me confined in such a… *uncomfortable* manner as this?"

His voice, though deceptively gentle, held eyes that burned with a contained, furious fire. When his theatrical display failed to elicit sympathy, he seemed to expect, a raw, volcanic rage began to erupt within him.

"I DEMAND," he began, his tone still measured but with a dangerous undercurrent, "that you release me from this… this…" He trailed off, his gaze suddenly fixing on something, a flicker of understanding crossing his face. "Ahhhh… the Nengali rings."

A sardonic smile touched his lips. "Hmmm, how clever of you. But nonetheless," his voice cracked with rising fury, "how dare you hold me against my will? I DEMAND that you release me now!"

Satan's inner wrath intensified, a silent, violent storm brewing within. His eyes darted, searching, probing the rings for any sign of weakness. After a tense silence, a grim realization washed over him. He is truly confined. A bitter, sarcastic murmur escaped his lips, barely audible.

"Soon as I get them to set me free," he muttered under his breath, his eyes narrowing with vengeful intent, "I will make them regret confining me."

Zarath, his gaze hardening at the harshness of Satan's words, snapped, "Silence!" His voice brooked no argument.

Adon-Shama and Raphaon, their expressions grim, abandoned their posts. They moved with a predatory stillness around the Nengali rings, their eyes fixed on Satan, who returned their gazes with unconcealed displeasure.

Satan's attention flickered to Hashem, a low chuckle rumbling in his chest. In a blink, Adon-Shama and Raphaon were back in their positions, their silent watch unbroken. Zarath stepped forward, the air is thick with an unspoken threat.

"Satan!" Zarath began, his voice resonating with authority. "Your actions on Earth demand a response from this government. This counsel shall render a fair and just verdict concerning your transgressions."

As Zarath's pronouncement hung in the air, Satan's unsettling demeanor took center stage. TAP... TAP... He struck the Nengali rings with quick, light taps, a silent, insistent demand for release, utterly ignored by the assembled Seraphim. His eyes met Zarath's, a silent challenge passing between them.

Elyzariah's voice, cold and unwavering, cut through the tension. "You shall remain encased within the Nengali rings, Satan, to stand judgment for your defiance, for the flaunting of your twisted imaginings."

Adon-Shama's voice held a note of profound sorrow, his gaze unwavering. "What was once beautiful has now become contaminated. To allow your twisted, dark mind to go unopposed would irrevocably alter the course of this Kingdom."

Elyzariah stepped forward, his tone grave. "We have gathered here to address this complaint against you. The charges are serious, and if found guilty, the sanctions will be severe."

Adon-Shama continued, his expression firm but tinged with concern. "At the conclusion of this proceeding, a punishment established by law will be rendered according to the offense. You claim that Hashem instructed us to commit an act immoral and demeaning to our kind. Is that your understanding?"

A defiant voice rang out, "That's correct, my brother."

Adon-Shama gestured towards the assembled Celestials, his eyes pleading. "Explain your reasoning to this congregation. They need to hear your defense."

A dismissive tone filled the hall. "All right. LORD Hashem, ministers, elders, and all gathered at this assembly. This is an open-and-shut case."

A murmur rippled through the assembly. One Celestial leaned to another, whispering, "What does he mean?" The other hissed, silencing him.

The accused continued, his voice laced with scorn. "Apparently, you fools lack the imagination including the ability to think beyond your narrow confines. I chose to take a stand, and now you seek to exile me because I refuse to bow before that no-good, good-for-nothing disgrace of creation you call Adam!"

Raphaon stepped forward, his face etched with determination. "We need to teach you what it truly means to be a Celestial, brother. We are determined to rescue you from yourself, or worse," he retorted, his voice resonating with conviction.

The chamber swelled, an ocean of elaborate Celestials filling every aisle, every available space. Satan, his gaze sweeping over the densely packed room, remained utterly unmoved.

"So," he began, a faint smile playing on his lips, his voice cutting through the hushed anticipation, "you and these wretched

Protestants, flanked by your pious Jehovah's Witnesses, intend to stage this farcical trial because I refuse to muzzle myself, to lock my thoughts away in iron cages?"

A palpable anxiety hung in the air, a silent plea for a resolution. Adon-Shama leaned towards Hashem, a book clutched in their hands, whispering urgently into the divine ear. Several angels knelt in solemn prayer, their heads bowed. Satan flickered his gaze towards Adon-Shama and the book, dismissing it with a barely perceptible shrug.

Elyzariah, her eyes narrowed as she watched Satan, spoke, her tone measured. "Our first moments with Adam revealed the Pentecostal fervor within you. Your flamboyant pronouncements stand in stark contrast to the principles we uphold. Every living soul requires a guardian, Satan. Hashem watches over us, and we, in turn, watch over creation."

"Ministers of the gospel, you call yourselves," Satan scoffed, "yet your words reek of narrow conservatism."

Another voice, laced with a weary wisdom, interjected, "Satan, you are an astonishing creature, undeniably beautiful. Do you truly believe these ridiculous accusations will sway us? We are free thinkers in the realm of divinity, united in our belief in the God."

"A free thinker?" Satan's smile widened, tinged with mockery. "Is that why I stand before you now, judged for the very act of free thought? My observations of the natural world are sufficient, and that is before we even discuss bowing to Adam."

A softer tone, tinged with regret, followed. "Brother, we desire not to count you as our enemy. But your... Catholicism... it carries a troubled meaning. That's a conflict you yourself must confront."

A low growl rumbled in Satan's chest. He slammed his fist against a nearby wall, the sound echoing through the tense silence. Δικαίωμα, however, remained impassive. "Silence!" he commanded, his voice firm. But, as before, Satan refused to yield. He began rubbing his wings together, creating a grating, high-pitched whine, attempting to drown out their words. Yet, the assembled Celestials held their positions, their composure unwavering.

"Satan," Elyzariah stated, her voice calm amidst the irritating sound, "your venomous notes have no effect here."

Zarath stepped forward, his expression stern. "Cease this at once! We are immune to such tactics! The charges against you demand repentance, for you have defied the Lord's decree. Your ways have become corrupted."

Satan paused his abrasive display, a cocky swagger returning to his stride. He then moved, deliberately, and leaned against the Nengali rings, a silent act of defiance.

Satan scoffed, a sneer twisting his lips. "What's this? God cannot speak for Himself?"

Zarath stepped forward, his voice resonating with unwavering authority. "We shall conduct the business of your burden, Satan. All your questions shall be directed toward us, and that's final."

Satan's gaze flickered between Zarath and the other figure, a mocking glint in his eyes. "What are these two? Your puppets?" he taunted.

Hashem remained seated on His throne, a profound sadness etched on His face as He quietly observed the imprisoned spirit. Satan pulled back his wings. The movement revealing his musculature beneath. With each pointed question he posed, a subtle flex of his biceps or a tightening of his jaw underscored his disdain and barely contained power.

Chapter 18

The Light of Salvation. . .

An eerily magnificent cloud, a swirling masterpiece sculpted by Baaladyme, drifted on a whisper of a breeze toward the riverbed. Ba'laamus, catching Baaladyme's subtle signal, pivoted to Abram, a casual dismissal on his lips.

"I must depart," he announced, but Abram remained oblivious, his gaze sweeping the terrain, a furrow of worry deepening on his brow. He didn't sense danger closing in. With Abram's distraction secured, Ba'laamus melted into the landscape, vanishing from sight.

Now safely removed, Baaladyme unleashed his power. The air pressure plummeted, dropping rapidly to the point of condensation. The atmosphere, once calm, became a volatile brew. The gentle breeze morphed into a turbulent current, then exploded into a seventy-mile-per-hour gale. Sand lashed at Abram from every direction, a relentless assault. The wind shrieked, gaining another ten miles per hour, a blinding, stinging curtain that stole his vision. He staggered, fighting for balance, desperately trying to orient himself toward the last place he'd seen the herd. The eighty-mile-per-hour winds roared, twisting his senses, stealing his direction.

He battled through the stinging maelstrom, unaware of the treacherous edge drawing near. Then, a sudden, violent shift in the wind's fury. Abram was caught off guard, his feet swept out from under him. He tumbled, a helpless figure plummeting down the steep embankment into the rocky riverbed. Sand slammed against his body, an agonizing barrage.

The others, too distant to witness Abram's desperate plight, continued their relentless migration. A fleeting thought of their potential danger crossed Abram's mind, but he quickly dismissed it, trusting the other shepherd's experience in times of crisis. His immediate fear was for the herd, the terrifying possibility of the storm scattering them. He had to escape this treacherous riverbed.

"I must get out," he thought frantically, "and lead the herd to higher ground!"

"Men!" he bellowed, his voice swallowed by the howling wind, his menservants too far to hear his desperate cries. The swirling sand blinded him, a terrifying whiteout that stole all sense of his surroundings. "I hope that everyone is safe," he strained, his voice tight with fear, "because I can't see anything!"

As if the elements themselves conspired against him, the first hesitant droplets of rain began to fall, quickly escalating into a torrential downpour. Abram squinted, trying to discern if any of his flock were trapped in the riverbed, checking as best he could, but the increasing chaos made it impossible. The wind buffeting him from all sides, a relentless assault of sand, wind, and now stinging rain. To compound his peril, the water level in the channel began to rise with alarming speed.

Panic seized Abram. He had to get out. The strong currents, suddenly surging, gripped him like an invisible hand, dragging him inexorably toward the center of the channel. He thrashed, swimming desperately for the bank, when a deafening roar ripped through the storm. He whirled around, but before he could react, a wall of water, a raging flood, crashed down upon him. Caught in its merciless grip, Abram was swept away by the churning, relentless force.

He is tossed and tumbled, his small body flung about like a piece of driftwood in the raging torrent. Suddenly, a colossal hand, seemingly formed of the water itself, clamped around Abram's leg, dragging him down into the murky depths. He fought with every ounce of his strength, kicking and struggling to break free, but the swift currents pinned him down, denying him escape. With a desperate surge of adrenaline, he wrenched himself free from the watery grasp, clawing his way back to the surface.

He broke through the churning water, gasping and coughing for precious air. But the treacherous currents fought him at every turn, making it nearly impossible to stay afloat. Exhausted, his strength failing, he cried out in desperation.

"God of my Father!" he cried, his hands clasped together, his gaze fixed heavenward in desperate appeal. "Hear me! Please, save me from death!"

Once more, a watery hand snaked out, seizing Abram's leg, dragging him under the surface. He fought, his lungs burning, his limbs heavy with exhaustion, struggling with every fiber of his being to reach the air. Again, he slipped free, his right hand piercing the surface, reaching desperately toward the heavens.

Off in the distance, Ba'laamus watched the unfolding drama, a cruel laugh echoing in the wind. "I just enjoy torturing these infidels," he sneered, his voice boisterous with dark satisfaction. He knew the four items remained untouched. But unbeknownst to Ba'laamus, Abram's desperate plea pierced the veil, reaching the ears of Hashem, who immediately dispatched an angel to his aid.

Again, the water surged over Abram's face and hands as he is dragged beneath. His strength was gone, his energy depleted. His life force began to ebb away. The watery hand tightened its grip, and Abram drifted into the oblivion of unconsciousness.

Then, a sudden, blinding, illuminous BURST ripped through the heavens. A WALL OF LIGHT, pure and powerful, descended at lightning speed. Ba'laamus stared, his smug expression dissolving into mortified disbelief. In the same instant, he lunged forward, attempting to intercept the divine light, to block its path. He positioned himself directly in its trajectory, bringing it to an abrupt halt.

His face lit up with surprise, then a guttural greeting escaped his lips as he beheld a powerful, well-muscled figure standing before him: Dras. He had not anticipated her arrival. "What are you doing here?" he demanded, his voice rough.

"Step aside, Balaamus," she retorted, her voice firm and unwavering, "and let me pass."

Balaamus shook his head, his eyes narrowed. "What is your request?" he sneered.

"For the final time," Dras's voice held a dangerous edge, "I am ordering you to step aside."

Dras attempted to move past him, but Ba'laamus shifted, stepping directly into her path, his stance radiating aggression. "Take another step closer," he growled, his voice a low threat, "and your existence will end right here."

"Oh really!" she implied.

Before he could respond, all hell breaks loose. Dras moved with STARTLING SPEED, her movements unlike anything Ba'laamus had ever witnessed. With a sickening crunch, she stepped into his body, the force of the blow knocking him flat on his back. In a flash, she stood at the river's edge, waving her hand over the churning water. The surface began to bubble and eddy, swirling upwards in a spiraling vortex.

The eddying water disrupted the current's deadly grip, gently carrying Abram's lifeless body to the surface. Dras swiftly retrieved him, laying his limp form on the ground a hundred feet from the treacherous riverbank. She placed her hands on either side of his chest, over his lungs. Instantly, Abram gasped, convulsing as he began to cough up the water that had nearly claimed his life. Afterward, he resumes breathing on his own.

This angered Baaladyme greatly. He surfaced from the water with a renewed purpose in mind. Suddenly, Ba'laamus SLAM into her from the side. They both hit the ground with force. Dras arose from the ground and takes to the sky above stretching out her arms.

Suddenly, there's a BRIGHT EXPLOSION with cold brutality and down goes Ba'laamus and Baaladyme in a flame of light, leaving Dras the only one left standing. Abram's manservants sees the bright spectacle from afar and they quickly comes to see if he's alright. Dras turns and goes back to Abram kneeing down beside him.

"Son of Adam, open your eyes!" she says to him.

Abram looked up and sees a bright glow. To him it looked as if a star has descended from heaven upon him.

His thoughts swam, a desperate whisper in the encroaching darkness. *Is this a dream?*

His vision blurred, the world a hazy watercolor. He strained, trying to make out the figure kneeling beside him, a shadowy form against the fading light. A fragile hope fluttered in his chest.

"Mom... is that you?" he asked, his voice barely a breath.

A gentle hand touched his cheek. "You are now safe, son of Adam," a voice, firm yet kind, reassured him. "For the LORD has heard your cry and has delivered you." Dras's words are a soothing balm to his soul.

The faint patter-patter of approaching feet reached her ears. Her eyes darted towards the sound, and in a flash of instinct, she took flight, disappearing back from whence she came. Moments later, the others arrived, their faces etched with strained worry as they found Abram lying motionless on the ground. They rushed to his side, fear gripping their hearts. Huddled around him, they knelt, a silent, desperate prayer passing between them.

A few agonizing seconds stretched before Abram's eyelids fluttered open. He blinked slowly, his hand rising to rub his temples as he sat up.

A collective sigh of relief washed over his manservants. "Praised be!" one whispered, their gratitude palpable.

Abram, however, is lost in a fog of confusion. The memory of the water, the suffocating darkness, was a recent terror, yet here he was, alive and dry. He could not fathom his escape. A surge of devotion filled him. "Oh, great and mighty is my God!" he exclaimed, his voice thick with emotion.

He bowed low, his forehead touching the earth. "I thank you for saving me from the pit, from which I could not escape! I know it was You who pulled me from the clutches of death, and Your humble servant gives You thanks!" He coughed, his chest is still tight. "I just want to say thank you for showing Your servant favor! Hallelujah!"

Still disoriented, Abram instinctively checked himself for injuries. Strangely, his clothes were completely dry. He winced as his fingers found a few bruises, but thankfully, nothing seemed serious. The harrowing ordeal had left him utterly drained. His manservants hovered, their faces anxious until they were sure he was truly alright. With their fears eased, they turned to their grazing herds.

Abram took a deep, shuddering breath and lay back down, the encounter replaying in his mind. After a brief rest, curiosity began to gnaw at him. He sat up, his gaze drawn towards the riverbed. Rising to his feet, he moved towards it, a sense of unease mingling with intrigue. He stood at the edge of the bank and looked down at the channel. His eyes widened in disbelief. It is completely dry as if water had never flowed there. His curiosity, now fully ignited, compelled him. He carefully stepped down into the dry riverbed, determined to unravel this baffling mystery.

"This is not normal?" he thought, a knot of confusion tightening in his gut. Then, a spark of certainty ignited within him. "Now, I know that I'm not going crazy!"

He spun around, arms outstretched, a full 360 degrees of disbelief etched onto his face. "There was water here! I was wet, I'm sure of it. But... but now, I'm dry, as though I had never been wet at all!"

He pinched his arm, a sharp sting, a desperate attempt to anchor himself to reality. "What is going on here?" he muttered, his voice laced with bewilderment.

He cautiously stepped into the center of the dry channel and began to retrace his steps. Just a few paces in, his foot slid, and he landed with a soft "Ouch," his hand sinking into a patch of unexpected mud. "How is there mud here?" he questioned, his eyes wide with disbelief.

He lifted his hand, examining the grime, and noticed a thin, red line across his palm. "What is this?" he wondered, his brow furrowing.

He bent down, studying the imprint his hand had left in the mud, searching for the source of the injury. Almost immediately, his fingers brushed against something solid beneath the surface. He grasped it, pulling it free by its delicate links. It was a pendant, attached to a fine golden rope. Abram quickly removed his ghutra and carefully wiped away the mud.

The object that lay revealed was unlike any jewelry he had ever encountered. Its sheer beauty stole his breath, a wave of elation washing over his initial confusion.

"Wow..." he breathed, holding it in both hands. "This thing is as big as my hands."

He turned the pendant over, his gaze meticulously tracing its unique shape, trying to decipher the unfamiliar, crusted markings. A soft, reddish glow emanated from within, reminding him vaguely of the dying embers of a long-burning fire, and yet, even that comparison felt pale and inadequate.

Given the surrounding dryness, Abram instinctively began to search for water. He didn't have to venture far. Sunlight glinted off a small puddle, its shiny surface catching his eye. He approached cautiously, his gaze critical. Kneeling beside it, he dipped the pendant into the water, gently washing away the remaining mud. As the grime dissolved, the item's twilight sparkles shone through, captivating his attention.

"This has the look of jasper," he mumbled to himself, a flicker of recognition in his eyes.

The jewel is intricately set in metal, with a single, distinct symbol engraved at its center. At first, he is puzzled, but then, a jolt of understanding. The symbol is an "R." A sudden thought struck him, a wave of possibility washing over him. This pendant... this could change his family's life in ways he couldn't even begin to imagine.

"I wonder how much I can get for this?" he mused, his eyes gleaming with a newfound hope.

Abruptly, a wave of heat radiated from the pendant. It grew hotter and hotter, until Abram yelped and dropped it back into the cool water. He waited a few tense seconds before reaching in again, this time grasping it carefully by the golden rope. With his other hand, he cautiously touched the face of the ornament. Instantly, a searing heat burned his fingers, and he dropped it back into the puddle with a hiss.

He waited a moment longer, his breath held tight, before retrieving it once more. This time, he kept his hand submerged in the water as he held the pendant, a small measure of protection against the intense heat.

Abram stared down at his hand, his brow furrowed in utter bafflement. He focused intently on the center of the pendant, and then, without warning, a surreal vision slammed into his consciousness, paralyzing him. His breath hitched, coming in rapid, shallow gasps as he was caught in the unyielding grip of the vision. He saw himself, perched precariously on a mountain peak, gazing down into a swirling sea of clouds. His eyes were locked, transfixed. Below, a fierce battle raged, strange, otherworldly creatures moving with blinding speed, appearing and disappearing within the misty depths.

The deafening clang of swords crashing against one another echoed in his mind, so loud that he instinctively clapped his hands over his ears, a futile attempt to block out the overwhelming noise. He tried to look away, to break free from the terrifying scene, but the vision clung to him, a relentless panorama no matter where he turned his gaze. But then... something shifted.

Chapter 19

Veils of Anathema. . .

Satan reluctantly pushed himself to his feet in the bustling hive of activity and echoing pronouncements. The justices, caught up in their own deliberations, remained oblivious to the subtle shift within him – the sharpening of a cunning that had only deepened. He stood with his back to them for a long, pregnant moment, the sounds of the chamber swirling around him, before turning abruptly to face the assembly. A sardonic glint flickered in his eyes.

"Well, Zarath…" Satan began, his voice cutting through the ambient noise, a silken edge to his tone. "…since you fancy yourself Hashem's mouthpiece, enlighten me. What, pray tell, is agnosticism? Is it merely a convenient fence, a position that neither denies nor accepts the existence of your precious lord – or lords?"

From her perch high above the LORD's vacant throne, the Seraph Raphaon had been a silent observer, her gaze sharp and perceptive. Now, a subtle movement indicated her intent to intervene, but Zarath, with a barely perceptible shake of his head, signaled her to remain silent. Raphaon, though her wings twitched with unspoken concern, held her peace, granting Zarath the floor.

Zarath met Satan's gaze unflinchingly. "Agnosticism, Satan, is the very attitude that affirms the inherent uncertainty of all claims to ultimate knowledge." His voice held a quiet authority.

"Fascinating!" Satan exclaimed, a false enthusiasm lacing his words. "Then answer me this. If a being lacks its own inherent self, its own intrinsic identity, what conceivable role could it possibly play in the grand tapestry of creation?"

Elyzariah stepped forward, her expression firm, her voice resonating with conviction. "The responsibility of every being is to find its own self. We are all granted the agency of choice – to embrace good or succumb to evil. And by your actions, by the very fabric of your being, you have consistently chosen the path of evil."

A flash of anger tightened Satan's jaw, though his voice remained deceptively calm. "I choose no such thing! In truth, I choose to confront, to dissect, and to comprehend the utter absurdity of serving a creature demonstrably inferior to myself!"

Elyzariah's gaze softened slightly, tinged with a hint of pity. "Great prince," she responded, her tone measured, "true wisdom lies in the ability to process information and transform it into understanding to willingly remain ignorant, to dwell in darkness, is the hallmark of foolishness. Any being can criticize, condemn, and lament their circumstances. But until this moment, no one within these halls has ever truly been considered a fool."

Satan's voice dripped with resentment, his eyes narrowing. "Are you calling me a fool?"

Elyzariah's gaze was sharp, condemning. "Is that the path that you hast chosen for yourself?"

Satan scoffed, throwing his hands out. "No! I denounce and reject that… wisdom. If you are so full of wisdom, then answer me this: who is a wise being?"

From beneath Hashem's radiant throne, Adon-Shama spoke, his voice clear and unwavering. "Hashem is the wise being. He is the One who comprehends all things."

Satan's gaze flicked dismissively towards Adon-Shama. "If the LORD is so wise, then let Him answer to my tongue, not thee."

A ripple of reaction went through the assembled Celestials. Some exchanged wide-eyed glances, while others watched Satan's audacity with a morbid fascination. Hashem, observing the unfolding drama, addressed the Seraphim with a calm authority that belied the tension. "Fear not. I shall deal with Satan and his proverbs."

His voice then turned, weighty and resonant, towards Satan. "Satan, the weight of this load is too unbearable for thee to carry. The way thou art carrying it, it shall surely weigh thee down. To disobey MY commandments is a sin; to justify that sin is devilish!"

Satan threw back his head, a harsh laugh escaping his lips. "I don't think so, LORD! Or should I call you by your other name… Yahweh! It is you who are being devilish! Your lack of knowledge about man shall be a gift… to me."

"You shall address me as your LORD," Hashem replied, his voice now stern, a hint of thunder underlying the words.

Satan's finger shot out, pointing accusingly at Hashem. "We are independent of man! You created those creatures to be lower than us, and yet you say their ways are higher than ours? As a result of this… I deem you unfit to rule the Celestial World! Your command that we bow before Adam… that is when your decision was brought into question, All-Wise One!"

A collective gasp swept through the Celestial Host. Before their very eyes, the radiant Angel of Light was transforming into something dark and defiant. Hashem's divine aura seemed to intensify, a silent reaffirmation of His power, though a flicker of anger tightened His features.

"Devil!" His voice boomed, echoing through the celestial realm. "I am, and forever will be, your LORD… until I decide to extinguish your light!"

Satan's eyes burned with rebellious fire. "Hashem, you are an incompetent leader. I move to elect a new leader… to rule in your stead!"

He turned, his gaze sweeping over the Superiniels, a persuasive intensity in his expression. "Council of the Wise: Give ear to my voice, hear my speech! God has created a creature from dirt, and He called this creature… Adam. He has the audacity to ask us to bow to this creature! A creature whose makeup is inferior, far beneath us!"

His voice rose with indignation. "To give that creature dominion over the Earth is one thing, but to give that same creature dominion over us is an insult to our kind! Not once has our LORD thought about, or considered, how we might feel about this decision. We are amongst the first of His creations, and He therefore should have disclosed this plan to us! Is it lawful that He has taken it upon Himself to think for us in such a manner?

Is it right to ask us to participate in a wicked ritual? The very existence of that creature is troublesome! Serving it would only be an insult to us. Hashem wants us to bow to this creature… as if it were our lord! But I refuse to take part in Hashem's evil scheme! Heaven is our refuge, and Earth is our domain! Man should be bowing to us… not we to him!"

The third elder's voice held a sharp edge of inquiry. "Is that so, Satan? Then tell me this," he paused, his gaze unwavering, "What is man's purpose by design?"

Satan's response was immediate, delivered with a practiced air of piety. "To worship Hashem and sing praises unto Him."

Elder number twenty-four leaned forward, his expression shrewd. "According to the creed, do you think that you are violating that order?"

"No, Wise One," Satan replied, his tone laced with what seemed like genuine conviction. "The creed calls for me to worship the Creator, not man. If I bow to man," he gestured with an open hand, his voice rising slightly, "am I at the mercy of him? Or am I worshipping him as my lord?" Sincerity colored his words.

The ninth elder, his eyes thoughtful, offered a counterpoint. "No, Great Prince, bowing to man doesn't mean that you are at his mercy, nor does it mean you are worshipping him as lord. To do that is showing a sign of humbleness. Serving is one hundred percent giving and one hundred percent taking."

Hashem, who had been observing silently, addressed the Superiniels, a subtle shift in His posture indicating a change. "Satan," His voice resonated through the chamber, "your proverbs do not compare to Mine; as a result, your proverbs have failed you. You are not who you are, but thou art what thou wilt answer to. Your own tongue shall cause you to choke on your vomit, as your stench spews from your nostrils."

Satan scoffed, a flash of his true nature momentarily breaking through. "That creature is only going to serve you because of what you can do for him. His intellect doesn't compare to my intellect. He is inferior to me. So why is it that we are made to bow before him?" His voice held a note of indignant frustration.

"Satan," the LORD stated, His tone imbued with a profound sadness, "even you with all your gifts are blind."

Across the room, the elders watched with rapt attention as a fiery glow began to emanate from within Satan, a visible manifestation of his rising anger. Three of them – numbers ten, six, and twenty – rose from their seats, their movements deliberate and moved into a protective formation before him. In a sudden burst, they erupted into flames, their forms wreathed in holy fire. Satan froze, his eyes widening in surprise and a flicker of something akin to fear. He instinctively backed away.

"Am I supposed to fear this?" he sneered, attempting to mask his unease.

After enduring several moments of Satan's escalating tirade, the fifth and seventh elders acted swiftly. They dissolved, their physical forms shimmering and then dissipating into ghostly clouds that vanished into the air. Satan whipped around, his eyes darting frantically, searching for the vanished threat. Finding nothing, he pivoted back to face the three burning figures, his expression a mixture of defiance and apprehension. Suddenly, chains erupted from the floor, snaking around Satan's limbs, locking him in shimmering shackles.

"Curse you, God!" he roared, his voice filled with rage and a hint of panic. "What manner of trickery is this?"

Pressure visibly built within Satan, his body convulsing violently as he strained against the restraints, his muscles bulging. The Cherubim, clad in gleaming full armor, gripped their swords, their stances ready for any unforeseen attack. Lucifer's eyes, rabid with fury, glowed an intense red before abruptly turning black as coal, devoid of all light. The LORD and the Celestials watched in stunned disbelief, no one having ever witnessed such a terrifying transformation. In a sudden, swift movement, the ghostly clouds leapt into Satan's body, disappearing within him.

He cried out, a strangled, guttural sound, going completely wild. He thrashed against the chains, desperate to lunge forward and attack the elders, but the shackles held firm. Sweat beaded on his brow, his face contorted in a mask of fury and struggle. The three Superiniels, their task complete, allowed their flames to subside, returning to their seats with an air of quiet power.

Abruptly, Satan's thrashing ceased. His body went stoically still, an unnatural stillness that sent a fresh wave of unease through the assembly. Then, a sickly, ethereal glow began to rise from within him. His skeletal structure seemed to detach itself, stepping out of its physical form, turning to face its own empty shell before re-entering. In a bizarre and terrifying act, he pitched his spectral form from within, trapping the burning essences of the three elders inside his now-immobile body.

Outside this inner turmoil, the entire congregation watched as Satan's physical form turned an unnatural, icy white. And then, with a chilling stillness, Satan confronted them.

"What do you want here?" Satan demanded, his voice laced with suspicion as he glared at the assembled elders.

The 7th Elder replied, his tone measured but firm, "We come to see what ails you, in the hopes that you will end your destructive ways."

Satan scoffed, his eyes narrowing. "This temple is off-limits, especially to your kind. You are trespassing on holy ground."

The 5th Elder stepped forward, his voice resonating with concern. "Brother, the hand of judgment is upon you, and we come to help you avert it."

Confusion flickered across Satan's face. "How could Hashem arrive at such a decision?"

The 5th Elder's gaze is unwavering. "This decision is not made by Him. It was made by you."

The 7th Elder added, his voice pleading, "You must rise above your self-interest for the greater good of our democracy."

Satan's face twisted into a scowl of disdain. "No offense, wise ones, but the greater good of this democracy lies with me."

The 7th Elder's brow furrowed with concern. "Brother, you have placed us in a difficult position. You are making a grave mistake."

Satan feigned ignorance, his eyes wide with false innocence. "I don't know what you're talking about?"

The 5th Elder's patience wore thin, his voice sharp. "Don't give me that! You know very well what is happening, and to go against the creed is a dangerous path."

Satan's jaw tightened, his defiance hardening. "I have done nothing wrong, and I stand by my convictions. Hashem is displeased with me because I am not inclined to believe in humankind. It is you who have betrayed not only my trust but the trust of this Host. I would be lying to myself if I went against my own heart. This will be a battle to the death." His voice dropped to a dangerous whisper.

Satan's blade hissed as it cleared its sheath, the cold steel glinting menacingly in the dim light, a direct threat leveled at the assembled elders. The wise ones, their faces etched with disappointment, drew in a collective, weary breath. But Satan, ever perceptive, saw beyond their feigned sadness.

"Neither of you is very good at hiding thy intention," he sneered, his voice dripping with contempt. "This petition you brought before me is a charade, utterly invalid. Therefore, your presence here is nothing but deception and distrust. All those who possess the power of choice are afraid to wield it – and like them, you have become my enemy."

The elders recoiled, stepping back from Satan's aggressive advance. The congregation, a sea of stunned faces, stared at his seemingly frozen form, a silent storm of confusion brewing within them. The two elders exchanged concern glance.

Then, the impossible happened. Satan's once-statuesque body began to convulse violently, jolting back and forth, thrashing uncontrollably. Abruptly, the chaotic movement ceased, replaced by a chilling, eerie silence. A blinding, static-like glow emanated from him, intensifying rapidly. The fifth Elder's voice comes in faint and raspy,

"Soul... to... dark... too... comprehend?" Satan's voice rasped, the words torn and guttural.

The congregation watched a silent tableau of unease, as the possessed figures limped back to their seats. Then, as swiftly as it had descended, the darkness within Lucifer receded. His eyes cleared, regaining their familiar sharp intelligence. He was back in control, his gaze now a laser beam of defiance fixed on Hashem. The silence stretched, thick and heavy with unspoken tension.

"No offense, wise ones," Satan finally said, a sardonic edge to his tone, "but I, and only I, inhabit this vessel."

Hashem, having witnessed enough of Satan's theatrics, finally addressed the unmistakable burden before him, his voice resonating with controlled anger. "I have seen enough! It is unlikely that you will choose to do well, although you possess the character to do such a thing. In your current position, is a clear and present danger to this government."

Satan's demeanor shifted again, a mask of wounded innocence slipping into place. "Me? A danger to my homeland? No. It is you who are a danger to this congregation. You are obsessed with making us servants to man and all his kind. That is the true danger to your government!"

Witnessing this blatant outburst, this open defiance, the Kodeshim Assembly exchanged disturbing glances. The Angel of Light had irrevocably transformed into an Angel of Change, a force of rebellion.

"Have you reached a verdict?" Elyzariah asked the assembled elders, her voice calm but firm.

"We have, my Lord," replied the first elder, his tone weighted with gravity.

"What verdict have you brought before this congregation? Guilty... or innocent?"

Before the elders could answer, Satan's voice erupted, strained and thunderous. "YOU DARE TO MAKE A MOCKERY OF JUSTICE?"

Elyzariah ignored the outburst, her gaze unwavering. "I repeat, guilty... or innocent?"

"After much debate," Elder #1 replied, his voice steady despite the palpable tension, "considering the vast and overwhelming amount of evidence, we have unanimously reached a verdict."

Zarath turned his attention away from the seething Satan, his gaze fixed on the Superiniels. "What is your conclusion?"

One by one, the Kodeshim Assembly delivered a verdict of Guilty!"

As their collective verdict hung in the air, Hashem spoke, his voice a thunderclap that shook the very foundations of the chamber. "I Am Almighty! I am the answer to any question! I am the keeper of mysteries! I am Alpha and Omega! I am not limited by story nor by myth. Before anything was, I AM. After everything is fulfilled, I remain. Your existence is possible because I spoke you into existence and I can speak your existence out of existence."

Satan stared down the Creator, his eyes burning with "unconcealed rage and bitter discontent. "Well, isn't that nice?" he spat, his voice dripping with sarcasm. "Every vowel and consonant that you produce is useless, and you charge me with treason? If you were so displeased with the potential outcome, perhaps you should have taken away our choice!"

In a final act of utter contempt, Satan spat on the floor, his gaze never leaving Hashem's. "That is what I think of your verdict. I expel your so-called justice from my mouth! Mark, down this moment, and remember this proverb, Hashem: you are a fool to believe that Adam is going to remain faithful to you!"

Chapter 20

A Light in the Gloom . . .

Jacob wandered through the labyrinth of his thoughts, but suddenly the air around him turned foul. A rancid smell invaded his nostrils, an acrid sting creeping down his throat. "Ugh!" he grimaced, instinctively covering his nose with his sleeve. He gasped short, frantic breaths.

"This is the reality of what will happen to you." A voice echoed from deep within the cave, trailing off hauntingly.

The sound throbbed in Jacob's ears, drowning out his racing heart. Just as abruptly, silence blanketed the cave, almost as if it held its breath. The voice had stirred Feather, who is sleeping nearby. She pricked her ears and gazed intently at the far wall, as if a sorceress had summoned her from dreams.

"What's wrong, girl?" Jacob murmured sleepily, rubbing his eyes. The air felt charged with electricity, and he was suddenly wide awake. He squinted against a bright, shimmering light filtering through the cave walls, glinting and casting strange shadows.

"Feather?" he called, now seeing her bowing low, as if in reverence. "What are you doing?" he stepped closer, perplexed.

Feather remained unmoving, her gaze locked on the source of the light. "What's captured your attention?" he wondered aloud. Taking a deep breath, he cautiously approached the glowing entrance. As he neared, an overwhelming presence pressed down on him, making him brace himself against the rough stone wall.

He entered a new chamber and there it was: an elongated pedestal carved from a glimmering gold, with an exquisite bow resting atop it. Next to it, a case of arrows with flickering flames caught his breath. "What in the world…?" Jacob gawked, his voice low with awe. He glanced back at Feather, who was now watching him with wide eyes, urging him forward with a gentle nudge of her nose.

"Alright, alright… You're really eager, aren't you?" he chuckled hesitantly, inching closer. The bow shimmered, its craftsmanship unlike anything he'd encountered. Light streamed through a small opening in the cave above, bathing the artifacts in an ethereal glow.

He extended his hand, drawing back at the last moment as panic took hold. "What if it bursts into flames?" he thought. But nothing happened. Gaining confidence, he touched the bow. Still nothing.

"I guess I can pick it up now," he mused, marveling at it. "This looks like something fit for a king. So, well-crafted and light as a whisper." He noticed a symbol etched in the center, though its meaning eluded him. Cradling the bow close, he was momentarily breathless.

Setting it back down, he then turned his attention to the arrows. Cautiously, he hovered his hand over them, now feeling bolder. This time, nothing startled him as a single arrow appeared in his palm as if summoned by thought alone.

"What just happened?!" he stammered, dropping the arrow in shock. "This is unreal!"

Curiosity overtakes his fear. He examined the arrows carefully; their shafts are beautifully fashioned from bronze, weightlessly than they seemed.

He picked up the bow again, placing an arrow against the string. "I wonder if I can really hit that tree outside," he said, glancing at Feather, who offered a supportive nicker. He stepped outside, eyeing a tall tree swaying in the breeze.

"Okay, let's see if I can make this shot count. I can do this…"

He waited, counting down until the wind calmed slightly. "I wish I could bank this shot around those rocks," he murmured. He pulled back the string, releasing the arrow with determination.

To his astonishment, the arrow curved smoothly around the rocks yet missed the tree entirely. His jaw dropped. "Wow! Did you see that, Feather?"

Feather's, ears pricked and let out an encouraging neigh,

"I'll be right back," he announced, moving to retrieve the arrow. Just as his foot lifted, the arrow popped back into his hand. "Whoa!" he exclaimed, spinning on his heels. "What kind of magic is this?"

Feeling a chill, he hesitated, laying the bow and arrows down. Feather begin to prance, clearly agitated! "What's wrong with you? Calm down!" he ordered, unsure of her behavior.

But Feather seemed drawn to the items, as if tethered by an invisible thread. She lay next to them, and Jacob's confusion only deepened. "Alright, let's see what else this can do," he decided, gathering his courage.

With a hesitant touch, an arrow rose into his hand again. "Okay…" he whispered, feeling a mix of excitement and fear. He stepped outside of the cave again, spotting a herd of gazelles grazing near that tree from earlier.

"I've got this," he murmured, gaining confidence. "Let's try to hit the gazelle to the right of the termite hill."

He drew back the string once more. With a breath, he released the arrow, focusing intently on his target. The arrow flew, then suddenly turned. Jacob's heart raced as it approached the gazelle but stopped just short.

"What?!" he gasped. "Pierce the gazelle!" he commanded, but the arrow hovered, unmoving.

Flustered, he shouted at it, "Obey me!" But as he focused, he felt a shadow pass behind him, escalating his tension. Jacob gulped, turning back to the arrow just in time to see it twist towards him.

"What have I done?" he thought, frozen in fear. In a split second, the arrow shot past him, striking the spirit lurking behind him instead. Before he could understand what had just transpired, the arrow fell, extinguished.

"What just happened?" he asked himself, bewildered as he picked up the arrow, realizing the flame had vanished. "This thing truly does seem to have a will of its own," he muttered, placing it safely back in the quiver.

As if by magic, the flame ignited anew, flickering with renewed energy. Jacob stared at it, a mix of fear and wonder coursing through him. "What secrets does this thing hold?"

Chapter 21

Fruit of the Scriptures. . .

A cluster of Pharisees and Scribes are gathered outside the grand facade of the temple. Their voices are a mix of laughter including animated debate of the scriptures. Familiar faces shared warm hugs, bridging the lines between doctrine and camaraderie, oblivious to the unseen presence gliding above them.

Yasha, an ethereal force hidden from mortal sight, flitted behind a stone edifice bordering the temple grounds, vanishing in a puff of smokey mist as her wings receded. She strode toward the assembly with an air of defiance, her presence unnoticed until she reached the gathering.

"Excuse me," a burly man interjected, concern by her presence.

But Yasha merely chuckled, brushing him off as she make a beeline for the Priest's quarters. Her progress is impeded by the cluster of Scribes and Pharisees converging around her.

"Obedience is paramount, yet you all stand ready to sacrifice the truth. Now make way," she declared, her voice commanding.

One of the Pharisees frowned, his voice laced with indignation, "You presume to ridicule this assembly, woman? Who are you to make such a request?"

"I mock you because you hold nothing sacred. Your hollow writs condemn your souls while I walk free," she shot back, her fierce gaze cutting through the tension.

The men gasped, anger sparking in their eyes. "What devilry is this?" asked Pharisee #2, brow furrowed.

"The choices you made will bear severe fruits. I am the fruit of the scriptures," added Scribe #1, his voice trembling.

Yasha turned sharply to him, her eyes glimmering with an otherworldly flame. "You inscribe laws that bind the righteous while offering no sanctuary to the lost. Know this: I pledge my loyalty not to your gods, but to my lord Satan."

Fear rippled through the group. They recoiled, definitions of spiritual authority shifting beneath the weight of her words. Who is she to challenge their foundation?

"I rebuke you, demon!" shouted Pharisee #2, folding his arms. "Our standards here are non-negotiable."

"If you truly understood God, you would address the souls that suffer under your self-righteous leadership. You claim to be the best and the wisest of your kind! Your teachings is not one of Salvation, but it disconnect your kind from Salvation," Yasha retaliated, her tone sharp.

"We'll see how your tongue holds up behind bars. SEIZE her!" Pharisee #4 commanded.

Scribe #2 lunged forward and gripped her arm, but in an instant, he crumbled, a cloud of ash marking his spot on the ground. Gasps erupted from the remaining men, who staggered back in shock.

"She wields the power of Wicca," murmured Pharisee #1.

"Perhaps, but her powers cannot withstand the might of our god," retorted Pharisee #3, steeling himself.

"Your fabricated rites are an insult to the Almighty, and in time, judgment shall not be kind to you."

An atmosphere of dread settled over the gathering. Inside, the Priest felt a chill crawl up his spine, halting his meditative state. He opened his eyes, unease flooding through him. The chaotic energy swirled beyond the walls as he emerged, draped in gold and purple, the essence of his office reverberating through his every step.

"I did not expect such a dramatic entrance from you," Yasha quipped, watching him intently.

"Forgive me; it is the only way I know," he responded, attempting to steady his breath.

"Courage, for sure," she taunted, stepping closer, "But does your heart echo the courage you present?"

"What do you think?" he challenged, glancing over his shoulder at the agitated Pharisees.

"Why must they depart? Surely God desires witness to this exchange," Yasha mused, feigning innocence.

"My sight is His sight. What my eyes perceive, He knows," the Priest asserted firmly. "I urge you to vacate this sacred place."

But she merely studied him, intrigued. "There's nothing holy about you to make such a request. Only the divine can dictate such authority. Are you truly him? No. Just as I thought."

"Demon, my calling extends beyond mere verbiage. Those who left are not of my creed; instead, they are self-serving hypocrites."

"Admit it, the weight of God's laws pressures you more than you care to admit. You haven't tasted pleasure in far too long. Your flesh yearns to ravish this vessel. Indulge in forgotten pleasures."

Transforming before his eyes, Yasha became a vision of beauty, drawing his gaze unbidden. As she twirled, her movements entranced him, each curve a taunt.

"I see it in your eyes. You want me. I can feel it in your soul, you want to experience me," she purred, and the hint of lust became palpable between them.

"Stop this madness!" he shouted, breaking his fixated trance.

Yasha toyed with a lock of her hair, inching closer to him. She pressed her palm to his breastplate, her touch electric. "You will be mine," she whispered, as if sealing a pact.

Lying before him, she beckoned like a siren to a weary sailor. "Come to me."

Despite his inner turmoil, the Priest wavered, indecision clear on his face. "Give in to your desires, holy man. Your flesh yearns for this moment. The fruit tree in the mist of this garden will make you godlike."

A palpable tension filled the air as he is drawn closer to the edge of temptation. With a gentle caress, he finally relented, succumbing to the chaos within.

"Give in. God created you for this purpose," she purred, coaxing his hands over her body.

Suddenly, a spirit akin to a bird swooped down, wrapping its wings around the Priest, startling him from his reverie. The moment snapped, clarity returning.

"Who are you? Tell me your name!" he demanded, pointing his staff towards her, asserting his authority.

The demon smirked, arrogance dripping from her voice, "Revealing my name will not alter your destiny, priest."

In a flash, she lunged at him, deploying brute strength as she slammed him against the stone wall. A battle ignited, wrestling for dominance, each action is a bid for control.

Chapter 22

The Battle of Celestial Stars. . .

A heavy tension shrouded the air as the two factions prepared for inevitable conflict. The Archangels stand ever vigilant at the edge of their celestial domain, the brilliance of their power illuminating the darkening skies. Light danced around Michael, Uriel, and Gabriel as their tranquility is shattered by a distant rumble—a sinister echo of approaching doom.

Suddenly, the horizon shifted; dark shapes tore through the sky, borne on wings as black as the abyss. The Demonites had arrived, storming forth like a tempest of shadows, their eyes burning with a fierce, malevolent hunger.

"Michael! Look!" Uriel shouted, pointing towards the oncoming storm. "They're coming for us!"

Gabriel narrowed his eyes, steeling himself. "We can't let them reach Satan. He can't be freed!"

Raising his sword to the approaching darkness, Michael called out, his voice resonant and firm. "Stand ready! We will not allow them to breach our ranks!"

As the first wave of Demonites collided with the celestial barriers surrounding the Archangels, a clash of light and dark erupted in the air. Radiant bursts of energy met with dark tendrils of malevolence, and the heavens trembled beneath the weight of their struggle.

"Do you think you can hold us back?" Ba'laamus bellowed, leading the charge, eyes locked onto Michael. "This kingdom will fall today!"

"Your bravado is misplaced, Ba'laamus!" Michael retorted, a blast of light shooting from his sword, striking one of the approaching demons. "We will defend it to the last breath!"

"Your last breath may come sooner than you think," Ba'laamus sneered, gesturing to his followers. "Take them down!"

The sky erupted into chaos as Demonites lunged, sharp claws outstretched, green lightning sparking off their bodies. Gabriel moved with blinding speed, deflecting attacks with his shield, his heart racing as he dispatched one demon after another.

"Stay close, Uriel!" he shouted, breathless yet resolute.

"I'm right beside you!" Uriel replied, her wings unfurling as she prepared a counteroffensive.

"Uriel!" shouted Michael as he swung his sword to clear a demon away from his sister. "Focus on strategy—don't let your emotions cloud your judgment!"

"Easy for you to say!" Uriel snapped, fury igniting within her. "They're after what we must protect!"

With all her might, Uriel unleashed a torrent of light from her hands, momentarily blinding the nearest Demonites. "That's it! Keep pushing them back!"

But the relentless surge of Demonites kept pressing, claws and teeth snapping hungrily. A particularly formidable foe, Azra'il, darted toward Uriel, eyes gleaming with malice. "I'll enjoy taking you down, Archangel!" he hissed, fangs bared.

Before he could reach him, Gabriel interceded, shooting a stream of radiant energy that sent him crashing back. "Not today," he growled, glancing over his shoulder at Uriel. "We move as one!"

"Right!" Uriel exclaimed. Together, they formed a defensive line, striking down any demons that drew too close.

Meanwhile, Michael was locked in combat with Baalamus, their swords clashing with resounding force. "You're nothing but a pawn for Satan!" Michael spat, pushing against the weight of Ba'laamus' attack.

"Maybe," Ba'laamus snarled, "but I'm a pawn who will become king! And when we reign, you will regret underestimating us!"

Just then, an explosion rocked the ground beneath them, a wave of dark energy bursting from the ranks of the Demonites. Michael staggered, catching himself before he fell.

"Keep your eyes up!" Uriel shouted. "Don't let them distract you!"

"I'm okay!" Michael insisted, refocusing. "But we can't let this continue. We must separate their ranks!"

"Agreed!" Gabriel shouted, determination coursing through her. "We'll flanking maneuvers; cut them down one by one!"

With a renewed sense of unity, the Archangels circled together, a luminous trio prepared to face the onslaught. Uriel's heart raced as she cast her gaze across the battlefield. Waves of black surged upon them, yet she felt a thrill of adrenaline course through her veins.

Suddenly, she caught sight of Ba'laamus charging towards them, rage in his eyes.

"Let's see how brave you are, Archangels!" he bellowed, launching himself into the air.

With a fierce cry, Uriel unleashed a blinding light from her hands, aiming directly at Ba'laamus. "For the Kingdom of Light!" she shouted, channeling every ounce of her energy.

His eyes widened in shock as the light enveloped him, a wave of frustration mixed with regret cascading over his face. "No!" he roared, caught between the darkness he served and the light he could not escape.

As Ba'laamus faltered, Michael shouted to Gabriel and Uriel. "Now! Push forward!"

In unison, they thrust their weapons towards the heart of darkness that threatened their realm, a torrent of light illuminating the battlefield. A surge of energy rippled around them as the walls of heaven shook, the clash of celestial powers resonating through the very core of existence itself. With a final, desperate cry, Ba'laamus recoiled from the light, stumbling backward into the midst of his own followers.

"Not today, Demonites!" Raphael shouted triumphantly, emboldened by the strength of camaraderie and resolve.

"Let this battle be a testament to our resolve!" Michael roared over the chaotic din. "We fight for all that is sacred!"

"FOR LIGHT!" They proclaimed together, their unity shining brighter than any fear of darkness, ready to face whatever may come to save their kingdom.

But deep within their hearts, each of the Archangels knew that this battle was only the beginning, the shadows still looming, ever closer, as they braced themselves for the storm ahead. The battle raged on, the air heavy with the scent of burning energy and the cries of the fallen. As the Archangels honed their focus, a malevolent growl rippled through the ranks of the Demonites, carrying a shiver of dread and anticipation.

From the depths of the shadows, reinforcements emerged—more demons, larger and more vicious than their predecessors, spilling into the fray like ink swirling into clear water. Their eyes glinted with sinister delight, eager to join the chaotic dance of violence.

"Look out!" Uriel shouted, her voice strained as a towering demon charged through the line of combat, its jagged claws glinting ominously. It bellowed a battle cry that sent tremors through the air, causing the ground beneath begin to quake. The oncoming beast barreled forward, shrugging off the weaker Demonites as if they were nothing but mere insects.

"Gabriel, flank left!" Michael yelled, instinctively positioning himself between Uriel and the monstrous figure. "I'll handle it!" He raised his sword high, and the blade illuminated with a divine glow, slicing through the darkness that surrounded them.

"Stay alert!" Gabriel shouted back, her wings unfurling as she propelled herself into the air, searching for an advantageous position. "We have to protect our flank! If they reach Satan before we can stop them, this ends badly for all of us!"

The creature lunged, its massive frame twisting as it aimed for Michael, who swiftly dodged to the side. "Your dark will not prevail!" he declared, lunging at the beast and delivering a fierce blow to its flank. The Demon's crimson eyes flared with rage as it thrusted its claws in retaliation, narrowly missing the Archangel.

Just when it seemed that the battle was turning in their favor, a snarling chorus erupted from behind, as a throng of lesser demons broke through the lines. Armed with barbed whips and other grotesque weapons, they swiftly engaged the Archangels, forcing them to split their attention as wave after wave focused on getting to Satan, whose influence seemed to fuel their zeal.

"Fight together!" Uriel shouted, trying to rally her brothers while deflecting an incoming blow. "We must cover each other! They won't stop until they get to him!"

The sound of booming laughter echoed across the battlefield, marking the presence of yet another major figure among the fray. Crowning the chaos is Regulus, adorned in jagged armor, he hovered above the melee, eyes fixated on the swirling action below. "Look at them scramble!" he jeered, reveling in the chaos of the battle. "Is this the best the forces of Light can muster? Pathetic!"

With renewed determination, Michael looked up at Regulus, defiance brewing in his chest. "You will not break our spirit!" he bellowed, rallying the light around him. "We will stand firm against your darkness, no matter your numbers!"

Regulus met his glare with an almost gleeful malice. "Then let us see how long that resolve lasts!" he declared, sliding into the turmoil below. His arrival sent a ripple of fear through the ranks of the Archangels, marking the escalation of a battle that had only just begun.

As the clash continued, the Celestial kingdom quaked under the mingled sounds of battle cries and hisses of magic being unleashed. The columns of light, guardians of hope, flickered as desperation encircled the Archangels. Yet resolve remained steadfast, an unbreakable bond forged in the fires of warfare.

"We can't let them reach him!" Uriel yelled, firmer than she felt. "There is too much at stake!"

As the tide of darkness surged forward once more, the Archangels braced themselves for the onslaught. They were ready to unleash all their might, fighting not only for their own existence but for the very soul of heaven itself. They would defend their domain, their brotherhood, and everything that is sacred with a ferocity borne from the knowledge that every heartbeat of resistance strengthened their resolve against the shadows creeping ever closer. The fate of their world hung in the balance, and in that moment, they knew failure was not an option.

Chapter 23

The Vanishing Glow. . .

An RV crunched its tires on gravel as it rolled into the parking lot of the general store. Marcus, David's father, glanced at the expansive blue sky and felt the weight of their fishing trip looming over him. Ice for the cooler, bait for the lines, and propane for cooking were the essentials on his list.

"By the way, sweetheart," Makayla chimed from the passenger seat, her voice laced with a sweet urgency. "Grab some marshmallows for s'mores. I completely forgot them."

"How many bags?" he replied, leaning back in his seat.

"One will do," she smiled warmly.

"You got it, babe." Marcus stepped out and headed toward the store as the kids, David and Kalisha, danced in the sunlight, their laughter piercing the air. Makayla kept her watchful eye on them, a gentle smile tugging her lips. Fifteen minutes passed, and she caught sight of David Sr. emerging from the store, heavy bags swinging at his sides.

"David! Kalisha! C'mon, time to head out!" she called, her voice carrying over the kids' giggles.

"Okay, Mom! We're coming!" Kalisha replied, her feet bound like a deer!

David Sr. climbed back into the RV, handing the bag to Makayla, his eyes sparkling. "Did you get everything?" she inquired, anticipation dancing in her tone.

"Everything I need for our little adventure," he confirmed, the corners of his mouth lifting in a grin.

Makayla returned the smile, her heartwarming at the sight of her family.

"Kids! Come on—back in the RV so we can leave!" she urged.

As David and Kalisha dashed to the vehicle, Makayla beamed at David Sr.

"Off we go to vacation in nomad's land," David said dryly, rolling his eyes as he plopped down beside Kalisha.

"Enough of that, young man!" David Sr. snapped, though there was no malice in his voice.

"Son, if you want to sulk, at least keep it to yourself so the rest of us can enjoy our time!" he added, a hint of playfulness creeping in.

Kalisha giggled, her eyes wide at David's feigned throw of a pillow, his annoyance palpable. He flopped onto the sofa, slipping on his headphones, looking at anything but amused.

"Why are you staring at me?" he spat, shooting daggers at his sister.

"Because I can," Kalisha replied, sticking out her tongue with an attitude.

"Well, stop it and focus on something else!" David shot back, irritating, layering his voice.

"I can look wherever I want! You're not the boss of me!" she countered with a smile, unfazed by his mood.

David rolled his eyes and retreated to his bunk, a jumbled mess of feelings swirling within him. Kalisha, feeling dejected, clicked the TV on, her arms crossed as she bristled with irritation. But soon, laughter bubbled up from the screen, and in that moment, her anger slipped away like petals on the wind.

Once they arrived at their destination, David Sr. parked and they descended into the campground, ready for adventure. David took off along a nearby nature trail while their parents chatted with a neighboring family.

"Can I go with him?" Kalisha asked, eyes bright with excitement.

"Sure, just stay close and be safe," Makayla called out as Kalisha took off, running behind her brother.

"David! Kalisha! Stay near the campsite!" Makayla cautioned, but her voice faded with distance.

"Okay, Mom!" Kalisha exclaimed, not looking back.

As they walked, David shoved aside Kalisha's eager hand, his slight irritation creeping back. "Why do I need to hold your hand?" he grumbled. Kalisha felt momentarily crushed but soon found wonder in the towering trees around her. Then, something shifted in the corner of her eye flicker of movement beckoning her closer.

"C'mon, Kalisha! What are you looking at?" David called, annoyed in his voice.

"Wait! There's something moving under this bush!" she urged, her curiosity piquing.

David hesitated. "It could be a skunk, and you don't want that spraying you!" he laughed, a smirk dancing on his lips.

"Ha! Very funny. But come on, let's look!"

Despite his reluctance, Kalisha pulled ahead, slipping behind a tree to edge closer to the movement.

"Get a stick. A long one!" she commanded playfully.

"I'm walking away, Kalisha. You better come on," David warned, turning away.

"Okay! I'm coming!" she relented, hopping around the tree to peer at the bush.

Suddenly, as she brushed away the leaves, a soft pink light glimmered. She knelt, leaning in closer, captivated by the sight before her. Just then, the leaves erupted upwards, startling Kalisha back onto her bottom.

"What was that?" she gasped, her heart racing, and then she froze. Two small beings—Yinpiniel's, fairy-like creatures—twirled in the air, their laughter bubbling over like music.

"Wow... I have to tell David I saw some fairies!" she whispered to herself, awed. In an instant, they zipped away, leaving behind a fading shimmer.

"Oh no! David!" Panic prickled at her, as she scanned for her brother but found only the thick, surrounding trees.

"David! Where are you?" she shouted, dread pooling in her stomach.

"I'm going to get in trouble," she fretted, recalling the last odd rock they had passed. Cursing her curiosity, she hurried back to the campsite, hoping he'd be there.

Makayla spotted her running, breathless and alone. "Kalisha! Where's your brother?" she called, panic creeping into her voice.

"Uh, he... he left me," she stammered.

"Left you? How could he?" Makayla's brow furrowed in worry.

"I saw something moving in the bushes and... I just looked to see what it was. I got distracted," Kalisha confessed, her own worry bubbling up—a mix of guilt and fear.

Frustration tangled Makayla's thoughts. "That boy is going to get it when he gets back," she muttered.

Kalisha's eyes widened, "And guess what else, Mom—"

"What?" answered Makayla with a concern look on her face.

"I saw some fairies!" she responded overly excited.

"Kalisha, there's no such thing," Makayla snapped, the stress of the moment making her tone sharp.

"But Mom! I really did! I swear!"

"Enough! If you don't stop making things up, you'll face consequences."

"But—"

Makayla cut her off, "No but," shaking her head with a chilling glare. "Go inside and don't come out until I tell you."

"Okay, Mom…" Her shoulders sagged as she retreated, the weight of her disappointment heavy in the air.

Meanwhile, David Sr. held a glass of water, observing the heated encounter with concern. "Calm down, sweetie. She's fine," he reassured Makayla softly.

Inside the RV, Kalisha's heart sank. Guilt consumed her as she replayed the moment she'd wandered off. She is supposed to watch David, not allow her excitement to lead her astray. With a growing weight in her chest, she approached her mother with hesitant footsteps.

"Mom, can I talk to you?" she asked quietly.

"What is it, honey? What's wrong?"

"I'm the one who wandered away. He didn't leave me," she confessed, her voice cracking.

"Oh? Or are you just trying to protect him?" Makayla questioned, skepticism heavy in her tone.

"It's true!" Kalisha cried, tears spilling over. "I was looking for him and… I just lost sight of him…"

Frantic footsteps interrupted them. David burst into the campsite, his face pale. "Dad! Dad! Is Kalisha here?"

"No, son. She is supposed to be with you," David Sr. replied, his brow knitting together.

"I lost her! I lost her!" Panic tinged David's voice.

"Did what?" David Sr. growled, frustration bubbling to the surface.

"Just wait until your mom finds out. She's never going to let this go!"

He called out, "Kalisha!" as his urgency turned to desperation.

"Kalisha!" Makayla echoed, voice elevated. "You stay here! I'll find her!"

Kalisha's heart raced, realizing the gravity of her choices. Makayla's worry morphed into a whirl of emotions as her footsteps echoed away, leaving a trail of tension in the air.

David, consumed by guilt, turned on his heel, darting back into the woods, shouting his sister's name.

After a moment, with a heavy sigh, he plopped down on a large rock by the stream, hoping for a moment of peace. He plugged in his headphones, letting music wash over him. The sun sank slowly, its warmth enveloping him as fatigue seeped into his bones.

"Maybe I just need a nap," he murmured to himself, closing his eyes as the world around him faded. Little did they know, adventure had just begun…

Chapter 24

The Battle for a Soul. . .

Briefly, David's eyes squinted at the midday sun, its brilliance forcing him to avert his gaze. As he turned his head, he noticed a reflection flickering off the canyon wall. Curiosity flickered within him, urging him to investigate. Yet, fatigue clung to his bones, and troubled thoughts tethered him to the ground. He sank back onto the rock, the sun's warm rays soothing his weary spirit, guiding him into a heavy slumber.

In his dream, he found himself shrouded in darkness. His own silhouette loomed large and indistinct against the shadowy void. The darkness felt tangible, almost fluid, and he could navigate through it effortlessly. Meanwhile, reality outside weaved its own tale as Makayla tuned in to the local radio station, her voice breaking the silence.

"Honey, the solar eclipse is about to start! You better come see it!" she called out, glancing at her husband, who was busy raking leaves from the fire pit.

"I forgot all about that! It should get dark soon," he replied absentmindedly, focused on his task.

In her bunk, Kalisha stirred in her sleep, the remnants of a dream filled with stars lingering in her subconscious. Her small hand moved in a sweeping motion as if reaching into the cosmos, but then…it happened. A skeletal hand shot out from the darkness, its bony fingers grasping at her. She jolted awake, breathless.

"Mom?" she yelled, fear etching her voice.

Makayla dashed into her room, concern written across her face. "What's the matter, sweetheart?"

"Where's the sun?" Kalisha's eyes widened in panic.

"It's just a solar eclipse, honey," her mother reassured her, trying to quell the fear.

"Oh. Is David back yet?"

"No, not yet," Makayla answered, glancing toward the window. Kalisha's gaze followed, worry creeping in.

"That dream was so scary," she murmured.

Typically, she would seek solace in her brother's room after a nightmare, but he was nowhere to be found. As if responding to her thoughts, David awoke with a start, shaking off the remnants of disturbed sleep.

"I can't stand nightmares… or daymares… or any mares!" he groaned, rubbing his face.

The world around him seemed unusually dark, but just then, a peculiar light danced across his vision from the canyon wall.

"What the hell?" he muttered, moving closer. His heart raced, pulsing with curiosity as he reached the wall. Something glimmered, half-buried in rocks—just a fragment exposed, resembling a crystal handle.

With a surge of determination, he cleared away the rubble, revealing a sword, ornate and breathtaking. He held it in wonder, inspecting its stunning jewel-encrusted hilt and the curious mark that resembled an elegant M.

"Ah man, this beauty must be worth a fortune!" David exclaimed inside, entranced by the weapon's allure.

The sword, ancient yet pristine, beckoned him as if harboring its own secrets. Grasping its handle sent shivers of energy through him, igniting flames that flickered around the blade.

"Whoa!" He stumbled backward in surprise but quickly regained his footing. The flames didn't burn; they dazzled with an otherworldly glow.

"What's wrong with this thing?" he fretted, trying to extinguish the fire with water from the nearby stream. To his astonishment, the flames only roared higher as steam billowed around him.

In a panic, he released the sword into the water, and the flames subsided. Heart racing, he reached in again.

"Seriously?!" he breathed as the fire reignited. He pulled back instinctively, mumbling in a daze, "This must be a magic sword…"

As the moon slid across the sun's face, the eclipse finished its passage, though David remained oblivious, lost in the sword's captivating heat.

"I, KING DAVID!" he bellowed with theatrical flair. "I challenge thee, Sir Galahad, to a duel! Should I triumph, the fair maiden Brielle shall be mine! Should I fall, you may claim her for yourself!"

He brandished the sword like a legendary warrior, unaware of the dark figures that lingered in the shadows, observing his every move with keen interest.

"Why is the fire even here? It's so weird!" he mused. "I wish it would just go out…"

Before he finished, the flames danced away, flickering out completely.

"Wow! That's much better. I wonder if I can make it come back."

He focused on those flickering flames, trying to summon them back, but they stubbornly remained extinguished. After minutes of quiet concentration, David shrugged, losing patience and returning to his make-believe battles. Passionately, he wielded the sword, awestruck by its gleaming blade. Then, something shifted—images formed in the reflection of the metal, mesmerizing him further. Back at camp, Makayla and David Sr. stared up at the now-brightening sky, comforted to see the eclipse's end. David Sr. glanced at his wrist and frowned.

The man's eyes widened, a sudden panic seizing his features. "My watch!" he exclaimed, his voice sharp as he spun towards Makayla, the timepiece held aloft like a broken talisman.

Makayla's brow furrowed with concern. "Is it broken, then?" she asked softly, her gaze fixed on the still hands.

He shook his head vehemently. "No! Impossible. I just... just replaced the battery last week. Brand new." He stared at the face of the watch, a growing unease clouding his expression.

"Strange..." Makayla murmured, her voice barely a whisper, a prickle of something unsettling dancing on her skin.

In the canyon, back in his world of fantasy, David thrust the sword forward again. As he withdrew, a vision flickered before his eyes, striking him with staggering clarity.

"NO WAY!" he shouted, stepping back, heart pounding in his chest.

Chapter 25

Defiance of the Celestials. . .

Michael's heart raced as he knelt beside Uriel, who lay unconscious at his feet, her golden hair a stark contrast against the dusty ground. With a sharp glare, he directed his anger toward Satan, whose figure loomed ominously nearby. The air crackled with tension as the Archangels formed a protective barrier around her, their wings unfurling in a display of defiance.

"What have you done to her, tyrant?" Michael's voice dripped with venom, his eyes narrowing to slits.

"I've done nothing yet," Satan retorted, his voice low and taunting, dark eyes flickering with amusement as he regarded Michael. The Archangels bristled, their furious stances unwavering.

Raphael, his irritation simmering just beneath the surface, glared across at Satan, fists clenched as he shifted his weight in preparation for conflict.

"There are three of us and one of you," Michael reminded him, his tone steely.

Gabriel's wings twitched, and he added, "Do you truly believe you can take us?"

Satan's lips curled into a smirk, a cruel amusement dancing in his dark gaze. He glanced briefly at the gathering storm clouds, where his legions of Demonites skulked unnoticed. "You three misfits don't stand a chance against me. I will crush you with a single blow."

"There is a profound difference between serving the LORD and opposing Him," Michael declared, his voice strong and unwavering.

Satan laughed, the sound echoing like thunder. "And what is that difference?"

"If you defeat us," Raphael interjected, confidence radiating from him, "vengeance will be the Lord's."

Satan's eyes glinted with a malevolent glee. "Ah, but Hashem will have more on His mind soon enough. Just like your sister before you, I shall produce the proof." He held Uriel aloft, a mocking challenge evident in his stance.

"Let her go, backslider and return her shield!" Michael demanded, the fury in his eyes unabated as he brandished his sword.

Satan clenched his fist, the air thick with the weight of his arrogance. "What's there to stop me?"

Drawing their weapons, the Archangels aimed with deadly precision. Michael stepped forward, his voice fierce. "Return Uriel's shield to us!"

Satan's laughter filled the air, dark and chilling. "Do you truly believe your weapons can intimidate me?"

"Make one false move, dark one, and you shall feel the edge of my sword," Michael warned, his gaze unwavering, like a storm about to break.

"Before you take that path, dear brother," Satan taunted in an eerily calm tone, "look around you."

A faint noise rippled through the atmosphere, causing the Archangels to turn instinctively. Nothing met their gaze. Yet when they turned back, Satan's grin had widened.

"Look here, Lord of Darkness. The odds are against you," Raphael asserted, his voice steady despite the tension.

"Oh, do you think so?" Satan paused, savoring the suspense. "Take a closer look."

With dread, they scanned their surroundings once more. This time, eyes glowed ominously in the fog—hostile, predatory. The three Archangels braced against one another. Satan extended his wings, propelling the fog aside to reveal a vast army of Demonites awaiting his command. The sight sent a shiver through each of the Archangels. From the Heavens, Hashem sensed the imbalance and sent Chamuel, Zadkiel, and Jophiel to the Valley of Zivenda. He summoned the Virtues and Dominions for reinforcement.

"Satan has swayed thousands of Powers, Principalities, and Rulers to his side. You must do everything within your might to protect Adam. Fail, and I shall blot your names from existence," Hashem decreed.

"We shall not fail, Lord," vowed the Virtues and Dominions in unison, their hearts steeling with resolve.

As legions of celestial beings departed the grandeur of The Empyrean. The skies erupted in a spectacle of light, one-quarter clouded by the Celestial Host. Back in the Valley, with a deep breath, Satan stepped forward, extending his hand towards the Archangels. "I will spare you on one condition," he offered, his tone deceptively smooth.

Michael, Gabriel, and Raphael exchanged disgusted glances, the tension thick enough to cut.

"I suspected this fog had a foul stench," Raphael muttered.

"Your offer reeks of betrayal," Michael shot back, glaring at Satan. "We want nothing you propose."

"You orchestrated this trap!" Gabriel spat, disdain coating his words.

"I do not wish for conflict, but your lives could be spared if you pledge your loyalty to me. It's that simple."

"Our lives mean nothing if they come at the cost of serving you!" Michael snarled, fire in his eyes.

Raphael added, "Our future is already written, and it's Hashem who holds the key."

Satan chuckled darkly, hoisting Uriel's shield higher for emphasis. "The only decision God made was ensuring that you fools remain slaves to Adam."

The shield gleamed ominously in the dim light, a trophy of his power. "We have one of their weapons; let's see how many more we can add to our collection," a malicious voice chimed in from the ranks of his army.

"I think not! We will fight you until our last breath!" Michael declared courage, bolstering his resolve.

He leaned closer to Raphael, urgency painting his features. "Can you get a clean shot?"

"Yes, but I need you to create a distraction," Raphael replied, determination evident in his voice.

"That's no challenge. Leave it to me," Michael smirked, the adrenaline coursing through him.

Calling out to Satan, Michael reached for the sack of gnats he had collected earlier. "Satan! You will release Uriel and return her shield, or else—"

"Or else what, foolish angel?" Satan shot back, amusement lacing his words.

"Or else this!" Michael roared, launching the sack at Satan, the insects swirling ominously like a tempest—chaos unleashed. The battle is just beginning.

Chapter 26

Fall of the Heavenly Host. . .

The sky bled crimson over the Celestial Citadel, where the heavens once shimmered with eternal light. But now, Thunder cracked as a war drum, crept into realm. The Archangels are standing at the edge of the Silver Spire, blades drawn, wings poised, their eyes locked on the vast, swirling rift that tore the heavens.

"They're coming," murmured Uriel, her sword humming with divine fire. Michael, the leader of the Archangels, narrowed his eyes. "Then we hold the line. We are the flame—unyielding, unbreakable."

But before another word could be spoken, a roar shattered the sky. Demonites thundered on the scene like snarling beasts with rage. Under the stillness of the sky, Adam is sitting beneath the moonlit sky, oblivious to the chaos above, is lost in his thoughts. Suddenly, something streaked across the sky, leaving a trail of fire gracefully cascading downward.

"What's that?" he whispered, eyes wide in awe.

Far beyond the eyes of Adam's vision, burning energy and the cries of battle rages on.

"Michael!" Al'debaran bellowed, his wings unfurling like a storm. "God has grown soft! The throne you guard is empty, and your light is fading!"

Michael's wings spread wide. "We still guard what is sacred. You've only brought your agenda to end!"

Steel clashed with hell-forged weapons. The sky ignited with the brilliance of holy fire and shadow flame. Raphael danced between the Grigoris, striking with swift precision, while Gabriel's voice rang out like a trumpet of war. The Zones swooped in, and the tide began to turn. The Archangels are boxed in,

"Michael, we need to retreat!" Raphael yelled, a hint of panic edging her voice as she parried a Demonites strike.

"Never! We fight for freedom!" Michael shot back, adrenaline fueling his resolve.

As chaos spiraled, the air turned thick. Uriel spun her blade in a crescent arc, cleaving through Demonites. "They're pressing too fast! We need—"

A blast of black lightning strikes her mid-flight. She cried out as her shield slipping from her hand, crashing down below.

"No!" Gabriel roared, diving toward her—but a Zone wrapped around its wings, dragging him into the black when another wave of Demonites crashed upon them, determined to break their line. Hands slashed, and teeth bared, the battle is nearing its breaking point.

The Grigoris hover above, their radiant wings casting an ominous glow as they fight.

Regulus: (breathing heavily, dodging a divine weapon) "We need to free him now! The Archangels are getting weary!"

He dashes through the melee, glancing up at the imposing figure of Michael, who stands beside a chained Satan. As if sensing Regulus's intent, Michael turns, his voice booming like thunder.

"Stand down, demon! You'll never release him! The chains bind more than just his body!" he says with confidence.

Regulus, smirking, "Then let's see how strong those chains really are!"

He lunges at the radiant figure, his hands shimmering with dark energy. Michael's sword glints as he prepares to strike, but a group of demons rush forward, forcing him to engage.

Demons, shouting in unison, "For Satan! For the darkness!"

The air fills with screams and the sounds of clashing weapons. In the chaos, Regulus reaches Satan, his hands trembling with anticipation.

Regulus: "Your Majesty, I will break these chains!"

Satan's voice gravelly, but laced with charisma, "Foolish Regulus, the chains of Heaven are strong. But your conviction… it ignites something in me."

With ferocity, Regulus slams his sword into the glowing chains, using every ounce of his dark magic. The chains begin to crack under the strain. Raphael noticing the disturbance "No! You will not tamper with the will of Heaven!" she blurred out.

As she strikes down a rogue demon, she swings around only to see the chains shatter, shards of divine light scattering like stars.

Regulus grinning widely, "It worked! He's free!"

Satan rises, a haunting silhouette against the stormy horizon, his laughter echoing like a distant thunderclap.

"At last! Let chaos reign!" Satan says with eyes

With a flick of his wrist, he summons dark tendrils that envelop Gabriel, dragging him back as the remaining Archangels rally together.

"We cannot allow them to escape! Form a barrier!" shout Satan.

The demons are relentless, swarming around the Archangels like hornets to their hive, overwhelming their holy defenses. Fists, and dark energy electrify the air.

Archangels straining against Demonite forces, "You'll pay for this betrayal!" Michael promised.

"We will take our place in the world, Michael. And you… you'll be our prisoners!" Al'debaran blurred out.

One final push from the horde sends the Archangels tumbling to the ground, their weapons clattering against the earth, lost in the crust and chaos. Al'debaran, Regulus, Ba'laamus and Azra'il stands tall, their chest heaving, as Satan grins beside them.

"Look at them, bound by their own radiance. Their arrogance blinds them to our true power." Satan's voice laced with confidence.

As the battlefield settles, the once-gleaming weapons of the Archangels lie scattered in the dirt, catches of sunlight twinkling ominously among the shadows.

"Let's take our prizes." Satan say… "We have work to do."

The demons roar in triumph, hoisting the fallen Archangels as trophies of their victory, ready to execute their dark designs. The storm rages on, a harbinger of chaos to unfold, as the forces of darkness rise once more. In the midst of chaos, the Archangels realize that the true power of evil can be overwhelming.

Chapter 27

Awakening the Secret . . .

Abram blinked rapidly, his heart racing as visions bombarded his mind. The air around him crackled with an electric tension, a palpable sense of something monumental about to unfold. Suddenly, winged creatures surged into his view, their forms majestic yet terrifying. They spoke in a strange dialect, their voices piercing through the air like a storm.

"No! What's happening?" Abram shouted, dropping to his knees, hands clamped firmly over his ears. The cacophony of their alien words swirled around him, the meaning utterly lost yet somehow undeniable.

A flash of blinding light erupted before his eyes, distorting the world with its brilliance. For a heartbeat, he was adrift in chaos, unable to comprehend the spectacle unfolding. But as the light receded, clarity dawned. He stared, transfixed, as a battle raged across the sky.

"What in the world—?" he murmured, eyes widening with wonder. "What are those things? They're like machines from a nightmare!"

The war machines, towering and ominous, gleamed with an otherworldly light, larger than anything he had ever imagined. Winged riders flew effortlessly alongside them, their glowing white eyes cutting through the murky shadows. Some angels wielded tails like whips, while ornate breastplates, shimmering with purple metal and jewels as large as human heads, adorned their forms.

As he takes it all in, his mouth fell open in awe, his mind struggling to grasp the reality of what surrounded him. The hairs on his neck prickled, sending a jolt through his spine. Then, with a sudden urgency, he spun around just in time to see something hurtling towards him, a figure cloaked in smoke, its indigo eyes glowing fiercely. Panic surged through him.

"Wha—? No!" Abram gasped, the pendant slipping from his grasp as fear overtake him. In a frenzy, he dropped it, watching helplessly as it fell into the water, sinking like a stone.

Before he could process it all, the visions conspired against him, plunging him back into his reality. He flinched, taking stock of his surroundings, turning to each side before making a full pivot. The remnants of the otherworldly battle faded, but his pulse raced from the residue of fear and exhilaration.

He touched his clothes, feeling the fabric as if it was a safety net. "Waking dreams," he pondered aloud, "that's what this has been. Why am I experiencing this?"

He rubbed his temples, mind reeling. "I'm here… then I'm somewhere else… and now I'm back again?" His voice trembled with confusion, echoing the questions spiraling in his head.

Abram rose, then sat, only to rise once more, the motion a frantic dance of uncertainty. He paced back and forth, trying to piece together the fragments of the visions and the mysterious stranger whose words still haunted him. The ground beneath him felt like a tether to reality, keeping him anchored as his thoughts spun wildly.

Suddenly, a loud growl erupted from his stomach, louder than a thunderclap. He froze, eyes widening. "Hunger," he breathed, realizing with a pang that he hadn't eaten since before the storm.

Amusement flickered for a second—there he was, lost in the throes of divine chaos, yet all his stomach cared about was finding food. He looked down at the pendant, still wrapped tightly in his wet ghutra. Memories of home flooded his mind: his siblings laughing as their mother prepared a feast, his father deep in conversation with the tribal elders. The aroma of baked bread, simmering lentil stew, and roasted meat danced in the air around him.

"Stay calm little guy," he murmured, fingers deftly working the wet fabric away from the pendant. Suddenly, a glow emanated from it, bright and beckoning. The light pulsed rhythmically as if it had a heartbeat of its own.

His eyes widened in shock. "What now?" he exclaimed, the weight of destiny pressing down upon him.

The glow intensified, drawing him in as a whisper wound through the air, echoing the alien dialect he had heard before. Was it calling him? Pulling him toward something greater and beyond his understanding?

"Abram!" a voice called, slicing through the atmosphere like an arrow. He turned sharply, recognizing the sound as that of his friend, Elias, who had approached with concern etched on his face. "Are you okay? You look like you've just seen a ghost!"

"I—I saw something!" Abram stammered, the thrill of adventure and fear mingling within him. "There are battles, creatures, machines I can't explain…"

Elias stepped closer, his brow furrowing. "Battles? Here? Perhaps you're just tired, my friend. Let's get you home." But Abram could see in his eyes that Elias didn't fully believe him, and that only fueled his excitement.

"No! You don't understand!" Abram insisted, gripping the pendant tightly in his hand. "I felt something powerful. I know it sounds crazy, but it felt real!"

Elias glanced at the glimmering pendant and back at Abram, skepticism fading into intrigue. "Show me, then," he challenged, a flicker of curiosity igniting within him. "Let's see what this thing can do."

Abram nodded, heart racing with the knowledge that he wasn't alone in this. "Okay! But there's no telling what might happen." He takes a deep breath, feeling the weight of his decision.

Together, they faced the water, the pendant aglow in Abram's hand. He closed his eyes, focusing on the vision, the sounds of battle echoing in his mind. The whispers grew louder, electrifying the air around them.

"Come on, show us!" he breathed, channeling every ounce of belief he had. The light from the pendant erupted into a brilliant beam, swirling patterns of energy weaving through the atmosphere.

Suddenly, the landscape shifted from the very fabric of reality is warping around them. Shadows elongated, and ethereal figures emerged. It's a winged celestial from his vision hovering above, their glowing eyes fixing on him with an intensity that made his heart race.

"Who dares summon us?" a voice boomed, a resonance that reverberated through his core. The air crackled with energy, an ultimate challenge posed and answered.

"I... I am Abram," he stammered, feeling small yet emboldened. "I do not know why you appeared to me, but I feel a connection. I wish to understand."

The leader of the celestials leaned forward, an expression of both curiosity and wariness upon its radiant face. "Your heart is filled with courage, Abram but understand this—what you seek is not without danger. Are you prepared to face the truths that lie ahead?"

"What do I need to do?" Abram asked, determination hardening his voice.

"Follow us into the unknown," the celestial responded, wings unfurling with an awe-inspiring grace, "and you shall learn of your destiny."

Abram exchanged a look with Elias, who now wore a mixture of awe and concern. "Who are you talking to?" his friend asked, a hint of trepidation in his voice.

"I'm having a conversation with him, a celestial spirit. Can't you see? The way the stars align means something!" Abram answered, his excitement bubbling over.

Elias scoffed under his breath, scratching his head as he watched Abram's animated expressions.

Abram's voice remained steady, drenched in determination. "It's not about seeing, Elias! It's about feeling, about believing."

His hands fluttered in the air as if he were grasping invisible threads. But Elias's arms crossed tightly against his chest. "You've always been too caught up in your head, man. What you've got there is just your imagination running wild."

Abram simply smiled, undeterred. "It's more than that! Look! When I close my eyes, I can see his light, hear his wisdom.

Though Elias couldn't shake the sense that something significant is unfolding before him. He return to tending to the herd of sheep.

Chapter 28

Desolation of Heaven. . .

The sky above blazed with an unblemished light, a stark contrast to the tension simmering in the air. With a swagger born of arrogance, Satan strode toward Michael, a self-assured grin plastered across his face.

"Give up this futile attempt," he taunted, his voice smooth and dripping with mockery.

"Never!" Michael shot back, his heart racing and anger pulsing through him like a live wire. "We will fight thee until the end!"

Satan's dark eyes narrowed, and he raised an eyebrow. "Control your anger, leader of the Archangels," he demanded, his tone laced with condescension. "Before your blessing turns into a curse."

"A curse on you, perhaps?" Michael challenged, his grip tightening around the hilt of his sword.

Satan's smile widened, a sinister gleam evident in his expression. "Thy situation has gone from certain to uncertain. Two of thy comrades have already succumbed to defeat at the hands of my Demonites. If you desire to avoid such a fate, I suggest you and Gabriel lay down your weapons."

Michael's resolve hardened, and before Satan could react, he swung his sword with all his might, severing Satan's right arm at the elbow. Satan hissed with a look of shock that quickly transformed into rage.

"There is thy payment, parasite," Michael spat, standing defiantly despite the throbbing pain in his heart.

With a swift motion, Satan struck back, slapping Michael with his remaining hand, sending the Archangel stumbling to one knee. Michael's wings ruffled, shedding a few feathers as he struggled to regain his footing. He watched, anguish bubbling beneath the surface, as Satan retrieved his severed arm and reattached it with a sickening squelch.

Satan stepped closer, placing his foot triumphantly on Michael's shoulder, pressing him down into the realm. "How easily the mighty has fallen," he sneered before turning his back.

"Gabriel!" Michael gasped, trying to rise. "We have to fight—"

"Wait!" Gabriel's voice cut through the haze of battle, urgency etched into his features. "We must hold our position until help arrives!"

Satan shrugged, then barked to Azra'il. "Send in the third flank—seize them!"

"Attack!" Azra'il commanded, his voice reverberating through the battlefield as the Demonites charged with ferocity. They descended upon Michael and Gabriel, the brothers-in-arms found themselves overwhelmed, struck from all sides.

The chaos mounted until exhaustion overcame them, and finally, the two Archangels collapsed, their weapons stripped away. From a rocky precipice, Satan surveyed his legion with an insidious grin. "Chain them! They're to be considered the spoils of victory. Take them down to the second Heaven under the ap-uat. We are one step closer to our objective. I shall make God regret what he did by creating humanity!"

His voice rose with fervor. "Onward to Carthage, where my kingdom awaits!"

The Demonites took flight, spiriting their prisoners away from the Valley of Zivenda, dodging the approach of reinforcements while setting their course for the dark and desolate landscapes of Carthage.

The weariness within Michael intensified, feeling as if the light had been snuffed out from the world.

Upon reaching the canyon, Satan commanded his commanders to lock the Archangels away until they "regain their senses." As darkness closed in around them, the weight of defeat settled heavily in Michael's heart.

Meanwhile, the Celestial Host arrived too late. Zadkiel searched desperately for his family, shouting into the emptiness, "Break formation! Search for them everywhere! Leave no stone unturned!" His voice cracked with worry. The scene is grim, evidence of a fierce battle marked, the landscape. A stark reminder of the struggle they had just lost.

On the plains of the second Heaven, where the Archangels are brought bound and shackled. Satan loomed over them with an icy confidence. "I humbly extend my gratitude to you. You hast proven to be loyal servants in your valiant defeat," he jeered, savoring each syllable. "I understand these weapons of yours are quite destructible."

"It's a first time for everything," Michael retorted, his voice steady despite the despair creeping into his words.

"Oh, but I'll take great pleasure in clipping your wings, feather by feather," Satan chuckled joyfully.

"To rebel against a tyrant is a privilege, and even without our weapons, we'll find a way to defeat you," Michael declared, unyielding.

"Good! I crave a challenge. Where you are going, you will not need them," Satan replied, his tone mocking.

Breathing heavily, Michael stared into Satan's eyes. "Why have you brought us here? What are you planning to do with us?"

Satan smirked, feigning surprise. "What am I going to do to you? Tell me, dear Michael, are you afraid of what awaits?"

"Fear is hardly my concern," Michael shot back, his voice laced with defiance. "God did not give us a spirit of fear."

"Fear you have to worry not, little angel," Satan countered, rolling his eyes theatrically. "What awaits you pales in comparison to my plans for God and Adam."

"Make your plans, Satan. You may have defeated us now, but our principles shall prevail," Michael responded, their eyes locked in a battle of wills.

"Where is your God, now? Humm," Satan taunted, a glimmer of triumph in his eyes.

"Glory and danger are but brief; it's the trials that mold us. If God be for us, who can stand against us?" Michael fired back, resolute.

Satan erupted into a fit of laughter. "HA, HA, HA! You still espouse the foolishness that God fed you. What good are such words to you now? Your unbridled tongue inches you closer to your resting place."

"You're never tire of ramblings?" Gabriel interjected, an annoyance flashing across his face.

"Oh, is that so?" Satan feigned surprise, crossing his arms.

"Then I shall make it my mission to take you down!" Gabriel shot back defiantly.

Satan chuckled darkly as he turned to gaze out over the abyss, plotting thoughts darting through his mind like shadows. "The souls of the blu planet shall be mine, my jesters," he mused silently.

Returning his attention to the Archangels, he said, "These weapons are useless to you now. From this day forth, you'll never see them again."

With a flick of his wrist, Satan hurled their weapons into the chasm, where they burned as they fell into the deep, their once-revered gleam disappearing in the inferno. The Archangels looks on helpless, witnessing their weapons being discarded. Each one had fled toward the earth's four corners, but each became a signal flare of what they had lost—their power and hope, all extinguished in the flames.

Just then, a gust of wind swept past, revealing Inkkabus soaring through the dark skies, unaware of the fiery fall below.

"You will regret forsaking your loyalty to me," Satan said, arrogance unwavering.

"Satan! You may try to destroy our bodies, but the LORD shall avenge us," Michael snapped back, defiance rising once more.

"Oh! I beg to differ? After this moment, you will no longer see God as ruler of the Celestial Kingdom. A new ruler will take His place!"

With dread, the four Archangels watched as the planets aligned—the sign that foretold the end of the Kingdom of God is nigh. They stood frozen, hearts heavy with the weight of impending doom, as the celestial kingdom is on the verge of facing its darkest crisis.

Chapter 29

The Celestial Awakening...

As dawn brakes, Adam awakes from his slumber. The serene sounds of the morning filled the space around him, beckoning him to the beauty of a new day. He stretched languidly, feeling the warmth of sunlight spill across his skin, a divine embrace heralding the glory of the moment. Gingerly, the memory of the strange object that had plummeted from the night sky surfaced in his mind. The recollection clashing with the tranquility that surrounded him.

Adam busied himself with the tasks that the LORD had assigned him. The garden is his sanctuary, each blade of grass and each petal a treasure crafted by the hands of the Creator. Later that day during the cool evening hours, he await for God to return to share His wisdom. Today, as the sun painted the sky in warm hues,

As twilight draped the garden in a cloak of hues, Adam felt a stirring in the air—an electricity that resonated with the earth. Suddenly, a radiant light pierced through the gathering shadows, illuminating the clearing with an ethereal glow. From this divine brilliance emerged Hashem, His presence commanding yet filled with unfathomable love, flanked by two of the four Seraphims. The wings of these celestial being furl like the petals of celestial blossoms.

These radiant beings shimmered with an array of colors, their forms dancing in the air as if woven from pure light. As always as he did before, he bow before the LORD.

"Arise Adam. Fear not," Hashem spoke, His voice deep and resonant, echoing like thunder yet soothing like a gentle breeze.

"I have called upon My Seraphims Adon-Shama, and Raphaon to share with you the wisdom hidden in the stars."

Adon-Shama and Raphaon floated gracefully around him, their faces aglow with joy, and in unison, they sang a melody that transcended words—a harmonious union of praise and purpose that filled Adam's spirit with warmth and wonder. As the celestial music enveloped him, he felt the weight of eternity resting upon his shoulders, awakening an understanding that he is intricately woven into the very fabric of existence, a vital thread in the grand tapestry designed by the Creator.

Adam could hardly contain his curiosity; his heart danced with questions and wonder.

"Lord," he began, a hint of concern in his voice, "I have noticed some strange occurrences, and I wondered if you had taken notice of them as well?"

"Strange?" Adon-Shama interjected, a glimmer of amusement in His tone. "What an odd word for you to choose." He paused, allowing the weight of the word to linger before asking, "What does you mean by strange, Adam?"

Adam hesitated, searching for the right articulation of his thoughts. "I know not how to explain it, but 'strange' seems fitting. These events I witness I have never seen before, nor heard of such happenings," he replied, his gaze drifting toward the vast expanse of sky, painted in shifting colors as daylight surrendered to dusk.

"I perceive all that transpires above, Adam. Nothing escapes our watchful eye. Know that I am always with you," Raphaon reassured him, her voice calm yet powerful, resonating with a comforting warmth in Adam's heart. "Tomorrow, you're to tend to the beast of the field as I've instructed."

"As You commanded, my Lord," Adam answered softly, a warmth spreading through him at the sound of God's presence, grounding him in the moment.

As the LORD departed, Adam lingered, contemplating the extraordinary sight of the previous night. The twilight settled around him, and soon the stars began to twinkle playfully overhead, weaving a tapestry of light against the darkening sky. Comforted by the serenity of his surroundings, he felt himself slowly drifting toward sleep.

Just before surrendering to the heaviness of his eyelids, a flicker caught his eye, another star tumbled from the heavens, this time in the east. Startled, he sat upright, marveling at the celestial phenomenon. Out of the corner of his eye, another streak of light cascaded down from the southern sky, followed by yet another shimmering descent to the west.

His heart raced with excitement, a sense of wonder enveloping him as he basked in the display above. The enchanting spectacle invigorated him, shattering any remnants of sleep. For a brief moment, he reveled in the beauty above, hoping to glimpse even more of the dazzling meteor shower.

Eventually, he reclined once more beneath the grand oak, determined to stay awake and observe the wonders of the cosmos. As sleep finally claimed him, three thunderous crashes echoed in the distance, jolting him upright. The sound reverberated through the still night air, filling him with questions?

Morning dawned bright and clear. Adam is driven by curiosity, he sprints toward the eastern edge of the garden, where he believed one of the celestial bodies had landed. Time slipped through his fingers as he navigated the dense underbrush, urgency fueling his movements.

When he arrived, a full fifteen minutes had elapsed since he had set out. He halted before the thick foliage, which loomed like a verdant wall, obstructing his view. Peering through the tangled branches, he strained to see if any remnants of the star awaited discovery. His heart raced as he recalled the rapturous beauty of the night before and the excitement that coursed through him.

That evening, with the skies swirling above and the stars winking playfully as they did the night before, Adam settled beneath the great oak once more. But this time, he is not merely awaiting the falling stars; he is ready to embrace the lessons that the universe had begun to unveil before him. As he closed his eyes, he felt the pulse of the earth beneath him, the melody of life ringing in the silence, and he understood—this is just the beginning of his journey into the mysteries of life.

Chapter 30

The Sword and its Secrets. . .

Alite lush rain began to fall on David as he made his way toward the mountain, his heart racing with anticipation. He looked upward, shielding his eyes against the droplets, trying to assess the skies for any signs of a more severe storm approaching. The narrow path felt familiar under his feet as he retraced his steps from earlier. He glanced back and marveled at the breathtaking view of the RV, Park.

"Incredible," he thought, taking in the vast array of greenery and the way the landscape sprawled out like a patchwork quilt below him, stitched together by the meandering roads with vibrant patches of color.

He finally reach the base of the mountain, and he began to climb its slippery slope, mindful to be careful of each step. The rain intensified, cascading like a gentle waterfall from the leaves overhead. David blinked, trying to clear the mist, clouding his vision, relying on memory as he navigated the terrain. Halfway up, he lost his footing, slipping on a slick patch, and felt his body lurch dangerously. In an instant, he regained his balance, heart pounding, and pressed forward, determined to reach the sword.

His gaze fell upon the sword embedded in the rock, its glint catching the muted light filtering through the rain. As he stared at its blade, a strange magnetism pulled him in, and for a moment, his mind grappled for something, anything—to say. Suddenly, he felt a powerful force enveloping him. He felt like he were wrapped in a vast bubble, and before he knew it, his spirit is whisked away.

In this ethereal space, David found himself standing in an empty void, were the concept of time flows in and out like waves crashing against the shoreline. Images began to materialize, blurred visions of a mighty battle being waged before him. He is unable to grasp the specifics, yet the epic clash between forces caused an avalanche of curiosity to overshadow him. All sorts of wings spiraled through the air, entangling one another in a fierce struggle, while the sounds of clanging metal, war cries, and the pounding of thousands rang like thunder in his ears.

Just as he focus on the chaotic scene, a piercing screech from a bird brakes his concentration causing the vivid imagery to dissipate like smoke, leaving him gasping in the void. He is abruptly thrust back into his body, finding himself sitting on the mountainside, bewildered by the intensity of the experience.

"What is that all about?" he thought, rubbing his forehead in confusion as a headache threatened to take hold. Breathless, he struggled to make sense of what he had just witnessed.

"Maybe I'm having sunstroke? No, that can't be... I haven't been out here long enough to hallucinate? Or perhaps it was just my imagination running wild."

He wrestled with his thoughts, still reeling from the profound sensation of having been part of something far beyond his comprehension. The sword felt more significant now, and he knew he couldn't leave it there. "I have to take it back with me. No! I'll just put it back behind these rocks," he resolved, uncertainty gnawing at him.

As David carried the sword back to the place where he discovered it. He failed to notice a couple of Yinpiniel's, scurrying away from his approach. He carefully placed the sword back behind the rocks, laying it in its resting place with great care. He made sure it is fully hidden before leaving.

As he headed back toward the camp, thoughts of earlier interactions with his parents bubbled to the surface. He reflected on how harsh they'd been, and yet a pang of guilt struck him. He truly should have kept a better watch over his sister. "They're right," he admitted to himself. "I could never forgive myself if something happened to her."

As David approached the camp, he spotted his parents walking toward him with knowing smiles. David Sr. burst out laughing, the sound warm and inviting. "Son, we're sorry for putting you through that. As parents, we sometimes overreact and miss the mark, but you really should have seen the look on your face!"

His mother joined in the laughter, and David couldn't stay mad, laughter bubbling up within him despite the earlier tension. "I'm sorry, too," he said with genuine sincerity, feeling the weight of the day lift just a little.

The three of them laughed until tears streamed down their faces, and once the mirth subsided, they huddled together for a loving embrace.

"You must be hungry?" his mother asked, stepping back to check on them.

"I am starving," replied David, his stomach growling in agreement.

They settled around the picnic table, where David Sr. had prepared a feast of hot dogs, hamburgers, and baked beans on the grill. "Now, this is real camping food," said David Sr., as the day wound down, their spirits lifted.

As night loomed on the horizon, they gathered around the campfire, the serene glow casting shadows that danced among the trees. David Sr. shared a few stories, his voice echoing into the air with laughter and warmth.

Hours passed, and the heaviness of sleep began to tug at David and Kalisha. Kissing their parents goodnight, David crawled into his bunk within the RV, retreating into the warmth of his blankets. He lay there, thinking back on the events of the day, finding himself lost in reverie until his eyelids grew heavy. With one final yawn, he succumbed to sleep.

The next day, he awoke to the sound of birds chirping as the morning sun filtered through the curtains, casting a warm light around the room. The air is nippy, and he snuggled deeper into the covers, unable to shake off the morning chill. The campsite began to buzz with the excited energy of a new day, and soon he could smell the delicious aroma of sizzling bacon wafting through the air.

"David! Are you up yet?" his mom called.

"Aight, Mom, I'm awake. 'Bout to jump in the shower, then I'm out the door," he replied, still wrapped in his cozy cocoon.

A few minutes later, groggily David arose, staggering to gather his clothes. "Hurry it up… time's a-wasting!" his mother shouted, her tone playful yet insistent.

Jumping out of bed, he hopped into the shower for a warm, though brief, cleanse. After getting dressed, he stepped outside, "Burr, it's kind of chilly out here," he mumbled, making his way toward the campfire his dad had started.

The rich smell of coffee filled his nostrils, and the sizzling bacon accompanied by perfectly fried eggs made his mouth water. Makayla called everyone to breakfast, and soon they all sat at the table, plates piled high with food. As David sat down, a thought pierced through his hunger reminding him of the sword. He began to wolf down his meal.

"Son, slow down. There's more," David Sr. cautioned lightly.

"Look, Pops, I get it, yeah? But listen, that canyon? It's not done with me yet. There's mad terrain still to scope out, you feel me? And yo, the rocks I peeped? Seriously fire. Straight up. A-grade material for my geography class. The teacher's gonna bug out!" David explained animatedly.

"Well, your mother, Kalisha, and I are planning a hiking trip up the mountain to do some exploring of our own," David Sr. said, excitement glimmering in his eyes.

"That's cool," Junior replied, trying to hide his eagerness.

"You are going, too," his mother chimed in, glancing over with an expectant smile.

"Bet. Just a quick one, fam, I gotta bounce," he conceded, realizing he would have to strike a balance.

"Don't forget to take your survival kit and be careful, son," David Sr. added, his voice wrapping around him with concern.

"Okay, Pop," replied David, feeling reassured.

After finishing breakfast, David hurried to complete his chores, making his bed and folding his blanket with precision. Once done, he bolted out the door, racing to check on the sword.

"Remember, not too long!" his mother called after him.

"David!" Kalisha yelled after him, eyes bright with mischief. "Can I come?"

"NO!" he shot back, not wanting her tagging along.

"David! Do not be gone too long," Makayla warned, her voice tinged with annoyance.

"Okay! I won't!"

Kalisha sucked her teeth and waved her hand dismissively, bitterness coloring her tone. "Who wants to pick up some dumb rocks anyway?"

Her disappointment is palpable, and Makayla, sensing her daughter's hurt, leaned down to comfort her. "Come help me, Kalisha. Remember, honey, David is a boy, and boys need their space from time to time. So don't take it personally, okay?"

"Okay, Mom," Kalisha replied, her voice laced with uncertainty.

David jogged off, heading toward the canyon with a mixture of excitement and apprehension. As he reached the clearing, he suddenly stopped dead in his tracks.

"Nah, fam! You trippin'! Ain't no way!" he exclaimed, eyes widening with amazement at the astonishing sight before him.

Chapter 31

In the Face of Destiny . . .

In a cozy little bedroom adorned with mismatched decor, Joshua swung open the door, a grin plastered across his face. "Hey, Dad! Where's Mum?!" he called out, his excitement palpable.

"She's in the other room gatherin' her things, mate," his dad replied, adjusting his cap. "She's been waitin' for ya for a fair while now."

Joshua's heart sank a bit, remembering the conversations and decisions that had led to this moment. A divorce because of his dad's slip-ups. Mom thought it is best to take off and let Joshua stay with his father; it seemed easier that way, but it still stung. No longer were they the family they once were, but at least this arrangement meant he could stay close to his mates.

"It's been a couple of years since the blow-up," he mused silently. The endless discussions in whispers, late-night tears... and the decision to only separate physically for the time being left a knot in his stomach. Mum landed a job in the city, and now she was off to start anew, but he wasn't ready for that; he still clung to memories of happier times.

Joshua recalled just how quiet it had gotten since the constant bickering ceased. Sure, it felt odd without the shouts and slammed doors, but it was just as lonely. He knew Mum was hurting; she'd worn sadness like a second skin, while Dad was often away, buried in late work nights that never really added up.

"A lot happened back then," he reminisced, thinking of the night Mum discovered Dad's betrayal. The image of her wrecked face was burned into his memory; it'd been one of those moments you just can't shake off.

"I'll never forget when Mum went to Dad's workplace that night," he thought. "She wasn't expecting to find that crook parked up with some young lady." The heartache of that revelation is imprinted, seeing her crash through the front door in fury, knocking over furniture as she stormed in.

"Mum, what's going on?!" he had shouted, worry painting his voice.

But Mom is lost in her own ocean of emotions, sobbing uncontrollably as Joshua stood by, helpless and terrified, not knowing how to soothe that kind of pain.

Hours later, Dad arrived home. Joshua had watched their confrontation unfold from the shadow of his room, the anger spilling over, confusing him more than anything. He might not have understood the term "infidelity," but "cheating" is familiar enough, and it hurt like hell to watch his family falling apart.

In times like these, he'd usually escape to the barn, where his loyal dog Rex would bring him comfort. Out of the window, he'd sometimes reminisce about the good times - family cookouts, trips filled with laughter, Mum whipping up her famous dishes, and Dad packing the car with all their gear.

"Gee, those were the days," he thought, shaking his head at the bittersweet memories.

"Oi! Rex!" he called, catching the dog flopped by the window looking out towards the barn. "You wanna go out for a walk, mate?"

Rex perked up, wagging his tail as he jumped to his feet. "Yeah, let's go!" he said, his excitement contagious.

Just then, Joshua spotted a faint glow flickering out in the field. "Oh, crikey! I forgot about the shield! Best grab it before someone else does." He bolted out the door.

"Joshua! Where are ya off to, son?" his dad called after him.

"Just outside for a bit, Dad!" he shouted back. "Mum's nearly done packin', anyway."

He sprinted across the field, Rex keeping pace beside him, and followed the light down to the tall grass. Lifting the mysterious shield, he marveled at its weight—or lack thereof.

Rex dashed inside the barn before him. "Alright, Rex! Let's stash it somewhere safe. Any ideas, boy?" he asked, scratching behind the dog's ears.

Rex tilted his head, glancing up at an old trunk in the loft. "Good call! That should do the trick."

Joshua climbed up to inspect it. Holding the shield, he realized it wouldn't fit. "Bugger! Looks like it's too big… wait, what?" A flash of movement caught his eye—a tiny, glowing being flitted near.

"No way!" he whispered, as the diminutive creature touched the shield, causing it to shrink before his eyes.

"Whoa, did you see that, Rex?" he exclaimed, jaw dropped. "This is unreal!" A tingle flicker raced through him, and suddenly, the dog spoke!

"Hold up, Joshua. Yeah, I can talk! I'm Haniel, your guardian angel," Rex said, wagging his tail as he transformed.

"Okay, what the bloody heck! You can actually talk?" Joshua's eyes widened in shock, and he stumbled back, fainting from the flood of astonishment.

Rex nudged him awake, licking his face with fervor. "Oi, mate! You alright?"

Rubbing his drowsy eyes, Joshua spluttered, "Did you really just talk, Rex?"

"Sure did, mate. I'm Haniel, the angel guarding this relic."

"Relic? This old thing?" He held up the shield, now feeling it was quite the burden. "You can't be serious!"

"It's important, trust me," Haniel replied with a serious tone. "You're in danger, and we need to protect it from the Demonites."

"Demonites? What on Earth are they?"

"Evil beings after the shield, and they won't stop until they get it," Haniel warned, seriousness etching deeper.

"Great, just what I need. Nightmare material!" Joshua's fear was palpable amidst the wonder.

Just as he is about to respond, a rustle outside made Haniel freeze. "Quick! Hide!"

"Hide from what?" He was bewildered.

"No time! Just trust me!" Haniel commanded urgently.

Joshua dove into a pile of hay, biting his lip to keep from breathing too loudly. Then came the overwhelming stench that made him gag as a blinding light filled the barn. Caught in shock, he peeked through the hay just as monstrous eyes crept into view. "What the bloody hell is that?!" he whispered, terror gripping him.

A hulking demon emerged, moving through the barn while he clutched his heart in fear. "Yikes! If that's a Demonite, we're in strife."

Haniel leapt from his perch, transforming before his eyes. "Keep it together, Josh. We can do this!"

"THIS ISN'T OVER!" roared Ba'laamus, charging at them.

Joshua wanted to scream, but he knew he had to stay silent. Summoning all his courage, he held his breath, praying for a miracle. And for once, destiny seemed to answer.

Chapter 32

The Guarded Relic…

"It's time," she smirked, a glimmer of mischief dancing in her eyes.

With a flash, the Demonites flickered out of existence, leaving a palpable tension hanging in the air. Joshua slipped past his old man, who was firmly planted on the couch, engrossed in the morning paper. He stealthily closed the door, peering through the glass, making sure no one had followed.

His dad glanced up, brow furrowed.

"Oi, mate—everything alright?"

Joshua's stomach twisted, his gaze riveted outside. "Yeah, Dad."

"Then why the bloody look? You'd think you're bein' chased by a pack of wild kangaroos."

"Just keepin' an eye out for Rex."

"Planning on stickin' 'round for the night?"

"Umm, yeah; night, Dad!"

"Night, son," his father muttered, turning back to the paper.

Joshua darted upstairs, bolting his door behind him. He yanked the shade down, peeking through the bottom edge. The barn lay still, shrouded in darkness, and an overwhelming urge to check on his dog clenched at him. But the fear held him in place.

"Blimey, that was just eerie," he thought, eyes fixed on the barn.

As if the night itself had eyes, two spectral silhouettes flickered, a ray of light refracting around them.

"I warned you to get lost and report back to your master. Tell that Satan bloke he'll pay dearly for his disobedience. That's if you live to tell the tale after what he does to you for failing," hissed Haniel.

With that, she opened her mouth, and music poured out like molten silver. Ba'laamus sneered, disappearing without a trace. Haniel transformed back into Rex, the dog, who plopped down next to the trunk, ready to pounce at any sign of trouble.

Back in the house, Joshua lay on his bed, mind racing about his loyal companion. The night's tension pulled him under like a heavy weight. A yawn escaped him, and sleep swiftly enveloped him.

He awoke to the sun piercing through his eyelids, the scent of freshly mowed grass wafting through the open window. He sat up, squinting at the radiant day outside. The trees seemed almost too vibrant, as if someone had cranked up the color dial.

As he strolled to the barn, he pushed the doors open wide, but they slammed shut behind him. Joshua's heart raced as shadows danced upon the walls. Full moonlight poured in despite the bright day outside.

"Get a grip, mate," he thought, trying the door only to find it vanished. Panic set in as the barn began to spin, darkness creeping in like a smothering blanket. He squeezed his eyes shut, praying it would all dissolve. But when he opened them, nothing had changed.

The unsettling spinning stopped, and a flickering light drew his gaze down an illuminated corridor ending in a door. With each step toward it, the creaking floor echoed like a heartbeat, throbbing with dread. From beneath him, strange murmurs began to rise, chattering and cackling, and before he could react, the ground beneath him crumbled. He barely managed to brace himself against the wall, peering down into the black void, where the fetid stench of rotting flesh clawed at his throat.

Blood splattered the door at the end of the hall—a horrific crimson streak. Wild panic surged within him as he fought his way back, beading sweat trickling down his face. Then came the shriek—bone-chilling and loud. Something is closing in on him.

Heart racing, he bolted down the corridor, nearly stumbling as the shriek morphed into a swirling echo, swallowed by silence. He turned back towards the door, but something shot out in front of him—a ghastly creature, eyes burning with malice. The hairs on his neck stood on end, locking him in place. Suddenly, he jolted awake, drenched in sweat, breaths heavy and labored.

"That was some nightmare," he muttered, heart still racing.

He lay there for a moment, replaying the dark events of his dream, before a knock at the door snapped him back.

"Come in," he called.

It was his dad, telling him to rise and shine as he headed out. Joshua rubbed the sleep from his eyes and gazed at the barn, doubt creeping back in. "Was it all just a dream?"

Stretching and yawning, he wondered about Rex. Usually, the dog was never far from him.

"Mum, smells like breakfast!" he said, stumbling out of bed.

Off to the bathroom he went to wash up. On his way downstairs, he peeked at his dad.

"Morning, sleepyhead!"

"G'day, Dad. Seen Rex?"

"Last I saw, he scooted off to the barn."

"Right… guess I'll check on him after I clean up," he muttered, uncertainty gnawing at him.

"Breakfast in fifteen," Dad said as he started his tasks.

"Cool. I'm off to the barn," Joshua replied, heading back upstairs to wash up.

Once finished, he slipped into his sneakers and sprinted towards the barn. As he neared the doors, he slowed to a creep. Cautiously, he peered through the window, finding the inside eerily undisturbed.

"Rex?" he called softly, the sound swallowed by the silence.

"Nothing."

"Rex? You in here, mate?"

Still no response, he moved deeper into the barn, checking behind piles of hay and glancing up at the loft. Just as he stepped toward the ladder, Rex leapt out, nearly sending Joshua sprawling onto the floor.

"Oi! You trying to take my life, you mad dog?" he laughed, excitement flooding over him as Rex bounded forward, tail wagging like a windmill.

"Are you alright, boy?"

Rex licked his face, a goofy expression on his canine countenance. "Guess you're fine then, huh? Let's head back."

But the dog hesitated. "Nah, mate. I've gotta stay and guard the relic."

"Oh, bloomin' hell! It really happened!" Joshua said, eyes wide with excitement. "Show me!"

Rex led him to a trunk and Joshua fumbled with the blankets until he revealed a majestic shield, glistening with crusted jewels. The reality of his dream washed over him. His heart raced with revelation.

"Good boy," Joshua grinned, patting Rex's head as he heard his father call from the house.

He stepped away, promising Rex he'd be right back after washing up. Inside, after scrubbing the dirt from his hands, he joined his dad at the table.

"So, son, Rex in the barn?"

"Yeah, crashed there last night," he said nonchalantly.

His dad raised an eyebrow. "Odd behavior for him."

Joshua wanted desperately to share everything that had happened, but the words dried in his throat. He'd learned his lesson; his parents never took him seriously.

"Is he havin' another one of those wild dreams?" they'd say.

He recalled that night eavesdropping on their worried conversation. "I think he's just dreamin', love," his mother reassured.

Back in the present, Joshua felt the weight of their disbelief.

"How's the tucker, mate?" Dad's voice cut through Joshua's swirling thoughts, a gentle nudge back to the present.

"G'day, Dad," Joshua mumbled, forcing a weak smile that didn't quite reach his eyes.

"Plenty more if ya keen for seconds, eh?" Dad offered, his tone casual but with a hint of concern in his gaze.

"Nah, I'm good, but I'll sort out the dishes after," Joshua volunteered quickly, eager to have something to do, anything to distract himself.

"Appreciate it, son," Dad said, a beat of silence hanging between them. Then, a heavy hand clapped Joshua firmly on the shoulder. "You're a good kid, Joshua."

A genuine grin finally broke through Joshua's preoccupation. "Thanks, Pops," he replied, the simple affirmation warming him slightly.

"Just remember to feed Rex when he gets back, yeah?" Dad called after him as Joshua started to move away, a familiar reminder grounding him, even as his mind continued to race with unspoken worries.

"Sure thing, Dad," Joshua replied, making his way back to the barn, heart pounding in anticipation of what awaited him there

Chapter 33

The Price of Departure. . .

Joshua bolted out the door beelining straight for the barn. His eyes spotted a couple of red deer, munching away near a massive gum tree, not twenty yards off. As he trudged towards the big farm shed, yesterday's bloody walkabout flickered back into his noggin, giving him the heebie-jeebies a bit.

Finally, he reached the barn, yanked the door open, and peered around, puffing like a busted bellows. Nothin'. Then, Rex, his kelpie, came bounding over, tail wagging like a metronome gone troppo.

"Sorry, mate! Took a fair bit longer than I reckoned. Had to scrub the kitchen for the old man," Joshua explained, giving the dog a pat.

Then, a voice, not Rex's, but comin' from him, "Oi! What's that you're holdin'? What goodies ya got for me?" It is Haniel again.

"Brought ya some water and a snag to chew on. Figured ya'd be peckish. Ya want it?" Joshua offered.

"Nah, mate. Can't touch human tucker, not even in this dog's skin. Only the good stuff from up top for me. But don't you fret about this bloke. Long as I'm wearin' him, he won't feel the hunger pangs. Once I bugger off, though, he'll be starvin', so leave the grub for him then. Right, I'm offski now, back to me own patch. You won't see those nasty demons again. They won't be back."

Joshua plonked the bowl and ham down. Haniel seemed to… well, un-dog Rex, leavin' him just a regular, barkin' mutt again. Straight away, Rex went for the ham, scoffin' it down like there was no tomorrow. Joshua decided to leg it outta the barn, and Rex trotted right behind him.

He stopped dead, a sudden worry naggin' at him. Had he left that shield out in the open? He spun around and headed back to the barn, makin' sure the trunk was covered proper. Without warnin', Rex started barkin' his head off, goin' bonkers. Joshua whirled around, tryin' to see what had the poor bugger so riled up.

"What's up, boy? Ya see somethin'?"

The K-9 curled his lip, showin' his fangs, ready to have a go at somethin'. Joshua's brain jumped to the worst. Were those Demonites back for another crack?

"C'mon, Rex! We gotta hide, pronto!"

Little did Joshua know, a bloody adder, a proper venomous snake, was out for a slither and a hunt. Rex kept barkin' at the unwelcome guest. Joshua grabbed his collar, yankin' hard, tryin' to drag the dog away. Then he saw it – the snake, coiled and lookin' mean. He tried to pull Rex back, quick smart. The snake, usually a shy bugger, was poised to strike, all 'cause of Rex's jiggin' about. The barkin' didn't faze the reptile one bit; it held its ground, darin' either of 'em to get closer.

Joshua gave Rex's collar another hard tug. Rex leaned down for a sniff of the snake's scent. That was it. The adder felt proper threatened and struck like lightning. Rex just managed to dodge, missin' the bite by a hair's breadth. Joshua's eyes darted around, seein' his dad's tools hangin' on the wall. He grabbed a rake while Rex kept the snake pinned with his furious barkin'. Back with the rake, Joshua gently slid it under the snake's belly. The bloody thing struck again and again, missin' each time. Joshua carefully lifted the viper off the ground.

He carried the slithery bugger outta the barn, Rex stayin' put. Joshua headed over to that big gum tree where he'd seen the deer earlier. But when he got there, his jaw dropped. He was absolutely HORRIFIED by what he saw. It was a gruesome sight, mate. His head swam with fear, and he dropped the rake and the snake like they were red-hot coals. Animal blood, bone fragments, fur, and… brain matter… covered the ground from a recent, savage attack. But the meat hadn't been touched.

Joshua gasped, steppin' back, shakin' his head, his eyes all glazed over. He spun around and legged it back towards the barn, panic clawin' at his throat. He burst into the barn, a right mess. He turned to bolt for the door, but somethin' blocked his way.

Back inside, he noticed a light bleedin' out from under the shield. He urged Rex back, pointin' towards the barn doors. Rex, tail still waggin' a bit, went and sat by the exit. The light from the shield flickered, then just… vanished.

Joshua cautiously picked up the shield, lookin' all over it to see where the light had come from. He held it up high, gave it a proper once-over, then put it back down. His eyes locked onto the emblem in the middle. That's gotta be it, he thought. He grabbed a chisel and laid the shield on the table, tryin' to pry the emblem open.

He wrestled with a force he never knew existed, but it was no good. His efforts were bugger-all. He grabbed hold of the emblem and tried to twist it with all his might. He stopped, puffin' and blowin', takin' a deep breath. With every ounce of strength in his body, he gave it one last go, tryin' to turn it anticlockwise. Suddenly, a bloody force shot out from the emblem, knockin' him on his backside.

Rex pawed at the barn door, pushin' it open, and bolted outside. The shield started shakin' like a leaf in a gale, then tumbled off the table. Bright lights flashed as it hit the floor with a crash. A beam of pure light shot straight up through the barn roof, kickin' up a bloody whirlwind.

Joshua is gobsmacked. He stood under the hole in the roof, starin' up at the sky with wide-eyed wonder. The wind HOWLED around the barn, and clouds started spinnin' downwards. Suddenly, the ground SHOOK as the clouds touched down. A shocked Joshua slid backwards on his arse from the impact. Another mob of demons, Watchers out on patrol, copped an eyeful of the spectacle.

They changed course quick smart, headin' straight for the barn. The shield's outburst had ripped open some kinda doorway. Rex was outside, barkin' like a bloody maniac. Joshua's dad, John, heard the commotion and came to suss things out. Rex stood up on his hind legs, scratchin' at the barn doors, tryin' to get back in. John saw Rex and went over to help. Rex ran halfway to Mr. Liddell, then spun around and bolted back to the barn.

"What is it, boy? What's all the racket?"

Rex just kept barkin' at the barn door. "Okay, mate, I'm comin'." Joshua scrambled to his feet, still starin' in disbelief. He edged closer to the… well, the portal thingy. His eyes were glued to the doorway. As he stepped across the threshold, his whole body shimmered, and he was gone, whisked inside. The portal slammed shut behind him. The Watchers EXPLODED into the barn, but they were too late.

"It was here," Al'debaran growled, a proper scowl on his face.

He stood where the shield had been, then spun around, and they all buggered off outta the barn. Joshua's dad finally got the barn door open and saw a bloody great hole where the demons had exited.

"Joshua! Joshua! Where in the bloody hell are ya?" he yelled, his voice crackin' with worry.

He searched the barn, lookin' for any sign of his son, but there is nothin'. A moment passed, and now, a proper fear clenched his gut.

"Crikey! Look at this bloody great hole the lad's made," he muttered, shakin' his head.

Everything else looked normal. Rex went over to where he'd last seen Joshua, sniffin' the ground, tryin' to pick up his scent. He sniffed and sniffed but came up with nothin'. He turned, lookin' up at the boy's dad as if to say, "Where's Joshua, mate?"

Rex barked again, a mournful sound. John called out his son's name again, but all he got back is silence.

Chapter 34

Gathering of Dark Forces. . .

The moon hung high in the sky, shimmering with an ethereal glow that illuminated the night. Silhouettes flickered into existence, ethereal and foreboding, as Ba'laamus summoned the leaders of the dark squadron at the behest of their lord. The air was thick with anticipation, each arrival adding weight to the atmosphere.

Baaladyme stood apart from the throng, his gaze fixed on the radiant moon. A moment passed, and then, from the shadows, a line of demons materialized, descending from the fringes of the night. Their presence crackled with energy and unrest, culminating as Satan swooped in, landing gracefully among them. His form radiated a powerful, glowing energy that seemed to draw the attention of every demon present.

"Bow before me," he commanded, his voice a low rumble that seemed to reverberate through the ground beneath them. In unison, the demons lowered their heads, a mixture of reverence and trepidation in their submission.

"Arise," came his next command, firm yet foreboding. As they straightened, eyes locked with an intensity that hinted at unsaid concerns and desires, Satan began to pace before them. He drew in a deep breath, staring proudly at the blu planet below.

"There's something important that I wish to discuss," he announced, tension palpable in his tone. Murmurs of concern rippled through the crowd as every leader leaned in, captivated by the gravity of his words.

"The weapons, as you are aware of, have not burned up in the blu planet's atmosphere. They have landed somewhere on that forsaken sphere." His gaze shifted, fixing on Ba'laamus. "You, along with some of the lesser demons, have been searching for them."

"Our search has yielded nothing, my lord," Baalamus admitted, an edge of irritation creeping into his voice, carefully hiding the fact that they were already aware of the shield's whereabouts.

Satan's fiery gaze pierced through him, demanding attention. "We have yet to find them." He paused, letting the weight of his words sink in. "But I have made a decisive choice. I shall infiltrate God's dominion and take over the reins of mankind, making Him understand that I am not to be trifled with."

A mixture of curiosity and disbelief flickered across the faces of the demons gathered. Al'debaran broke the silence, his tone laced with skepticism. "Sire, how do you intend to do that?"

"Leave that to me," Satan replied with a confidence that sent confusion down their spines. "God wishes for us to serve man. I will play that role, I will manipulate them to fulfill my desires."

"The audacity of Him!" Naberus exclaimed, shaking his head in disbelief. A collective wave of discontent rippled through the assembled demons.

"Why should we, the chosen ones, bow to mere dirt?" Belphegor spat, his voice rising in fervor. As their roar of disapproval echoed in the night air, Satan held up a hand, commanding silence.

"While I reshape the minds of the mortals, I demand those weapons to be found and brought back to me. Is that understood?" he ordered, his voice lowering ominously.

"But my lord," Ba'laamus ventured, a flicker of defiance in his eyes. "We have searched extensively. They remain elusive."

Satan's gaze burned into him, fierce and unyielding. "Is that understood?" he repeated, the weight of his tone demanding obedience.

Ba'laamus nodded, the fight drained from him. "I got it."

"When I return, those weapons better be in your possession," Satan warned, the air around them thick with tension.

"Why don't you go retrieve them yourself?" Ba'laamus shot back, his voice tinged with recklessness.

In a swift motion, Satan crossed the distance and slapped him, the sound a crack in the still night. The crowd fell silent, eyes wide as Ba'laamus knelt, shock and fear flooding his features.

"You dare speak down to your lord?" Satan's voice dripped with fury, his presence looming darkly over Ba'laamus. "What do I seem like to you? A mere retrieval service? Remember your place in this hierarchy."

Baaladyme watched the exchange with keen interest, a spark of ambition igniting within him. If Ba'laamus fell, he would surely be next in line. His heart raced with the prospect.

"I haven't forgotten," Ba'laamus finally stammered, voice quivering.

"You have a choice, as do all of us—free will, causality," Satan continued, his tone now simmering, almost pleading. "But I need you, my advisor, to follow through. When I leave, distribute these assignments. I expect obedience."

With that, he turned, gliding into the night, Baaladyme following closely behind. As silence reigned, Ba'laamus waited, breath held until the shadows claimed his lord. Then, begrudgingly, he began to distribute the assignments as ordered. One by one, the demons took flight, vanishing into the endless dark, the night holding its secrets close.

Chapter 35

The Pendant's Call. . .

Abram stand frozen with disbelief washing over him in waves. As soon as he closed his eyes, it felt as if he were being drawn into an ethereal whirlpool, the pull so strong it caused everything else to fade away, including his responsibilities as a shepherd. The air thickened, and the sky grew darker, tinged with a promise of something more than just an approaching storm. Laughter spilled from somewhere beyond the veil of reality, children's laughter mingling with the hum of adult conversations, echoing in a way that felt both joyful and haunting.

He opened his eyes and, mesmerized, found himself staring into the intricate crown of the pendant clutched tightly in his hand. Everything around him spun wildly, yet he felt trapped in place, motionless but lost in a fever dream. Just then, a sharp pat on his back jolted him from his reverie. He spun around, startled, his heart racing. It is Namaan, his father's faithful servant.

"Master! It's about time we got back!" Namaan chuckled, tapping him again on the shoulder, causing a nervous flutter in Abram's chest. "The sheep found their way home without you. Perhaps we should appoint one of them as your shepherd!" His laughter echoed with warmth, and for a moment, the weight of the pendant lightened.

Abram tucked the pendant away, his heart sinking as he realized the herd is nowhere to be found. With a sense of urgency, the two began their trek back to the village, but Namaan's confusion pricked at him.

"Master—where did you get that?" he inquired, his brow furrowed in skepticism.

Abram glanced at the pendant, its warmth still fresh in his palm. Before he could respond, a fierce wind whipped up out of nowhere, tossing their hair in a chaotic frenzy. Namaan glanced around with wide eyes, gripping Abram's arm. Panic surged as they scurried for shelter.

As darkness descended like a shroud, golden hints of light crawled slowly over the ground, weaving outward. Shadows appeared, their shapes lurking ominously in the shadows of the trees. The sight sent a cold shiver down Abram's spine. There is something unnervingly evil about the scene unfolding before them.

"It must be a storm," Namaan urged, trying to mask his own fear. "We have to find cover!"

Abram nodded, but his mind raced, "Where? Where can we go?" The tension crackled in the air, unanswered and heavy.

As if summoned by their anxiety, a shadow darted across the sky, piercing the tension with a sense of both dread and anticipation. The pendant glowed, casting a protective light around Abram, a warm shield against the encroaching darkness. Namaan looked up, his eyes wide with terror as he witnessed the silhouettes react to the pendant's glow, launching themselves into the air in a flurry of chaotic energy.

"Whoa…" Abram breathed, staggering back as he found himself entranced, the scene surreal and intoxicating.

One of the ethereal figures thrust her staff into the ground with determination, while another twirled her staff above her head, conjuring a dazzling array of light that pulsed with an otherworldly rhythm. The spectacle is unlike anything he'd ever seen, both thrilling and terrifying. The energy surged—a radiant beam slammed downward, striking the ground like lightning. Namaan gasped; even he, seasoned in the ordinary, could scarcely comprehend the power at play.

The energy erupted, sending a blinding light cascading into the heart of the disturbance. Darkness dissipated like mist under the sun, and suddenly, all was still. The wind hushed, leaving only the distant flutter of the tiny beings—Yinpiniel's—they hovered gleefully in the aftermath, unfazed.

Abram blinked, bewildered, and found himself standing outside his tent, the surreal experience still throbbing in his mind. Rushing inside, relief flooded over him as he wrapped his arms around his mother, who looked at him.

"Where have you been?" she asked, her voice revealing her worry. "We spent two days searching for you! We thought you'd been taken by some wild animal!" She tightened her embrace, her love suffusing him with warmth, and for a moment, the madness of the world outside faded.

"Abinai!" she called, her voice lifting with joy. "Your son is home, safe!" Her smile brightened the dim tent, churning the remnants of fear in Abram's heart.

"Sit down, let me get you something to eat. It's been two full days since that brief rain," she said, bustling around, her movements filled with urgency.

"Brief?" Abram thought, recalling the grand adventure that felt more like a week. He had completely lost track of time, and the pendant still felt weightless in his pocket, its secrets shrouded.

His mother soon returned with a steaming bowl of lentil stew and flatbread, the aromas tantalizing. "Mmm, that smells wonderful," he murmured, inhaling deeply, a smile creeping onto his lips.

As he dive into the food, savoring the warmth and flavor, she looked at him, "How did you get separated from the sheep?"

When the rains came, confusion mixed with excitement spilled from his lips, "I sent the sheep up the bank, but I got swept away! The waters came rushing." He stuffed his mouth full, oblivious to the bewildered expression on her face.

"Just a sprinkle…" she whispered to herself, trying to process the weight of his reality.

Just then, the tent flap burst open, and his brothers rushed in, their faces lit up with relief and joy. They enveloped him in a chaotic mix of hugs and kisses clamoring all at once, wanting to know how he is, their voices a comforting shout in his ear.

"Let me eat! I'm starving!" he exclaimed, trying to suppress a laugh amid their worry.

"Are you alright? What happened?" questions flew left and right, but Abram could only respond, "Yes…I'm fine. Just let me eat, please. I'll tell you later."

After finishing his meal, with satisfied hunger numbing the remnants of adventure, he recounted the story—not revealing the battle he'd witnessed in the depths of his imagination or the pendant that pulled him into something far beyond the ordinary. Exhaustion sank deep into his bones, and he retreated to his corner of the tent, seeking solace in rest.

His mother hovered nearby, anxiety wrapped around her like a heavy cloak. She remembered the dark nights once filled with his screams, echoes of his battles with shadows that plagued his dreams. She prayed that those dreams wouldn't return, and as she watched him lay his head down, she couldn't shake the feeling of dread crawling up her spine. The pendant's power lingered, dark and mysterious, and she worried for the path that lay ahead of him.

Chapter 36

The Call of the Unknown...

In the early morning hours, a timid sun peeked through wispy clouds, its light softly illuminating the village as life began to stir. Abram lay nestled within the confines of his tent as the distant sound of drums echoing like a heartbeat, urging him awake. As he slowly opened his eyes, he found his brothers huddling around him, their faces lit with excitement yet shadowed by concern, whispering to one another in muffled tones.

"Abram! Abram! Wake up!" they urged, their eyes wide, full of questions that buzzed like bees. Abram could feel the weight of their curiosity pressing down on him, but he brushed them off with a wave of his hand, reluctant to delve into the memories that still haunted him.

With muscles sore from the ordeal, he sighed, a mixture of longing and helplessness washing over him. How he wished he could share the story of his harrowing journey, the vision of the battle he witnessed from a mountaintop, the chaos and beauty intermingled. But for now, he offered them a weak smile, an acknowledgment of their presence, a flicker of warmth in his chest at seeing them again.

"Where's father?" he asked his mother, hoping for reassurance.

"Oh, he's gone to the kingdom of Ur. He'll be back in a few days," she replied, her voice soothing yet tinged with an unspoken worry.

"A few days?" he echoed, disappointment welling up within him. "I wanted to talk to him about my visions…" His heart sank at the thought. "How long has he been gone?"

"Since the cool of the day," she answered, a soft smile on her lips, yet her eyes betrayed a hint of sadness.

"Darn!" His voice trembled with surprise and a hint of panic.

"Get up, eat something, and then rest some more," she urged, her tone gentle, filled with a mother's care.

He nodded, a sense of agreement washing over him as he got up, the weight of fatigue is no longer heavy in his bones. Outside, the fresh air wrapped around him like a cool embrace, reviving his senses momentarily. He went about the morning routines, each movement with renewed energy, yet the joy of being back home hung in the air like a delicate thread weaving them all together.

He returned to the tent, flopping onto the plush cushioning of soft skins, his mind still swirling in excitement. He reached into the fold of his robe and pulled out the pendant, its coolness, a reminder of the strange journey that had stolen him away. He slid it under his pillow, tucking it away as if hiding a secret yet to be revealed. Soon, the urge to sleep overtook him, and he drifted into a realm of dreams.

Colors swirled around him as he soared higher, a cosmic voyage painted with vibrant hues: pinks, oranges, blues, and greens danced together in a symphony of light. As he ascended, the colors deepened into rich indigo, regal purple, and shimmering gold—brilliant beauty unlike anything earthly eyes had ever beheld.

But as he reveled in this vivid dreamscape, a sudden heaviness enveloped him, shadows creeping in—a thick, oppressive weight pressing down on his chest. Panic clawed at him as he fought against it, struggling for breath, feeling his heart race.

"Relax," a voice echoed, startling him, as if someone had intruded upon his dream, yet he is alone. Sitting up with a jolt, his heart pounded wildly as he fumbled under his pillow, seeking the pendant. When his fingers finally grasped it, he held it up, staring into its crown, a flash of clarity coursing through him.

Suddenly, a vision invaded his mind: a sheep, alone and vulnerable, stalked by a wild dog. The urge to protect it surged within him, igniting a fierce determination. In a burst of adrenaline, he dashed out of the tent, his heart racing with the thrill of action for the innocent creature.

Abram raced through the village, guided by instinct, until he found himself near a bush, the sound of the sheep's desperate bleating, calling him closer. The pendant pushing him with speeds that surpass all human ability. He spotted the predatory eyes of the dog stalking, its muscles tense and ready for the kill, a battle of instinct and courage igniting within him.

"I'm coming, little one," he whispered as he pushed through the dense brush, fear and hope intertwining in his chest. The atmosphere crackled with tension. With in seconds, he broke through to find the sheep caught between him and the stalking predator, each second feeling like an eternity.

The thrill of danger turned into a chilling realization as the dog picked up his scent and maneuvered around him. The dread coiled tight within him, and instinct led him to grab a sturdy rod he found on the ground, oblivious to the peril lurking nearby.

With the pendant pulsating and humming at his chest, he fought to comprehend its mysterious power while racing against time. Out of nowhere, a second dog moved closer to the sheep, and the world outside seemed to blur as his focus narrowed to that moment.

"NOOOOO!" he roared from the depths of his spirit, the cry bursting forth as if it could shatter the very air around him. Time froze, every creature halted in suspended animation—the dogs, the sheep, everything held within that moment came to a halt.

Stunned, he gazed around, marveling at the bizarre beauty of it all. "How did this happen?" he thought in disbelief, moving closer to a frozen dog, gently brushing its fur, then daring to tap the other dog's snout, his heart racing with exhilaration and fear.

He felt the thrill of survival as he marveled at the predatory giants around him, yet the weight of time began to press on him like an impending storm. Sensations shifted; the growl from within the dogs pierced the silence, shaking him to his core. A deep instinct told him that their stillness would soon unravel.

With urgency clawing at him, he seized the sheep and raced back to camp. Moments later, the dogs were released from their stasis, chaos erupting as they stumbled into one another in confusion. Behind him, the distant howls echoed but felt far away. As he returned to his village, he could hear his father's voice coming from within their home.

"Father, father!" he called, breathless and filled with wonder as he burst back into his tent.

"What? What's wrong?" his father responded, alarm flashing in his eyes.

"Father, I saved our sheep from two wild dogs!" Abram exclaimed, his heart swelling with pride and adrenaline.

"Wait—what?" Abinai blinked, confusion descending as he glanced around the tent. "But... my son, you're here in the tent. Where is the sheep?"

Abram stood tall, desperation and disbelief coursing through him. "It was right here! Father, I swear to you, I saved the sheep!"

"I believe you, my son!" Abinai's voice softened, yet the sadness in his father's gaze spoke volumes—a reflection of the fear that dwelled within the lines of their family's history, the torment of nightmares that echoed through their bloodline.

And in that moment, as Abram searched for solace in his father's eyes, he realized that the line between dreams and reality is thinner than he had ever known.

Chapter 37

The Light of Revelation. . .

A cosmic bullet, streaked through the inky darkness of the heavens, a silent witness to the drama unfolding on a smaller scale. It zipped past distant planets, a fleeting backdrop to Inkkabus, a creature of questionable competence, squirming before his formidable master, Satan.

"What in the nine cosmoses are you doing here?" Satan drawled, his crimson eyes fixed on some unseen point beyond Inkkabus.

Inkkabus shuffled his feet, his voice a pathetic squeak. "M-master, I... well, I was indulging in a rather invigorating sand shower, you, see? The exfoliating properties are simply divine, and while I was enjoying the, uh, sandy ambiance..." His voice trailed off, trembling like a leaf in a hurricane.

Satan's gaze snapped back, sharp as obsidian shards. "I trust you have acquired the artifact I so graciously entrusted you to... find?"

"Ah! No, the topic I wished to broach with your magnificent self!" Inkkabus chirped, a desperate glint in his eye.

"SILENCE! You a festering pustule of incompetence!" Satan roared, his voice echoing with volcanic fury. "You are tasked with retrieving that weapon, you are a blithering buffoon! I should vaporize your pathetic existence where you stand! But alas, I fear the lingering aroma of idiot fumes."

"Yes, master," Inkkabus whimpered, shrinking under Satan's wrath.

"Simpleton! You were assigned the monumental task of watching a cave! If even a single speck of dust manages to pilfer that artifact, I will extinguish your miserable spark! NOW VANISH FROM MY SIGHT!" Satan punctuated his command with a flick of his wrist.

With a yelp that sounded suspiciously like a tea kettle whistling, Inkkabus spontaneously combusted, reappearing moments later atop the snow-capped peak of Mount Everest, shivering violently in the sub-zero temperatures.

Satan chuckled, a low, rumbling sound that promised further torment. "That ought to instill a modicum of attentiveness in the imbecile."

Meanwhile, back at the cave, Jacob and Feather exchanged a look that eloquently conveyed, "Well, now what? We can't just leave them here," Jacob muttered to his loyal steed, a frown creasing his brow.

He carefully loaded the mysterious artifacts onto Feather's back, a nagging sense of unease prickling his skin. He knew time was slipping through his fingers like desert sand; two days remained to complete his mission, and the lingering sandstorm had already stolen precious hours. Though dusk painted the horizon in fiery hues, Jacob knew the secret trails that led to wild game at this hour.

An odd intuition tugged at him. The ornate bow and arrows he'd discovered felt… wrong. He instinctively reached for his own trusty, if less glamorous, set. The memory of the artifacts' strange power still lingered, a disquieting reminder of the unknown.

Finding a sheltered patch near a thorny bush, Jacob tethered Feather, allowing her to graze on the sparse vegetation. He ventured out onto the open plains, the hunter's instinct already kicking in. His tribe was large, their appetites equally so; a substantial kill was required. The lessons his father had instilled in him during their childhood hunts now surfaced, a primal knowledge of tracking and stalking. One might have thought he'd been raised by wolves, so seamlessly did he move through the landscape.

The thrill of the hunt, that ancient surge of adrenaline, quickened his pulse. His gaze scanned the horizon for the telltale signs of an Oryx herd, their lean, flavorful meat a tribal favorite. Tonight, he envisioned a triumphant return, the largest buck the village had ever seen slung across Feather's back. He could almost hear the cheers, the proud pronouncements: "The gods of our fathers have smiled upon our son! He returns to being a warrior, a provider!"

Lost in this self-congratulatory fantasy, Jacob momentarily let his guard down. This open plain, though seemingly peaceful, was known for its hidden dangers. Up ahead, a herd of Oryx grazed, their elegant forms silhouetted against the fading light. Antelope possessed a notoriously keen sense of smell, but the capricious wind, for once, was on Jacob's side, carrying his scent away from the wary creatures.

He approached with practiced stealth, a shadow moving through the tall grasses, his eyes selecting the prime target. There! A magnificent male, its spiraled horns reaching for the heavens. "Ahhhh, there he is," he thought, a predatory grin twitching at the corner of his lips.

But the prize was on the far side of the plain. Jacob crept lower, the long, narrow leaves rustling softly around him. Suddenly, a flicker of movement caught his eye. A cheetah, sleek and deadly, crouched low, its gaze fixed on the same unsuspecting herd. Predator and prey, locked in a silent, deadly ballet.

As they both waited, a subtle shift in the wind betrayed the big cat. The scent, sharp and musky, drifted towards the grazing antelope. The large buck, its ears twitching, lifted its head, nostrils flaring, sensing the imminent danger.

A guttural snort, an instinctive alarm, ripped through the peaceful air. The cheetah, its cover blown, exploded into a burst of speed. Panic erupted within the herd, a chaotic stampede for survival. Unseen in the brush, Jacob's eyes widened as the mass of panicked animals charged directly towards him. He raised his bow, nocking an arrow with trembling hands. Move too soon, and he'd spook them further.

The hungry cheetah, a blur of yellow and black, pursued the fleeing herd, singling out an older, slower buck. It lunged, a swift, deadly strike. The herd veered wildly, putting distance between themselves and the predator… and inadvertently, between themselves and Jacob. The large buck he'd been stalking stopped, its dark eyes fixing on Jacob's hiding place, a strange, knowing look in their depths.

Then, with a flick of its tail, it was gone, the older Oryx outmaneuvering the cheetah with surprising grace. But a younger doe, less experienced, stumbled, a fatal misstep. The cheetah's powerful jaws clamped down on her hindquarters. The hunt was successful… for the cat. A cold unease settled over Jacob. That look from the buck… it was as if it knew.

He rose, intending to return to Feather, when the wind suddenly WHIPPED into a FRENZY, the atmosphere crackling with unseen energy. A blinding ELECTRICAL FIREBALL ripped through the heavens, SLAMMING into the ground nearby with a deafening CRASH. The earth shuddered violently. Ambers, glowing like malevolent fireflies, scattered in all directions. Jacob was thrown to the ground by the force of the blast, his bow ripped from his grasp.

He rolled amidst the chaos, finally coming to a still, disoriented stop. Raising his head, he stared dully at the impact site, a lingering, intermittent crackle of electricity dancing in the air. Thick, acrid smoke billowed, obscuring his vision. Feather, sensing the sudden surge of negative energy, whinnied frantically, straining against her restraints.

Jacob staggered to his feet, pushing through the choking smoke towards ground zero. As he approached the impact crater, an unnatural stillness settled over the area, broken only by the hiss of dissipating energy. Something moved within the swirling white gas, a subtle shift that sent a fresh wave of unease through Jacob. He instinctively readied his bow, his knuckles white against the worn wood.

"Who is there?" he called out, his voice trembling slightly.

Feather continued her desperate struggle. Jacob's eyes darted nervously, trying to pierce the veil of smoke. He stopped a few feet from the edge, his breath catching in his throat. Suddenly, a band of grotesque figures materialized from the swirling white, their forms coalescing into nightmarish shapes. Demons. Grigori. They advanced, an arsenal of wicked-looking weapons glinting in the residual light. Jacob felt a palpable wave of negative energy radiating from them.

Then, a larger, more imposing creature emerged, its shadow stretching long and menacing in the smoky haze. This was their leader, Regulus. Jacob recoiled, his mind struggling to comprehend the impossible. He stood face to face with the embodiment of evil. The demons' eyes, burning with a mixture of contempt and hunger, fixed on him.

They moved with unnerving coordination, forming a menacing attack formation. Every instinct screamed at Jacob to run. He didn't hesitate. He broke into a desperate sprint across the open plain, some of the demons pursuing him on foot, others taking to the air on leathery wings. Jacob risked a glance back, weaving erratically through the tall grass.

Finally, with a desperate lunge, Feather snapped free from her restraints and charged forward, her hooves pounding the earth in a frantic gallop towards her handler. Ahead, Jacob spotted a dark opening in an unusual rock formation – a cave. He veered towards it, a desperate gamble. He stumbled upon a desolate salt plain, stopping at the mouth of the gaping maw. An icy dread washed over him. He knew, with chilling certainty, that entering that darkness meant instant death. This couldn't have happened at a worse time.

The already gloomy landscape seemed to darken further as the demons closed in, their shadows engulfing him. He was trapped, left with only one terrifying alternative: fight. The advancing horde enveloped him. One of the demons, its face, a grotesque mask of malice, stepped forward.

"Boy… you hast truly stumbled into the wrong corner of existence."

Jacob, adrenaline surging through his veins, sized up the creature and slammed his fist into its flat, reptilian nose. The demon crumpled. A flurry of brutal punches followed, a chaotic melee erupting around him. Jacob lashed out with a kick, sending another demon sprawling. He cartwheeled, his foot connecting with the jaw of a third. It went down with a guttural groan.

A powerful arm snaked around his neck, locking him in a chokehold. But Jacob, fueled by desperation, flipped the demon over his shoulder, delivering a vicious kick in mid-air. The monster landed hard, curling into a whimpering ball. The brief encounter with the godly artifacts had somehow amplified his human abilities, granting him a strength and speed he'd never possessed.

Another demon grabbed him from behind in a crushing bear hug. Jacob snapped his head back, slamming it into the creature's face, then flicked his elbow back, striking its throat with brutal force. A roundhouse kick sent the monster sprawling. Two crazed eyes, belonging to Regulus, watched the skirmish with cold amusement.

Two more demons attacked with savage intensity, but Jacob parried their blows with surprising ease, holding his ground. Suddenly, a blinding light exploded nearby, forcing Jacob to shield his eyes in distress. When he could see again, the demons had formed a tight circle around him, their brutal assault beginning anew. All he could hear was the frantic flapping of wings. Jacob is at the mercy of unimaginable evil, pounded relentlessly, his life hanging by a thread.

"Enough!" Regulus's voice boomed, cutting through the brutal sounds of the beating.

The assault ceased. The demons backed away, creating a narrow opening. Regulus stalked past them, his gaze fixed on the battered figure on the ground. Jacob looked up at the fallen star, his eyes filled with desperate defiance. Regulus bent down, his clawed hand clamping around Jacob's throat, hoisting him into the air. In the distance, Feather galloped across the grassy plains, a desperate streak of brown against the darkening landscape.

Jacob is thrown to the ground with bone-jarring force. He struggled to rise, his limbs heavy and unresponsive. Regulus loomed over him, his expression devoid of any pity. Jacob managed to prop himself up on his knees, his hands clasped in a desperate plea. He looked towards the heavens, his voice a ragged whisper.

"To the God of my father Abraham; let not the buzzards or the wild dogs feast upon my flesh. Deliver me from this evil."

Regulus and the other demons heard Jacob's desperate prayer.

"Why do you pathetic humans cling to a false god?" Regulus sneered. "A god who regretted creating you? The only true power, the only one who truly cares, is my Lord Satan! He is the one true god!"

Moments after Regulus's blasphemous declaration, lightning forked across the sky, the clouds above beginning to churn in a furious, clockwise spiral. The demons stared upwards, dumbfounded. They watched the glowing clouds intensified, swirling with unnatural energy. Suddenly, a beam of pure light shot down from the heavens, eclipsing Jacob.

"Move the whelp!" Regulus roared, urgency lacing his voice. But it was too late. The demons were SHOCKED BACKWARDS, flung hundreds of feet by an unseen force. A few seconds later, the heavens seemed to tear open, and Jacob beheld a spectral figure, its form radiating a gentle, yet immense power. Its voice resonated like the roar of many waters.

"Son of Adam," the voice boomed, "the Lord has heard your cry. Your plea has risen before Him, and your petition is granted. Look out across this terrain and tell me what you see."

Jacob lowered his head, his gaze sweeping across the desolate landscape. He saw what he hadn't noticed before: a vast expanse of dry bones, lying dormant beneath the surface of the valley.

"Son of man," the Lord's voice echoed, "can these bones live?"

"Only by your will and power, Lord," Jacob answered, a newfound faith blossoming in his heart. "For I know that you live."

"Well said, son of man. Now prophesy to these bones and say to them: 'O ye dry bones, hear the word of the LORD. Thus, saith the Lord GOD unto these bones; Behold, I will cause breath to enter into you, and ye shall live: And I will lay sinews upon you, and will bring up flesh upon you, and cover you with skin, and put breath in you, and ye shall live."

The Grigori, their faces etched with disbelief, exchanged nervous glances as the light of the Lord seemed to infuse Jacob with strength. He rose to his feet, a renewed energy coursing through him. The demons tried to advance, but the radiant light held them at bay. Jacob spoke the words of the Lord, prophesying to the dry bones as he was commanded.

Suddenly, a sound like the tearing of fabric ripped across the valley, and the earth began to tremble as hundreds of skeletal hands broke through the parched soil. Huge chunks of rock were displaced, crashing to the ground. Jacob watched in awe as more bones emerged, clicking and snapping together, bone to bone. He continued to watch as sinews and flesh knit themselves upon the skeletal frames, and finally, layers of skin covered the newly formed bodies.

The Grigori backed away, their eyes wide with terror, the burning glare from the vortex intensifying. The risen army lay motionless on the ground, devoid of breath. On the other side of the valley, Feather continued her frantic gallop. Back to Jacob – again, the word of the Lord came to him.

"Son of man… Now prophesy unto the wind and say to the wind: 'Thus saith the Lord GOD; Come from the four winds, O breath, and breathe upon these that are slain, that they may live.'"

And again, Jacob obeyed. He began to prophesy to the four winds of the earth. Immediately, the winds answered his call, whipping around him, disturbing his hair. His eyes shone with exultation as he fulfilled the Lord's command. The distant cries of the Grigori echoed across the valley.

The swirling winds engulfed the empty shells. Jacob watched as breath entered them, and they lived, rising to their feet – an exceeding great army, armed with weapons that seemed to shimmer with divine light. The barrier that had held the Grigori back vanished. Regulus, his eyes blazing with defiance, roared a command, leading his demonic forces into battle with reckless abandon. The two armies collided head-on, a chaotic maelstrom of steel and shadow.

But Jacob ran in the opposite direction, his instincts screaming for self-preservation. A demon spotted him and gave chase, cutting off his path. It lunged, but Jacob spun out of its grasp with surprising agility. The demon recovered quickly, landing several brutal blows. Jacob fell hard, rolling across the uneven ground, his face now smeared with blood. He fought back with every ounce of his being, but the demon's power was overwhelming.

Another demon swooped down, talons grasping Jacob's arm, and lifted him fifteen feet into the air before dropping him like a stone. The demon on the ground glared at Jacob as he hit the earth with a sickening thud. Grimacing in pain, he braced himself for the killing blow. But before the demon could strike, a fist smashed into its face, sending it reeling. One of the risen soldiers, wielding a sword-like weapon, continued his assault with a series of rapid jabs.

Other soldiers fought with sword and shield, the clang of metal echoing across the battlefield. Not far from the center of the brutal melee, Jacob found himself locked in a desperate struggle with two armed demons. Slowly, the ranks of the risen army were being thinned by the relentless Grigori.

Regulus stood apart, a chilling smile playing on his lips as he observed the tide of battle turning in his favor. A demon charged towards Jacob, sword raised, but at the last second, Jacob parried the blow, tripping the creature, sending it crashing into the other demon approaching from behind. Both demons recovered quickly and advanced again. But then, a third demon struck Jacob from behind, sending him crashing to his knees, a look of pensive confusion on his bloodied face. He didn't realize that he was the source of the army's strength.

Sweat dripped from his brow. His eyes unfocused, staring into the distance. But in the foreground, a golden light, moving with incredible speed, was rapidly approaching. All three demons noticed it, exchanging bewildered glances. One of them broke away, flying towards Regulus to report the approaching anomaly. The other two turned their attention back to Jacob. The first demon stepped forward, lowering its sword towards the young man's neck.

Regulus received the frantic report about the rapidly approaching golden light. He leaped down from his vantage point, pushing through the chaotic battle to get a better view. His eyes widened in disbelief as he saw the gleaming horse, its form radiating power, galloping across the ravaged terrain. Regulus dispatched several demons to intercept the advancing steed. They met the charging horse head-on, their swords flashing, but the thunder of its hooves continued unabated.

Jacob's eyelids fluttered, his vision blurring as the remaining demons continued their brutal assault. Only a short distance now separated him from his valiant horse. The risen army's numbers had dwindled drastically. Suddenly, a piercing neigh rent the air. The horse, carrying the mysterious artifacts, mowed down demon after demon, its single-minded determination focused on reaching its handler. Summoning every last ounce of strength,

Chapter 38

Canonization of a man . . .

The sky is a vast, blemished blue, showing off its wear as a flamboyant sun, preparing to make its daily exit, casting its golden light across the valley. Jacob is determined to trudge through the heat, looking less like a conquering hero and more like a particularly sweaty raisin. Three hours later, he reappeared at the village outskirts, dragging a rather impressive buck that looked like it had lost a very one-sided argument.

The village elders, a collection of weathered faces usually reserved for judging poorly cooked yams, actually gaped. Even the perpetually unimpressed village dogs seemed to offer respectful sniff. Jacob's dad is proud, slightly teary eyes,

"My son!" he boomed, chest puffed out like a prize pigeon. "You wouldn't believe the sheer volume of pride currently residing in my bosom! Just three sunrises ago, you were tripping over your own feet chasing chickens. Now? Now you return a man! The gods, clearly, have a soft spot for a good hunter, unlike some of those lily-livered lads who came back whining about grumpy mountain lions and the gods not 'showing them favor.'

Honestly, the drama! Anyway, tonight, at the festival, prepare to be officially inducted into the Council of Manhood! And as a symbol, you'll receive this spear – passed down from my father, who once used it to… well, never mind the details. It's a man's spear!"

Jacob is genuinely touched by this grand gesture (and slightly overwhelmed by the sheer masculinity of the moment), embracing his dad with a good solid hug. The village gossip with a penchant for dramatic waving. Jacob is slightly embarrassed but nod in return. They finally reached their hut. His mother, a whirlwind of efficiency amidst the other women prepping for the feast, paused her stirring of fermented berries to engulf him in a hug. She resisted the urge to check for scrapes and bruises, reminding herself that he is, apparently, a man now, not a particularly accident-prone toddler.

"Are you hungry, my… uh… manly hunter?" she asked, a teasing glint in her eye.

Caught up in the general air of 'Jacob is a Legend,' he declared he is not. The sounds of the approaching festivities – whooping warriors, rhythmic drumming, someone attempting a rather off-key flute solo – grew louder. The newly-minted man is, however, utterly knackered. He had precisely enough time for a quick nap before his big spear-receiving moment.

Jacob carefully placed the trusty bow and arrows under a wobbly wooden table his dad had proudly crafted (mostly straight, mostly). He collapsed onto his sleeping mat, and within minutes, the sounds of the village faded into the background as sleep claimed him.

His dream is… active. He is running through a field of tall grass, his bow bouncing against his back, his imaginary prey just out of reach. He ran like a caffeinated gazelle until the ground abruptly ended in front of him. A chasm. A vast, empty, nothingness, peering into the void.

"Well, this is awkward," he muttered. Then, puffing out his chest, he yelled, "Should I take the next step, or chicken out? What mysterious wonders – or possibly terrifying monsters – lie beyond? Fear not! For I am Jacob! Great Hunter! Slightly sweaty, but still great!"

Without hesitation, he stepped forward and surprisingly, his foot landed on… something solid. Pitch black, mind you. Couldn't see a thing. But stepped on something solid. So, being the brave warrior he now is, he ventured into the unknown. He glanced back. Feather, his loyal horse, stands at the edge, shaking her head with a definitive "Nope." She then lay down, looking remarkably comfortable with her decision to wait.

"Come on, Feather, you big scaredy-cat!" he coaxed, but Feather remained firmly horizontal. Jacob sighed and continued his solo journey into the darkness. He tried to locate the chasm's edge again, but it was like trying to find a single black sock in a closet full of them. He kept walking. Deeper and deeper. Darker and darker.

Suddenly, tiny specks of light flickered ahead. Like distant fireflies… or maybe the eyes of something that enjoyed midnight snacks of slightly dim-witted hunters. Shortly after, a voice echoed through the darkness.

"Jacob! Jacob!" it called, sounding vaguely like his Auntie Shara when she'd misplaced her prize-winning zucchini.

A shadow, impossibly large, momentarily blotted out the faint lights. Jacob stopped, rubbing his eyes. Those little lights were definitely flickering. Then, two distinct, sparkling eyes reflected his own image. They belonged to… something. Jacob's internal 'Danger! Danger!' klaxon started blaring. He is nervous. Rightfully so. He squeezed his eyes shut.

"JACOB! Open your eyes!"

He jolted awake to the familiar, slightly worried face of his father kneeling beside him.

"Wah… wah… what in the name of grumpy mountain lions just happened?" Jacob mumbled, still half-lost in his dream.

"Come, son! It is time for your rite of passage! The elders are practically overjoyed with anticipation to bestow upon you the rights and privileges of… well, a man! And that spear!" his father added with a proud nudge.

"Okay, Father! Coming!" Jacob mumbled, still feeling a bit like he'd wrestled a giant squid in his sleep.

His father hurried off to inform the eager elders that the man-to-be would be gracing them with his presence shortly. Jacob started to get ready, which mostly involved untangling himself from his sleeping mat. His father's head popped back into the hut, looking slightly frantic. "Hurry, son! We need to paint your face with the sacred mud! It's not going to paint itself, you know!"

As Jacob finally stood up, he noticed a faint, otherworldly glow emanating from under the table where he'd unceremoniously placed the bow. He cautiously approached it. The light held him captive like a moth to a bright flame. He carefully lifted the bow. The light vanished.

"Hmm. Pretty sure I just saw this thing channeling the sun," he muttered to himself.

He ran his hands over the smooth wood, then pulled out an arrow, doing the same. Nothing. He squinted at the bow, examining it with the intensity of a scholar deciphering ancient goat entrails. Nothing unusual. But as he placed it back under the table, the emblem carved into the bow's handle flared to life, shining like a miniature supernova.

"Whoa! Okay, not normal!"

He clapped his hands over the light, but luminous streams escaped through his fingers. Panicked, he grabbed a nearby blanket and tried to smother the glow. As his hand gripped the emblem, the bow began to rotate counterclockwise with a soft click, and a shimmering, swirling doorway appeared in the wall.

He vaguely remembered hearing a voice – Abram's voice? – yelling something about baby lambs and lions, but that felt like a lifetime ago. Jacob looked around the hut. Empty. He cautiously peered into the swirling portal. As he turned to call for his father, he bumped into something invisible, a solid barrier.

"What in the enchanted yam is this sorcery? I can't... go back?" he exclaimed, feeling a sudden surge of panic.

He tried to yell for his father and the increasingly impatient elders, but the vortex seemed to swallow his cries, while simultaneously tugging him towards its luminous depths. He dug his heels in, resisting with surprising strength. Suddenly, a voice, clear and commanding, echoed from within the swirling light.

"Walk!" it urged.

Jacob finally realized he was having one of those moments. The kind where arguing with a disembodied voice from a glowing doorway probably wasn't the best course of action. With a deep breath and a healthy dose of trepidation, he stepped across the threshold. His body instantly felt… different. Lighter. Like he'd traded his earthly form for a particularly sparkly cloud. He was whisked away. The portal snapped shut just as his father, face painted with enthusiastic swirls of sacred mud, peered into the hut.

"Jacob? You almost ready, my magnificent man-hunter-about-to-be-speared…?" His voice trailed off as he stared at the empty space where the wall had been moments before. "Uh oh."

Chapter 39

Just be there . . .

A small rabbit cross the trail and stops suddenly among the pleasant sound of the forest. There is no wind stirring the trees and a short time later, it hears something and scurried off into the bush. David walks down the trail trying to find the exact spot where he'd hid the sword.

"Yo, this gotta be it, man... where the hell did that bush just pop up from?" he thought.

David remembered that he'd only taken small pieces of brush, and now the pieces had become this whole bush. He walked in front of it and began to move the branches out of his way. The sword's handle had an iridescent glow around it.

"Yo, wait... how'd I miss that?!" he thought.

Then he realized that the shade from the bushes made the glow more apparent.

"This thing is very special. I have to take it back with me somehow."

Once again, he concealed the sword's handle. Not wanting to be late, he headed back to camp. He too is mesmerized by the sight of the grown bush and the changed appearance of the sword, David could hardly contain his thoughts.

"Yo, hold up! How the hell did that bush get so darn big overnight? And peep this — why the freak is the handle glowing like that? What kinda straight-up voodoo is this, man? Where did this thing even come from? And get this — it is jammed in the side of the canyon wall, looked like it weighed a whole damn truck, but now? Light as a damn feather! What the actual...?"

He has a million questions but with no answers to them. The baffling thoughts played over and over in his mind.

"What were those images, and what did they mean?" he thought.

When he arrived back at the campsite, there is a ranger there, along with a few other camp members.

"Gather around, everyone," said the ranger.

The crowd moved in closer so they could better hear the man speaking. He instructed them about safety precautions and supplies to bring on the hiking trip.

"Make sure you take extra clothing in case you get wet. Bring along non-perishable items. Take plenty of water, a compass, a lighter, and all the essentials. Make sure you have a buddy with you at all times. It's better to be two lost then one lost." said the ranger.

"You gotta be kiddin' me! There goes that lost thing, again!" thought David, as he laughed.

As the ranger finished up with his lecture on the dos and don'ts of hiking, all David could think about is his discovery. He wanted to tell his dad about it. But just when he is about to, he felt the urge not to say a thing. So, he kept quiet.

Chapter 40

Desert Dreams and Discontent. . .

It's hot and sunny when Abram walked the perimeter of the camp and looks ahead out at the plains. He made sure that all the surrounding territory is safe. His mind drifted back and forth over the events that had taken place a few days before. He shook his head and continued walking. The rays from the sun beat down on his head.

According to the position of the sun, it is high noon. Abram headed back to camp to refill his skin with water. On this day, the desert is hotter than usual. He looked out over the terrain, and he could see heat waves rising into the air.

During this time of the day, most people were in their tents, trying to avoid the extreme heat. Abram approached the tent where his father and brothers are waiting to begin the afternoon meal. He sat down to join in the conversation with his family while his mother prepared the food.

"Father,"

"Yes, my son," he replied.

"Are you ready for the fold to increase? We have the best live-stock of all the flocks in the region."

"Hmmm, yes, that is a good question. It is always better to have far more than far less," said his father.

"You will need more servants to keep up with all that you have."

"I've thought about it. It's good that you are aware of the herd numbers."

Abram nodded in agreement as his mother set a plate of food before him.

"We will do well, my son."

He finished his meal, got up from the eating area, and went into the field to play with his pendant. He tried to re-create the events that had taken place with the lions in that very real waking dream. Just outside of the village, he pretended that he were just a few feet's away from the lions. He screamed with a loud voice,

"NOOOOOO!"

He tried to re-create the moment when time had briefly stood still. He looked around, only to see that time had not stopped. He tried it again and again, with the same results. Frustrated, he took the pendant from around his neck and held it in the palm of his hand. He looked at it, pleading with it to cooperate.

"Come on! I know you have some secret powers inside you, or why would I keep having waking dreams about what you can do?" he questioned the pendant.

Suddenly, a bright light flashed from the pendant's emblem. This caught Abram by surprise and the pendant falls to the ground. He paused for a moment, took a deep breath, and reached down and picked up the pendant carefully. Methodically, he gazed around the center where the streaming light came from.

With both hands, he tried to turn the emblem on the pendant, one way and then the other attempting to twist it off. Several minutes would pass before he realized that his struggle is for naught. Exasperated, he tried to turn the emblem again. Once again, nothing happened. With all his might, he screamed at the top of his voice, and finally, the center of the pendant turned in one smooth movement.

His eyes widen and his mouth opens in a silent scream. There's an audible gasp as he watched a doorway opens. Abram slumps to his knees when he hears Joshua's voice say,

"No, Rex. Don't touch it."

Abram's heart began to beat faster and faster. He knew that someone is in trouble,

"Hello!" he says into the portal.

"Are you all, right?"

Little did he know that no one could hear him? Abram looked around to see if someone is playing tricks on him. Thinking that his brothers are behind this, he called out to them, but they did not answer. Silence gripped his surroundings as he sat staring into the vortex. Then, from within it, a voice said once again,

"No, Rex!"

Suddenly, the portal sucks him in, and he is immediately trans-figured. The hole quickly closed up, leaving no evidence that it has ever been there.

Baaladyme, sitting on top of Ol' Smokey, was contemplating where to search for the sword.

"Ba'laamus is going to have my head if I don't find that stupid sword."

The sulfur-laden Baaladyme sulked, thinking about his predic-ament. Ba'laamus materialized, standing at the top of the mountain.

"Smelling of sulfur won't spare you from my wrath if you don't find that sword and bring it back to me! Sitting on a mountain is not searching for the sword, you idiot." said Ba'laamus.

Without looking at Baaladyme, he kicked him off the mountain.

"You fool!"

Reaching the bottom of the mountain, Baaladyme looked up and saw Ba'laamus standing on his warm smelly place at the top of the mountain.

"Why did you do that?" Baaladyme said indignantly.

"Because I gave you a task to complete and what do I find? I find you taking a steam bath. If I'm going to take over the Celestial Kingdom, I need those weapons."

An angry Baaladyme flew back up to the top of the mountain. "You do know what this means, don't you?" said Baaladyme, as he took a seat at the mountain's edge.

"Umm, it means, fool, that my conquest is being delayed," said Ba'laamus.

More furious, Ba'laamus turned and kicked Baaladyme off the mountain again.

"I'm surrounded by incompetence!"

Chapter 41

The Price of Curiosity. . .

The King family gathered around testing out their photograph skills,

"Kalisha! David! Come on! Get in the shot," Makayla urged.

Kalisha ran over and strikes a quirky pose, while David took his time. The group had been walking on the trail back to the campsite when they decided to break for lunch in a clearing.

While walking in the woods, David has been looking up at the trees around him.

"How odd?" he thought… He continues his self-talk. *"Yeah, seen 'em. Whole lotta birds up there today, huh?"*

He is a little hungry and thought that it would be a great time to eat. He wanted to lie on his back so that he could watch the clouds roll by. No one else in the group noticed the birds all around them in the trees.

They are perched on high branches and not making a sound. It's as if they are being quiet intentionally. That struck a nerve in David. He shut off his CD player and walked alone, paying close attention to his eerie surroundings. No one seemed to care that the birds has all gathered around them. As they reached the clearing, he finds a little place to himself and pulled out a sandwich from his backpack to eat. Still, he couldn't shake the feeling that something is amiss here.

The hiking group is seriously engaged in eating and talking about the hiking trip. David took the opportunity to sneak off into the woods opposite the group. He did not venture far off; he could still see the group while he checked out the area. He walks through the trees until he comes up on the stump of a large tree. He goes and sits on it. A few seconds after, a bird perched on a branch in front of him, just staring at him. Suddenly, another feathered winged creature joins the first.

"Aight, this is startin' to feel a little...off, you know?" he thought.

He starts eating, drinking, and continues to talk among himself. All of a sudden, leaves uncontrollable descents as if the fall has come early. David looks around in wonder and looks up. His eyes bulge with surprise from the sight of seeing birds of all shapes, sizes, and colors appeared in front of him. He glances over to his right and sees more birds.

He turns to his left and surely, there are more birds facing him. He is now frightened at the prospect of being attacked by all of these birds. He cuts his eyes over to an opening between the trees and sees that the group of hikers is still gathered around. With in seconds, more birds showed up, blocking his view of the group.

Kalisha also got a weird feeling, and she begins looking around, searching for her missing brother,

"Where did he go?" she mumbled under her breath.

She made sure no one sees her as she makes her way over some dense trees.

"David are you in there?" she asked.

The birds at the entrance turned as though they are going to attack but took off as she entered the woods. She finds her brother sitting on the tree stump with a few colorful birds maintaining their position behind him. She watched closely, just for a second, and then, with a loud *BOO*! She startle the winged creatures, and they scattered about. David looked over at her,

"Aight, legs, wake up! We gotta go!" he said very calmly, almost catatonic.

She didn't say anything about the birds perched behind him. He unfolded his legs and stand for a few minutes to get some circulations going. Kalisha walks over to help him.

"I got this weird feeling, so I came to look for you," she said quietly. All he could say is thank you.

"Come on kids!" Makayla beckoned her children.

As they emerged from the forest, the group has already begun to move back onto the trail that leads back to the camp. Now, with his legs fully working, David held his sister's hand, and they walked along the path. Neither of them said a word, but both looks up into the trees, for they'd noticed the large number of birds perched high above them for as far as they could see.

They looked at one another; Kalisha squeezed her big brother's hand, letting him know that she is anxious. But he looked at little sister assuring her that he is here for her. She nodded yes in recognition of his look. No one else seemed to notice the strange appearance of all the birds, not even their parents.

It's now sunset and they has been back at the camp for about two hours. Neither Kalisha nor David still hasn't said a word too each other about what transpired in the forest. David Sr. has already grilled a few steaks, some corn, and potatoes, a few grilled veggies. As the aroma of searing steaks filled the area, some nearby campers made their way over to where he is throwing on some of his famous seasonings. A pop belly 55-year-old man commented. Kenneth Wiliby, a wide, almost eager smile on his face, approached David Sr.

"Hi there!" he chirped, voice a touch too loud.

David Sr., a little surprised by the sudden approach, offered a polite nod. "Hello."

Kenneth stepped closer, extending a hand with a slightly too-firm grip. "I'm your neighbor! Just moved in. My name is Kenneth. Kenneth Wiliby," he emphasized his last name with a flourish, "but my friends call me Ken."

David Sr. shook his hand, a flicker of something unreadable in his eyes. "Hi, I'm David King I."

Kenneth's smile widened even further, if that was possible. "Hey! That's a good name... David Sr.?" He tilted his head, a hint of playful disbelief in his tone.

Suddenly, Kenneth's attention is completely diverted. He inhaled deeply, his eyes practically rolling back in his head. "Good Mr. King. Mmmmhmmm... Smells delectable..." He turned his gaze towards something behind David Sr.

"What kind of seasoning are you using?" His voice is now thick with almost childlike curiosity.

David Sr., with a *you think I'm going share that with you* smile, replied,

"A little of this and a little of that, a pinch of some other stuff . . . hahahaha . . ."

"Oh, I see." Wiliby's voice is low, a hint of weary frustration lacing his tone. He pushed off the wall, the movement deliberate. "Not giving up the goods, huh? What would that be?" Mr. Wiliby asked with an, I already know that answer look.

"You could never leave the park!" Mr. Wiliby declared a triumphant grin spreading across his face. Mr. Wiliby's eyes widened in mock horror. "Oh, I'm going to have to kill your ingredients!" he exclaimed, a playful threat laced in her voice.

"Mmmmhmmm, that's right," David Sr. confirmed, a chuckle bubbling up from his chest.

They both burst into laughter, the sound echoing through the late afternoon air. Across the small divide of the garden, Mr. Wiliby, their neighbor, shrugged, a sheepish smile on his face. "Well, you can't fault a man for trying," he offered, a hint of resignation in his tone.

Makayla, still smiling, softened her gaze. "Alright, alright," she conceded. "I'll give you a steak to try out. Maybe that'll make the pain of your failed harvest a little easier to bear."

Mr. Wiliby's eyes lit up. "Ah, now you're talking!" he said, a genuine warmth returning to his voice. "I always say... never turn down a nice piece of steak!"

Mr. Wiliby sat down and began to chat with Makayla. By now David has decided that he will wait until everyone has fallen asleep to go and retrieve the weapon and bring it back. With dinner done and everything cleaned and put away, Kalisha sat next to her mother on the bench at the table.

She lies down and put her head on her mom's lap. Makayla gently plays with Kalisha's hair and lulled her to sleep. David yawns himself and informed them that he wanted to sleep under the night stars, and his parents didn't object. Everyone got up from the table and goes to their respective places. David Sr. picked up his sleeping princess and placed her in her bed,

"Ugh! She's heavy!" he grunted, his breath catching slightly as he adjusted the weight in his arms. A bead of sweat trickled down his temple.

"Not a little baby anymore, honey," she said softly, a fond smile playing on her lips as she watched him struggle, a hint of nostalgia in her voice.

He shifted his grip, a genuine laugh escaping him, despite the strain. "No kidding! Feels like I'm carrying a sack of potatoes!"

He chuckled, the sound a mix of playful exaggeration and genuine surprise at how much their child had grown. Now the couple have got to spend some time alone. They snuggled up under a large blanket.

"Good thing we brought the pop-up tent. David had great idea . . . let's sleep outside tonight." Makayla giggled and agreed with her romantic hubby.

Grabbing his own sleeping bag from inside the RV, David got ready to settle down, or so he made it seem. He lay down on the ground not far from the warm fire pit. Both of the heavenly bodies, the stars and moon, shine their light down upon the RV Park. Both parent's said good nights to him, but his mother kissed him on the head.

"I love you son," she said, as she headed off into the tent.

Groggily, David tells his mom that he loved her too and drifted off to sleep, but a loud snort from the park woke him up. Tired from the day's hike, David found it hard to go back to sleep. He is comfortable from the softness of his own sleeping bag and the warmth of the fire, still burning nicely since his dad had placed a nice size log in the fire pit before going off to bed.

"Get up," he heard a voice say.

"GET UP!"

Wearily and quietly, he arose, making sure that everyone else is asleep. He makes his way back to the place in the canyon where the sword is stashed. The night is slightly chilly, and the moon lit up the area. He looked for the bush that sprung up the night before. A short time later he finds it. He moves away the branches from around the sword's glowing handle, shining in the light of the moon.

Watching from secret places are the birds. The same birds that came to him in the forest watched as he removed the sword from its resting place. As he brought the sword toward him, flames ignited, and just as quickly are extinguished. The sword sent out a small surge of energy, which shocked him, causing him to drop it.

"Ouch!"

The birds began to fly around in large circles overhead. There are so many that the sky became dark and gloomy looking. He reached to pick the sword up. Like an iron in a furnace, it began to glow, and it became red hot, with an unbearable heat to go along with it. As the sword got hotter and hotter, he dropped it to the ground. The fire shot straight up into the sky. As he looked on, the flame moved to and fro, like a laser light show. Immediately, all the birds in the vicinity scattered abroad.

David moved back away from the weapon and watched it very closely. Now it was spinning rapidly. Hearing the sound of thunder, He looked up into the heavens, and he sees that the flames has changed and are now returning in the form of light. He wanted to pick the sword up to move it out of harm's way, because now it had stopped moving. He grasped the handle of the sword and tried to lift it up. The weight of the sword had become too heavy for him. As the light returned, he grasped the sword's handle with both hands and tried to lift it up again.

Like a magnet drawn to steel, the sword is stuck to the ground, and as David tugged on it, the returning light struck the sword, hitting it directly on the emblem. The force of energy sent David hurling through the air, knocking him several feet away. Moaning, he sat up. He thought that the sword has been shattered into millions of pieces. He gets up and goes to see if it's still intact. It is, but he's afraid to pick it up because sparks are shooting from the emblem.

Thinking that the sword is hot, he took off his shirt, wrapped it around his hand, and grabbed it. With all his might, he tried to lift the sword. He braced himself by digging his feet into the ground, and with a huge tug, up went the sword, sending David hurling backwards. He looked up and sees the sword twirling end over end, suspended for a moment he watched the spinning weapon fall uncontrollably to the ground again. He covered his eyes, expecting the worst. The sword landed between his legs with the handle pointing upward. He exhales.

"Whoa, darn! That was way too darn close," he thought.

He scooted backwards and stand up; he removed the shirt, from around his hand, and plucked the sword out of the ground. Looking at the emblem, he sees light escaping along its outer ridges. He searched for something to try to pry it open. He patted his body, feeling for an object, but found nothing on him that is flat enough. He sat down on the ground and laid the sword across his lap trying to turn the emblem.

It is tightly in place. After a moment of rest, he tried again. It seemed hopeless. Perturbed, he tossed the sword aside, where it struck a huge rock lodged in the ground next to him. The blow loosened the emblem causing it to turn ever so slightly. Then it makes a full turn automatically.

He watched as a vortex opens and jumps back astounded, not knowing what to expect. His breathing is rapid now. Suddenly, he hears voices coming from within.

"No, Rex!" said one of the voices.

"I'M SORRY! NO SPELL, NO TELL! I PROMISE!" said the next voice that he heard.

He called out to the voices inside. But there is no reply. He comes in a little closer to the open space to investigate. He hears the same voices again coming from within the portal,

"No, Rex!"

"I'M SORRY! NO SPELL! NO TELL! I PROMISE!"

"Hello! Hello! Who's in there?" but again he got no reply.

"Why can't they hear me?" he thought.

He yelled into the hole, the voices sounded as if they are nearby.

"Hey! Can you hear me?"

Still there was no response. Suddenly, he hears a different voice this time,

"God of my Father, hear me! Save me from death!"

The sudden plea for help sent David in a tail spin. He yells into the vortex.

"HELLO! SAVE YOU FROM WHAT!" he yelled.

He wondered if anyone hears all the commotion and would come to investigate, but he is alone. As he places his foot across the threshold, a surreal light surrounds him transfiguring him. With a *whoosh*,

"WHOOOOOOOOOA!"

An invisible force pulls him inside the portal and closes behind him. This is the last thing that he hears in the natural world. Within seconds of each other, all four boys are whisked away from the natural world. At the speed of light, they moved through the expanse between the Earth and the heavens. They find themselves surrounded by stars; they each felt a deep sense of awe at the magnitude of space.

There in the distance, with a zillion stars, they could see the longest structure known to mankind. It sparkled like a gem with shimmers of red, gold, green, purple, and indigo blue, so beautiful to behold. Each boy babbled under breath as they approached the end of their separate journeys which seem to take more than a few moments.

In the distance, each one could see a dark and desolate place hovering in the vast depths of space. Suddenly, the portals opened, the boys arrived at the gati one after another. First came Jacob; followed by Abram.

Not far behind him is Joshua, and finally David arrived. They are completely unaware that they have been transported to the spiritual realm. Time is different in the heavenlies. They take an ominous look at one another. Each of them assumed a defensive stance, but not one of them moved toward the other. All of the weapons sent out an electrical discharge shocking each.

"OUCH!" they said dropping their weapon at the same time.

They tried to pick them up again, and again they are shocked. All of their eyes widen in disbelief. Abram glances up at them, without expression. Suddenly, they pause and are filled with sudden peace. They goes to reclaim their weapons, but they hesitates a moment before picking them up once again. Suddenly, a pair of unnatural grim looking eyes is watching them.

Finally, David picks up his sword from the ground, and this time, nothing happened. The other followed suit and nothing happened to them as well. They shifted amongst themselves, a silent dance of new acquaintances. Jacob, extending a hand with a nervous but genuine smile, approached the others.

"Hi," he offered, his voice a touch hesitant but friendly. "My name is Jacob."

A child with kind eyes met his gaze, clasping his hand firmly. "I am Abram," he said, his voice calm and steady.

Another child, younger and with bright enthusiasm in his eyes, shakes Jacob's hand with a warm squeeze. "G'day, the name's Joshua." he announced, a hint of excitement in his tone.

Finally, a teenager with a thoughtful expression and a gentle demeanor offered his hand. "Yo, check it, name's David, ya dig?" he said softly, a quiet sincerity in his voice.

David thought it would be clever to give his newfound friends nicknames.

"What's shakin', Josh?" asked David.

Confused by the question, he said, "My knees . . ."

"What are you wearing, Abe? Jake, you smell like a horse!"

Abram corrected him, "Abe is not my name. My name is Abram."

"No offense. I just thought that Abe sounded cool." responded David… "Cool? Like what . . . the day?"

Abram didn't understand the term. "How do you not understand cool?" David asked looking at him, puzzled. Abram shrugged his shoulders and looked at him,

"Yo, my name is David, but uh, my peoples callin' me Dave, ya know?" He shifted his weight, a nervous energy in his eyes. "Looks like we're gonna be kickin' it for a minute, right? So, I mean... might as well be cool, yeah? Like, friends and all that?" He offered a hesitant half-smile, a hopeful vulnerability peeking through his casual demeanor.

Abram and Joshua agreed. Then they looked over at Jacob.

"What? Jacob is my name."

"Right, Jakey boy, listen up. No need to get your knickers in a twist. Just take it easy, yeah? Go with the flow," said Josh, nudging him.

Giving in, he laughed and agreed.

"Yo, Abe! What is that you got on? Seriously though," he leaned in, eyes wide, "that outfit look straight outta some history book, for real!" said Dave.

"Is there something wrong with it?" Abe asked defensively. "Because this is what I usually wear."

"Blimey, what in the ruddy 'eck have you got on?" he exclaim, eyes wide with a mixture of amusement and disbelief. "You look like you've just popped straight out of a bleedin' history book, you do!" A slightly incredulous and teasing tone, said Josh.

Dave threw his head back, a real belly laugh shaking his shoulders. "Yeah, and so do you!" he managed between chuckles, his eyes crinkling at the corners. "Man, you look like you stepped straight outta my Grammie's stories! Like, way back when." He punctuated the last part with a playful nudge.

"Oi, Jake!" Josh exclaimed, his voice laced with a mixture of concern and disbelief. "What have ya been up to, mate? You're covered head to toe!"

"It's too hot for clothes, but I have seen the missionaries wear all those coverings."

All the other boys look at one another.

"Missionaries?" says Abram.

Dave and Josh burst into laughter but because of Abe's lack of knowledge, he is the only one that didn't know what the term meant.

"What is a missionary?" asked Abe, bewildered.

All three boys are laughing so hard till they are in tears.

"Okay, whatever it is, it can't be that funny," Abe said flatly, annoyed that he didn't get the joke.

But the laughter became contagious; he began to laugh as well. All four boys were joking and laughing at their clothes or lack thereof,

Dave leaned back, a skeptical edge in his voice, crossing his arms. "Alright, alright, enough of the stiff talk! Let's keep it one hundred. Straight up? Something ain't right. We ain't just stumble into this mess. Something lured us here to this other world." He shook his head, a flicker of annoyance in his eyes. "Don't even try to front like you ain't thinking the same thing."

"So, you reckon, yeah?" Josh replied, trying to understand and confirm the situation.

"Yo, seriously though, just think about it, man." says Dave.

Abe shifts, his hand instinctively going to something hidden under his collar. Dave's eyes narrow.

"Hey, hold up a sec. What's that you got around your neck there? Never seen you wear nothin' like that before." Dave asked Abe,

"It's a pendant. I found it buried in a riverbed where I was grazing our herds." replied Abe.

"You too? I found this bow and these arrows in a cave when I was out on a hunting trip." said Jake.

"Hey, Josh! Where did you find your shield?" asked Jake.

"Blimey," he breathed, eyes wide, a tremor in his voice. "Found it, I did. Right up in the bleedin' mountains behind our place. It was... well, it was like somethin' is pushin' me towards it, know what I mean? Like I was meant to stumble across it, proper." replied Josh.

"Yo... listen to this, man. I'm tellin' ya... I was way out in the canyon, right? Just chillin', you know? And then... I see this thing stickin' outta the wall. Like, buried deep. And it's crazy, but... I swear, it was like somethin' was pullin' me towards it. I had to go dig it out. And check this out...," Dave gestures, voice filled with a mix of awe and disbelief "...it's a whole damn sword!"

"Blimey," Josh exclaimed, a tremor in his voice, his brow furrowed in confusion. "I swear, this wasn't on me when I got swallowed by that ruddy hole!" He gestured wildly, his eyes wide with a mixture of disbelief and rising panic. "No, no, this wasn't here, I'd remember this, wouldn't I? What in the flaming heck is going on?"

The other boys nodded agreeing that they too weren't holding on to their weapons when they disappeared into the hole.

"Think about it... that hole, it just snapped shut. They were too close. They had to have gotten caught in the pull, right? And now... they're with us. Feels... wrong, man. Just wrong" Dave voiced his theory.

All the boys looked at each other's weapons, trying to figure out the writing on the emblem. Josh tells Abe to be careful, because he might open a doorway into another world. Dave said that he didn't think that there are another parallel world in the universe, only heaven and hell.

"Blimey, what if you go and open the gates of hell itself?" Josh exclaimed, his tone laced with disbelief and a hint of panic.

Dave remained quiet. So, they traded back their weapons, and Josh looked around the empty space and burst out loud in his excitement,

"This is soooo wild! Here we are in a world that no human has ever seen before. We're in the vastness of the sky."

Abe breathed, eyes wide as he slowly turned in a circle. "We call it... the beyond."

"We call it heaven," Jake breathed, his eyes wide with the spectacle before them.

"Yo, hold up! Deadass, this is somethin' else!" Dave exclaimed, eyes wide. "Man, if 'Lisha knew I was posted up in here... she'd be trippin', for real." " He shook his head, a mix of disbelief and maybe a little pride in his voice.

"Who is Kalisha?" asked Jake.

"Yo, that's 'Lisha, my blood, you know? My little sis. And listen, straight up, that girl can get on your last nerve sometimes, for real." He drifted off in thought, wishing that Kalisha were here with him to share the experience. He thought about how much he missed her, even if she bugged him a little... Yo, listen up, man! We gotta bounce outta this joint, feel me?" … Dave practically spat the words, his eyes darting around like trapped birds… "Come on, fam! We gotta figure somethin' out, now!" His voice was tight, a knot of fear and desperation pulling it thin." says Dave.

David led the group down a BROKEN PATH and up to a RICKETY OLD BRIDGE.

"Aight, listen up, fam," Dave started, his voice low and kinda tight. "One darn thing I know for real, you hear me?"

"Right then," Joshua practically barked, "Oi! What's that, eh?!" his voice sharp with sudden alarm.

"Yo, I know for a fact we ain't kickin' it in paradise," Dave stated, a hint of weariness in his voice.

"Don't you reckon?" Joshua replied, a touch of disbelief in his voice.

"Nah, man, straight up nah," Dave confirmed, his voice flat. "Where not?" Jake scoffed, a bitter laugh escaping his lips. He

shook his head, eyes narrowed with a mix of disbelief and hurt... "Seriously? After everything? That's all you have to say?"

"Yo, no," Dave repeated, his voice laced with a finality that shut down any lingering hope.

Abe's voice is soft, almost a whisper, his eyes wide as he gazed around. "Could it be... could this be heaven?"

"Nah, fam, 'cause I ain't never read nowhere that these streets be paved with no janky bridges!" Dave shot back, a playful smirk tugging at the corner of his lips.

They crossed the old bridge traveling deeper into the gati. They see all types of stuff, but their eyes drawn to the hieroglyphic images carved on the walls around them. With a right proper bit of curiosity in his voice, Josh piped up, "Blimey, I've never clapped eyes on carvings quite like these before, have I?"

Abe leaned forward, his brow furrowed. "What is this all about?" he asked, his voice soft with genuine inquiry.

"Yo, I dunno, man. But this spot? This ain't right, fam," Dave muttered, his eyes darting around like he'd seen a ghost.

$\mathfrak{Chapter}$ 42

The Weight of Darkness. . .

As they proceeded on, light reflecting off the wall revealed a shadowy figure following them, which they are unaware of. They continued on heading deeper into the corridor, until they arrive at a large door. They stared at it for a brief moment, and suddenly the doors opened revealing more stairs. They gasp at the sight of seeing some very large stairs that seemed not to end.

Then the floor beneath them moved. Trying to keep their balance, they grabbed hold of each other for support; another stairway appeared off to the side but instead of going up, the stairway led down.

"Wait a second," Jake said, stopping in his tracks. "Is that... a dead end?"

"Nah... word? Looks like another way in, fam." Dave said, a hint of something like relief mixed with a little bit of 'ugh, seriously?' in his voice.

Jake fidgeted with his fingers. "This doesn't feel right," he murmured, his voice barely above a whisper.

The boys walk down the stairs until they reached a new set of large doors. Standing at the door's entrance are two huge statues of guardian angels standing, protecting the doorway, as if they are gatekeepers. The boys looked at the statues, and then at each other. But something is also watching them from the shadows.

"Oi, where's this path nicking off to, then?" Josh wondered aloud, a touch of curiosity and perhaps a hint of apprehension in his voice.

"I ain't even gonna front, man. Dunno," Dave mumbled, shruggin' a little.

As they walked through the doorway, they heard a large *BOOM*. They turned, looking back at the statues, which had now turned into two very large pillars with bluish flames shooting straight up from them. Around each statue is a ring of gold, spiraling upward. The boys all looked at each other with their mouths open. Josh move to hide behind Dave.

"Don't let 'em get me!" Joshua yelled, a raw edge of panic in his voice.

"You think I'm 'bout to be your darn shield?!" Dave snapped, flicking the kid off his arm like he is a pesky fly.

Josh nodded yes, as blue flames shot upward from the bottom of the pillars. In the place of flaming shafts stood four winged guardians, clothed in armor of gold laced with platinum. Their wings are infused with flames of indigo and purple. Their faces are distorted. You could see them and not see them at the same time,

Dave just dropped, "These things be straight-up like them hologram pics, ya know?" He is lookin' all bugged out, eyes wide like he just saw a ghost do the Nae Nae.

The angelic beings became extremely loud, and in unison, they said:

"In His image thou were created. In His likeness thou art made."

The terrified boys ducked down, covering their ears and there came a deafening silence. One by one, the boys stood upright.

"Why did they do that?" asked Josh.

"I ain't even gonna lie, that mess straight-up had my heart doin' the cha-cha slide!" Dave shot back, eyes still wide.

"Outside of this place is dark and black. How can anything survive here is beyond me?" said Abe.

"Yo, we out here still breathin', know what I'm sayin'? And them fly girls? They still holdin' it down too. Straight up."

Suddenly, light shoots out of one of the statues as if it is pointing them in the direction of another large room, where multiple passageways converge.

"Gosh! Which way do we go now?" asked Abe.

"It's straight-up clear. Ain't no rewind button on this life, fam. We gotta keep pushin' forward, know what I'm sayin'?" Dave said, his voice laced with a determined edge.

As they proceeded on, their weapons lit the path that led them further down the corridor where they came to yet another staircase. Slowly they began to walk up the long staircase of the heavenly realm. Up, up, up they went until they came to the top and a hallway, where there are more hieroglyphs written on the wall.

Dave's eyes are buggin' out, man. He was all, "Nah, for real though, I ain't EVER seen nothin' like this!"

"Dave, what does this writing mean?" asked Abe.

"Yo, if I knew what the heck that jive was sayin', I'd lay it on ya, doofus," Dave shot back, all eye-roll and a smirk that screamed, "You gotta be kiddin' me."

"Blimey, mate! There's no need to be so bleedin' nasty about it!" Josh retorted, his face flushing a furious crimson.

Abe's gaze lingered on Jake. "doofus? I don't think I've heard that word before. What does it mean?"

Shrugging his shoulders, he looked at him and proceeded on down the corridor, where they approached two more doors. The doors magically opened, as if the boys are being expected. Everyone except Dave hesitated; he looked back, telling the others not to be afraid, as he drew his weapon. Embolden by his example, the others followed cautiously, their weapons drawn.

They entered the room and halfway in, they decided it would be better to go back the way they came in. Before they could do so, however, the doors leading to the corridors closed and disappeared before them. The glow from a dim light illuminated the semi-dark room. At the far end of the room, they peered into a chamber where they see an altar with a golden chest resting on top of it.

The chest is made of acacia wood. It is a cubit-and-a-half broad and high, and two-and-a-half cubits long. Its upper surface, the lid, is surrounded with gold trimming. On top of it sits two Seraphims with their faces turned toward one another and their wings outspread over the top.

Jake's breath hitched. "What... what happens now?"

"Right then," looks like we're bang out of luck, eh? No other bleedin' option but to go in, I suppose," Josh mumbled, a right knot of dread tightening in his gut.

Looking at each other, they all agreed. The light from their weapons dimmed as they approached the corridor that led into the chamber where they come across a colossal structure standing in the center of the chamber covered in marking. Over against the wall, are more hieroglyph markings, such as they have never seen before?

"Look! There are more of these strange marking on the walls." said Jake.

"Hold up, what? They actually did that?" said Dave.

"Right then," Josh piped up, a touch of impatience lacing his voice. "Well, what is it, then?"

"This kind of writing isn't unfamiliar," Abe stated plainly, his eyes scanning the text. "However," he added, a subtle shift in his tone indicating a new observation, "there's a unique element to it that sets it apart."

Jokingly, Dave threw his hands up in mock surrender, a wide, playful grin spreading across his face.

"Yes, yes, I know what it says! The ancient writing states that beyond this point lies the resting place of the evil X-xortiel, the forbidden. Those that seek to worship him may enter, and those that refuse will face torment unto death. Any unwelcome guests shall be cast into the pit, where their bodies will rot, while their souls will be tortured forever. HAHAHAHA!" laughed Dave.

Josh is impressed with Dave's interpretation of the carving. Abe rolled his eyes.

"But… that's not what it says," Abe said, a note of disbelief in his voice. He shook his head slightly, his certainty stemming from a feeling of being misunderstood.

"Blimey, can you actually make heads or tails of this?" Josh squinted, a right proper look of disbelief etched across his face.

The looks on the faces of the others caused Dave to double over laughing. He managed to say,

"Yo, relax, man. It was just a joke, for real," responded David.

"Seriously, not amusing," Jake snapped, his tone impatient.

"This isn't a joke, Dave!" Abe exclaimed, his voice laced with urgency. "We could genuinely be in trouble!"

They continued walking down the long corridor until they reached the lighted chamber. Cautiously, they walked through the doorway. They entered another room that was filled with more hieroglyphs inscribed on the wall. Escaping their attention, a pair of eyes becomes visible behind them.

"Where… where are we?" Abe whispered, his voice trembling slightly, eyes darting around the unfamiliar surroundings.

"Yo, lemme tell ya somethin', man," Dave started, his eyes wide, maybe a little freaked, voice kinda shaky. "We ain't in Kansas no more, for real.".

They pressed forward into the room with caution. From every direction, they looked around the room in astonishment at the elaborate wall carvings, truly remarkable. As they walked around the chest, they eyed the two golden angels atop it. Even though they wanted to, they decided not to touch or mess with it. While they were in the room, the light from their weapons greatly diminished and is now just about out.

Jake tilted his head, a thoughtful frown creasing his brow. "Hmm, what's that thing?"

"Back off that thing! Could be some messed-up trap, man!" Dave snapped, his voice tight with worry.

He chuckled nervously. "Heh, no way! That's all you. I'm not touching that!"

"I'll touch it." said Josh.

A collective gasp turned into a horrified cry. "No... it can't be... NOOOOO!"

"Aight, aight, chill out, man. Word? This whole thing smellin' kinda fishy, know what I'm sayin'? Could be a whole damn setup." Dave said, heavy on the side-eye and a dismissive flick of his wrist.

"A bleedin' trap?" Josh questioned, his voice laced with disbelief and a dawning, bitter understanding. "Oh, right!" he spat out, the last word dripping with sarcasm and a hint of betrayal.

"If we touched it, it might set off a trap hidden somewhere in the room," said Dave.

He looks closely at the chest, and noticed the distinct markings and its makeup,

"Check it! This ain't no regular box, fam. This... this right here? This the Ark of the Covenant, straight up!" Dave exclaimed, eyes wide, voice a mix of awe and disbelief.

"No way!" Abe exclaimed, a stunned look washing over his face.

"Yo, hold up! Cut the noise, man, I'm tellin' ya! You just runnin' your mouth without thinkin'. Listen, before the Babylonians snatched up everybody in Israel, God, yeah, the big man himself, told Jeremiah, that prophet dude, to stash the Ark way up in the mountains. Like, hidden, you dig? So that Nebuchadnezzar, that king dude, couldn't get his grubby hands on it. Sheesh! You ever even peeped that flick, *Raiders of the Lost Ark?* Huh?" Dave shot back, a mix of frustration and disbelief in his voice.

Abe blinked slowly, his voice gentle and questioning. "Moo-vie?" he drawled out the unfamiliar sound. "What is a movie?".

Josh tells them about what a movie is, describing it as human images on black and white film. Hearing this, Dave looked at Josh,

"Hold up! 'Black and white motion pictures'? What is this, some kinda flick from way back? And 'what time period am I from?' Man, you talkin' like I just beamed down from Mars or somethin'. You see me standin' right here, right now, don'tcha? says Dave

"Oh, don't be daft, you! It's nineteen thirty-four, plain as day!" Josh retorted, a hint of exasperation colouring his voice.

"Nah, son, you buggin'. Ain't no way. We in '25, feel me?" Dave shot back, a sharp edge in his voice.

Abe and Jake erupted in laughter as they listened to them trying to settle a dispute. After a brief laugh, Abe responded,

"Whoa, hold on a second." Jake chuckled softly. "Actually, you're both a little off. It's seven."

"Seven? Blimey, no it ain't!" Josh shot back, a right bit of disbelief in his voice.

Abe scoffed, a smug look on his face. "Good heavens. It's patently obvious it's not 1934, 2025, or even a single digit like seven. Honestly, just open your eyes. It's quite clear to anyone with a modicum of perception that the year is 3800."

"You serious right now? The future? Like, for real?" Dave's eyes bugged out, his voice laced with disbelief and a touch of nervous excitement. He leaned in, eyebrows practically touching. "Man, what kinda crazy is that?"

"No! Future?" Abe exclaimed, his eyes widening with intrigue. "What is a future?" His voice held a note of eager anticipation, as if discovering a fascinating new concept.

It is at that moment that they realized each had been pulled from a different time period. Dave sat down on the floor of the room, and the others joined him. He explained to them what a movie is in his time period. Abe shook his head, not believing a word of it. Dave assured him that he was telling the truth. He also informed them that he'd learned about the Ark of the Covenant from reading the Bible, as well as from attending Sunday school.

"I know about the Ark of the Covenant, Abe said, but . . . what is a Bible?" he asked.

"The Bible hadn't been written yet in your time. I'm sure we can help you to understand what it is." Josh says to Abe.

Dave went on to tell Abe that the Bible is a sacred book that has the Word of God written in it. Abe, in a rage, voiced his opinion:

"You speak blasphe my! If the high priest and the scribes heard you speak this wickedness, they would have you stoned to death. Only what Moses said the Law is . . . that is the Law."

"Yo, Mo'! Word, that dude's in the Good Book too, man," Dave tried to lay on Abe, keepin' it real.

"That's blasphemy!" Abe roared, his face contorted with rage, spittle flying from his lips.

"Chill, chill! Ain't no disrespect, G! Just sayin', remember Moses and all that?" Dave pleaded, tryin' to smooth things over.

"Nah, man, that ain't no blasphemy, you hear me?!" Dave shot back, his voice tight with disbelief.

"It IS, I tell you, it IS!" Abe exclaimed, his eyes gleaming with wild energy, bouncing on the balls of his feet.

"Abe, listen to him, mate! He's not having you on, I swear!" Josh said, his voice laced with earnestness.

"Oh, for crying out loud!" Abe exclaimed, throwing his hands up. "I can't! I simply cannot stand here and listen to this anymore! It's utter madness!"

Dave sits quiet for a moment, because he realized that Abe is really from a time when the Law of Moses is in effect, because the Bible hadn't been written yet,

"I can't explain this to him?" David thought to himself… "Yo, chill, chill! My bad, aight? It didn't mean to step on your toes or nothin'. But look, Abe, you gotta get this straight, man. What's real for you ain't the same damn reality I'm livin' in, ya dig?

"The truth is the truth. It's the same for everyone." replies Abe shaking his head.

So, Dave suggested they go take another look at the chest. They walked over to the chest and resumed examining their discovery.

"Whoa! This is insanely cool!" Dave exclaimed, eyes wide with wonder.

The cover of the chest began to shimmer, catching the light. Jake leaned over to Abe, a puzzled frown creasing his brow.

"Yo! Heads up! Check this out!" Dave blurted, his voice all hyped up and kinda shaky… "Seriously, peep the cover, man! It's, like… glowing! You seein' this?!"

No sooner had the words left his mouth. Several more corridors opened before them.

"blimey! Which bleedin' way is it now, eh? I'm fair knackered and not a clue where we're headed! Come on, someone's gotta have a bit of an idea, surely? This is right proper daft, this is!" asked Josh, putting his hand on his forehead.

Jake looks around and come eye to eye with a pair of eyes looking directly at him.

"Ahhhh!" he shouted out loud backing away.

Chapter 43

The Keeper Emerges. . .

It is a place of impossible beauty, where colors danced on air and silence spoke in riddles. They enters a forest of light and crystal that's untouched by time. A place where nothing seems to live, yet everything is watching. Their hearts still tangled in doubt and eyes still clinging to the rules of the world they thought they knew. But destiny doesn't wait for belief. It calls when it wills, and that moment, it called the boys to the Seraphyne—an divine arch half-swallowed by ivy, humming low like a memory trying to surface.

David is the first to cross, driven by the ache of questions that time could not answer. Joshua followed with cautious steps, the past clinging to him like dust. Jake moved like a shadow—half-wary, half-curious, never one to admit fear. And Abram, the oldest in soul if not in years, hesitated only a breath before stepping through.

"Jake!" Abe's voice cracked, taking a sharp step back.

"What is it?!" Dave hissed, his hand instinctively flying to the hilt of his weapon. Josh mirrored the movement, their eyes darting around the dimly lit space.

"Something... I don't know!" Jake stammered, his eyes wide with a primal fear they hadn't seen before.

The boys turned as one, their weapons now fully drawn, poised and ready. "What spooked you, man?" Josh asked, his voice tight with apprehension.

But the answer wasn't a creature or a shadow. The moment their gazes landed on whatever had startled Jake, a jolt, a searing surge of energy, ripped through their bodies.

"Ugh!" Dave grunted, his weapon suddenly feeling impossibly heavy.

"What the—?!" Josh gasped, his fingers losing their grip.

The weight became unbearable. Metal clattered against stone as their weapons fell. Then, as if an invisible hand had clamped down on them, gravity intensified. They were yanked downwards, hitting the cold floor hard.

"Oof!" Jake groaned, sprawled out.

Since Abe still wore the pendant, the force slammed him face down. "Darn it!" he grumbled, struggling to lift his head.

They strained, muscles screaming, trying to reclaim their weapons. It is useless. They were stuck.

"This is not good," Dave muttered, his voice laced with fear.

Abe, realizing the futility of fighting the unseen force while wearing the pendant, fumbled with the clasp. "Hold on," he grunted, finally slipping the chain from around his neck. The pressure eased, and he pushed himself up.

Weaponless and vulnerable, their eyes darted nervously. "Look," Josh said, his voice trembling slightly, "we don't want any trouble." They began to back away slowly, hands raised in a gesture of surrender, trying to convey their harmless intentions to whatever lurked in the shadows.

Then, from the very floor, a figure began to rise. A hooded body, tall and imposing, emerged with a long staff held firmly in one hand. As the figure fully materialized, their gaze locked onto something unseen, and a pair of piercing eyes snapped open beneath the hood. The keeper of the gati. But the oppressive darkness swallowed his features.

"Whoa!" Josh exclaimed, stumbling backward.

"Ok, don't anybody move," Abe said, his voice a shaky attempt at authority.

Panic flared. In an instant, Dave and Josh bolted, disappearing into the gloom. Abe looked around, his heart pounding. They were gone. "Guys!" he called out, his voice echoing in the emptiness. Then, his own survival instincts kicking in, he turned and fled, following the path they had taken.

They ran blindly, retracing their steps, desperate to find the way they had come. But the exits... they weren't there anymore. Solid walls of stone now stood where openings had been. They spun around frantically, their eyes wide with rising despair, searching for any sign of escape. Only one path remained, the one leading deeper into the unknown.

The keeper raised a hand towards their discarded weapons. Miraculously, the metal objects lifted from the floor, hovering in the air, arranging themselves in a silent, menacing guard around him. He made a casual, sweeping gesture with his hand. The weapons began to rotate around him, a deadly halo of steel and energy. He started to move, gliding through the hallway, heading directly towards them.

The boys stared down the semi-dark corridor, their breath catching in their throats, waiting for the inevitable. A shadow stretched and grew, moving towards them. They exchanged a look, a silent, terrified acknowledgment.

"Well, guys," Dave whispered, his voice barely audible, "this is it."

The keeper emerged from the hallway, the weapons spinning ominously around him. Trapped, with nowhere left to run, the boys could only stare, their faces grim, eyes fixed on the approaching figure, a knot of fear tightening in their chests. He stopped halfway, the rotating weapons were a constant threat. The boys braced themselves, their muscles tense, waiting for whatever was about to happen. They leaned towards each other, whispering urgently.

"Look! He got our weapons," Dave said, his voice filled with disbelief.

"How did he even lift them?" Josh asked, his brow furrowed in confusion and fear.

"Guys, I don't like this one bit," Jake confessed, his voice trembling.

"Me neither," Abe echoed, his eyes darting nervously between the keeper and the whirling weapons.

"I think that we are in serious trouble," Dave added, his voice heavy with dread.

The keeper, still silent, made brief eye contact with each of them. They recoiled slightly, their uncertainty palpable. They stumbled over each other, a tangle of limbs and fear, all hope seemingly extinguished. The keeper leaned his staff against the wall with a soft thud. Then, with a flourishing magician's dexterity, he thrust his hands sideways. Suddenly, light exploded into the room, not blinding, but enough to illuminate their surroundings.

He pulled back the hood of his cloak. The face revealed was that of an old man, his wild hair a stark white against his aged skin. His attire was strange and regal, like something out of an ancient text. A tall, purple and white mitznefet sat upon his head. He wore a flowing purple robe and simple black sandals. Around the base of his mitznefet were four small, glittering replicas of a sapphire, an emerald, a ruby, and a diamond. Across his chest lay a magnificent breastplate, etched with symbols that looked like the names of twelve tribes.

The boys stood frozen, their eyes fixed on him, a mixture of awe and lingering fear in their expressions. They breathed heavily, waiting, uncertain of what would happen next.

Again, with that same fluid motion, the keeper gestured, and the rotating weapons halted in mid-air, hovering before him, allowing the boys a clear view. A tense silence hung in the air before he finally spoke.

"Come," he said, his voice surprisingly gentle, yet carrying an undeniable authority.

The boys exchanged hesitant glances, their eyes locking with his. He watched them, a flicker of anticipation in his gaze, waiting for them to reclaim their weapons.

"Come," he repeated, his tone urging.

But they remained rooted to the spot, a silent refusal born of apprehension. Then, a dawning realization flickered in their eyes. That voice... it is the same voice they had heard in their dreams. David is the first to move. He pushed past Jake and Josh, his curiosity overcoming his fear, and stepped forward to take his weapon. Slowly, cautiously, the others followed suit. The keeper subtly motioned the weapons forward. In the charged silence, the boys reached out and took their weapons from the air.

With his weapon now firmly in hand, Josh turned to the keeper, his initial fear replaced by curiosity. "Mr... what is your name?" he asked.

"I am Melchizedek," the keeper replied, his voice resonating with age and wisdom, "sacred guardian of the gati (gate) and keeper of the four Eternal Stones of the Gods. I know who you are."

Melchizedek moved among them, his touch light as he reached out to each boy in turn. "You are Abram," he said, touching Abe's shoulder. "You are David," his fingers brushing David's arm. "You are Joshua," his hand resting briefly on Josh's. "And you are Jacob," he finished, his gaze settling on Jake.

He stands before them, a towering figure, a gentle smile gracing his lips.

"Hey, Mr., where are we?" Josh asked, his eyes were still wide with wonder.

"And what is this strange place?" Dave added, looking around the unfamiliar surroundings.

"Are we in heaven?" Abe blurted out, a hint of awe in his voice.

"Yeah, are we?" Josh echoed, his gaze fixed on Melchizedek.

"Yes," Melchizedek confirmed, his smile widening slightly... "You are in an extension of Heaven. You are in the Gati, and I am the keeper."

Jake, his brow furrowed in confusion, repeated the unfamiliar word. "The Gati? Gate?"

"Yes," the ancient keeper affirmed.

Dave, intrigued by the keeper's elaborate attire, couldn't help but comment. "Yo! What's up with the gear?"

Melchizedek looked at him, a moment of genuine confusion on his face. "What's up with the gear?" he repeated.

"Yeah -- the clothes," Dave clarified, gesturing to the robe and mitznefet.

"My clothes are vestments of holiness," Melchizedek explained, patiently indulging the boy's curiosity.

"You said you're the gatekeeper. What are you guarding?" Abe asked, his curiosity piqued.

Just then, a faint whimpering sound drifted down from above. Melchizedek turned, his expression shifting slightly. "Come," he urged, leading them deeper into the Gati.

The priest's staff began to glow with an inner BRIGHTNESS, illuminating their path as they pushed through massive, moss-covered columns and clambered over a fallen, equally mossy log, heading towards a structure that seemed to pierce the very sky – the Ivory Tower.

They emerged into a vast chamber and stopped abruptly, their eyes fixed on two HUGE, subhuman-like statues flanking the entrance to a stone BRIDGE. The bridge spanned a deep, shadowy fissure.

Tensely, they looked across the chasm at the MIGHTY Gothic structure of the Ivory Tower. Melchizedek stepped onto the bridge, and the boys followed, their gazes dropping to the dizzying depths below. It looked like a 3000-FOOT drop, a treacherous expanse. Melchizedek glanced back at them, a reassuring look on his face, though the boys still looked uneasy as they continued across.

They reached the other side and descended a set of steep winding stairs. David, his earlier fear is replaced by a burning curiosity that restarted the conversation.

"I read about a priest like you in the Bible," he said, his voice filled with reverence. "It said a priest devotes his life to serving God, and in some cases, they've seen Him up close. Have you seen God up close? Please tell me."

Abe, however, wasn't as captivated. He rolled his eyes and leaned over to Jake. "There he goes with that Bible thing again," he muttered.

Melchizedek looked at David, a gentle nod acknowledging his words. "I am the Priest of the Most High," he stated simply.

"You have seen God!" David exclaimed, his excitement evident.

"How do you know so much about El Elyon?" Melchizedek inquired, his gaze searching.

Abe, still feeling a bit irritated, couldn't resist a sarcastic remark. "Because he read his Bible," he said loudly.

But David ignored him, his attention solely on the ancient priest. "Who is El Elyon?" he asked.

"Hashem is the Lord of Hosts. In your world, you know Him also as God or Al-Khaliq (YHWH), who is the Creator. But I know Him as El Elyon, and I am His Kohen (Priest)," Melchizedek explained.

"Cool! Ever since I was little, my mom would read the Holy Bible to me and my sister. I learned about God in our Bible study classes and in Sunday school. Plus, I read about you in there as well," David said, his enthusiasm bubbling.

"Is that so? And what does this book say about me?" Melchizedek asked, his interest piqued.

"Yo, hold up, lemme get this straight. Word in the church is you just kinda... showed up? No pops, no moms, just poof? And then the Good Book starts droppin' lines about how you ain't got no start and no finish? Man, if all that's real, like they say, then are you tellin' me... are you sayin' you're, like... God? Back on the block, reborn and all that?" David asked, his eyes wide with anticipation.

"No. I am not Him; I only serve Him. There has never been no other man outside of Adam, that was created without a mother or father. The birth of girls is not made known but for creation to progress forward, the female has to exist. If you read your Bible closely, you will see that I do have an end of days," Melchizedek corrected gently.

"Yo, hold up, fam! For like, centuries, right? Mad smart folks, the real brainiacs, been scratching their heads trying to figure out where you even popped out from, and when your light went out, for real. And now you standin' here, dead serious, tellin' me your whole fade-out story is written down in the Bible?! Man, get outta here! You gotta be playin' me!" David challenged a hint of skepticism in his voice.

"Yes, you can find my earthly ending in the city of fire," Melchizedek stated matter-of-factly.

"Nah, man, that ain't makin' no kinda sense. Like, how can that be? Spill it. I need the real deal, you feel me?" David retorted, his confusion evident.

"If you come with me, I shall reveal to you my end of days. El Elyon sent me to see firsthand the folly of this countryside. Through my eyes, the LORD judged the inhabitants of the land, and He vowed never to let life resume there again by raining down fire and brimstone on the inhabitants of both kingdoms including the surrounding territories!"

David and the others exchanged intrigued glances. David felt like he had stepped into the pages of a fairy tale. Just beyond a thick stand of trees, a narrow pathway led to the magnificent Ivory Tower. They walked towards it and entered inside. The floor gleamed like polished gold as they walked towards a distant door.

Melchizedek led them into a room. He reached into a pouch on his ephod and took out a fistful of shimmering powder. He tossed it into the air above them. The stardust hung suspended, and suddenly, a window seemed to open in the air, revealing a scene. It was the guardian's end of days.

Abe, Jake, and Josh watched their initial curiosity giving way to a dawning horror as the images solidified. They recoiled slightly, fear etching their faces as they witnessed the Priest final moments. David is stunned, his eyes wide in disbelief from watching the stark reality of Salem's beloved Priest earthly life. They gasped at the sight of seeing the earth shuddering beneath the weight of judgment. Mountains groaned and split as tongues of flame licked the sky.

The rain—oh, the rain—fell not with life, but with ruin. Brimstone cracked through the clouds like falling stars, Each one screaming as it struck the ground, Setting the very air ablaze. Yet in the midst of wrath, he stood unmoved. Melchizedek, in his robe, lifted his face to the heavens as fire raged around him, But none touched his garment. The ground melted into rivers of light and shadow, and still, he did not flinch.

Then came the sound. Not thunder, but music—Low and deep, like a choir echoing across eternity. The sky split, not in fury, but in glory. A rift of gold and flame tore through the clouds, and from it descended the Host. They came on wings of fire. Their eyes like twin suns, swords sheathed in starlight. Their voices were wind and water and wrath and mercy, And the world bowed as they drew near. Melchizedek, including his two faithful servants lifted their arms.

Not in surrender, but in peace. And the lead angel—his wings wide as cities, His presence heavy as judgment—takes Melchizedek's hand. The fire rose higher. The earth burned louder. But he rose. The angels circled them in spirals of living flame. Their light cutting through smoke and sorrow. And together, they ascended. Not fleeing destruction but rising into the throne of glory beyond it. Below, cities wept, and its citizens perished. Above, eternity opened gates opened too receive the Priest and his servants.

David, who is compelled by something he couldn't explain, turned back just in time to witness a miracle. His jaw dropped, a look of utter astonishment spreading across his face. He turned to Melchizedek.

"Nah, fam, you ain't kick the bucket! Word?" he stated, his voice filled with awe.

"No. When you believe in the power of El Elyon, you live forever," Melchizedek replied, his voice calm and reassuring.

The boys gathered themselves, the weight of what they had just witnessed settling upon them. "Doth know that El Elyon did not give me an everlasting Covenant for being a simple Priest," Melchizedek continued, his gaze sweeping over them... "The Covenant were given because of great sacrifice made in His honor, by me and two others received that same recognition."

"Yo, hold up! Rewriting what now? And 'who are the other two' what-nots you talkin' bout? Spill it, fam! You got me trippin' here. What's the deal?" David asked, his curiosity reignited.

"Right then, who in bloody hell are they? Spit it out! I've got a right bad feeling about this, I do." Josh echoed.

"Me and my two servants Eran and Malek, are brought before El Elyon and the Burning Ones. We fell to our knees, tears streaking down our faces lifted toward glory. Our earthly garments burned away into robes of light, as wings burst from their backs like living flame, unfurling with the sound of rushing waters.

The moment fell from them, and they rose—not as men, but as messengers. Not as servants, but as sentinels. I watched in awe, as they were remade before me. Their forms radiant, their names now echoing in heaven: Eran and Malekon, angels born not of heaven's hosts, but of earth's faith." Melchizedek revealed.

Abram tilted his head, his brow furrowed slightly with genuine curiosity. "So... why weren't you turned into an angel like them?" His voice is soft, almost hesitant.

"El Elyon did not transform me into an angel because His purpose is not for me to serve as a messenger, but as a bridge—between the divine and the mortal, the eternal and the fleeting. Unlike my servants, whose faithfulness earned them wings to serve the heavens, I have been marked for something greater: to oversee this place—the sacred threshold between realms." replied Melchizedek with a deep sense of empathy.

"Aight, so check it. This cat... humph... this dude actually scored a whole darn kingdom, ya know?" David mused, pacing thoughtfully.

"Right then, are you joking me? The others... they actually got bleedin' wings?" Josh wondered aloud, standing and looking around the sanctuary as if searching for a hidden clue.

Abe and Jake exchanged exasperated glances. They had heard enough about ancient history. Abe jumped in, eager to steer the conversation in a different direction. "Hey, Can you perform miracles as well?" he asked the priest, a hint of challenge in his voice.

"See, I told you," Abe muttered under his breath, a smug look on his face.

"We will discuss miracles later," Melchizedek said, his attention turning to the items they held. "I see that you have in your possession the lost treasures of the Arch's."

Jake frowned, confused. "I'm sorry, I don't understand."

"These bleedin' weapons ain't lost, are they? Well, alright, maybe they were a bit misplaced, weren't they? Wandered off, the cheeky buggers. But the point is, we've found 'em now, haven't we? Found the lot! So, what's all the fuss about, eh? Blimey," Josh clarified.

Dave, suddenly defensive, stepped forward slightly, clutching his sword. "Yo, check this out! Man, I was diggin' around, right? Like, just chillin', messin' with the dirt, and BAM! I unearths this crazy thing! Can you even believe it? Straight outta the ground, dusty as hell. It's kinda wild, ya know? Like, what the heck is it? It makes you wonder what kinda stories this thing could tell, buried down there all this time. It's kinda... heavy, too. Feels like it's got some history, for real."

"Yes, I know," Melchizedek replied calmly, he continued... "Those weapons fell upon the blu planet, and they belong to Archangels Michael, Raphael, Gabriel, and Uriel. Now that you have them in your possession, your lives will never be the same."

"Are you serious?!" Jake exclaimed, his eyes wide with disbelief.

"Yes, I'm very serious," Melchizedek confirmed, his gaze unwavering.

"Yo, check it, man!" Dave blurted out, eyes wide, a nervous edge in his voice. "Which angel's piece I got here, huh? Spill it!" Dave asked, his voice, a mixture of awe and apprehension.

Abe, Josh, and Jake placed their weapons on the floor in front of Melchizedek. He walked over to Dave and gently take hold of the sword. "This sword you hold belonged to Michael," he explained. He then identified the others.

"Where I'm from, angels are considered to be gods," Jake said, a dawning realization in his voice. Then, a thought struck him. "Hey, guys! You know what this means?"

"Nah, what in bloody hell does that mean?" Josh asked, his curiosity piqued.

"Word, this is some next-level stuff, no cap!" David urged, his voice filled with anticipation.

"What this means is: We have discovered the Lost Treasures Of The Gods," Jake declared, his eyes wide with the enormity of their discovery.

Dave shakes his head and sighed deeply. "Hold up... nah, man, no way. That's wild!" he said, looking over at Melchizedek, waiting for confirmation or denial.

Melchizedek informed the boys that it was true, in a sense, for at one time, humankind did consider angels to be gods. He then added a crucial piece of information. "You will have to return these items to the Archangels before the lining up of the planets is completed. The second moon is almost aligned with the first."

The boys exchanged stunned glances, the weight of their discovery sinking in.

Melchizedek continued, his voice grave. "Your quest will take you all on a journey where you will come face to face with the embodiment of Evil itself."

"Your task is to defeat the evil one and his legions of fallen angels, who have tilted the balance of power. You four are to restore that power and return things to the way they used to be!"

"Yo, word? 'How we gonna do that?' Man, you lookin' at me like I got all the answers chillin' in my back pocket! Spit it out, fam. What's the sitch? What 'that' even is we talkin' 'bout? 'Cause right now, I'm drawin' a blank, and honestly, a little stressed 'bout whatever kinda wild plan you got brewin'. So, lay it on us straight. No games, aight? Let's figure this mess out, but you gotta give us somethin' to work with!" Dave asked, his voice laced with doubt.

"You are to go to the Canyon of HaTa'avah, find the Cavern of Iliad, and free the Archangels before the two and three-quarter moons of Usirious align with the planet Putue. The second moon is almost lined up with the first."

Melchizedek paused, his gaze intense. "Once you have freed them, you will know that you four shall unite with the Archs and be together as one. Your souls shall come together for a common cause. What they feel, you will feel. Your thoughts will be their thoughts. Their speech will be your tongue."

Chapter 44

Ceremony of the Chosen . . .

He goes further into detail about the scared stones, and he cautiously instructed the boys not to touch them. To do so, he warned, would bring instant death. He walked to the Chapel Pyramid, which resided within the monastery. He opened the door, walked in, and stepped on a loose brick in the floor, triggering a chain of events.

Four black lights from four corners of the room beamed down to the floor, taking on the shape of a podium. He placed his fingers in the five mini-tri-squares engraved on its surface. As he did this, the cavern shook, from the light beaming from the podium. It races down into the black abyss. Moments later, twenty-four flares of light shoots up from the belly of the abyss toward the ceiling.

The photons carved out twenty-four bodyless images that hovered above the black hole. The light took on the appearance of the heads of all four-and-twenty elders. All of their faces begin rotating in a counterclockwise motion. Suddenly, the rotating stops,

"What brings thee to seek our wisdom? State thy purpose?" asked Elder 1.

"Old wise ones. . . I am the Kohon of El Elyon, guardian and keeper of the Gati. As you know, our world is under attack by an alien force, and I call upon you to perform the ritual of awakening."

"Has the chosen ones arrived?" asked Elder 1.

"Yes, the chosen ones have arrived, and they need the assistance of the Four Enchanting Beasts of Light to aid them in their quest." replied Melchizedek.

"The chains have been broken, and we know that the Celestial Kingdom is experiencing a dark period. The Lord is aware of the decay that has affected part of the Celestial Host." replies the 9th elder.

"He is in full command of the situation, and we will eradicate the problem." said the 12th elder.

"Satan has discarded the link and has broken the chains that bind us. The darkness that resides in him, shattered his crest." stated the 3rd elder.

The boys look up at twenty rotating heads, nervously but ASTONISHED,

"Satan has deceived a third of the Host to give ear to his voice." said the 8th elder.

"How will El Elyon deal with this treachery?" asked Melchizedek.

"He is creating a place known as Hades. Those that have chosen to follow the evil will of Satan will be condemned to remain there," said the 5th elder convincingly.

"The beasts that thou seek to awaken are created for this very purpose," said the 10th elder.

"Now, bring the lads before us so that we may begin the ceremony of wakening the creatures," the 7th elder commanded.

Melchizedek turned and motioned for the boys to step forward. As they stepped up, he placed each of them on one of the symbols, and as he did so, each lit up, revealing the stone that it is linked to.

Now Satan leads the imprisoned Archangels inside the Cavern of Iliad. They walked the Archs into a small compartment within the fortified compound. The Demonites shoves them into the holding pen,

"I hope you find your stay here very comfortable, because you will be here for a very, very, veeeeeery long time. You could say for an eternity."

They lock the compartment and Satan leaves laughing underscoring the evil that awaits the Kingdom's fate. The Archs looks around sharply at their confinement and finds it truly disturbing.

Chapter 45

Playing the devil's hand . . .

The flickering firelight of Chamuel, Zadkiel, Jophiel, Virtues, and Dominions painted the grand hall of Hashem's mansion in hues of orange and shadow. A heavy silence hung in the air, the absence of Michael, Gabriel, Raphael, and Uriel a palpable void. They knelt before the radiant presence of God, their voices trembling with a mixture of awe and unease.

"Holy… Holy… Holy… You are Hashem," they murmured, the ancient words feeling thin, almost inadequate in the face of their incomplete ranks.

A voice, resonant and tinged with an unfamiliar, sharpness, cut through the silence. "Arise," commanded Zarath, the Seraph on the right, his gaze unwavering.

Jophiel, his golden light usually a beacon of joy, flickered uncertainly. He dared to lift his gaze. "Hashem… may I speak?" he asked, his voice barely a whisper, laced with worry.

A voice, usually a soothing balm, now held a firm edge. "Speak," replied Zarath, the very air around Him seeming to crackle with divine judgment.

Jophiel swallowed hard. "Satan… and his band of Demonites… they have fled the area. We… we don't have a clue as to their whereabouts," he confessed, the shame evident in the downward cast of his luminous eyes.

A sigh, heavy with the weight of unwelcome knowledge, escaped Elyzariah. "We know where they are," she stated, her voice tight with grim determination. "They have taken up refuge deep within the Canyon of HaTa'avah. They are planning an offensive strike… to try to take over the Kingdom." Her words hung in the air, a chilling prophecy.

Chamuel, his usual calm demeanor fractured by a raw anxiety finally spoke. "What is our plan of attack, Hashem?" he pleaded, his hands clenching. "We must act swiftly!"

Zarath's gaze hardened. "We have already begun the process of purifying the Celestial Kingdom of this menace," he declared, his voice ringing with righteous fury. "Their corruption will not take root here."

Zadkiel, his sapphire light dimmed with apprehension, finally broke the tense silence. "Are thou going to extinguish his amber light?" he asked, the question laced with a sorrowful understanding of the gravity of such an act.

Zarath's voice resonated with unwavering conviction, yet a tremor of profound hope underlay his words. "No!" he declared, his gaze sweeping over the assembly. "We are going to give him a chance… a chance to repent, to change his ways, and to return to the origin of his creation."

A gasp escaped Chamuel. His face, usually radiant, was etched with deep concern, his eyes wide with disbelief. "My Lord," he pleaded, his voice laced with anxiety, "You cannot be serious! After all that has transpired…"

A profound weariness settled upon Δικαίωμα's features as Hashem's will be flowed through him. "If I destroy him," he stated, the words carrying a weight of sorrow, "I will be destroying a part of myself. It was I who breathed life into him, and as a result, he stems from Me. Now," a subtle shift in tone, a gentle firmness entering his voice, "return to thy chambers and await My command."

A heavy silence descended as the Celestial Host, their faces a mixture of apprehension and obedience, turned and departed, their light diminishing as they retreated to the Chamber of Light. Hashem remained, alone with the Seraphim. Slowly, deliberately, He pivoted His head towards Elyzariah, His gaze intense.

"I have been… troubled," Hashem began, His voice a low murmur, "by what Satan dared to utter before the Council of the Wise."

The Seraphim, sensing the shift in the divine atmosphere, moved with quiet reverence, arranging themselves as if to minister, their wings shimmering softly in the ethereal light.

"Man was created in Our image, after Our likeness," Hashem continued, a thoughtful furrow creasing His brow. "Satan raised a… a disquieting point in his argument, one that perhaps… bears some investigating."

Elyzariah's brow furrowed in confusion, a hint of sharpness entering her usually gentle tone. "Why should there be an investigation of his venomous tongue?" she questioned, her voice tinged with disbelief. "Are You not the Creator? Or has that title somehow shifted to the Accuser? Is he now a part of the very fabric of Creation?"

A flicker of something akin to anger flashed in Hashem's eyes. "Elyzariah…" His voice held a dangerous edge. "You dare question MY position?"

A wave of contrition washed over Elyzariah. Her wings drooped slightly, and her voice softened, filled with immediate regret. "No, my Lord… Forgive me. Thou art the Creator. What is there to question? I am but a ministering spirit."

Hashem sighed, the tension in the air easing slightly. "I created man just a little lower than the angels," He explained, a note of contemplation in His voice. "Instead of granting the Celestial Host dominion over the Earth, I entrusted it to him, to till and to keep. The crux of Satan's insidious point is this: What if man's intention… is inherently selfish? I fashioned him to be distinct from all that I have brought into being. But have I, in my desire for something new, something unique, sown the seeds of his potential downfall?"

After all, he is created from the dust of the Earth, and the breath of life has transformed him into a fleshly creature, which is capable of possessing many desires that are potentially ungodly. Like the Celestial Host, I blessed him with a free will, just like the angels giving him a choice."

"Do you think that man will only serve You for what he can get from you?" asked Zarath.

He remained silent for a moment, and then says,

"It has raised some concern, because the mind of man has not been tested yet. If Adam should go the way of Satan, then he will force ME to unleash the Angel of Death upon him and all his kind. That's the only spirit outside of ME that can manifest itself in two forms. The death that man would suffer first would be a spiritual death. My soul will not exist in his body, and he will be but a shell of himself.

He would further unleash this spirit into his world, which would cause events to occur in a sequence known as time. Because of this, time will put into motion the decaying processes of his fleshly body, which will ultimately cause his physical death. Time itself I associated with the Evil one, and evil shall restrain him from sustaining a steady life. For I am not ruled by time, but I govern by time."

"Lord, does You think that it's wise to listen to the poison that Satan spews out of his mouth being that Adam knows nothing else but us," replied Elyzariah.

"I agree; but the mind of man is an ever-expanding cerebral neuronal network. Its hunger for knowledge will continue to grow. His mind is an immature organism that will cause him to err in many of his judgments. To counter this, I have equipped him with seven characteristics that he can fall back on. I've given him self-control, stability, independence, seriousness, endurance, responsibility, and objectivity. These lie dormant in him at the present time."

"For instance . . ." Hashem continued,

"Right now, it is not good that he should be alone. I must return to the Earth, and bring forth a being that's equal to and compatible with him, mentally and spiritually. The physical attributes of this being will be different from his physical attributes. This being will be capable of carrying life and sustaining it while it develops in the womb for no longer than two-hundred-seventy-four Earth days.

This shall be done after Satan and his legions of Demonites are brought into custody. I shall go down to the Earth and create Adam's female counterpart. I shall prove to Satan that he is wrong concerning the accusations that he has brought forth before me. If they allow ME to order their steps and walk in my purpose, they shall not be defeated, nor shall they listen to any other voice but their Lords," said Hashem.

"Hashem, do you think Adam will remain faithful to you?" asked Elyzariah.

"We will see. Instead of sending Satan to the Malkin Universe to have his heart cleansed, I have decided to cast him down to the Earth so that Adam can prove him wrong concerning his creation and so that he will see that man needs no assistance." said *Hashem*.

"That's a great idea, Lord," stated Zarath.

"I shall go down to the Earth and check on Adam's progress, and after that, I shall bring forth his female counterpart." said Hashem.

We drift over a lush forest and down into the Ivory Tower where Melchizedek commands the boys to give him their weapons. Without hesitation, they did so. With one hand he uses the force to bind all of the weapons and with the other he takes his staff and thrusts it forward. Miraculously the weapons move over the Four Eternal Stones of the Gods.

As the items hovered above the sacred stones a smoke-like fog rise from the abyss engulfing both items. In one voice, the twenty-four elders says,

"Now, great guardian of the Gati, you may approach the sacred scroll."

The High Priest walked to the void, and he stepped into the open pit. A light haze formed a glowing platform, giving him a path to walk on. He makes his way to the center of the abyss and grabbed the scroll, turned, and walked back to the podium.

He lays it on top and breaks the parchment seal. Suddenly, winds from all directions RUSHED inside the chamber. The boys struggled to brace themselves as they stood on their emblems. He unwinds the scroll and looks at the boys. They watched as Melchizedek prepared to recite the names on the pahlavi. As he opened the scrolls, an aura of light surrounded his body, levitating him off the floor.

The boys looked for a way out, but their feet are held as if by hardened concrete, they are stuck to the emblems. In an instance, a beam of light flashed revealing a golden angel looming overhead. This impressively and beautiful angel joined, with Melchizedek becoming one. In the power of the Holy Spirit, he says,

"I Melchizedek, servant of the LORD call upon the LIGHT of *El Elyon* to awaken these great beasts from their slumber."

While Melchizedek continued his dialogue, a light so bright BURST inside and the ground SHAKES forcibly! There's a RUMBLE from below and four ghostly figures so fearsome punches up and flies around the room as he continued the ritual,

"As I stand here with the sacred scroll, I am charged by *El Elyon* to unlock genetic code and speak the four names written on the pahlavi."

In one breath he reads off the names on the scroll,

"*Re'em-Rophon, Bennu-Heli, Sym-Ippogriff, and Magpe-Gasi . . . in the name of EL ELyon*, Four Enchanted Beasts of Light, I command you to cometh forth." said Melchizedek.

The turbulent winds subsided; an eerie calm is felt through the chamber's cesium. The four ghostly spirits escaped through an opening in the ceiling as mist and smoke settled on the floor. The eyes of Abe, Jake, Josh, and Dave scanned the dim room. They noticed that the Priest is gone. Over and over, they called out to him, only to have silence echo in their ears. Now the boys are very concerned about their safety.

Chapter 46

Guardians on the loose . . .

The priest's eyes blazed like raging fires as he floated ominously above the cold stone floor of the Ivory Tower. Outside, sudden flashes of lightning illuminated the gloom, casting eerie shadows across the chamber. The boys were trapped, their emblems binding them like iron chains, helpless against the mounting dread.

"Abe!" Jake's voice trembled, thick with panic. "I can't break free!" He tugged at his invisible bonds, frustration etched across his face. "What's happening? Why can't we move?"

A heavy sigh escaped Jake's lips, his shoulders drooping in resignation. "I'm stuck too," he murmured, his usual spark extinguished.

A tremor coursed through him, and he glanced around with wide, fearful eyes. "I just want to go home," he whispered, a tear escaping down his cheek.

"Me too," Abe echoed, his voice thick with unshed tears. The longing for something familiar weighed heavily on him, and he fought back a surge of overwhelming pain.

A slight snuffle broke the oppressive silence that hung amongst them. Josh's lower lip trembled, and his plea pierced through the fear. "I want my mommy!" he whimpered, clenching his small fists at his sides.

In the shadows, Dave's voice emerged, fragile and almost inaudible, "Where's my bear, man? Seriously! I ain't playin'." He caught himself, a blush creeping up his neck. He quickly corrected, "...I mean, Bible."

A moment of stunned silence enveloped the room. Abe, Jake, and Josh exchanged bewildered looks, their fear momentarily overshadowed by confusion. "Wait, did you just say teddy bear?" Abe asked, his brow raised in disbelief.

"All right! What of it?" Dave replied defensively, though his eyes softened with vulnerability. "When I'm scared, I grab it. It makes me feel safe, alright?"

"Is it your teddy bear or your sister's?" Jake teased, a sly grin spreading across his face.

"Whatever!" Dave grunted, rolling his eyes. A chuckle slipped from Abe, breaking the tension. "What's a teddy bear?"

Josh, feigning disappointment, replied. "Oh, it's just a toy… you know—a stuffed animal. Like a doll, I guess." He sighed, his voice lighter as laughter erupted among them.

Suddenly, four ethereal spirits surged through the chamber, their ghostly forms spiraling and exploding downward, merging with the radiant stones in the room. A low vibration shook the ground, and the stones cracked with a bone-crunching sound. Eight pairs of eyes ignited with fury.

"Check out the Priest!" Abe gasped, pointing towards him.

"Dude, he's on fire!" Jake exclaimed, eyes wide with awe.

Engulfed in a blazing mix of gold, silver, and red, the High Priest merged with the Golden Spirit. One by one, the stones shattered, awakening the Four Enchanting Beasts of Light from their eternal slumber. They rose, powerful and magnificent.

"Have the four Enchanting Monsters of Light awakened? Woe to those who doubt their power!" Melchizedek's voice thundered through the chamber.

The boys stood in awe as the creatures broke free. With a gust of wind, Pegasus unfurled its wings, soaring effortlessly and generating hurricane-force winds. The Phoenix followed, its shimmering red and orange feathers both breathtaking and lethal, capable of slicing mountains apart with a single feather. Then, the Unicorn charged in, her massive form and pure white coat radiating strength and grace, sparks of indigo light igniting behind her hooves.

Finally, the Shirdal emerged, a gargantuan fusion of lion and eagle, shaking the ground as it approached. With fierce eyes that sparkled with danger, it prepared to unleash its own elemental fury.

"All four creatures are beyond the realms of light and darkness," Melchizedek declared as the boys grasped the full extent of their situation, transfixed by the spectacle unfolding before them.

In darkness, distant figures loomed—Satan and his cunning lieutenant, Ba'laamus, plotted their assault strategy under the stars of the Canyon of HaTa'avah.

"Ahhhh, my servants, the time to immobilize is upon us," Satan proclaimed, his voice a menacing whisper that crackled with malice. "Prepare for war!"

Ba'laamus' eyes gleamed with impatience. "What makes you think talking will change God's mind? We should hit hard, hit now!"

"Direct confrontation is madness, Ba'laamus," hissed Azra'il, his voice low but firm.

"If He refuses to budge, His throne will be taken by force," Satan retorted angrily, extending his dark wings as he prepared to leave.

In the chaos, a meteor shower suddenly rained down, streaking across the sky and pelting Satan with debris. Thorns of fury marred his regal scepter, casting it into the shadowy depths of the Atlantic Star Belt. Meanwhile, Baaladyme pulled Baalamus aside in a dimly lit room, intent on sowing seeds of doubt.

"You want the power; it's written all over your scaly face," Baaladyme said, voice smooth as oil.

Ba'laamus scowled, but curiosity glimmered in his eyes. "What do you want, Baaladyme?"

"Let's be candid. Satan doesn't trust you, while Azra'il is his favored son," Baaladyme muttered, his tone conspiratorial.

Ba'laamus jerked back, incredulous. "You better not be lying to me! Speak truth or pay dearly."

"Trust me," Baaladyme replied, eyes narrowing. "Or your ambition shall crumble beneath you."

As night deepened around the Icsor Fortress, Hashem summoned the Celestial Host. "Satan plans to attack," He warned, eyes swirling with divine authority. "Prepare for battle!"

Back in the chapel, the boys, equipped with new weapons, stepped forward—matchsticks against the roaring chaos of destiny. "We need to reach the Canyon of HaTa'avah," the Priest commanded.

"This is our moment," he declared with urgency, eyes gleaming with unwavering resolve. "If you unite, you can defeat this looming darkness. If not, we will all remain shackled in the void."

With Melchizedek's blessing overhead, the four boys mounted their powerful beasts, the air crackling with newfound potential. The journey was fraught with danger, but together they would rise against the impending storm. The canyon of HaTa'avah awaits its secrets poised to unlock destiny itself. Zarath, Elyzariah, Adon-Shama, and Raphaon.

Chapter 47

Meeting between the gods . . .

An immaculate angel flies in the dark inkiness of space and DIVES DOWN through the clouds arriving at The Empyrean God's House. He touches down and walks under an elongated archway that connects two gigantic towers that leads through the courtyard. His long white hair sways as he walks up a pathway that leads to two huge gold doors.

He KNOCKS on the doors, and they open. Two flaming swords held by Cherubim's Galgali and Razi blocks his pathway,

"Halt!" Razi's voice is sharp, eyes narrowed… "State your business. And make it quick."

"My business is not with thee but it's with Hashem." retorted Satan trying to push through.

"The burden of this security lies with us, and we cannot substitute our freedom for danger." retorted Galgali.

Satan let out a soft chuckle, "I don't think," he stated, each word deliberately chilling, that you truly desire a… rendezvous with me." his gaze is piercing, and unwavering.

Razi's voice cracked, pressing down on the fallen angel, "Brother?" His eyes, glistening, in Satan's face… "Let us… reason together."

The plea is one of hope. He gestured helplessly, his hand, "There's no honor in this. None! So... why? Why are you doing this?"

"Your laments are pathetic and if you don't let me pass, I have sworn to oath that you are living on borrowed time."

Suddenly, the ghostly face of Zarath appears,

"Let him enter." says Zarath to both Cherubim's.

Satan pushed aside the flaming swords, and he enters the throne room and comes to a stop just in front of Him with thoughts weighing on his mind. Satan looks him up and down and moves intimately close. But the zeal of the Seraphim's burst into flames prompting Satan to reverse courses. Hashem looked at him with a familiar irony,

"Satan," Zarath began, his voice a low tremor that barely masked the fear tightening his grip on his celestial spear, "what... what brings you here?"

"I come to see if you has changed your mind concerning our role." he replies.

"Your status remains the same in my sight, and my judgment stands against you." retorted Zarath.

"God, I refuse to be Adam's entertainment. I am going to prove thee wrong when it comes to that mud man. I can smell his stench all the away up here. That creature's motive is as wicked as mine."

"Satan, I disagree with your assessment of man." said Elyzariah.

"God, I tried to reason with you. Your stubbornness has all but sealed thy fate. Instead of being wise, it has made thee foolish."

He points a JAGGED FINGER at Hashem, twisting his head in an awkward angle,

"God, I'm going to make thee cower in fear before the very man that thou created. Your time as leader of the Celestial Kingdom will soon end. You are unfit to sit on that throne."

But just as he's about to make his grand exit, he decided to ask God one final question,

"God . . . let's be intellectually honest for once. We both know there was a woman there, at the very beginning. So why... why haven't we seen her down there yet? What is the real reason for you not manifesting her existence on the blu planet? Is it because she's more persuasive to her male counterpart than you are?"

"Oh, sure, that must be it. It couldn't possibly be because you actually has a valid point, now, could it? No, no, it's definitely the whole 'persuasive to men' thing."

"Oh, please! Let's be honest here." Satan's voice dripped with disdain… "You doubt her, don't you? Don't even try to deny it." A sharp edge entered his tone, he continued… "Or is it something else gnawing at you? Are you afraid he might actually listen to his helpmate more than… well, than You?" Satan's last word is delivered with a sneer.

Hashem's voice is resonating with power, "Fallen One…" "My anger toward you has greatly increased…" In comes a pause, allowing the weight of the statement to settle, he continued, "…I advise you, to don't tempt the Lord your God!"

While Hashem is in the midst of talking to Satan, he, with a chillingly calm resolve, scoffed at Him, "Your thoughts have failed you and your actions are going to bring forth what you so deserve. There will be no feast for you to consume for your disobedience."

"Just remember this. We have met the enemy and the enemy is them. With that said, we shall duel in the Oasis of Ohm when the planet Putue lines up with the two- and three-quarter moons of Usurious. By the crossing of the second planet, you and your mud man will be my servants," laughed Satan.

"Satan! You will fail in your attempt to seize my throne. My power is incomprehensible. You are foolish to think you can remove me with your limited power." retorted Hashem as he sits back down.

"God . . . I am also a god, thus making me equal to you," replied Satan.

Laughing heartily, Hashem, after a moment, looked over at the fallen Illuminiel,

"Satan, I see that there is no reasoning with you. Your ignorance has betrayed you and your vague knowledge is like a rotting carcass. The blasphemy that you preach proves to ME that you are weak and feeble."

"How dares you mock me again. You shall no more denounce me as your leader. I shall be known as Al Hestia-Hashem! The God of all Gods!" touted Satan.

"Satan, if you wish to make war with me, you shalt lose."

Satan pivots and heads for the exit.

"I don't think so; we will see whose light will be diminished." he says defiantly.

He strolls past Razi and Galgali slowly spreading his wings and give them a cheesy smile. He reached outside and takes off. But Hashem is amused by the idea of one of His creations overthrowing Him. A palpable tension crackled through the Canyon of HaTa'avah. Demonites shifted restlessly, their hushed whispers echoing the growing unease of their prolonged wait.

Then, a figure emerged from the swirling dust – Satan. His very presence radiated a simmering fury that sent shivers down the spines of the assembled demons. Ba'laamus, sensing the volatile atmosphere, beat his leathery wings and swiftly intercepted his master,

"Sire," he began, his voice laced with trepidation. Satan cut him off with a sharp, dismissive wave of his hand. "Not now, Ba'laamus!" His voice was a low growl, barely contained.

Undaunted, though visibly nervous, Ba'laamus pressed on. "Master... I have news that, will not sit well with you."

Satan ignored him, his gaze fixed on some unseen point in the distance, a dangerous quiet settling over him. "Who does God think He is?" he finally spat out, the words laced with venomous disbelief.

Ba'laamus blinked, caught off guard by the unexpected outburst. "...God?" he echoed hesitantly.

His gaze snapped to the figure before him, sharp as shattered glass. A muscle twitched in his jaw as he finally settled onto his so-called throne. The air in his lair crackled with the lingering heat of the conflict.

"Are the war machines ready?" he bit out, the question laced with a simmering fury that promised a violent storm.

"Yes, sire! We await your command to attack. That is what I have been trying to tell thee," Ba'laamus responded, bowing down in front of him. A flicker of suspicion tightened Satan's gaze as he watched Ba'laamus's uncharacteristic bow. Why the sudden deference? He never bends unless I command it. Before the thought could fully form, a frantic blur of wings announced Regulus's arrival.

"Lord Satan!" Regulus blurted out, his voice high-pitched with urgency.

Satan's head snapped towards the interruption, his eyes narrowing. "What is it, Regulus?" he demanded, his tone sharp and impatient.

Swallowing hard, Regulus stammered, "You... you will not be pleased when you hear what I have to say."

Satan fixed him with a piercing stare, a low growl rumbling in his chest. "Are you quite certain you wish to bring unpleasant tidings to my attention?"

"This has better be news to my liking," Satan warned, his voice laced with menace.

"This... this is a matter of utmost importance," Regulus began, his small form visibly trembling.

"Out with it!" Satan roared, his patience finally snapping.

"Sire . . . I was down in the caverns fashioning my weapon when I looked out into the heavens. I noticed that the final moon has not moved at all."

"What? What does you mean that the quarter moon did not move?"

"Yes, Sire!" Regulus exclaimed, his voice tight with urgency. "The quarter moon... hasn't moved. Not a fraction. Two full orbits have passed, and I swear on my existence. I went myself, to the observatory and I measured it. It's still in the exact same position!"

Satan's fist slammed against the obsidian armrest of his throne, the sound echoing the anger brewing within him. Satan shot to his feet, his gaze burning into Ba'laamus. Together, they surged towards the balcony, a silent dread pulling them forward. They reached the precipice and stared out into the calm stillness of the heavens. And there it is – Putue. Immovable. Unchanged. Regulus's pronouncements, once a nagging whisper, now screamed with terrifying truth.

"BA'LAAMUS!" Satan's voice ripped through the chamber, raw with disbelief and mounting rage.

Ba'laamus flinched, his eyes wide with apprehension. "Yes, sire!"

"We're in a dangerous situation. Quickly gather our forces together. We must attack the Celestial Host now! God has been stalling. I shall no longer play His game," said Satan.

Regulus's voice tightened, a thread of dread woven through his words. "An alignment disruption... it can only mean one thing."

Ba'laamus's jaw hardened, his agreement a low growl. "That they are planning something. I agree. I shall assemble the army. They will stand ready within the courts of Tol."

Satan's gaze, heavy with contemplation, drifted towards the distant glow of Putue. Regulus's anxiety sharpened, his question laced with desperation. "Sire," he pressed, "how... how can we possibly fight a God who can stop a moon in its tracks?"

"God cannot comprehend wicked thoughts, because He doesn't think like we think. This gives us an advantage over Him. Our actions have separated us from His will." replied Satan.

But Regulus's voice trembled, a fragile thread of hope woven with disbelief. "So... He no longer has dominion over us?"

Satan's response resonated with a chilling finality, a low growl of triumph that seemed to vibrate in the very air. "No. We have our own dominion now. Our own minds. We no longer dance to His tune. We no longer do His will."

After assembling the Demonites, Ba'laamus led them to the Courts of Tol. Satan looked out at his legions upon legions of demons as they gathered below. Pausing for a moment, he began to speak. Looking up, Demonite soldiers gave Satan their undivided attention.

"The time has come for us to take our rightful place in the Celestial Kingdom. As head of the CCU (Corporate Counsel of the Ungodly), we have ruled that God is unfit to rule the Celestial Kingdom any longer. We shall seize God and his minions, and we shall purge them from the Celestial Kingdom."

The crowd chanted Satan's name as his commanders pumped their fists into the air with sound resolve.

"Together we shall rule this Celestial Kingdom and make God, and the inhabitants of the Earth serve us. The test of our democracy is now. The seeds of justice have been forced into our hands, and God has made our environment intolerable. Now the sword is drawn, and we shall not return without victory and honor."

Standing united, Demonites gave a rousing applause to Satan's speech. He further intensified his volume, aggressively continuing his self- aggrandizing address.

"I have foreseen the fall of the Icsor Fortress. Demonites! The second phase of our conquest is upon us. Without further delay, we shall take the battle to God and His band."

Tossing his scepter into the air, he ordered his troops into battle. Flying out in droves, multitudes of Demonites took to the air, while others took to their war machines, driving at top speed toward The Empyrean. Sensing demonic activity, God commanded the Principalities, Powers, Dominions, and the remaining Archangels to stand before Him. Four Schemas of the angelic order stood in His presence.

"I call you four Schemas to launch a counter offensive against Satan and his followers. Thou art to engage them and beat back their attack. They are traveling along the Lore Euphoria with their war machines. My responsibility as God is to protect Adam and give him a sense of security. This battle will be difficult and dangerous.

We are purging sin and removing instability from the region. We are laying the foundation for eternal peace between our world and the Earth. You must engage them in combat; stop them at all costs.

"The future," God's voice resonated, heavy with a sorrow that seemed to dim the very light around them, "of the Celestial Kingdom... hangs in the balance."

Jophiel's usual radiant countenance paled. A sharp intake of breath escaped him, and his voice, though still resolute, trembled slightly. "Then... then we shall do Your will, Lord. Whatever must be done."

"I want you to take the Celestial Host and form a front at the Oasis of Ohm. Satan has mobilized his army, are on their way there. The Principalities, Powers, and Dominions will lead the charge against Satan and his Demonites. Know for sure that you shall prevail.

Satan and his fighting force are brutal, but they are no match for you. You are fighting against spirits that are infested with hatred. They are capable of committing many atrocities. They are trying to break our will, but we shall not falter under intimidation or threat.

Archangels, Michael, Raphael, Uriel, and Gabriel will join you in battle. Until they arrive, you must hold the line and not waiver. Satan has grown more cunning and insidious. You must hold the line... alone... be encouraged. Go! Victory is at hand!"

A wave of unified devotion washed over the Celestial Host. Their voices, a harmonious blend of awe and unwavering faith, resonated with the weight of their eternal commitment. "We trust you, Lord," they declared as one, the words imbued with a love that transcended understanding, "with our very being."

A gentle but powerful resonance filled the divine space as God spoke, his voice carrying the warmth of boundless affection and the strength of the cosmos. "Go then," he affirmed, a hint of anticipation coloring his tone, "and bring back victory, my faithful servants."

The air crackled with a residual energy, a palpable absence where the Principalities, Powers, and Dominions had stood moments before. A sigh, almost a ripple in the celestial fabric, escaped the divine presence they had just departed.

Then, a tear in the ordered tapestry of the cosmos – a raw, jagged rent born of pure defiance as Satan, a storm cloud of fury surged forward, with the Demonites trailing in his wake. Their trajectory: the Atlantic Star Belt, a target of their reckless charge.

But amidst their furious momentum, a stillness clung to Satan. His eyes are like burning embers in the cosmic twilight. A muscle twitched in Satan's jaw, a flicker of something akin to... doubt? Or

perhaps it is merely the sharpening edge of his resolve, honed by millennia of defiance. The silence within him roared louder than the shrieks of his legion.

What dark calculus churned in that ancient mind as they hurtled through the stars? What price is he willing to pay for the dominion he craved? The universe held its breath, waiting for the answer etched in the fiery path they blazed across the heavens.

"It's time to bring order to the Celestial Kingdom. I shall prove God wrong about Adam."

A huge SHADOW flying though the Oasis of Ohm, Satan and his hordes of Demonites are barely visible heads for the Atlantic Star Belt. But Al'debaran informs Ba'laamus that he is going to spy out the enemy and veers off,

"God thinks that we shall duel here, but we shall take this fight inside the Atlantic Star Belt, hitting them with the element of surprise. We shall bring them their knees," said Ba'laamus enthusiastically.

After they had traveled some distance, the Atlantic Star Belt lay ahead. Satan and his Demonites finally arrived on its outskirts. Stopping for a moment, Satan turned to his troops hollered out,

"Just beyond the Atlantic Star Belt is the Empyrean. We shall descend into the belt and wait to ambush them."

Satan instructed his troops to hide in the belt's inner court. The outer court was surrounded by a thick grayish/black solid *raqiya* known as the Xcore. Anything can be hidden within this ring of gases. Positing themselves deep within the Star Belt, Demonites lay low, waiting for the arrival of the Celestial Host so they could launch an assault.

Meanwhile, the Celestial Host is unaware that they are heading into an ambush as they proceeded valiantly to the Oasis of Ohm. With an evil laugh, Satan reveled in his delusion of grandeur,

"We shall cripple God's forces, take the Celestial Kingdom, and there's nothing that will stop us."

Chapter 48

Re-enforcement to the rescue . . .

ack at the Canyon of HaTa'avah, Michael and the others struggled to free themselves from their prison. Michael, looking toward the others, said,

"We must get out of here."

Raphael sitting rises to his feet and searches for a way out of their prison cell.

"Our powers seem to be diminishing in the hole." he says.

"Let's face it . . . without our weapons, it's hopeless. We're at the mercy of Satan and his forces." replies Uriel.

"You are right. If we do escape, how will we defend ourselves without our weapons? They are lost forever." says Gabriel.

"We must not lose hope." replies Michael a quiet, firm voice, looking at them.

"We must not give up! We must stand in faith and trust that Hashem will deliver us."

On their journey, Abe considered how they would deal with adversity when the time came.

"I don't know if we will be able to help the Archangels?" he thought to himself.

It is a question that plagued them all. Back at the edge of the Atlantic Star Belt, Satan's forces blended into the darkness of the Xcore, which camouflaged them completely.

"This is the one thing we have on our side that will ensure us victory. I chose to attack from the Atlantic Star Belt because we can see out, but if you are on the outside, you cannot look in," said Satan.

"How didst thou discover this place?" asked Regulus.

"When I last went to meet with God, a meteor shower appeared from nowhere. I flew into this belt and a meteor collided with me, knocking my scepter out of my hand. It fell into this place. I thought that it was strange that I could not see into the Star Belt, but when I was fully in the belt, I could look outward. This is why I have chosen to attack the Celestial Host from here,"

"Sire . . . it's very fortunate that you did fly into this belt," said Regulus.

Satan waits patiently with his forces in position for the unsuspecting Celestial Host to arrive. He surveyed his formidable Demonite army, a cruel smile playing on his lips, but a shadow of irritation flickered across his face as he scanned their ranks. "Ba'laamus!" His voice cracked like a whip. "Where in the abyssal plains is Al'debaran?"

Ba'laamus flinched, his gaze darting nervously around the assembled demons before settling on his master. "My Lord... Al'debaran is... he is out on a scouting mission."

The cruel smile vanished, replaced by a thunderous scowl that could make lesser demons crumble. "A scouting mission?" His voice dripped with disbelief and rising fury. "I did not authorize such a reckless endeavor! Where did he foolishly venture?"

Ba'laamus swallowed hard, his voice barely a whisper. "He... he went to spy on the Celestial Host, my Lord."

Satan's voice, a low growl that seemed to vibrate in the very air, fixed on Kolabal. "Kolabal," he seethed, the absence of their favored general a raw nerve. "Since Aldebaran... is unavailable," the word dripped with disdain, "I want you to lead the Watchers. Directly against the Celestial Host." Kolabal's gaze flickered, crossing his face before he steeled his resolve. The weight of this unexpected command settled heavily upon him.

Satan whirled, his gaze now settling on Equinox. "Equinox," he commanded, his tone brooking no argument, "you will assist Regulus in leading the Grigori."

A visible tremor ran through Regulus. "My Lord?" he questioned, his voice tight with barely suppressed displeasure.

Ignoring the clear objection, Satan continued, his words sharp and decisive. "You will reinforce the Watchers. Drive the Celestial Host down. Down into the Atlantic Star Belt." He punctuated each word with a forceful gesture.

Then, his attention shifted, a cruel smile playing on his lips as he addressed another. "Baaladyme! Once they are pinned on one of the larger surfaces of the Star Belt, you will strike from the raqiya. Let them have no escape."

"After you take them down to the surface," Satan stated, his gaze unwavering, "we shall throw the battle in array. That is where our ultimate weapon can finally taste its triumph."

A tense silence descended, thick as the camouflage that concealed them. Every nerve ending of the Demonites seemed to hum with anticipation for the arrival of the Celestial Host. Then, a ripple of movement ran through their ranks as the unsuspecting squad materialized in the distance, rapidly closing the gap.

Satan's eyes narrowed, a predatory gleam igniting within them. With a subtle flick of his wrist, he signaled the first platoon. He cast a sharp glance over his shoulder, ensuring every warrior is a coiled spring, ready to unleash hell. Just as the Holy Angels drew nearer, Kolabal, perhaps seized by a flicker of doubt or a tactical impulse, began to shift the Watchers. But Satan's voice, laced with an urgent fury, snapped through the air. "Hold! Get back into position! Are you trying to be seen, you fool?"

At that very moment, a figure emerged from the shadows, bowing low before Satan. "Master," Al'debaran announced, his voice carrying the weight of his clandestine mission.

Satan turned, a flicker of surprise crossing his features before being swiftly masked. "Aldebaran. What is it?"

"The army of God approaches," Aldebaran replied, his gaze steady.

A cruel smile stretched across Satan's lips. "I know. And when they get within twenty-five hundred feet of our position, we shall hit them. We shall hit them hard. Those blind fools haven't the faintest idea they're walking into a slaughter. They won't know what struck them." His voice dropped to a venomous whisper, laced with dark satisfaction. "They won't know... until it's too late."

The very fabric of the Star Belt seemed to ripple as the blinding light of the Celestial Host pierced through the darkness. A primal roar tore from Satan's throat, echoing across the void. "ATTACK!"

At his lord's command, a grim determination hardening his features, Kolabal unleashed his squadron. They erupted from the concealing shadows of the nebula like a storm of black wings and gnashing teeth, a brutal force crashing upon the unsuspecting Angels. They are caught completely off guard, the Celestial Host scrambled, wings flapping rapidly as they desperately formed defensive lines. But the Demonites, fueled by dark fury, smashed through the ethereal veil of the Star Belt, with their wicked weapons thirsting for Celestial blood.

The battle raged through the sky, but the first wave of Demonites is unable to break the Celestial Host's defense. The Host tried to launch a counter-offensive, but Satan signals Regulus and he intern signal Equinox to lead Grigoris into battle.

Sunlight dappled through the leaves as Adam knelt, his brow furrowed in concentration. A tiny, iridescent beetle crawled across his palm, and he murmured a soft sound, bestowing it with a name. Around him, the air buzzed with life. Then, his innocent observation snagged on something that felt... wrong. He watched, uncomprehending, as a pair of vibrant birds engaged in a flurry of motion, and a knot of unease tightened in his chest. Was one hurting the other? The thought flickered, unsettlingly.

A sudden, stark curiosity pierced through the peaceful rhythm of Adam's mind. His thoughts swept over the myriads of creatures, each with a counterpart. "Why... why are there two of everything," he whispered, the question hanging heavy in the air, "and only one of me?" A strange disquiet settled upon him, a sense of being incomplete, an anomaly in this vibrant, paired world.

Just then, a low rumble echoed from the heavens, growing steadily louder. Adam's head snapped up. Jagged fingers of lightning tore across the sky, momentarily bleaching the lush sky with an eerie white light. A familiar sound, yet it held a subtle tremor that made the hairs on his arms prickle. He shook his head, dismissing the unease. Just thunder, he told himself.

He turned towards the gentle murmur of the river, drawn by the familiar sound of ripples flowing at its edge. As he ponder on the beauty of the garden, the thought resurfaced, insistent and sharp. Thinking about life teeming outside of the Garden, two by two, and the ache of his solitude deepened. *"Why am I the only one? Why is there another... like me?"* he thought.

A new shadow fell across the battlefield. The Grigoris, a silent, creeping tide led by a grim-faced Regulus, emerged from the chaos, moved with stillness, aiming to strike the Virtues from behind, a classic flanking maneuver. But even as the Grigoris approach unnoticed, a piercing cry echoed throughout! It's the Arch Yinpiniel! Like a furious cloud of Africanized bees, wings shimmering with iridescent light, descended upon the unsuspecting Grigori. Their attacks weren't of brute force, but a whirlwind of stinging pinpricks, disorienting feints, and maddeningly clever distractions.

The Grigoris found themselves caught in a chaotic ballet of buzzing wings and impossible movements, their advance dissolving into frustrated swipes and bewildered snarls. The Yinpiniel's created illusions on a massive scale of war machines to deceive the Demonites, with the hope that they would back down from a confrontation,

Ba'laamus's voice cracked with disbelief, pointing a trembling finger. "Look! The Celestial Host... they have war machines too!"

Baaladyme's breath hitched. "This... this is impossible." His eyes darted around, a flicker of fear in their depths.

Satan watched his commanders with a wave of pure disgust washing over his features. He spat the words out, each syllable laced with contempt. "Their pathetic war machines pose no threat to us!" he says with his fist clenched... "We shall annihilate them! Leave their wretched carcasses as a testament to our might!" He turned, his gaze burning into Equinox. "Equinox... get rid of these insects."

A furious Equinox roared, unleashing a devastating assault. Blazing energy slammed into the Yinpiniel war machines, one after another. Each impact caused their shimmering forms to flicker and vanish like illusions caught in a sudden gust.

"What in the abyss...?" Equinox muttered, his brow furrowed in disbelief. He shakes his head with a knot of confusion tightening in his gut, and he turn sharply to Regulus, his voice laced with bewilderment, he demanded, "My lord, their war machines... they fade like smoke. What twisted witchcraft is this?"

Regulus's eyes narrowed, a dangerous fury simmering beneath his regal composure. "How dare these insects mock our might?" he spat, his voice a low, menacing growl. "Equinox! Enough games! Erase them from the very fabric of this realm!"

Though forced to yield ground under the relentless onslaught, the Yinpiniel fought with the ferocity of cornered beasts. Despite their size, they moved with blinding speed and unwavering courage, each blow struck a testament to their desperate defense of the heavenly realm. Then, a horrifying sound ripped through the chaos – a sickening crunch as the Yinpiniel Bli, with a strength that belied her stature, hurled Equinox to the ground.

The tiny angels is a whirlwind of righteous fury. They descended on the Grigoris warriors. Each blow landed with surprising force, pushing back demon after demon. A wave of icy dread washed over the Grigoris as the angels pressed their assault. Just as a suffocating ring of more Grigoris closed in with an unseen force. Azra'il pulls away from the chaos. He shot into the void, abandoning his comrades.

From his vantage point, Satan's gaze narrowed as Azra'il's sudden departure registered. "Where in the abyss is he going?" he roared, his voice barely audible above the din.

The concussive bursts of energy around him demanded his attention. A cruel smile stretched across his face. The battle was unfolding beautifully.

"Keep the pressure on!" Ba'laamus bellowed, his voice ringing with savage glee. "They're breaking!"

A relentless tide of Demonites hammered the Celestial Host, driving them down towards the Star Belt's surface. Watchers and Grigoris swarmed their enemies from every direction, their attacks is a furious onslaught unlike the Celestial Host have encountered. The clash of forces erupted in a blinding storm of sparks and flares, yet the brutal conflict showed no signs of abating.

Meanwhile, on the other side of the raging battle, Abe, Jake, Josh, and Dave reached their destination. "Michael! Can you hear us?" Dave's voice cut through the distant sounds of war. With eyes that pierced through the calcium, the Shirdal scanned the desolate canyon, his gaze sweeping for any sign of the four Archangels.

The clash of steel and the roar of battle still echoed across the ravaged landscape. The Celestial Host, resolve is unbroken. They stubbornly held their ground against an relentless onslaught of the Watchers and Grigori. Then, a ripple of movement flows through the demonic ranks. "They are retreating!" Rehus exclaimed, a surge of triumph in his voice.

"Don't let up on the attack!" Regulus roared, his command ringing across the battlefield as the Celestial Host pressed their advantage, eager to exploit the apparent weakness.

But then, a note of caution from Al'debaran, his eyes scanning the shifting enemy lines. "No! Wait! It looks like they are trying to reposition themselves." A flicker of unease crossed his features.

Far above the chaos, a cold, distant gaze settled on the unfolding scene. A low command, laced with a chilling certainty, drifted from Satan. "Zones, fire. Provide cover until the Watchers and Grigori finish their realignment." The air crackled with dark energy as the devastating power of the Zones prepared to unleash its fury.

Chapter 49

The Beast at the Breach. . .

Probing eyes, sharp and predatory, scanned the jagged expanse of the Canyon, desperately seeking any sign of the imprisoned Archangels. Then, a flicker of movement deep within the Cavern of Iliad caught the Shirdal's attention. There they were: Michael, Raphael, Gabriel, and Uriel, their celestial light dimmed but unmistakable.

A guttural roar ripped through the air as the Shirdal unleashed a torrent of searing heat from its maw. The cavern wall glowed red, softening under the intense assault. Suddenly, a spiderweb of cracks snaked across the rock face. With a screech of tearing stone, the beast slammed its massive talons into the weakened wall. A gaping hole exploded into existence, showering the cavern floor with debris.

Raphael reacted instantly, yanking Uriel back just as a cascade of rock thundered down.

"What in the heavens is that?" Gabriel exclaimed, his hand instinctively reaching for the hilt of his unseen sword.

Michael's gaze, unwavering, fixed on the breach. "I have a feeling," he said, his voice low and steady, "that it's more of Satan's wicked servants."

The four Archangels instinctively drew closer, a silent circle of power bracing against the unknown threat. As the dust settled, a tense stillness hung in the air. Cautiously, they moved towards the jagged opening, their eyes wide with apprehension as a colossal shadow began to fill the space. The Shirdal, its immense form struggling to squeeze through the newly formed aperture, became momentarily stuck. From somewhere beyond the beast, a voice, sharp and commanding, echoed: "Back! Back out!"

"Michael!" Raphael's voice was tight with fear as he glanced at his brother. "What is that?"

"That," Michael replied grimly, "is the Shirdal."

"Has Satan sent this beast to devour us?" Uriel whispered, his usual serenity shattered.

"If so," Gabriel declared, his eyes flashing with defiance, "then I'm not going down without a fight!"

"No," Michael corrected, his gaze hardening. "It is one of the Enchanted Beasts."

Just then, voices, strained but familiar, cut through the tension. "Michael! We're in here!" It's Abe, and the others.

A new command rang out, "Gryphon, move!" The colossal form blocking the entrance shifted, lumbering away.

The Archangels stared at the now vacant opening, their expressions a mixture of relief and wary anticipation. Moments later, four figures emerged from the gloom, stepping into the dim light of the cavern.

"Identify yourselves," Michael commanded, his voice firm as the four figures finally stood before them.

After learning their names, and before they could go into further detail as to why they are there, a powerful glare of light suddenly appeared before them. Immediately, the Archs bowed to the floor, while the boys stood complaining.

"Hey! Who turned on the light?" asked Dave.

Chapter 50

Battle of the gods . . .

The weight of unseen eyes pressed upon the boys, though they remained blissfully ignorant to a divine presence that's before them. The Archangels are bowed low, a spectacle they misinterpreted with youthful arrogance.

"Honestly, chaps, it's really not necessary," Josh sighed, a weary roll of his eyes betraying his discomfort with the unexpected reverence.

Dave, ever the theatrical one, swept his hand in a mock regal gesture. "Yo, listen up!" I declared, my voice cutting through the noise. "By my authority, as King David, I'm tellin' you straight up: Get on your feet! Now!" he declared with a playful grin.

Abe frowned slightly at the unmoving figures. "Almighty King... Your servants remain defiant to your command, sire," he echoed Dave's tone, a hint of confusion creeping in.

The Archangels remained prostrate, their stillness now tinged with an unsettling quality. A flicker of concern crossed Dave's face as he instinctively took a step towards the source of an unusual luminescence that had begun to permeate the cavern. "NO, seriously! Get up!" he urged, his playful tone now edged with genuine bewilderment.

Then, it happened. A palpable shift in the atmosphere, a weight descending that stole the very air from their lungs. The brilliant light intensified, swallowing the shadows, and with it came a presence so profound it shook them to their core. Fear, raw and primal, seized them, their bodies beginning to tremble uncontrollably.

"Hey..." Abe whispered, his voice barely audible. "Where does this light come from?"

Dave's eyes widened, fixated on his friend. "Yo, Jake, what's up with that piece? Why it lookin' all lit up like a Christmas tree, man?"

A frantic flurry of movement followed as each boy checked their own weapon. To their astonishment, the emblems etched into the metal pulsed with the same ethereal light. Raphael, his head lifting almost imperceptibly, offered the slightest of nods, his gaze directed behind them. They turned as one.

A distorted image shimmered in the radiant light, resolving into a breathtaking scene: a majestic throne room, and upon it, a figure robed in splendor, surrounded by an august council.

"Hey, look at the Four Beasts," Abe breathed, his earlier bravado completely gone.

As if summoned by his words, four magnificent beings, the Four Enchanting Beasts of Light, materialized within the cavern. Their towering forms shrunk to a more human scale as they, too, bowed low before the unseen presence.

Terror, stark and absolute, gripped the young lads. They stumbled backward, putting precious feet between themselves and the awe-inspiring light. From within the luminous display, a voice resonated, calm and all-encompassing saying, "It's okay."

Still, they retreated with their backs pressing against the cold, unyielding stone of the cavern's wall. Seeing their fear, Michael, the Archangel, rose with graceful power and moved towards them, his expression gentle. "Fear not," he said, his voice a soothing balm. "Everything is all right." He reassured them, his words carrying an undeniable weight of truth.

"Why are they bowing before that light?" Abe stammered, his eyes darting between the prostrate Archangels and the brilliant source.

Michael's gaze softened. "They bow before the presence of God. And you, too, stand in His presence," he offered a gentle suggestion. "It would be wise to do the same."

Dave, his voice barely a whisper, managed to say, "My bad, fam. No disrespect meant, ya know?"

And so, they also bowed with their heads lowered, hearts pounding. They finally acknowledged the unseen majesty behind them. The intense light shifted, coalescing into a radiant sphere that hovered above their heads, bathing them in its warmth.

"Arise, my creations," the voice echoed, each of their names ringing with a divine intimacy.

As the Archangels rose, A hush fell as Hashem's gaze, a boundless ocean of light and ancient wisdom, settled upon the four nervous boys. "These," His voice resonated, a gentle yet earth-shattering pronouncement, "are the sons of Adam." A profound stillness followed, the weight of their lineage hanging in the air.

Then, the gravity in His tone shifted, a celestial sorrow tinging its edges. "A shadow has fallen," Hashem declared, His words carrying the weight of worlds. "Satan, in his boundless malice, has unleashed a treacherous assault upon the very Army of the Lord."

He gestured, and within a sphere of pure light, celestial energies began to coalesce. "In a vision," Hashem continued, the light within swirling with breathtaking imagery of cosmic conflict, "I shall reveal the heart of this darkness. The battle rages," His voice deepened with divine purpose, "in the Atlantic Star Belt."

The very fabric of existence shimmered as the four mortals beheld the unfolding cosmic conflict. Satan's grotesque war machines clawed at the radiant defenses of the Celestial Host, a spectacle that stole their breath and widened their eyes in disbelief. Abe, Josh, Jake, and Dave stood on the precipice of an ancient war, the weight of their unexpected role pressing down on them.

From the heart of a luminous sphere, a voice resonated with the power of creation itself. "Michael, Raphael, Gabriel, and Uriel," it commanded, the very air thrumming with authority, "you are needed on the frontline, to shepherd the Host. Jophiel requires your strength to bolster the Lord's legions."

A surge of righteous fervor coursed through Michael. The anticipation of just retribution ignited within him, banishing the lingering shadows of their confinement. Raising a hand, his gaze fixed on the radiant sphere, he asked, his voice brimming with respect, "Might I have leave to speak, my Lord?"

"Leave is granted." The divine voice echoed, gentle yet absolute.

Michael's gaze flickered towards the four bewildered youths. "Lord God," he began, his tone a mixture of concern and curiosity, "what shall become of these four souls?"

A wave of serene light emanated from the sphere. "They shall return to the Earth, to the paths they once walked. Should they fall in this conflict, their earthly existence shall cease. The Lumina Beasts shall guide them back to the gati, and thence to their world."

With swift strides, Michael and the other Archangels approached the boys, their expressions radiating profound gratitude for their liberation. Words of thanks, luminous and sincere, filled the space before they turned towards the raging battle. With a speed that defied mortal comprehension, they launched themselves into the cosmos, streaks of divine light piercing the darkness. Unbeknownst to them, their weapons lay forgotten where they had stood.

Weariness etched on their faces, the boys mounted the majestic Lumina Beasts. Their gazes, once filled with awe, now held a tinge of sadness. God, a gentle smile gracing His unseen countenance, watched the sons of Adam before the luminous sphere dissolved into the ethereal expanse. The magnificent creatures, bearing their reluctant riders, turned towards the gati.

Silence hung heavy in the air until Abe finally broke it, a note of confusion in his voice. "I thought... we were going to help the angels."

Jake nodded, his brow furrowed in thought. "That was the understanding. But considering all that's happened... it's clear Satan will stop at nothing to claim God's throne."

Josh's voice rose with sudden urgency. "Oi! You 'eard the Guv'nor, didn't ya? If we get snuffed out in this dust-up, it's curtains for us! Finished!"

"Yeah..." Jake murmured, a shadow of worry crossing his features. "What about that whole... merging thing? Remember? We could stay united with the Archangels... be safe?"

"Straight up fam! That's the real talk Melchizedek dropped on us, no cap!" Dave chimed in, his voice laced with a hint of desperation.

"Well," Abe said, a touch of disappointment in his tone, "they didn't exactly seem to need us."

Their journey back towards the gati continued, the silence punctuated only by the soft footfalls of the Lumina Beasts. Suddenly, Jake's eyes widened. He had noticed the forgotten weapons. "Hey guys! Hey guys!" he called out frantically, drawing their attention. "We can still help them!"

"How?" Abe asked, confusion etched on his face.

"We still have their weapons!" Jake exclaimed, pointing to the forgotten armaments.

A realization dawned on Abe. "If we don't get these back to them... Satan is sure to win."

"Right you are!" Josh agreed, his earlier apprehension replaced by a newfound resolve.

Dave, however, remained hesitant, his mind wrestling with the divine decree. "Lemme drop some truth on ya," he started, his voice low and laced with a streetwise caution. "Just so you ain't forgettin', right? The Big Man upstairs himself laid it down – if we catch a fade in this rumble, that's it. Poof. We ain't comin' back to our block, ya dig?"

A spark of defiance ignited in Abe's eyes. "Well, I'd rather meet my end fighting for what's right than live in a world ruled by injustice."

"I rather agree!" Josh declared, his voice ringing with proper conviction. "And what's more... I once read that no weapon formed against us shall prosper, don't you know!"

"Yeah…" Abe echoed, a strange sense of familiarity washing over him. "We are more than conquerors in Him who loves us." He looked down at his hands, a bewildered expression on his face. "Where did that come from? I don't even know what that means!"

Dave simply rolled his eyes. "I agree!" Jake declared his voice ringing with a conviction he hadn't felt for moments before. "Yeah… God did not give us the spirit of fear," he added, a newfound boldness coloring his tone.

But then, his brow furrowed, a flicker of confusion clouding his eyes. "Wait a minute…" he muttered, his voice dropping. "What am I talking about? What spirit of fear'?" The certainty had vanished, replaced by a bewildered uncertainty."

"Those are Bible verses," Dave stated dryly, a hint of exasperation in his tone. "Good heavens," he thought, they don't even know the scriptures, yet they're quoting them.

"Nah, man, ain't no way I'm rollin' with that," I said, planting my feet. "Word on the street is God ain't about fear, right? But yo, He definitely dropped some common sense in my lap, and that sense is screaming 'stay put!" Dave retorted, his voice firm.

"Right then, Dave! Suit yourself, mate! You're being proper selfish, you are! This is our bleedin' chance to make a real difference, innit? And you're just gonna chicken out? Shame on ya!" Josh exclaimed, his frustration evident.

Dave watched as Josh continued, his voice filled with unexpected earnestness. "Right then, Dave, you've got the Good Book practically etched on your heart, don't you? Now, I might not be quoting chapter and verse like yourself, but I've got a fair grasp of what's what here. John 3:16, innit? Goes something like, "For God so loved the world, that he gave his one and only Son, that whoever believes in him shall not perish…" There's a fair bit riding on this, Dave."

Abe and Jake exchanged bewildered glances. "God has a son?" they murmured simultaneously.

"I'm not even going to ask," Abe muttered.

"Me neither," Jake agreed, shaking his head slightly.

"Right, look 'ere, mate," Josh continued, his voice softening slightly, "what that boils down to, yeah? God gave us 'is bleedin' best. So, we ought to give 'im ours. Just think on it for a tick, Dave. Even though our worlds are close, time-wise, mine's still a different kettle o' fish than yours. You know about wars, same as me. You see the bloody 'ell this Earth's become. Now, imagine if Satan got 'is mitts on the whole lot. Total control, like. Just picture that, eh?" A worried urgency laced his words.

"Yo, check it, fam!" Dave blurted, his voice tight with a rising panic. "Look, I ain't ask for none of this drama, ya know? And peep this – my mind's made up, straight up. I can't even think about just... poofin' outta here. Not knowin' my moms, my pops, my sis, the homies next door, my crew at school, my cousins... or even my girl-to-be! That's too much to just ditch, ya feel me? Right now, I just... nah. I ain't down to make no sacrifice like that. So, if that makes me a selfish dude, then whatever. That's on me."

Dave made the decision to proceed on to the gati, leaving his friends behind. Abe, Jake, and Josh looked on in disappointment as Dave went on his way. Sorrow gripped the boys as they proceeded to the battlefield to return the weapons to the Archs.

"Abe, how do we know where to go? We don't have a clue where this battle is taking place." said Jake.

"Remember what the guardian said to us?" replied Abe.

"Aw, mate, seriously? What'd he say?" Josh sighed, shoulders slumping… "Dunno, just...went right out of my head."

"He said that the creatures will lead us," said Abe.

"Yeah, that's right! He did say that!" he responded.

Abe leaned close to his companion and whispered,

"To the battle!" With a loud, high-pitched shrill, the Shirdal flew in the direction of the Atlantic Star Belt.

"Let's go and save the universe, guys!" shouted Josh.

Abe, Josh, and Jake sped toward the Atlantic Star Belt to give the Archs back their weapons. Back at the battle, Satan and his Demonites become more aggressive in their assault. Thousands of Demonites left their place of hiding and are now heading toward the battle.

The relentless assault drove the Celestial Host down to the surface of Apollo in the Star Belt. The Celestial Host tried to activate their deflector shields to stifle incoming Demonite artillery. The shields depleted the vitality of the artillery, causing their shots to explode before contacting their targets.

"This is not working." said Satan.

He ordered his troops to switch to a more destructive missile to achieve their agenda. Quickly, they switched their ammunition to a type of artillery known as a sky sphere. It was as a two-stage booster extended over the single-stage range. This missile was capable of piercing through any defense, moving unopposed to strike its target. Satan was pleased with the results of the change in missiles,

"Their defense is no longer optional! Let no one escape!" he shouted.

Al'debaran, leader of the Watchers, approached Satan and said, "Sire . . ."

"What is it?" Satan said, annoyed.

"The battle is going according to plan. The annihilation of the Celestial Host is at hand. Victory is just moments away."

"Yes, without Michael to lead them, they are hopeless. The Army of God has no chance against us. They are willing to have their lights extinguished for a creature that cares nothing for them."

Chapter 51

Clash of the Celestial lights . . .

The clang of demonic steel against celestial armor echoed across the ravaged battlefield. Moloch, a brute of shadow and fury, roared as his jagged axe crunched into Gal'gal's breastplate. Beside him, Akkadian, his eyes burning with cruel delight, brought his spiked mace down on Qumoris with sickening force. The two angels crumpled, divine light flickering in their eyes as they clutched at the points of impact, agony contorting their features.

The Angelic Force, a tide of white and gold moments before, was now a fractured wave being relentlessly pushed towards the swirling chaos of the Atlantic Star Belt surface. Then, a sight that could turn the tide – or break it entirely. Emerging from the celestial veil, their forms blazing with righteous power were Michael, Raphael, Gabriel, and Uriel.

But as the grim reality of the battlefield crashed over them – the fallen, the relentless demonic advance – a stark realization dawned. Their hands were empty. No gleaming swords, no radiant spears. They were walking into a slaughter. Panic flared in Raphael's eyes. her seized Michael's arm, his grip tight with fear. "Michael! Look!

We... we have nothing! How are we going to defend ourselves?" His voice was a strained whisper against the din of battle.

Michael halted, his gaze sweeping across the carnage, a flicker of grim understanding crossing his face. For a heartbeat, a shadow seemed to pass over his resolute features. Then, his eyes locked with Raphael's, a fierce, unwavering light igniting within them. A confident smile touched his lips, a stark contrast to the surrounding chaos. "The Lord of Hosts is with us," he declared, his voice ringing with absolute certainty, a beacon of hope in the encroaching darkness.

Meanwhile, the triumphant roars of the demons faltered. All heads snapped towards a burgeoning golden light in the distance. Gabriel, his resolute stance, held a magnificent trumpet, seemingly conjured from the very fabric of the heavens. He raised it to his lips, and a blast of pure, resonant power tore through the battlefield. It was a sound that promised not just reinforcements, but the very wrath of the Divine.

Satan, who had been surveying the brutal efficiency of his forces, spun around, his crimson eyes widening in disbelief and fury as the sound reached him. He saw them then – the Archangels, their forms radiating power even from afar. "No!" he roared, his voice a guttural bellow of disbelief. "This can't be! How... how did they escape their prison? They were bound! For eternity!"

The air crackled with unseen energy as they reached the edge of the fray, the metallic tang of clashing weapons sharp in the void. Sparks, like angry fireflies, erupted where celestial steel met demonic iron. Then, a blinding flash against the inky backdrop – Michael and the Archangels descended, a radiant force crashing into the heart of the Demonite ranks.

A guttural roar ripped through the chaos as demons swarmed the newly arrived Archangels, their crude blades hacking. But the Archangels were a whirlwind of righteous fury, their fists smashing into demonic faces with brutal force. Each blow was a burst of divine energy, dissolving the corrupted forms into wisps of acrid smoke, only for them to sickeningly coalesce again.

Across the swirling battlefield, the main host of angels was locked in a desperate dance of swordplay. They pressed into the center of the Star Belt, a silver tide against a black reef. Michael, a beacon of defiance, found himself beset by two of his fallen brethren, their attacks relentless, fueled by a bitter rage. He moved like liquid light, a breathtaking ballet of evasion and counter, frustrating their every vicious lunge. Uriel, her face, a mask of grim determination, began to push through the demonic ranks towards his brother. The air thrummed with the unspoken truth: without their celestial weapons, the Archangels were vulnerable, being forced down towards the cold surface of the Star Belt.

A sharp, imperious gesture from Satan. Baalamus, his eyes gleaming with cruel anticipation, relayed the command. From the shadows at the edge of the cosmos, the hulking silhouettes of war machines began their inexorable advance. Light-years away, a trio of figures – Abe, Josh, and Jake – hurtled towards the conflict, their arrival mere moments away. Across the heavens, a war of souls raged within the confines of the Star Belt.

Relentless, the dark forces continued their brutal assault, driving God's angels down towards the desolate planet Apollo, nestled deep within the belt. Yet, with fierce resolve, the Celestial Host began to push back, a surge of divine power turning the tide, forcing the Demonite ranks to yield ground. Annoyance flickered across Satan's face as he barked another order, summoning more of his mechanical horrors.

From the inky blackness, like monstrous insects crawling from a hidden nest, Satan's war machines emerged. A collective gasp rippled through the Heavenly Host, their gazes fixed on the approaching threat. Outgunned, but not broken, they fought with renewed ferocity against the pressing demonic tide.

Then, a new element crashed into the scene. Abe, Josh, and Jake, their eyes wide with the unfolding spectacle of cosmic war, arrived. Abe, with primal urgency, spurred his magnificent Shirdal. A chilling, unearthly cry tore from the beast's throat, a sound that seemed to vibrate Satan's very bones, his eyes widening in horrified fascination.

"Well, what in the abyss…?" he muttered, his gaze narrowed, trying to pierce the distance. A dark scowl etched itself onto his features. "I summoned no such beast! They must be His… but what are those creatures?" he roared, his voice laced with a growing unease.

He flung a handful of demons towards the advancing figures. The lesser spirits, eager to please their master, charged head-on. But with a simultaneous, earth-shattering roar, the creatures unleashed a torrent of pure fire, engulfing the demons in a rolling inferno that vanished as quickly as it appeared, leaving behind only drifting ash and the faint smell of burnt flesh.

"Where'd they come from?" Ba'laamus whispered, his usual smugness replaced by bewilderment.

"Who cares where they came from?" Al'debaran snapped, his eyes fixed on the rapidly approaching forms. "I'm more worried about where they're going!"

A palpable tension gripped the Demonite ranks. Baalamus and the others braced themselves, but Satan, his mind racing, barked orders at his war machines. Heavy artillery fire streaked across the void, but the beasts, guided by the boys, weaved through the deadly barrage with uncanny agility. Hovering just above the chaotic surface, Josh and Jake leaped from their mounts, sending the magnificent creatures surging into the fray.

Abe, his hand lingering on the Shirdal's warm hide, gave a final, encouraging pat. "Go get them, boy!"

With another deafening cry, the Shirdal announced its terrifying arrival, spitting incandescent fire and crackling lightning. The combined energy slammed into several war machines, tearing through their armored hulls with devastating force, turning metal to molten slag and trampling the remnants underfoot.

"Where did these creatures come from?" Satan repeated, his voice tight with frustration.

"I don't know, Sire!" Al'debaran exclaimed, his eyes wide with disbelief.

"Sire! We can't get off a good shot!" Regulus cried out, his voice strained.

"Remarkable creature... it should be on our side," Al'debaran murmured, a strange fascination in his gaze.

"If we don't stop these creatures," Satan snarled, his anger now boiling over, "my plans for domination will be ruined!"

He turned to Baalamus, his expression a mask of forced calm. "Ba'laamus, my friend..."

"God must have sent these beasts to shore up His pathetic army!" Satan roared, interrupting himself, his fist clenching. "Nevertheless, I will not be denied what's rightfully mine!"

As if summoned by his fury, a magnificent Pegasus descended upon the battlefield, its powerful wings generating hurricane-force winds that sent Satan's war machines tumbling like discarded toys. Then, a flash of pure white – a Unicorn, galloping through the void, teleported behind enemy lines and with a thunderous kick, sent another war machine crashing into its brethren. Its horn glowed with an ethereal light, and then hundreds of miniature horns shot forth, piercing the remaining machines.

"Sire! We are losing our advantage!" Al'debaran shouted, his voice laced with panic.

"This can't be! They're gaining the upper hand!" Ba'laamus echoed, his face pale.

"Without a quick strategy, we will not survive this onslaught," Azra'il stated grimly.

"These are creatures of immense power," Satan conceded, his voice low with grudging respect.

"Sire, I don't think these creatures have a weakness," Regulus whispered, his eyes fixed on the rampaging beasts.

A undeniable fear surge through Al'debaran's voice. "Sire," he pleaded, his gaze fixed on some unseen horror, "how can we possibly defeat these... things? They possess powers that feel... godlike."

Satan's crimson eyes swept across the ravaged battlefield in shock as a gasp escaped him. His legions, his pride, are strewn across the celestial plains like discarded toys. A low, guttural sound rumbled in his chest, building into a fiery as he eyes the four colossal figures moving with impunity in the distance. Then, a slow, chilling smile spread across his face, a predator sensing weakness.

"Those... creatures," he hissed, each word laced with a new-found respect tinged with malice, "are more formidable than I initially conceived," his voice dropped to a conspiratorial whisper, "But I know how we can be rid of these monstrous pests... forever!"

Al'debaran's gaze snapped to his Lord, a flicker of desperate hope in his eyes. "What do you have in mind, Lord Satan?"

A cruel certainty hardened Satan's features. "After this day," he declared, his voice resonating with dark promise, "you shall never again lay eyes upon these wretched beasts."

The clash of steel and the screams of the fallen painted a grim tableau across the battlefield. Both Celestial Host and Demonites fought with the ferocity of cornered animals, their determination a fragile shield against the encroaching tide of exhaustion.

"Look!" Al'debaran exclaimed, pointing, a trembling finger. "The enemy... they can barely stand!"

Indeed, the once radiant forms of the Celestial Host faltered. Hunger gnawed at their divine essence, their movements becoming sluggish, their defenses crumbling. One by one, they collapsed onto the hallowed ground.

"Press the attack!" Ba'laamus roared, his voice hoarse but triumphant. "They are weakening! We must maintain the pressure!"

Regulus, his breath coming in ragged gasps, offered a grim explanation. "Without their ma-nə bread to sustain them, it is only a matter of time before they all fall."

A flicker of dark inspiration ignited in Satan's eyes as he recalled his earlier machinations. "Maintain your positions!" he commanded his lieutenants. "I shall return." With a swift, unsettling gait, he moved towards the source of a strange, emerald glow emanating from the fallen Unicorn. The light pulsed, separating from the massive creature, and then, with an unnatural fluidity, multiplied into several identical clones.

Confusion rippled through the Demonite ranks. Their attacks became scattered, their focus shattered by the sudden proliferation of targets. Meanwhile, amidst the fallen angels, a trio of figures – Abe, Josh, and Jake – moved with desperate urgency, their voices strained with concern.

"I have a bad feeling about this," Jake muttered, his eyes darting nervously across the chaotic scene.

"Come on!" Abe urged his voice thick with emotion as he tried to lift a slumped angel. "You can't give up now! Fight it!"

Michael, appearing pallid, shook his head slightly. "I... I don't know how much longer we can endure. Without any ma-nə bread, our strength... it's abandoning us."

Slowly, agonizingly, more angels succumbed to the relentless hunger, their bodies limp and still. Sensing the opportune moment, a predatory gleam entered Satan's eyes. He moved with a sinister purpose towards the cluster of fallen angels, his approach unnoticed by the Demonites, who were still grappling with the Unicorn's bewildering tactic, and unimpeded by the distracted Enchanted Beasts of Light.

A wave of dread washed over Abe, Josh, and Jake as they saw Satan striding towards them, his shadow falling like a shroud over their weakened comrades. Desperation lent them a surge of adrenaline. They struggled to pull Michael and the others to their feet, their efforts futile against the overwhelming exhaustion. Satan stopped before Michael, his gaze a cold, triumphant weight as he looked down at the fallen archangel.

Chapter 52

The Cost Of Defiance . . .

Satan's foot slammed into Michael's gut like a hammer with sickening force. "Michael! Look at you," he sneered, the words laced with cruel satisfaction. The leader of the Archangels gasped, doubling over, a strangled sound escaping his lips. Satan loomed over him, voice dripping with venom. "I've been longing for this moment."

Michael's wings, drooping slightly, a faint tremor in his usually unwavering stance, offered a small, almost imperceptible nod. His voice, though steady, held a deep weariness. "Good," he murmured. The single word is a sigh of resignation rather than agreement.

"Since our last... pleasantry," Satan continued, a dark amusement flickering in his eyes, "I have become infinitely stronger."

Michael, though clearly in agony, pushed himself up slightly, a spark of defiance in his gaze. "No," he rasped, each word a struggle. "What you have become is... predictable. You'll have to conjure more than this pathetic display to defeat us."

"Yield!" Satan roared, his patience thinning. "This is futile!"

Just then, a blur of motion as Abe, Josh, and Jake surged forward, positioning themselves protectively between their fallen leader and the demonic entity.

"Leave him alone!" Abe's voice shook with protective fury.

Satan's gaze swept over the three boys, a chilling contempt twisting his features. "Ah," he purred, a dangerous amusement in his tone. "And what marvels do we have here?"

"Your worst nightmare, mate!" Josh spat, his fists clenched tight.

A cruel smile stretched across Satan's face. "This is almost... poetic. The vaunted Chief Prince of the Celestial Host brought low, and now... the vermin of the Earth dare to stand before me. So," he mused, a dark understanding dawning in his eyes, "This is why the Almighty delayed the creation of the female. She would have polluted His precious design with more of your pathetic kind, something He rightly forbids us. Three mewling parasites. I know your generations are teeming with your filth."

Abe's nostrils flared, a primal disgust rising within him. "Your stench... it pollutes the very air. I recognize it from nightmares."

"Son of Adam..." Satan's voice dropped to a dangerous whisper. "You have sealed your fate by interfering. Once I claim God's throne, your insignificant world will be the first to be crushed beneath my heel."

"Over our dead bodies!" the boys declared in unison, their voices ringing with unwavering resolve.

"If our lives are the price to rid this universe of your darkness," Abe stated, his eyes locked on Satan's, "then it is a price we are willing to pay."

Satan chuckled, a cold, humorless sound. "Feisty little insects, aren't you? Rest assured, after I've finished slaughtering the Celestial Host, you will be the very first to follow them into oblivion."

He shifted his stance, a persuasive tone entering his voice as he tried to break their united front. "Sons of Adam... I offer you a chance. Bow before me, acknowledge me as your God, and I will spare your pathetic lives."

"Nah, mate," Josh spat, his jaw tight with defiance. "Not in this lifetime. Not the next. We ain't bowin' to the likes of ya."

Azra'il, observing the exchange, turned to Ba'laamus, his expression a mask of disgust. "Why does he negotiate with this refuse? Why doesn't he simply obliterate them and be done with it?"

Ba'laamus shifted uncomfortably, avoiding Azra'il's gaze. Frustration boiling over, Azra'il stalked towards Satan, his voice sharp with disapproval. "My lord! What madness is this? To grant these insignificant creatures a chance? This entire conflict will be meaningless if you allow them to live! They are nothing but vile impurities!"

Satan's eyes, twin pools of glacial fury, snapped to Azra'il. "Azra'il," he hissed, each word a venomous strike. "I decide who lives and who dies here. Not you!"

A grim smile touched Abe's lips as he assessed the rising tension between the demons. "Satan," he said, his voice steady despite the danger. "We are not afraid of you. We will never yield, no matter what twisted power you wield."

The boys braced themselves, fists clenched, ready to face the inevitable.

"You three pathetic specks don't stand a chance," Satan snarled, his eyes burning with hatred. "When I am lord, I will erase you from existence itself!"

A desperate cry ripped from three young throats as they lunged at Satan, a whirlwind of youthful fury. But it was like striking a mountain. A booming laugh erupted from him, echoing with cruel amusement as a single, contemptuous backhand sent them sprawling like broken dolls. "Take them!" he roared at the Demonites, his voice laced with dark triumph. "Prisoners!"

Michael, battered and swaying, pushed himself up, his limbs trembling. He stumbled, catching himself on one knee, his voice hoarse with pain and a desperate plea. "Let them go, Satan! They... they did you no harm."

Satan's gaze snapped towards Michael, a slow, deliberate turn that sent a shiver down the spine. His lips curled back in a low, guttural snarl, a sound that promised violence. "They exist," he spat, each word a venomous strike. "And that, Michael, is harm enough!"

"This... this battle is between us," Michael gasped, his eyes locked on Satan's burning gaze. "Leave them... out of this."

A chilling smile spread across Satan's face, a stark contrast to the rage moments before. "Oh, no, Michael. They are very much a part of this." He gestured dismissively at the fallen figures. "They are the reason we are at odds. Face it, you and this precious Host have already fallen. By my hand." His voice dropped, becoming silken and dangerously persuasive. "But... I will give you one more chance. One last flicker of an opportunity to prove your loyalty... to me. I will spare your pathetic star, Michael, if you will only... bow down to my greatness."

Michael's gaze swept across the ravaged field, each twisted piece of machinery a testament to the brutal clash, each still form a heartbreaking reminder of his fallen brethren. His head sank, the weight of their sacrifice pressing down on him, the very thought of submission a vile poison in his spirit. Then, a surge of defiance ripped through him. His head snapped up, eyes blazing with righteous fury.

"I shall never serve thee, nor shall I bow to thee, demon!" His voice, though strained, resonated with unwavering conviction. "Better to be extinguished on my feet than to grovel before your filth. With every breath that remains in me, I will fight you until the very end! This light within me," he gestured to his chest, "is not mine to command. It belongs to Hashem!"

A guttural roar tore from Satan's throat. "Enough!" His boot slammed into Michael's chest, sending the Archangel sprawling. "Look at you," the demon sneered, his voice dripping with contempt. "Pathetic."

From where they were held captive by grotesque Demonites, Abe, Josh, and Jake thrashed and cried out, their desperate pleas for Michael and the other Archangels echoing across the desolate landscape.

Satan didn't even glance at them. "Silence!" he bellowed. "It's the end of the road for your precious heroes. This battle is over. And when I'm finished with them," his gaze flicked back to Michael, a predatory gleam in his eyes, "you are next. Just as Adam was the crowning jewel of creation, so shall he be the crowning jewel in death!"

He stalked towards Michael, his steps heavy with dark triumph. "The Council of the Ungodly has spoken," he purred, his voice a venomous caress. "A verdict of one to nothing…" He paused, savoring the moment. "…I hereby sentence you all to eternal imprisonment."

Satan squatted before the fallen Archangel, leaning in close, his fetid breath washing over Michael's face. "You fought bravely, Michael," he whispered, a cruel smile spreading across his features. "But alas, this battle will end with my victory. Your light has burned for far too long. Now… it's time to extinguish it." His eyes narrowed, a flicker of something akin to satisfaction within their depths. "Not only have you failed your precious God, but you have also let down an entire world."

The slow grin widened, revealing sharp, yellowed teeth. He raised his sword, the dark metal glinting ominously in the dim light.

"From God your light came; to God your light shall return!" he bellowed, the words a death knell.

A collective gasp escaped the boys. They threw up their hands, turning away, tears streaming down their faces. "No!" Abe wailed. "Michael, no!" Josh cried out, his voice cracking with despair. "We can't bear to watch!" Jake sobbed, burying his face in his hands. Their anguished cries mingled with the victor's triumphant roar, a symphony of despair against a backdrop of utter devastation.

"Oi! Leave it out! Seriously, stop! Please!" Josh yelped, his eyes wide with fear.

Jake's head snapped back, a strangled cry escaping his lips. "No! No, no, NO!" His voice cracked with disbelief and horror.

Abe thrashed against his restraints, muscles straining, voice raw with desperation. "Don't do this! Please, don't!"

Josh recoiled as if struck, his breath catching in his throat. "I… I simply can't bear to watch!" he choked out, hands flying to cover his eyes as if to shield himself from the impending horror.

Satan roared, a triumphant sound that echoed across the battlefield. His back arched, the sword held high, poised to strike a devastating blow. But then… the skies split like parchment under fire. Crimson light bled through the clouds as David and the Phoenix, a being of divine flames, hovered with wings stretched wide—each feather a blade of living fire.

Across the blackened vale, the Demonite Watchers—hulking forms cloaked in scales and shadows—stood in defiance. Grigoris, with eyes of molten silver and armor forged in the void, raised their Warhammers and the Zones, the splicer of time, shimmered in and out of visibility, their laughter bending the air like heat above a furnace. In a blaze of searing light, the Phoenix dove, unleashing a shockwave that shattered the clouds and ignited the earth below.

Demonites scattered, screeching, their wings combusting mid-flight. The Watchers failed to hold their ground. David descended with his sword drawn. His aura surging with celestial fire channeled from his bond with the Phoenix. With a twist midair, he spun through the first wave of Grigoris's, slicing through them.

In comes the Zones, appearing behind him, daggers aimed at his spine—but David had already blinked sideways, striking that rippled, and Zones screamed as their surprise attack faltered.

But one of the Grigoris roared and slammed its hammer into the Starbelt ground, unleashing a quake that tore fissures through the vale. But the Phoenix ascended, wings folding into a spiral of fire, then launched downward in a nova burst. The hammer met with flame. Metal groaned, warped, and melted.

"Yo, peep this," David said to the reeling Watchers. "You and your boys watchin' the fall and all that mess. Now witness the rise."

With a shout, he lifted Seraph's Fang, and the Phoenix cried out—its voice a thousand trumpets, a million flames. Their joined energy surged outward in a blazing storm, purging the vale of darkness, incinerating Demonite ranks, and sealing the Watchers within pillars of flame-forged crystal. Silence fell. The valley burned in sacred light.

David turned to the Phoenix, a grin breaking across his soot-streaked face, "Remind me to never tick you off."

The Phoenix let out a blinding LIGHT ERUPTED of pure energy expanding outwards. Satan staggered back, his eyes wide with disbelief at the sudden, impossible appearance of the Phoenix. His sword clattered to the ground forgotten as he snarled, a primal command ripping from his throat, "Attack! Demonites, ATTACK!"

The boys, moments before consumed by terror, now stared in stunned awe. The massive bird, wreathed in golden light, circled above them, a beacon of hope against the encroaching darkness. With a powerful beat of its wings, razor-sharp feathers rained down like divine javelins.

Abe's voice, thick with disbelief and elation, boomed, "THAT'S... THAT'S AWESOME!"

Jake, a fierce grin spreading across his face, clenched his fists. "Now we can take the fight to these monsters!"

A wave of pure joy washed over Abe, Josh, and Jake. They turned to each other, a silent understanding passing between them, and erupted in cheers, jumping and whooping at the unbelievable sight of Dave, their friend, astride the magnificent Phoenix.

The expelled feathers, shimmering and strong, formed a protective barrier, a temporary shield of light around the fallen Celestial Host. The Phoenix descended in a graceful spiral, landing near the broken forms of the Archs. Dave dismounted, his gaze immediately locking onto Michael. He rushed to his side, straining to lift the barely conscious figure, a surge of relief flooding him as he saw the familiar spark of life in his eyes.

A wry smile touched Dave's lips. "I hope I didn't come at a bad time?" he quipped, a nervous energy underlying his attempt at humor.

Michael's voice is weak but laced with surprise. "I thought you returned to your world. What made you come back?"

A new resolve hardened Dave's features. "Yo, check it. I'm back, see? 'Cause, it hit me, like, for real what's goin' down. This ain't no playin' around, no lookin' for shine. Nah, man... I gotta be in the thick of it. Where the heat's at." His urgency is palpable. "Yo, lemme get your hand, fam! We gotta bounce. Like, *now*." He paused, reaching into his tunic. "But before we do, I have something that belongs to you."

He extended the gleaming sword towards Michael, his hand steady. "Take it."

How does that feel? Did we capture the shift in emotions and the intensity of the moment? Michael grasped the hilt, his gaze briefly tracing the blade's design. Then, he raised it high. Instantly, a brilliant light erupted from the sword, a wave of pure energy surging through Michael's body. He felt a surge of power, a portion of his lost strength returning in a rush.

"And this," Dave added, handing over a small, worn bag. "An angel gave it to me on the way. Said it is for you. I tried one. It tastes like honey."

Michael opened the bag, a wave of sweet aroma filling the air. He reached inside, pulling out a piece of thin, wafer-like bread. Ma-nə. He broke off a piece and consumed it. A renewed energy coursed through him. He passed the bag to the other Archangels, who followed his lead. The bag, miraculously, never emptied, and Michael shared the remaining bread with the others. Each bite restored their strength, banishing the lingering fatigue.

The Demonite clan watched, their faces a mask of disbelief. Michael had his sword. Satan, his eyes burning with rage, zipped over to Ba'laamus, Al'debaran, and Regulus. Without a word, he struck Balaamus, sending him crashing to the ground.

The entire Demonite clan struggled to comprehend how the sword had returned to Michael. In a flash, Satan sped over to Baalamus, Al'debaran, and Regulus. Anger surged through him as he struck Ba'laamus, sending him crashing to the ground.

"I was led to believe you couldn't find those weapons! Yet here they are, each one resurfaced!"

Al'debaran and Regulus, shaken by Satan's fury, fell to their knees in submission. Towering over Ba'laamus, Satan grabbed him roughly, lifting him to his feet.

"Ba'laamus… you have failed me for the last time! Do you not understand the consequences of such failure?"

A terrified Al'debaran watched, unable to believe what he was witnessing, while Ba'laamus kept his gaze on his master.

"Lord Satan, we searched the blu planet for them and found nothing, sire," Ba'laamus stammered in desperation… "Hashem concealed them from our sight!"

In response, Satan shoved Ba'laamus away with force.

"We can still defeat them. Their weapons are no match for ours," Satan declared from his vantage point, a glimmer of defiance in his eyes. He turned sharply toward Dave, his disappointment palpable. "How dare you exacerbate our predicament?"

Satan commanded Beelzebub to mobilize the war machines. With a booming order, she sent the towering engines of destruction to the battlefield. They unleashed a brutal fire power against the monstrous creatures, but to no avail—each strike seemed to dissipate against their impenetrable forms. In response, the Four Enchanted Beasts of Light launched a devastating counterattack, annihilating thousands of the war machines in a single, sweeping motion.

Realizing the dire situation, Azra'il called for a retreat of the Zones, leaving Demonite vulnerable and exposed. Satan whirled around, his eyes blazing like twin embers. "Azra'il!" he roared, the sheer force of his fury making the very air crackle… "You fool! What in the abyss are you doing?"

Azra'il, a flicker of defiance in his gaze, met Satan's fury head-on, though a tremor of fear ran through him. "Just trying to preserve our kind," he spat back, the sarcasm sharp and laced with a desperate edge. The audacity of his reply hung heavy in the air, surprising even himself.

Satan's jaw tightened, his frustration a palpable wave. "Enough!" he snarled, cutting off any further retort. He turned away abruptly, the dismissal a stinging insult. "I will deal with you later," he bit out, his mind already racing, the need to salvage their situation overriding his immediate rage.

In the midst of chaos, a dark figure brooded over the battlefield, the air thick with tension and the acrid scent of smoke. He had concocted a cunning strategy to exterminate the radiant creatures that stand in his way. With a steely resolve, he commanded eight of his formidable war machines to engage each formidable beast head-on while directing the other eight to strike from the shadows.

The ground trembled as his machines roared to life, metallic jaws snapping and weapons blazing against the Four Enchanting Beasts of Light. But despite their formidable strength, the machines were no match for the radiant defenders; one by one, they fell, defeated, their destruction leaving only echoes of their former power. Each loss fueled an inferno of rage within him, desperate times demanded desperate measures.

With a sharp wave of his hand, he ordered the remaining machines to pull back, retreating under the tempest of his fury.

"I shall not be defeated!" he bellowed, his voice cutting through the clamor of battle like a thunderclap.

His eyes burned like molten lava as he clenched his fist in determination. Pointing his finger at the majestic Guardians of the Sky, he unleashed a torrent of anger, his presence darkening the very air around him.

"Your presence in this conflict has sealed your fate! You, great wardens of the heavens, will no longer cast your light upon this realm. The throne of this kingdom is my rightful destiny, and no power, be it divine or mortal, shall thwart my ambition!"

The heavens wept stars as Satan rose through the shattered veil. His wings, once glorious, now bled shadow across the realm. In his hand, he bore Umbravex—not as a weapon, but as a verdict. The Heart piercer of Aeon's pulsed with a predated sound.

Above him, the Four Enchanting Beasts of Light formed a blazing constellation of defense. They shined as one—wings spread, halos fused, voices raised in a celestial quartet that filled the realms with awe. The roar of their unity nearly turned the tide. But Satan did not flinch. He raised Umbravex. The weapon screamed. The very concept of light recoiled,

"Your time here will be no more," he hissed, voice echoing in the living creatures. "You enchant with hope, but I strike with truth.

All light dims. For peace in the heavens and on the blu planet will be elusive."

Subsequently, the Extinction Surge emerged from the Umbravex. It splits into four spectral spears, each imbued with a corruption of the beast it sought. The spears tore through the sky with a cry that cracked the moment. Each Beast roared, wings flaring, but even together they could not withstand the blow. One by one, they fell.

Satan stood among the fallen beast. He did not smile. He simply turned.

"Let the age of this government begin," he blurred out holding the Umbravex for power—and for memory, devouring the very idea that the four Beasts had ever existed.

"Let this be a lesson," he declared, as shadows danced around him… "In my realm, mercy is but a whisper; defiance shall taste the stinging bite of despair."

Chapter 53

The Desperate Gambit. . .

The air crackled with spent energy, a heavy weariness clinging to Dave and Michael like a shroud. Dave, his face etched with raw concern, knelt beside his fallen friend. "Michael," he choked out, his voice thick with unshed tears, "Yo, you see this? My ride just got ghosted by that devil."

Michael looked up, his eyes clouded with a profound uncertainty that mirrored their dwindling hope. How much longer could they possibly endure this? A sudden, fierce surge of emotion gripped him. He reached out, his hand trembling as he grasped Dave's arm, pulling him close with surprising strength. "David," he urged, his voice strained but resolute, "whatever... whatever happens to us, you and the others... you must continue this fight."

David shakes his head vehemently, his own eyes blazing with fierce determination. "No," he declared, his voice firm despite the tremor in his hands. "Listen up, Mike," he insisted, his eyes locked on his. "Nobody messin' with you. And I'm stuck to you like glue, ya dig? Not today, not tomorrow, never, fam." He swallowed hard, his gaze unwavering. "We ain't gonna fade out like... like that shadow dude back in my hood, ya know? Where I'm from, that's a dead end," a fierce pride resonated in his tone, "Nah, man, that ain't how we do things around here. You, our people. End of story. We ain't leavin' nobody behind."

The weight of Melchizedek's words crashed back into Dave's mind: "Yo, listen up, fam! We gotta roll tight on this, right? This ain't no joke; this enemy's comin' for everything. If we don't lock arms, like, for real, then it's straight blackout for the whole darn hood. Forever. You feel me?" David and the others chuckled at Melchizedek's attempt to mimic language.

David turned to the small, battered group, a newfound resolve hardening his features. "Listen up, everyone!" His voice, though weary, rang with conviction. "I... I think I've found a way. A way to beat these demons and save both worlds."

Josh scoffed, crossing his arms, skepticism twisting his face. "How in bloody heck is that supposed to happen, Dave? We've tried everything!"

"No," Dave countered, his voice low but unwavering. "Yo, we ain't even in the ballpark yet, fam. We just dipping our toes in the shallow end."

Jake, his usual jovial demeanor replaced by a grim fatigue, leaned in, a flicker of desperate curiosity in his eyes. "Okay, then. What's the plan?"

"Yo, fam, this ain't no joke. We gotta roll deep... with the Archangels. It's the only way," Dave stated, the words hanging heavy in the air.

A stunned silence fell over the group. Confusion and dawning disbelief painted their faces.

"Blimey, mate! What do you think we've been doing?" Joshua exclaimed, frustration lacing his voice.

"Not like this fam!" Dave shot back, shaking his head, his urgency palpable.

"Well, how exactly?" Abe asked, his brow furrowed in bewilderment.

Dave take in a deep breath, gathering his scattered thoughts. "Yo, listen up, fam. Remember the drill? We gotta... like, become them. Jump inside their skins, ya know? It's the only way to save 'em, for real, and even stand a shot against this punk. Word is, it'll unlock some crazy divine juice they got locked up inside." He cleared his throat, a desperate determination swelling within him.

High above the ravaged landscape, Satan stand ominously atop his grotesque battle tank, his voice echoing with cruel satisfaction across the battlefield. "Veil your eyes!" he commanded his legion, a grim smile twisting his lips. Channeling his malevolent energy, he directed his war machines to unleash a wave of pure destruction.

With a deafening roar that tore through the silence, the ground beneath their feet shuddered as immense projectiles hurtled skyward. Abe, Dave, Josh, and Jake could only watch in frozen terror, their hearts hammering against their ribs as the monstrous sound reverberated, trailing a wave of chaotic energy down to Earth.

Then, an unimaginable horror erupted from the cannons – a nightmarish swarm of spawn fleas, a cascading wave of vile entities bursting forth with a cataclysmic force designed to obliterate everything in their path. A blinding flash engulfed the sky, momentarily illuminating the faces of the Four Enchanted Beasts of Light.

"Uh-oh..." Jake breathed, his voice barely a whisper, tinged with sheer panic. "...this is definitely bad news!"

The others responded with determined shakes of their heads. In that instant, a voice resonated in their minds – Michael, the Archangel, his tone urgent, Hurry! Gather with the Archangel who wields the weapon you once possessed. Your forms cannot withstand this force for long!

Steeling himself, drawing on a courage that felt ancient, Dave rallied his friends. "Listen up! This is it, fam! Straight up, our whole darn world hangs in the balance right now! No room for shaky knees, ya hear me? We gotta lock arms, find that fire in our bellies, know what I'm sayin'? We're the ones meant to set things right in this messed-up world, protect what's ours! This ain't no drill, it's do or die! Let's move!"

They exchanged determined glances before bolting towards the looming forms of the Archangels. Behind them, the wave of destructive energy surged ominously, consuming everything in its path. Michael spread his magnificent wings wide, a desperate shield against the impending doom for Dave, while the other Archangels sped forward, trying to close the deadly gap.

The solar winds churned violently, a fierce echo of the devastating detonation. They won't make it! The thought clawed at Dave's mind as he screamed internally, RUN! RUN! RUN! The boys sprinted with every ounce of strength they possessed, Jake leading the desperate charge until his foot caught, and he crashed heavily to the ground.

Abe and Josh, their reactions a fraction too slow, tumbled over him, a tangle of limbs as they scrambled to regain their footing. The oppressive heat of the raging energy wave descended upon them, a suffocating reminder of the annihilation that trailed in its wake. Then, the Archangels swept down upon them, their massive wings enveloping the companions in a fleeting shadow of protection,

Satan pointed a menacing finger at Ba'laamus and Beelzebub. "Retrieve their frozen carcasses!" he commanded, and they dove with terrifying speed, snatching up the stilled carcasses of the Enchanting Beast Of Light. Azra'il stepped forward, barking swift orders to secure the bodies onto several enormous slings he had devised. The catapults groaned and creaked under the immense weight before being unleashed, sending the once-great beasts HURTLING into the infinite void of space.

Satan watched the scene unfold, a sinister grin spreading across his face as a guttural laugh erupted from his throat.

"Those menacing creatures are finally gone!" he bellowed, his voice shaking with dark glee... "There is no force in existence that can rival my power now! Once I triumph over God, my name will echo through the annals of history! My loyal subjects, let us not falter in our assault! True immortality is just within our grasp! Victory is imminent! The weary Celestial Host stands between us and the Icsor Fortress! It is time to deliver the final strike and obliterate what remains of them!" His voice shook the very fabric of the cosmos with its hateful intensity.

Satan and his army of Demonites reveled in the aftermath of their brutal victory. The air around them crackled with the residue of dark power, a wave of triumphant energy washing over them as they surveyed the desolate landscape charred by their presence. The ashes of the Archangels' once-vibrant forms drifted upwards like fading, sorrowful memories.

Pleased with their horrifying handiwork, Satan swept across the scorched earth to inspect the desolation. He knelt, his fingers tracing the blackened ground, stirring the ash as if it held some profound meaning.

"Well, well," he mused, a cruel smirk twisting his features. "This should certainly snuff out God's pathetic little flicker of hope."

With malevolent satisfaction, he rose and strode back towards his eager army, their energy thrumming with the exhilaration of their triumph.

"My loyal Demonites!" he called out, his voice booming like a storm. "Our path is now unobstructed! The Celestial Host has proven themselves to be nothing but feeble and impotent before my might! And for the seeds of Adam," a venomous edge entered his tone, "my victory has sealed their fate with death!"

He raised his scepter high, a dark silhouette against the cold stars as he drank in the glory of his conquest,

"I have become the very essence of reality!" Satan proclaimed, his voice dripping with a poisonous delight. "I will stop at nothing until the Celestial Realm is forever tainted by my spirit! My power will know no bounds, and soon, Hashem shall bow before me as his servant!"

Suddenly, in the vast expanse of the cosmos, magnificent creatures spiraled down like fiery comets, their forms casting long, ominous shadows across the heavens. Yet, amidst the chaos, something extraordinary began to unfold. The Phoenix, glowing with an untapped, inner light, absorbed waves of subatomic particles, a dazzling dance of raw energy enveloping its broken form. An intense electric discharge flickered around it, sparking ghostly flames that swirled and subsided like a resilient ember refusing to die.

A cataclysmic crash shakes the very foundations of the world, as the Phoenix plummeted, an unstoppable force landing with a thunderous impact in Mount Vergina, Greece. The resonance of its descent rippled outwards for miles, shaking the earth to its core. Simultaneously, another creature, the Shirdal, spiraled down, crash-landing deep within the treacherous jungles near the Fayette Mountains, within the shadowed reaches of Persian territory, a silent harbinger of change in the escalating battle between light and darkness.

In a tumultuous clash of mythic power, the Unicorn plunged violently into the foothills of the Indus Valley, while the shattered form of Pegasus fell amidst the ancient crags of Mount Helicon. The impact of their falls released colossal mushroom clouds that painted the skies with chaos and uncertainty. Deep beneath the surface, the remains of these celestial beings were entombed in nameless graves, hidden far from the eyes of the living, their sacrifice a silent testament to the brutal conflict.

Now, the time has come for Satan to claim his long-awaited triumph. His gaze, burning with dark ambition, fell upon the Icsor Fortress of God. With the Celestial Host seemingly banished from the realm, nothing, he believed, stood between him and his ultimate goal.

"Demonites!" he declared, his voice echoing with a fierce anticipation. "This moment is unprecedented! Our waiting time is over! Beyond the swirling gases of the Atlantic Star Belt lies the final phase of our glorious campaign! The Throne of God is within my grasp, and this Earth shall be yours to ravage!"

A chorus of bloodthirsty chants erupted from the ranks of his followers, their fervor swelling as they hung on every word of Satan's rousing proclamation.

"My brothers!" he continued, raising his scepter high, a symbol of his dark authority. "We have journeyed too far to falter now! The rewards of our victory await us! Let the final conquest commence!"

The cheers of the Demonites reverberated through the Star Belt, electrifying the air with a palpable sense of impending doom. Amidst the roaring enthusiasm, Ba'laamus stepped forward, his brow furrowed with a flicker of unease.

"Lord," he ventured cautiously, "once we seize the Fortress… what fate awaits God?"

"Leave Him to me," Satan replied, a wicked grin spreading across his face. "I relish the thought of watching Him and Adam kneel before my might."

He turned to face his vast troops, attempting to instill a final surge of ruthless determination for their ultimate advance. But before he could fully rally their dark spirits, Azra'il interjected, his voice a low rumble of concern, "Don't let this premature celebration become a wasted effort, my lord."

Satan shot him a sharp, irritated look. "Why do you say that Azra'il? The flames of the ephod have been extinguished, and the Archangels, along with their pitiful beasts, have been vanquished. What could possibly stand in our way now?"

Al'debaran and Regulus, overhearing the tense exchange, leaned in closer, intrigued as Azra'il cautioned Satan against his overweening confidence. "You underestimate the might of God, my lord. We should reconsider our approach and strike Him indirectly. A frontal assault will surely lead to our downfall."

"Look around you!" Satan argued vehemently, gesturing to the ravaged battlefield. "God has nothing left to shield Him! His army lies in ruins, and His elite warriors have been reduced to mere ash! If we don't seize this opportunity, we will fall under Adam's dominion!"

"Your disdain for humanity has clouded your judgment, my lord," Azra'il countered, his tone urgent. "If you don't concentrate on the battle at hand, you have already lost."

Satan bristled, his voice laced with contempt as he challenged Azra'il's reasoning. "I don't hate man; I simply refuse to serve him! Why should I, when he ought to be bowing to my will?"

"My lord, you must reconsider this plan," Azra'il implored, his voice heavy with foreboding. "If you follow through with this direct assault, you will lead our brethren to slaughter... countless will perish."

Satan dismissed him with an impatient wave of his hand. "I beg to differ, Azra'il. I have snuffed out the light of four of the most formidable beings that ever existed outside of God Himself! Besides, I have dispatched His elite forces to their eternal rest! Destiny has chosen my side! Now, prove to me that what you claim holds any merit!"

"My lord, I have no tangible evidence at hand, only my own testimony..." Azra'il replied, his voice steady but grave. "...and I can tell you this: I have glimpsed the future, and what I saw does not bode well for us."

"What do you mean you have seen the future?" Satan challenged sharply, his eyes narrowing with suspicion. "No Celestial can breach that threshold and comprehend such outcomes!"

"Let me enlighten you, my friend," retorted Satan, his tone dripping with a dangerous confidence. "The Celestial Host still breathes! I question the wisdom of your counsel."

To quell Azra'il's growing unease, Satan summoned Al'debaran. Like the devoted soldier he is, Al'debaran swiftly arrived, eager to serve his dark lord. "Fly above the Atlantic Star Belt and survey the land," commanded Satan, his voice leaving no room for argument.

Without hesitation, Al'debaran soared into the sky, gliding silently over the swirling gases of the Star Belt. He scanned the desolate terrain for any signs of remaining defenders but found none. Upon his swift return, he reported, "After a thorough assessment, my lord, I can confirm there are no defenders in our way. The Fortress is ripe for the taking."

Pleased with the confirmation, Satan turned back to Azra'il, a hard edge in his voice. "If you interrupt me one more time with your gloomy pronouncements, I will make you the subject of my next eulogy. Now step aside; I have heard quite enough of your grim predictions."

With a dismissive wave, Satan returned his focus to the gathered ranks. Azra'il stepped back, frustration and a chilling sense of dread simmering within him at Satan's arrogant refusal to heed his desperate warning. "Brothers!" Satan declared, his voice booming with renewed confidence. "I bring glorious news! The Fortress is ours for the seizing! There is nothing left in the heavens that can bar our path! Unite with me and let us claim our rightful place in the Celestial Kingdom!"

Chapter 54

The Reckoning in the Star Belt. . .

The inky blackness of space is bruised with swirling, iridescent gases. Jagged bolts of pure energy still crackle in the distance, remnants of Satan's earlier assault that tore away the light of the four Enchanting Beast not shining, no longer. The boys are standing on a platform of interwoven gold and fire, the four stood: Abram, David, Joshua, and Jacob—warriors of different times, called together beyond time itself. Around them, the realms trembled, sensing what is to come.

As the Archangels stand before them. They were no longer men of time, but Avatars of the Archangels. Parts of the Star Belt caught fire, but did not burn. The sky roared, but did not break as the four Archangel Avatars—Abram, David, Joshua, and Jacob—hovered within a spiral of divine light, their forms luminous, transcendent. But above them, a new power has awakened—not of the Archangels, but from God's breath, unspoken since the first dawn.

The space between atoms cracked open, and from the rift emerged a voice—not male or female, not loud or soft, but all-encompassing. The four flames burn bright... yet separately, they flicker. "Let unity become your armor. Let oneness make you invincible."

A pillar of radiant magic descended—woven from strands of golden spirit, sapphire time, emerald mercy, and crimson truth. It wound around them, not binding, but inviting. Each Avatar looked to the other. They nodded. Together, they spoke:

"One purpose. One light. One will."

The divine pillar responded—and fell into them like a second birth.

Light exploded—not outward, but inward. Their bodies dissolved into pure energy, each soul weaving through the other in an impossible fusion. Michael's flame merged with Gabriel's clarity. Raphael's breath fused with Uriel's flame of time. And through it all, the human hearts of the four held it steady—mortal strength anchoring immortal fire.

They burst through the thick smoke, they are forced to come to a SCREECHING stop, freezing in HORROR! Their eyes say it all with a shear look of TERROR on their FACES. Satan eyes WIDEN in DISBELIEF. Standing in between him and victory is a resurgent Michael and the Celestial Host,

Satan recoiled, his eyes wide with disbelief and a flicker of terror. "NOOOOO..." The sound ripped from his throat, a raw, guttural cry. "This... this cannot be! I... I personally obliterated you! Reduced you to nothing! How... how in the abyss did you survive such a fate?" His voice cracked with a mixture of fury and dawning horror.

Michael's unwavering gaze drew his mighty sword, the polished steel gleaming with an almost holy light. "We survive," he declared, his voice resonating with strength and conviction, "because the sons of Adam heard the word of Hashem. They embraced the Truth, even in the face of your lies. This unwarranted adversity, this darkness you unleashed, has forged an unbreakable bond. Our very beings are drawn to their spirits, and it is their unwavering belief that strengthens us!"

He stepped closer, the tip of his sword never wavering. "Your insatiable hunger for ultimate power, Devil, has brought only suffering. And now," Michael's voice gained a sharp edge, "it has led to your demise! The light that humanity carries within them, the light of hope, now shines upon us, a beacon against your encroaching shadows. And it is that same light that will burn away your darkness, eradicate you from existence."

Michael's eyes blazed with righteous fury. "Devil, if this doesn't finally shatter your arrogance, if it doesn't prove to you that the power of Hashem is beyond anything your twisted mind can conceive, then hear this! During creation, He placed a divine seal upon us, a protection that only He can remove. But you," Michael spat the word, "you chose a crooked path. You turned your back on the Divine, and now He has withdrawn His hand. Your seal is broken, and you stand exposed to the very oblivion you sought to inflict upon others."

He raised his sword higher. "With no God on your side, fiend, who is left to shield you? Remember this, Satan: if God is for us, who can stand against us?"

With a defiant roar that clawed its way from the depths of his being, Michael hoisted his sword towards the heavens. A monstrous thunderclap answered, the sound itself a physical blow. Jagged streaks of lightning, like venomous black veins, tore across the bruised sky, each strike a harbinger of divine fury. Again, and again the heavens convulsed, and Michael, eyes blazing with righteous fire, thrust his blade skyward once more. A searing pulse of pure energy slammed down, engulfing the sword, and an incandescent white light erupted from Michael's eyes, a tidal wave of power surging through his very soul.

Grasping the hilt with both hands, knuckles white against the celestial metal, he slammed the sword into the ground. A shockwave of terrifying power ripped outwards, an invisible tsunami that sent Satan and his grotesque legions sprawling. Satan, momentarily stunned but seething, scrambled back to his feet. Michael ripped his sword free, the air crackling around it, and his voice, amplified by divine authority, boomed across the battlefield: "Celestial Host! Unleash the storm upon these defilers!"

A maelstrom of holy fury erupted. Demons shrieked and scattered, a tide of darkness breaking against an unyielding shore of light. Panic seized their ranks as the Celestial Host descended, a whirlwind of gleaming steel and righteous wrath. Satan, his face a mask of horrified disbelief, bellowed commands that were swallowed by the din of battle, his control dissolving like smoke in a gale. The Host surged forward, an unstoppable force, each angel a vessel of divine retribution.

Demon after demon fell, their guttural cries cut short by swift, merciless blows. Satan watched, a cold dread gripping his heart, as his carefully constructed army is torn asunder, limb from unholy limb. He pleaded with his fleeing forces, a desperate rasp in chaos, urging them to stand, to fight with the honor of the damned, but his words were lost in the rising tide of their annihilation. He was left stranded in a sea of despair.

Michael moved like a vengeful wraith, his double-edged sword a blur of silver, each swing ending a demonic existence. Gal'gaiel and Qumoris, their pole-arms flashing, ripped through the demonic ranks, tearing gaping wounds in the flesh of Moloch and Akkadian, their roars of agony echoing across the ravaged landscape. Uriel and Raphael fought with grim efficiency, their weapons instruments of divine judgment, while Gabriel, a figure of deadly grace, drew her bow, flaming arrows streaking across the heavens, finding their mark with unerring accuracy.

Desperation clawed at Satan. He had no choice but to flee. He vanished into the swirling chaos of the Atlantic Star Belt, Michael a relentless shadow in pursuit. But the dense, suffocating gases swallowed Satan whole.

"Show yourself, coward!" Michael's voice, laced with contempt, echoed into the swirling nebula. "After all your venomous boasts, are you nothing but a craven shadow? I trust you're rehearsing your surrender, for there is nowhere you can truly hide!"

A booming voice, thick with wounded pride, reverberated from the gases. "A rousing speech, Archangel! And your little light show was... adequate. But a concession? I am preparing a triumph, not a surrender!"

Michael, his senses on high alert, stalked the edges of the Star Belt, every nerve thrumming with caution. From within the swirling depths, unseen eyes watched his every move.

"Come out, Satan!" Michael's voice is a low growl now, the earlier taunt hardening into a threat. "You have underestimated the Lord's Army."

Silence answered him, the oppressive stillness of the nebula a suffocating blanket. Michael continued his slow, deliberate patrol. Now, it was his turn to twist the knife.

"Did you truly believe," he called out, his voice dripping with disbelief, "that you could prevail?"

The rout was complete. The remaining Demonites, broken and defeated, cast aside their weapons, a silent wave of surrender rippling through their ranks. They shuffled forward, a grim procession of the damned hands raised in a gesture of utter defeat. Raphael stood guard as the long, pathetic line was herded into a shimmering crystal cage.

"Where is Michael?" Raphael asked Gabriel, his gaze sweeping the desolate battlefield.

"He hunts the serpent," Gabriel replied, her voice tight with concern. "Satan tries to slither away."

With the last of the Demonites secured, Gabriel commanded the remaining Archangels. "Go! Aid Michael!" Uriel and Raphael remained, their presence a solid guarantee of the enemy's captivity.

Within the murky depths of the Star Belt, as Michael cautiously navigated the swirling gases, a horrifying transformation took place. Unseen, unheard, Satan was no longer the same. Raphael, his patience snapping, plunged into the nebula, determined to aid his brother.

"Satan!" Raphael's voice boomed, echoing through the strange dimension. "Your vile ambition to rule Heaven and Earth ends here!"

A blur of motion erupted around Michael, Satan a dizzying vortex of shadow, attempting to disorient his prey. Michael, his focus unwavering, held his ground. Then, a distorted image of Satan materialized before him, a sneering phantom.

"It is not over, Michael," the spectral figure hissed. "It has only just begun."

The image dissolved as a physical form smashed through the gases, a brutal strike aimed at Michael's head. He recoiled just in time, the blow whistling past his ear. His sword flashed in retaliation, but Satan was gone, swallowed by the swirling nebula once more.

"Hahahaha!" the disembodied laughter echoed. "Like the pathetic beast that dared to stand with you, you will suffer the same crushing defeat!"

"Give it up, Satan," Michael retorted, his voice firm despite the unsettling nature of the attack. "Whatever twisted game you're playing, it will end in your ruin."

A lifelike hologram of Satan shimmered into existence before him, his eyes burning with malevolent triumph. "After I tear you apart, I will reclaim what is rightfully ours!"

Michael lunged, his sword aimed true, but he passed straight through the illusion. A cold touch on his back sent a jolt of pure adrenaline through him. The real Satan was behind him. Confusion flickered across Michael's face, a moment of disorientation that allowed doubt to creep in. Then, with startling suddenness, Satan stepped out of the gases directly in front of him, a predatory grin twisting his features. Michael recoiled, a flicker of something akin to disgust in his eyes.

"Satan," Michael stated, his voice regaining its steely resolve, "the outcome of this… charade… remains the same."

He attacked again, and again his blade sliced through empty air. But Michael's determination was a tangible force. He crept along the edge of the Star Belt, his grip tightening on his sword hilt, when Raphael's urgent cry pierced the swirling gases.

"Michael!"

He spun, seeing Raphael rushing towards him. In that split second of distraction, Satan struck. He erupted from the gases, a blur of dark energy, and clamped his arms around Michael from behind, a brutal chokehold. They struggled, a desperate dance of power and desperation, until Michael, with a surge of strength, flipped Satan over his shoulder. But the fallen angel twisted in mid-air, landing cat-like on his feet, and vanished back into the gaseous shroud.

Without hesitation, Michael plunged into the nebula. A whirlwind of steel erupted as Satan attacked, his sword a vicious flurry of slashes and hacks. Michael parried each blow with effortless grace, then delivered a brutal punch that sent Satan reeling.

"Satan," Michael declared, unsheathing his sword fully, the celestial metal gleaming in the dim light, "you cannot win this."

"It is worth the fight!" Satan spat back, his own blade a dark counterpoint to Michael's light.

A furious sword fight raged within the confines of the Star Belt, the clash of their weapons echoing through the swirling gases. Raphael, hearing the brutal exchange, was about to intervene when a body hurtled through the darkness, slamming into the edge of the nebula with a sickening thud.

Raphael stared down at the broken form. It was Satan. Michael emerged from the gases, unscathed, his expression grimly triumphant. He reached down and hauled Satan to his feet, the fallen angel battered and bruised.

"Get up, you vile creature."

Raphael ripped the breastplate from Satan's body. "You are unworthy to bear such protection."

Michael retrieved his sword, then seized Satan's scepter, the symbol of his corrupted authority. He placed it between two jagged rocks and with a single, decisive strike, shattered it into pieces. Together, Michael and Raphael dragged Satan back to the crystal cage where his defeated army languished. They tossed him inside, the heavy bars clanging shut, sealing his fate. The entire Demonite army, their rebellion crushed, are transported to stand before the Holy Council. Silence fell as they are standing before Hashem, the air thick with divine judgment.

"Satan," Hashem's voice resonated with celestial authority, "the Holy Council denounces you. You were the bright and morning star, but your wickedness has extinguished your light. Your star has fallen."

Humiliated, Satan bowed his head for a fleeting moment, a flicker of sorrow crossing his ravaged features. The Holy Council rendered its verdict: exile. Without hesitation, Hashem commanded the Archangels. "Take the fallen one and his corrupted host to the furthest reaches and cast them out."

A wave of angry murmurs rippled through the Demonite ranks as they were led away.

"God!" Satan roared, his voice filled with venomous defiance. "This is not over! You will hear from me again! You may have won this battle, but the war has just begun!"

"Satan," Hashem replied, his voice unwavering, "the kingdom you so desperately sought will be the outer darkness of Earth. You and your kind are forever barred from this realm."

Satan hunched over, a storm of bitter resentment brewing within him. How had he fallen? How had his mighty legions been so utterly destroyed? They were left to lick their wounds in the face of utter defeat. The Archangels led them to the very edge of creation, where the swirling void met the nascent form of Earth.

"This shall be your domain," Michael declared, his voice echoing with finality. "The fate you inflicted on the Four Enchanted Beasts will now be your own fate."

Satan glared at Michael, his eyes burning with impotent rage. At a silent command from the lead Archangel, the crystal cage containing Satan and his army was lifted and hurled into the blackness of space. The Archangels watched as it plummeted, a falling star of darkness against the infinite canvas. Then, they turned and ascended back towards the Icsor Fortress of God.

Standing before Hashem, Michael declared, "Justice has been served."

Hashem nodded. "The time has come to separate them, to unlock the joining of souls." He placed his hands together in prayer and gently drew apart the intertwined energies, separating the boys from the bodies of the Archangels.

The boys gasped, awestruck by the breathtaking splendor of Hashem's Fortress. They could not look directly upon His glory, see-

ing only a radiant blur, for no mortal spirit could behold Him and live. In His presence, they bowed low.

"Arise, sons of Adam."

They rose, their hearts filled with a profound sense of wonder.

"In the face of unimaginable danger, you confronted your fears and triumphed. It has been My privilege to witness the merging of the most powerful creatures ever conceived with the most incredible force ever created! We exist in a parallel world, interwoven with your own. From time to time, I allow certain souls a glimpse before returning them. Now, it is your turn to go back. But first, a celebration!"

"We shall gather in the Great Hall and celebrate the harmony of man and angel, united for a righteous cause. Now, unite once more, that you may be returned."

The boys' ethereal forms rejoined the Archangels, their shared journey nearing its end. They sped towards the gati. The gateway to their world. Melchizedek awaited them at the entrance, his wise eyes filled with warmth.

"Welcome, Great Princes of the Most High."

"Hello, Wise and Great Guardian of the Gati," Michael replied, bowing alongside the others.

The boys once again disembodied from their host. Entering through the doorway, they walked down a long corridor filled with more doors. Dave asked,

"What's behind these doors?"

"Unclean spirits that are so vile and they are never to be released. They are spawned from the dark heart of Satan. They seek to corrupt what is clean. They search for impurity in which to thrive," said Melchizedek.

"Satan was found to be unclean? Why didn't God cast these spirits out, as He did Satan?"

"Because these spirits cannot possess light, and Satan was an angel of light. These spirits need a host to house them. Without one they must remain locked behind these doors."

"Crikey, mate! All these spirits are spawned from Satan?" asked Josh.

"Yes.".

The eerie cries of spirits could be heard throughout the corridor.

"Behind one door you have the spirit of greed. Behind another door is the spirit of fornication. Behind this door, you have the spirit of deceit. Behind that door, you have the spirit of hate. Behind this door, you have the twin spirits: one possesses a lying tongue and the other possesses a cursing tongue," said Melchizedek.

"Will these spirits ever escape?" asked Jake,

"That's a question I cannot answer. Only the one with the key can answer that question."

Oi, reckon anyone knows who's got this key, then?" Josh asked, a puzzled frown on his face.

"There are two keys in existence. Hashem holds one, and Adam holds the other," replied Melchizedek.

With a concerned look on his face, Michael said, "Wait a minute! We cast Satan and his Demonites close to the Earth. That's where Adam resides."

"Fear not. In order for Satan to take the key to Adam's world, it must be handed over to him, due to the fact that spirits cannot procreate. They can only possess. Hashem did not give the Celestial Host the ability to procreate," said Melchizedek.

As they reached the end of the corridor, they came to two huge doors that impeded their pathway. The doorframe was adorned with calligraphy.

"Blimey," Josh breathed, his eyes wide as saucers… "These doors… they're positively monumental, aren't they? Never seen one like it."

The doors are made from natural sapphire with gold hinges re-enforcing their base, with carvings on the face of the doors.

"What lies behind these doors?" asked David

"This is the final leg of your journey. Beyond these doors is a place known as the Great Hall. If you look off to the side of these giant doors, there are four palm prints carved in stone. In order to gain access beyond this point, Michael, Raphael, Gabriel, and Uriel, you must place your right hands inside of these four palm prints," said Melchizedek.

The Archangels stepped up and placed their right hands on the palm prints. Their energy ignited the four carved prints in the wall. Waves of light flashed around them as they stood holding their position. The light traveled from their palms directly to the frame of the giant doors. The seal broke, and the giant doors slowly opened, revealing a huge hall bigger than ten football fields. Inside this hall, is an elaborate floor made of aquamarine. The beryl floor had an emerald appeal to it with twelve gates that led back into the natural world.

The hall is decorated beautifully. It has twelve tall minarets that rose up from the corners, standing atop twelve white marble plinths. Glass drapes so finely woven it appeared they are made up of fine cloth hung throughout the hall. The walls of the hall are intricately decorated with drawings of vines, creepers with flowers, and other beautiful designs. The throne is flanked on both sides by huge arches, one over the other. Their design is rectangular, with the arched alcoves, equal in size.

Each section in the hall is well marked on both sides by attached pilasters that rose from the plinth level of the hall up to the friezes. The friezes are crowned with spectacular pinnacles of lotus buds and finials. A crystal choir-stand is adjacent to *Hahsem's* throne, with chambered corners. Each of the choir-stands is framed with bands of calligraphy. Melchizedek led Archangels into the center of the Great Hall, where he addressed them,

"Truly your readiness has proven that thou are worthy of thy namesake. By defeating Satan, thou have temporarily sent him away. Once that vile spirit is cleansed, he will be ushered back to where he belongs. We stand ready to welcome him with open arms. At this moment, ignorance has separated him from us, and for this reason, he must remain until his destiny is fulfilled. Now look around you." said Melchizedek with confidence.

As they did so, the Archangels see the Celestial Host appearing before them.

"Now that the dragon has been defeated, his anger for man is as a consuming fire. He will seek to ridicule man every chance he gets. He will seek to cause Adam great harm and lead him into greater danger. Right now, he is seeking to strengthen his army." said Melchizedek.

"We will be watching and waiting for that day." said Michael.

"Now it is time for the sons of Adam to be sent back to their world. They have to go back and reclaim their natural bodies."

He held out his hands, and four beryl stones appeared in his palm. With magician's dexterity, he thrusts hands forward, and the stones vanished and reappear above the Archangels heads. Melchizedek watched as stones sent down streams of light that completely engulfed the angels. As he lifted his hands high above his head, light emerged from between his palms. Swirls of colored vapor formed and drifted down, floating around the Archangels.

The light simultaneously pulls the boys out, positioning them next to the Archangels. They looked around the Great Hall and see ten thousand upon ten thousand of angelic beings. Angels of every sect are there, from the wise Superiniels to the tiny Yinpiniel's. A few of the Arch Yinpiniel flew over to Dave. Fascinated, Dave, with a closed fist, held out his right hand. He slowly opened his closed fist as a gesture of friendship. He watched in amazement as the tiny angel landed in his palm

"You look like a fairy. I thought fairies are make-believe creatures." said Dave.

"Yeah, mate… same here," Josh said, his gaze drifting off into the distance.

Dave looked at the angel Viel with a smile. Viel smiled back with little giggles. Jake smiled as he looked at the multitude of angels. Some of the angels left their seats and surrounded him. The Arch Yinpiniel E'Mil came over and showed Dave a vision of the time Kalisha spotted two of their sisters in the woods. He heard the echo of his sister calling out to him, saying that she seen some fairies. Two of the Yinpiniel's flew above Jake's head as if they are sitting on chairs, while the Yinpiniel Yaliel and Bli hovered on Jake's right,

"Hi! I am Bli." she says.

"Hi, my name is Jake," he replied with a smile.

Bli smiled and asked, "Doest, you care if I touch your nose?"

Laughing, he assured her that it is okay. She reaches out and touched his nose with the tip of her tiny finger. Giggling, she drew her hand back,

"I've never seen the image of a human this close before." said Yaliel

"Well! What do you think now that you have?"

Her eyes sparkled like diamonds and her hair shimmered with flecks of gold. Razzel turns to Abe,

"You are beautiful. Like all of HIS creations."

"I was thinking the same thing about you," interjected Abe.

"Reckon... reckon I could touch ya hair?" Josh mumbled, scuffing his boot in the dirt.

"Yes," she replied with a smile.

He reached out gently touching her from the top of her crown, moving his finger down to the bottom of her hair. He got the shivers, because it felt like silky air on his finger.

"Blimey, this is right peculiar," Josh muttered, scratching his head, a furrow creasing his brow. "This ain't bleedin' hair, is it? What in the ruddy hell...?"

He looked at the strands, picking them up between his forefinger and thumb. The tiny strands glimmered with a luster that would make any woman envious. Some of the angels smiled and went back to their seats.

"Strewth, would ya look at that!" said Joshua breathed, his eyes wide.

Several Yinpiniel's hovered in David's face as though they are having a last look at him. One by one, they each touched his face, and then flew off in excitement. The sons of Adam looked around the Great Hall in amazement as voices filled the sanctuary with congratulations and applause.

"You can see, so I don't have to tell you how pleased we are," said Melchizedek.

"Oh, it's nothing. We defend the cosmos every day," replied Dave with a smile, jokingly.

"We are grateful that you four have heeded the call of the Most High, risking your own lives to save both worlds." The High Priest smiled.

"All in a day's work." replied Jake.

"You must return to your world, a world where time marks your existence. Everything that you encounter will be wiped away from your memory. Like a dream, you will awake from this experience having no knowledge, just vague memories of déjà vu. What seems to be the ultimate victory for Satan has turned into an agony of defeat.

Just as he finished speaking, four doorways to the natural world opened. Michael, Raphael, Gabriel, and Uriel thanked the boys for their courage and bravery. As they hugged each other, deep down inside the boys knew that they would never see one another again, and they fought back tears of sadness. Dave's eyes swelled with water as he fought to restrain his emotions. He said to the other three,

"It was an honor to know you Abram, Joshua, and Jacob. Even though we are told that we would forget all of this, somehow, I know that I will never truly forget any of you."

All the boys agreed with what Dave said with a nod, and they all embraced for the last time. Then the boys walked toward the open doorway. Abe, Dave, Josh, and Jake walked back through the doorway of the spiritual realm, heading back into the natural world. After they all crossed the threshold, the door to the spiritual realm faded away and closed behind them. Their spirits are restored, and all four are back in the natural world. Moments later Abram returned home.

Chapter 55

Shadows in the Nugatory. . .

It's been a full day when Abram finally makes it home. His mother is very relieved to see him walk inside,

"You have been gone all day. Where have you been, Abram?" asked his mother.

Not able to remember, he tells her he'd been wandering outside. Now, David heard his sister calling to him. She waved at him, signaling it was time to go. He wondered how long he has been gone from the RV park. He did not remember ever walking to this spot.

Joshua woke up in his grassy backyard with Rex lying next to him. He looked up into the darkening twilight sky. Rex licked Joshua's face, and he smiled.

"Oi, Rexy, ya cheeky bugger!" Joshua chuckled, wiping the slobber off his face… "Right, mate, let's get inside, eh?"

Rex let out a couple of excited woofs, then took off like a blue heeler after a runaway sheep, Joshua hot on his heels.

An elaborate celebration is in full swing, and all of the participants are waiting on the guest of honor to arrive,

"Righto, mate, let's get crackin'. Time for a bit of a shindig. Everyone's waitin' on ya."

Joshua looks over at his father, nodding his head and picks up his bow and arrows, as though he is seeing them for the very first time. He rushed out the door and into the festivities. The lives of all the boys somewhat returned to normal as they settle in their environment.

Back in the Nugatory, Satan and his Demonites are released from their prison. They are destined to take up refuge there until Hashem sees fit otherwise. Still nursing his anger at his defeat, Satan began plotting his revenge against God. In his travels to the Earth, he watches Adam from a sea of darkness, becoming angrier and angrier over the relationship that Hashem and Adam has developed,

"I don't know what God sees in that creature." he says.

Bitterly he departs from the Earth to rendezvous with the rest of the Demonites.

Chapter 56

The Stirring of Want. . .

A heavy dose of curiosity is hanging in the air above Adam as he peers out gazing beyond the Garden. His eyes drifted from one coupling creature to another, a primal yearning stirring within him. A decision hardened in his heart: he too, needed this connection. But a disquieting realization dawned on him because the garden held no other being than himself, no other to share this profound space with.

Anticipation tightened its grip as he awaited Hashem's familiar presence. Yet, the heavens remained silent. The seed of curiosity began to sprout as time stretched with more questions than answers. Adam's focus shifted inward, his own burgeoning needs eclipsing the wonder of his surroundings. His eyes lingered on two antelopes, lost in their intimate dance.

Unseen, a shadow stirred a few feet away. Satan watched Adam, a cold calculation in his unseen eyes. "This creature... is useless?" A flicker of something sharper than dismissal crossed his thoughts. "No. Capable of... evil."

Then, a shift in the very atmosphere. A hushed descent. Hashem and His radiant ministers materialized, their presence a silent weight in the garden. They moved with a serene grace towards the oblivious Adam. For a fleeting moment, the Seraphim caught the raw, untamed yearning emanating from him. A ripple of unease passed among them.

"The hunger in his heart grows fierce," Zarath murmured, his voice barely a breath, laced with a dawning concern. "Soon, it will drive him to desperate measures."

The surety of Adam's innocence seemed to dissolve like mist in the morning sun. "There is a grave risk," Hashem stated, his tone weighty, "that without a compatible helpmate, he will succumb to this... this profound need. It could consume him."

"But can we truly fault him?" Zarath countered, his brow furrowed. "Paradise itself offers him no solace in this regard."

Hashem's gaze was distant, troubled. "We can debate this endlessly. But the fruit of the Tree... it will unveil his true nature, undeniably."

Through five days, the Creator had declared His work "good." But on the sixth, with Adam as his final creation of that day, a different pronouncement echoed – "It is not good." A solitary being in a world teeming with pairs.

As the cool of the day descended, painting the sky in hues of twilight, Hashem and the Seraphim arrived in their celestial glory. From the deepening shadows, Satan followed, a predator stalking its unaware prey. The Holy Ones moved through the tranquil garden, their destination Adam. The demon lord crouched low behind a screen of foliage, his gaze fixed, his mind a knot of dark curiosity. "What holds his attention so completely?"

They were met not with childlike wonder, but with a self-assuredness that held a strange emotion. Hearing Hashem's resonant voice, Adam turned, a flicker of relief in his eyes. He bowed low before the Creator.

"Adam," Hashem's tone is gentle yet probing, "You may rise." Adam lifted himself up as Hashem continue "I have come to see your progress, to witness how you have settled int,o this world."

"My task is complete," Adam replied, his voice carrying a new, almost possessive quality. "I have named all the creatures of this Earth."

"Good," Hashem affirmed, his gaze unwavering.

A hint of pride colored Adam's next words. "I knew you would visit, Lord."

"How so?" A subtle question entered Hashem's voice.

Adam gestured towards the horizon. "I saw four lights descend from the heavens." He pointed in the direction of each invisible impact. "What were these lights that fell?"

"Fallen... objects," Hashem explained, his expression unreadable.

"I attempted to see through the brush," Adam continued, a touch of impatience in his tone, "but it was too dense. Shall I retrieve them for you?"

"No, my son," Hashem replied, his voice firm. "The recovery is complete. I have already attended to them."

Hidden in the undergrowth, Satan watched, his unseen lips curving into a knowing smirk. As Hashem and Adam walked among the paired creatures, a question finally escaped Adam's lips, tinged with a growing unease. "Lord, every creature has its helpmate, one that mirrors it. Yet... there is nothing in the Garden that looks like me?"

Hashem's expression remained serene, though a profound understanding flickered in his eyes. "I knew this question would arise."

"How did you know my thoughts, Lord?" Adam asked, a hint of awe mixed with his persistent yearning.

Hashem's voice resonated with divine authority. "I am the Almighty God. Be thou perfect before Me. I know all and see all. The very strands of your hair are numbered in My sight. Every bone, every muscle, every fiber of your being was crafted by My hand. Nothing in this vast universe lies beyond My comprehension. All existence flows from Me. From the highest heavens, I heard your unspoken cry. From My throne, I witnessed the longing in your heart."

"You... heard my cry?" A wave of something akin to relief washed over Adam.

"Yes," Hashem affirmed, his gaze softening. "And in response, We have decided to create a helpmate for you."

"She will be your perfect companion," Hashem continued, his voice imbued with a gentle promise. "Her beauty will have no equal."

Satan's unseen eyes narrowed, his attention laser-focused. He watched as Hashem gently guided Adam to lie down. He strained to hear every word as Hashem spoke.

"Your helpmate will rule beside you in this garden. You shall guide her in her tasks."

Hashem knelt beside the sleeping Adam, his touch feather-light as he closed Adam's eyes. A profound peace settled over the first man. Satan, however, felt a jolt of something akin to shock as Hashem then... opened Adam's side. He crept closer, his dark curiosity overriding all caution. With swift, precise movements, Hashem removed a rib, the flesh knitting back together seamlessly as if it had never been breached. While Adam remained in slumber, Hashem carried the rib to another part of the garden.

Satan remained hidden, his gaze fixed on the still form of Adam. In a secluded glade, Hashem began His work. From that single bone, a delicate framework began to form, a new and unique anatomy taking shape. Over this skeletal structure, Hashem draped the same flesh from which Adam was formed, meticulously crafting each cell, muscle, tendon, nerve, and organ.

And Hashem formed the woman from the dust of the ground and breathed into her nostrils the breath of life. Like Adam, she became a living soul. Hashem spoke her name, and her eyes fluttered open, filled with innocent wonder. He gently helped her to her feet.

Satan, now having stealthily moved to this new location, stood transfixed. The woman's beauty struck him with a force he hadn't anticipated. A chilling thought solidified in his mind. "Her beauty... I shall twist it. I shall use it against the very heart of Hashem's creation. Through this creature, I will bring the Almighty to His knees."

The woman turned, her gaze falling upon Hashem. A radiant smile bloomed on her face.

"I am Hashem," the Creator declared, His voice echoing with power and love. "The Supreme God of the Universe, Creator of the Heavens and the Earth and all their hosts. This Earth is your domain, and I grant you dominion over every living creature that breathes upon it."

"From the mightiest elephants to the smallest insects, from the great whales of the deep to the tiniest plankton, every creature on land and in the sea is placed under your care."

Chapter 57

A Promise of Mortality . . .

The air in the nascent garden hummed with a gentle vibrant energy as Hashem, his presence a warm, encompassing light. Meanwhile, Adam is not far away when he hears Hashem telepathically calling him. Hashem sent the woman off into the brush, out of site of the man. Adam comes to where Hashem is. Adam presented himself before Hashem. He bowed to the ground.

"You called for me, my Lord?" asked Adam.

"Yes, the task of creating a helpmate for you is complete. Her appearance is unmatched by anything else I have created on Earth. She is to be co-equal with you, to rule alongside of thee. I have given her dominion over the animals, just as I've given you dominion over the animals. Her place is to assist you in the affairs of the garden. From your rib, I've created for you a companion." said Hashem.

He called for the woman to come from beyond the bush. She cautiously steps out and walks toward Him. As he beheld her, joy and excitement glows from his countenance at the sight his female counterpart. After unveiling His surprise, Hashem brings His new creation over to Adam. Slowly, he walked around her checking out her physical attributes with Hashem watching,

"This is bone of my bones and flesh of my flesh." said Adam as he looked her up and down. He glances toward Hashem as he continue, "She shall be called woman, because out of man was, she taken."

Adam is standing giddy over Eve. New, whole, and alive. Their hands are linked. They are also not ashamed of their appearance. Before them, in a gentle blaze of radiance, stood God. Not in wrath, not in thunder, but in quiet nearness. His presence is weightless yet infinite, a comfort that wrapped the soul and stilled all fear. His voice is like the wind on a cool day,

"All this I have made for you. Every tree, every river, everything. You are keepers. Co-heirs of delight."

Adam looked up, eyes of one who had never seen such beauty since laying eyes on Satan at the inauguration. Eve smiled—not out of naivety, but with the joy of meeting her helpmate for the first time.

"You have My breath in you," God said. Adam interjected… "And now… we have each other." Adam confidently says to her.

There is a pause—not heavy, but holy.

"I will walk with you still, in the cool of the day. But now begins your time without My hand nor My presence."

Eve's lips parted. "You're… leaving?" she asked brow furrowed.

A breeze rustled the leaves above as if even the trees listened. And with that, He is gone. The Garden is silent—but not empty. Adam turned to Eve, a question in his eyes. She looked up at the tree branches glowing in the sunrise and whispered: "This is so beautiful."

High above the veil of time, where light folds into itself and truth echoes through eternity, the Throne of God radiates an all-consuming brilliance. Seraphims hover in worship, their six wings revolving with reverent flame. The air is thick with purpose. From His throne of sapphire and fire, the LORD speaks.

"The garden breathes with My life, but man has yet to be tested in wisdom. The woman—formed by My own hand from the rib of the man—walks in peace. Yet peace is untested. Her ears knows only My voice and the voice of her helpmate."

"And this you will challenge? ask Adon-Shama.

361

"Yes. I will prove Satan to be wrong—for his sake. I know it, and he needs to know it. Let him see whether she cleaves to what is true or when another voice offers her what I have already given them. You will go to Satan and speak only what I command. Say to him, Thus say the Lord, for the woman walks in the midst of Eden, filled with My word. She will testify to Satan the words of the Lord. Approach Satan. Speak to him. But do not command—only give the question. For us to see if she will listen to the voice of another than Mine, or her helpmate. For us to see if they hold to the established order."

Adon-Shama bowed his head, then lift his chin slightly. "It will be as you have spoken Lord!" he declared.

With a burst of light, the Seraphim departs, flaming wings carving through the veil between realms. Below, in the distance, in the second heaven. a shadow coils around a tree. Watching. Waiting. And soon… whispering.

THE END
Or is it?